Praise for beloved author Betty Neels

"Neels is especially good at painting her scenes with choice words, and this adds to the charm of the story."
—*USATODAY.com's Happy Ever After* blog on *Tulips for Augusta*

"Betty Neels surpasses herself with an excellent storyline, a hearty conflict and pleasing characters."
—*RT Book Reviews* on *The Right Kind of Girl*

"Once again Betty Neels delights readers with a sweet tale in which love conquers all."
—*RT Book Reviews* on *Fate Takes a Hand*

"One of the first Harlequin authors I remember reading. I was completely enthralled by the exotic locales… Her books will always be some of my favorites to re-read."
—*Goodreads* on *A Valentine for Daisy*

"I just love Betty Neels!… If you like a good old-fashioned romance…you can't go wrong with this author."
—*Goodreads* on *Caroline's Waterloo*

Romance readers around the world were sad to note the passing of **Betty Neels** in June 2001. Her career spanned thirty years, and she continued to write into her ninetieth year. To her millions of fans, Betty epitomized the romance writer, and yet she began writing almost by accident. She had retired from nursing, but her inquiring mind still sought stimulation. Her new career was born when she heard a lady in her local library bemoaning the lack of good romance novels. Betty's first book, *Sister Peters in Amsterdam*, was published in 1969, and she eventually completed 134 books. Her novels offer a reassuring warmth that was very much a part of her own personality. She was a wonderful writer, and she is greatly missed. Her spirit and genuine talent live on in all her stories.

BETTY NEELS

A Kiss for Julie
& The Doubtful Marriage

HARLEQUIN® SPECIAL RELEASE

ISBN-13: 978-1-335-00786-5

A Kiss for Julie & The Doubtful Marriage

Copyright © 2019 by Harlequin Books S.A.

The publisher acknowledges the copyright holder of the individual works as follows:

A Kiss for Julie
Copyright © 1996 by Betty Neels

The Doubtful Marriage
Copyright © 1987 by Betty Neels

Recycling programs for this product may not exist in your area.

HARLEQUIN®
www.Harlequin.com

Printed in U.S.A.

CONTENTS

A KISS FOR JULIE

Chapter 1

Professor Smythe sat behind his cluttered desk, peering over his spectacles at the girl sitting on the other side of it. A very pretty girl, indeed, he considered her beautiful, with bronze hair piled on top of her head, a charming nose, a gentle mouth and large green eyes fringed with bronze lashes.

She looked up from her notebook and smiled at him.

He took off his spectacles, polished them and put them back on again, ran his hand through the fringe of white hair encircling his bald patch and tugged his goatee beard. 'I've a surprise for you, Julie.' And at her sudden sharp glance he added, 'No, no, you're not being made redundant—I'm retiring at the end of the week. There, I meant to lead up to it gently—'

She said at once, 'You're ill—that must be the reason. No one would ever let you retire, sir.'

'Yes, I'm ill—not prostrate in bed, by any means, but I have to lead a quiet life, it seems, without delay.' He sighed. 'I shall miss this place and I shall miss you, Julie. How long is it since you started working for me?'

'Three years. I shall miss you too, Professor.'

'Do you want to know what is to happen to you?' he asked.

'Yes—yes, please, I do.'

'I am handing over to a Professor van der Driesma— a Dutchman widely acclaimed in our particular field of medicine. He works mostly at Leiden but he's been over here for some time, working at Birmingham and Edinburgh. What he doesn't know about haematology would barely cover a pin's head.' He smiled. 'I should know; he was my registrar at Edinburgh.' He went on, 'I'm handing you over to him, Julie; you'll be able to help him find his feet and make sure that he knows where to go and keep his appointments and so on. You've no objection?'

'No, sir. I'm truly sorry that you are retiring but I'll do my best to please Professor whatever-his-name-is.'

Professor Smythe sighed. 'Well, that's that. Now, what about Mrs Collins? Did you manage to get her old notes for me?'

Julie pushed a folder a little nearer to him. 'They go back a long way...'

'Yes, a most interesting case. I'll read them and then I shall want you to make a summary for me.' He tossed the papers on his desk around in front of him. 'Wasn't there a report I had to deal with?'

Julie got up, tall, splendidly built and unfussed. 'It's here, under your elbow, sir.' She fished the paper out for him and put it down under his nose.

He went away presently to see his patients and she settled down to her day's work. Secretary to someone as important as Professor Smythe was a job which didn't allow for slacking; her private worries about his leaving and the prospect of working for a stranger who might not approve of her had to be put aside until the evening.

Professor Smythe didn't refer to his departure again that day. She took the letters he dictated and went to her slip of a room adjoining his office, dealt with mislaid notes, answered the telephone and kept at bay anyone threatening to waste his precious time. A usual day, she reflected, wishing him goodnight at last and going out into the busy streets.

It was late September and the evening dusk cast a kindly veil over the dinginess of the rows of small houses and shabby shops encircling the hospital. Julie took a breath of unfresh air and went to queue for her bus.

St Bravo's was in Shoreditch, a large, ugly building with a long history and a splendid reputation, and since her home was close to Victoria Park the bus ride was fairly short.

She walked along the little street bordered by red-brick terraced houses, rounded the corner at its end, turned into a short drive leading to a solid Victorian house and went in through the back door. The kitchen was large and old-fashioned and there was an elderly man standing at the table, cutting bread and butter.

Julie took off her jacket. 'Hello, Luscombe. Lovely to be home; it seems to have been a long day.'

'Mondays always is, Miss Julie. Your ma's in the sitting room; I'll be along with the tea in two ticks.'

She took a slice of bread and butter as she went past him and crammed it into her pretty mouth. 'I'll come and help you with supper presently. Is it something nice? It was corned beef and those ready-made potatoes for lunch.'

'As nice a macaroni cheese as you'll find anywhere. I'll leave you to see to the pudding.'

She went out of the room, crossed the hall and opened the door of a room on the other side of the house. Mrs Beckworth was sitting at the table writing, but she pushed the papers away as Julie went in.

'Hello, love. You're early; how nice. I'm dying for a cup of tea...'

'Luscombe's bringing it.' Julie sat down near her mother. 'I can't imagine life without him, can you, Mother?'

'No, dear. I've been checking the bills. Do you suppose we could afford to get Esme that hockey stick she says she simply must have? Yours is a bit old, I suppose.'

Julie thought. 'I had it for my fifteenth birthday; that's almost twelve years ago. Let's afford it.'

Her mother said unexpectedly, 'You ought to be enjoying yourself, Julie—finding a husband...'

'I'll wait until he finds me, Mother, dear. I'm very happy at St Bravo's. Professor Smythe's a dear.' She hesitated. 'He's leaving at the end of the week—he's not well. I'm to be handed over to his successor—a Dutchman with the kind of name you never remember!'

'Do you mind?'

'I shall miss Professor Smythe—he's a dear old man—but no, I don't mind.' She would have minded, she reflected, if she had been told that her services were no longer required; her salary was something that they couldn't do without.

Luscombe came in with the tea then, and they talked of other things—Michael, Julie's elder brother, a houseman at a Birmingham hospital; David, still at Cambridge, reading ancient history and intent on becoming a schoolmaster, and Esme, the baby of the family, fourteen years old and a pupil at the local grammar school.

'Where is she, by the way?' asked Julie.

'Having tea at the Thompsons'. She promised to be back here by half past six. The Thompson boy will walk her round.'

Julie peered into the empty teapot. 'Well, I'll go and make a bread-and-butter pudding, shall I?'

'That would be nice, dear. Esme popped in on her way from school and took Blotto with her. The Thompsons don't mind.'

'Good. I'll give him a run in the park later on.'

Her mother frowned. 'I don't like you going out after dark.'

'I'll not be alone, dear; Blotto will be with me.' She smiled widely. 'Besides, I'm hardly what you would describe as a delicate female, am I?'

She was in the kitchen when Esme came home, bringing with her the Thompson boy, Freddie, and Blotto, a dog of assorted ancestry with a long, sweeping tail and a rough coat. He was a large dog and he looked fierce, but his disposition was that of a lamb. However, as Julie pointed out, what did that matter when he looked fierce?

Freddie didn't stay; he was a frequent visitor to the house and came and went casually. He bade Julie a polite goodbye, lifted a hand in farewell to Esme and took himself off, leaving the younger girl to feed Blotto and then, spurred on by Julie, to finish her homework. 'And we'll go on Saturday and get that hockey stick,' said Julie.

Esme flung herself at her. 'Julie, you darling. Really? The one I want? Not one of those horrid cheap ones.'

'The one you want, love.'

Getting ready for bed in her room later that evening, Julie allowed her thoughts to dwell on the future. She did this seldom, for as far as she could see there wasn't much point in doing so. She must learn to be content with her life.

No one had expected her father to die of a heart attack and they were lucky to have this house to live in. It was too large and needed a lot done to it, but it was cheaper to continue to live in it than to find something more modern and smaller. Besides, when she had made tentative enquiries of a house agent, he had told her that if they sold the place they would get a very poor price—barely enough to buy anything worth living in. It was a pity that there had been very little money, and what there had been had gone to get the boys started.

Julie sighed and picked up her hairbrush. It would be nice to get married—to meet a man who wouldn't mind shouldering the burden of a widowed mother, two brothers and a schoolgirl sister. Her sensible mind told her that she might as well wish for the moon.

She brushed her mane of hair and jumped into bed. She hoped that the professor who was taking her over would be as nice an old man as Professor Smythe. Perhaps, she thought sleepily, as he was Dutch, he would go back to Holland from time to time, leaving her to deal with things or be loaned out to other consultants as and when required. It would make a change.

There was a good deal of extra work to be done during the rest of the week; Professor Smythe tended to be forgetful and occasionally peevish when he mislaid something. Julie dealt with him patiently, used to his sudden little spurts of temper. Besides, she reasoned after a particularly trying morning, he wasn't well.

It was on the last morning—Friday—as she patiently waded through the filing cabinet for notes which Professor Smythe simply had to have when the door opened behind her and she turned to see who it was.

Any girl's dream, she thought, and, since he had ignored her and crossed to Professor Smythe's office, turned back to her files. But she had even in those few seconds taken a good look. Tall—six and a half feet, perhaps—and enormous with it, and pale hair—so pale that there might be grey hair too. His eyes, she felt sure, would be blue.

'Come here, Julie, and meet your new boss,' called Professor Smythe.

She entered his office, closed the door carefully and

crossed the room, glad for once that she was a tall girl and wouldn't have to stretch her neck to look at him.

'Professor van der Driesma,' said Professor Smythe. 'Simon, this is Julie Beckworth; I'm sure you'll get on famously.'

She held out a polite hand and had it crushed briefly. She wasn't as sure as Professor Smythe about getting on famously, though. His eyes *were* blue; they were cold too, and indifferent. He wasn't going to like her. She sought frantically for the right thing to say and murmured, 'How do you do?' which didn't sound right somehow.

He didn't waste words but nodded at her and turned to Professor Smythe. 'I wonder if we might go over these notes—that patient in the women's ward—Mrs Collins—there are several problems...'

'Ah, yes, you are quite right, Simon. Now, as I see it...'

Julie went back to her filing cabinet, and when told to take her coffee-break went away thankfully. When she got back her new boss had gone.

He came again that afternoon when she was at her desk, dealing with the last of the paperwork before Professor Smythe handed over. The door separating her office from Professor Smythe's was open but when he came in he paused to close it—an action which caused her to sit up very straight and let out an explosive word. Did he imagine that she would eavesdrop? Professor Smythe had conducted countless interviews with the door wide open. A bad start, reflected Julie, thumping the computer with unnecessary force.

* * *

She would have been even more indignant if she could have heard what the two men were talking about.

'I should like to know more about Miss Beckworth,' observed Professor van der Driesma. 'I am indeed fortunate to have her, but if I were to know rather more of her background it might make for a speedier rapport between us.'

'Of course, Simon. I should have thought of that sooner. She has been with me for three years; I believe I told you that. Her father had a practice near Victoria Park, died suddenly of a massive heart attack—he was barely fifty-six years old. A splendid man, had a big practice, never expected to die young, of course, and left almost no money.

'Luckily the house was his; they still live in it— Julie, her mother and her young sister. There are two boys—the eldest's at the Birmingham General, his first post after qualifying, and the other boy's at Cambridge. I imagine they are poor, but Julie is hardly a young woman to talk about herself and I wouldn't presume to ask. She's a clever girl, very patient and hard-working, well liked too; you will find her a splendid right hand when you need one.' He chuckled. 'All this and beautiful besides.'

His companion smiled. 'How old is she? There is no question of her leaving to marry?'

'Twenty-six. Never heard of a boyfriend let alone a prospective husband. Even if she didn't tell me, the hospital grapevine would have got hold of it. Her home is nearby and she doesn't watch the clock and I've never known her to be late.'

'A paragon,' observed his companion drily.

'Indeed, yes. You are a lucky man, Simon.'

To which Professor van der Driesma made no reply. He glanced at his watch. 'I'm due on the wards; I'd better go. I shall hope to see something of you when you have retired, sir.'

'Of course, Mary and I will be delighted to see you at any time. I shall be interested to know how you get on. I'm sure you'll like the post.'

'I'm looking forward to it. I'll see you tomorrow before you leave.'

He went away, adding insult to injury by leaving the door open on his way out.

Professor Smythe had refused an official leave-taking but his friends and colleagues poured into his office on Saturday morning. Julie, who didn't work on a Saturday, was there, keeping in the background as well as her splendid shape allowed, making coffee, finding chairs and answering the phone, which rang incessantly. Presently the last of the visitors went away and Professor Smythe was left with just his successor and Julie.

'I'm off,' he told them. 'Thank you, Julie, for coming in to give a hand.' He trotted over to her and kissed her cheek. 'My right hand; I shall miss you. You must come and see us.'

She shook his hand and saw how tired he looked. 'Oh, I will, please.' She proffered a small book. 'I hope you'll like this—a kind of memento...'

It was a small book on birds and probably he had it already, for he was a keen bird-watcher, but he received it with delight, kissed her again and said, 'Be off with you, Julie.'

He would want to talk to Professor van der Driesma she thought, and went silently, closing the door behind her. She was crossing the forecourt when a dark grey Bentley crept up beside her and stopped. Professor van der Driesma got out.

He said without preamble, 'I'll drive you home.'

'My bus goes from across the street. Thank you for the offer, though.' She was coolly polite, remembering the closed door. Rude man…

'Get in.' Nicely said, but he wasn't prepared to argue. After all, she was working for him from now on. She got in

He got in beside her. 'Somewhere on the other side of Victoria Park, isn't it? Professor Smythe told me that your father was a GP.'

'Yes.' She added baldly, 'He died.'

'I'm sorry,' he said, and strangely enough she knew that he meant it.

'I think that I should warn you that I may work at a slightly faster pace than Professor Smythe.'

'That's to be expected,' said Julie crisply. 'He's very elderly and ill too, and you're…' she paused. 'You're not quite middle-aged, are you?'

'Not quite. If I work you too hard you must tell me, Miss Beckworth.'

Put neatly in her place, she said, 'You can turn left here and then right. It's a short cut.'

If he was surprised to see the roomy house with its rather untidy garden, surrounded by narrow streets of small dwellings, he said nothing. He drew up in the road and got out to open her door—an action which impressed her, even if against her will. He might have a nasty tongue but his manners were perfect and effortless.

'Thank you, Professor,' she said politely, not to be outdone. 'I'll be at the office at eight forty-five on Monday morning.'

He closed the gate behind her, aware of faces peering from several windows in the house, waited until she had reached the door and opened it and then got into his car and drove away. He smiled as he drove.

Julie was met in the hall by her mother, Esme and Luscombe.

'Whoever was that?' her mother wanted to know.

'That's a smashing car,' observed Luscombe.

'He's a giant,' said Esme.

'That's my new boss. He gave me a lift home. His name is Simon van der Driesma; I don't think he likes me...'

'Why ever not?' Her mother was simply astonished; everyone liked Julie. 'Why did he give you a lift, then?'

'I think he may have wanted to see where I lived.'

Mrs Beckworth, who had hoped that there might be other reasons—after all, Julie was a beautiful girl and excellent company—said in a disappointed voice, 'Oh, well, perhaps. We waited lunch for you, love. One of Luscombe's splendid casseroles.'

Luscombe, besides having been with them for as

long as Julie could remember, first as a general facto-
tum in her father's surgery and then somehow taking
over the housekeeping, was a splendid cook. 'I'm rav-
enous,' said Julie.

They went to the sports shop after lunch and bought
Esme's hockey stick, and Esme went round to the
Thompsons' later to show it off to Freddie while Julie
took Blotto for his evening walk.

Sunday, as all Sundays, went too quickly—church,
home to an economical pot-roast, and then a few lazy
hours reading the Sunday papers until it was time to
get the tea.

Luscombe went to see his married sister on Sunday
afternoons, so Julie got their supper, loaded the washing
machine ready to switch it on in the morning, did some
ironing, made sure that Esme had everything ready for
school, had a cosy chat with her mother and took herself
off to bed. She went to sleep quickly, but only after a
few anxious thoughts about the next morning. Even if
Professor van der Driesma didn't like her overmuch, as
long as she did as he wished and remembered to hold
her tongue it might not be so bad.

It was a bad start on Monday morning. She was
punctual as always, but he was already there, sitting at
his desk, his reading glasses perched on his patrician
nose, perusing some papers lying before him then laying them tidily aside.

'Good morning, sir,' said Julie, and waited.

He glanced up. His 'good morning' was grave; she

hoped that he would soon get out of the habit of calling her Miss Beckworth; it made her feel old.

'I believe I am to do a ward round at ten o'clock. Perhaps you will get the patients' notes and bring them to me here.' When she hesitated, he said, 'Yes, I am aware that the ward sister should have them, but I simply wish to glance through them before I do my round.'

Julie went up to the women's medical ward and found Sister in her office. Sister was small and dainty, never lacking dates with the more senior housemen. She was drinking strong tea from a battered mug and waved Julie to the only chair. 'Have some tea—I'll get one of the nurses—'

'I'd love a cup, but I don't dare,' said Julie. 'Professor van der Driesma wants the notes of his patients on the ward so's he can study them before his round.'

'A bit different to Professor Smythe?' asked Sister, hunting up folders on her desk. 'I must say he's remarkably good-looking; my nurses are drooling over him but I don't think he's even noticed them. A bit reserved?'

'I don't know, but I think you may be right.' She took the bundle of notes. 'I'll get these back to you as soon as I can, Sister.'

'I'll have your head if you don't,' said Sister. 'It's his first round and it has to be perfect.'

Julie skimmed back through the hospital, laid the folders on the professor's desk and waited.

He said thank you without looking up and she slid away to her own desk to type up notes and reports and answer the telephone. Just before ten o'clock, however, she went back to his desk.

'Shall I take the patients' notes back now, sir?' she asked the bowed head; his glasses were on the end of his nose and he was making pencil notes in the margin of the report that he was reading.

He glanced up and spoke mildly. 'Is there any need? I can take them with me.' When she hesitated he said, 'Well?'

'Sister Griffiths wanted them back before you went on the ward.'

He gave her a brief look and said, 'Indeed? Then we mustn't disappoint her, must we? Oh, and you may as well stay on the ward and take notes.'

She gathered up the folders. 'Very well, sir. Do you want me to come back here for you? It is almost ten o'clock.'

'No, no, save your foot!'

It was a remark which made her feel as if she had bunions or painful corns. It rankled, for she had excellent feet, narrow and high-arched, and while she spent little money on her clothes she bought good shoes. Plain court shoes with not too high heels, kept beautifully polished.

From his desk the professor watched her go, aware that he had annoyed her and irritated by it. He hoped that her prickly manner would soften, totally unaware that it was he who was making it prickly. He didn't waste time thinking about her; he put the notes he had been making in his pocket and took himself off to Women's Medical.

He had a number of patients there; a rare case of aplastic anaemia—the only treatment of which was frequent blood transfusions, two young women with leukaemia, an older woman with Hodgkin's disease and two cases of polycythaemia. To each he gave his full attention, taking twice as long as Sister had expected, dictating to Julie as he went in a quiet, unhurried voice.

She, wrestling with long words like agranulocytosis and lymphosarcoma, could see that the patients liked him. So did Sister, her annoyance at the length of the round giving way to her obvious pleasure in his company. It was a pity that he didn't appear to show any pleasure in hers; his attention was focused on his patients; he had few words to say to her and those he had were of a purely professional kind.

As for Julie, he dictated to her at length, over one shoulder, never once looking to see if she knew what he was talking about. Luckily, she did; Professor Smythe had been a good deal slower but the words he had used had been just as long. She had taken care over the years to have a medical directory handy when she was typing up notes, although from time to time she had asked him to explain a word or a medical term to her and he had done so readily.

She thought that it would be unlikely for Professor van der Driesma to do that. Nor would he invite her to share his coffee-break while he told her about his grandchildren... He was too young for grandchildren, of course, but probably he had children. Pretty little girls, handsome little boys, a beautiful wife.

She became aware that he had stopped speaking and looked up. He was staring at her so coldly that she had a moment's fright that she had missed something he had said. If she had, she would get it from Sister later.

She shut her notebook with a snap and he said, 'I'd like those notes as soon as you can get them typed, Miss Beckworth.'

'Very well, sir,' said Julie, and promised herself silently that she would have her coffee first.

Which she did, prudently not spending too much time doing so; somehow the professor struck her as a man not given to wasting time in Sister's office chatting over coffee and a tin of biscuits. She was right; she was halfway through the first batch of notes when he returned.

'I shall be in the path lab if I'm wanted,' he told her, and went away again.

Julie applied herself to her work. It was all going to be quite different, she thought regretfully; life would never be the same again.

The professor stayed away for a long time; she finished her notes, placed them on his desk and took herself off to the canteen for her midday meal. She shared her table with two other secretaries and one of the receptionists, all of them agog to know about the new professor.

'What's he like?' asked the receptionist, young and pretty and aware of it.

'Well, I don't really know, do I?' said Julie reasonably. 'I mean, I've only seen him for a few minutes this morning and on the ward round.' She added cautiously, 'He seems very nice.'

'You'll miss Professor Smythe,' said one of the secretaries, middle-aged and placid. 'He was an old dear...'

The receptionist laughed, 'Well, this one certainly

isn't that. He's got more than his fair share of good looks too. Hope he comes to my desk one day!'

Julie thought that unlikely, but she didn't say so. She ate her cold meat, potatoes, lettuce leaf and half a tomato, followed this wholesome but dull fare with prunes and custard and went back to her little office. She would make herself tea; Professor Smythe had installed an electric kettle and she kept a teapot and mugs in the bottom drawer of one of the filing cabinets—sugar too, and tiny plastic pots of milk.

Professor van der Driesma was sitting at his desk. He looked up as she went in. 'You have been to your lunch?' he asked smoothly. 'Perhaps you would let me know when you will be absent from the office.'

Julie glowered; never mind if he was a highly important member of the medical profession, there was such a thing as pleasant manners between colleagues. 'If you had been here to tell, I would have told you,' she pointed out in a chilly voice. 'And it's not lunch, it's midday dinner.'

He sat back in his chair, watching her. Presently he said, coldly polite, 'Miss Beckworth, shall we begin as we intend to go on? I am aware that I am a poor substitute for Professor Smythe; nevertheless, we have inherited each other whether we wish it or not. Shall we endeavour to make the best of things?

'I must confess that you are not quite what I would have wished for and I believe that you hold the same opinion of me. If you find it difficult to work for me, then by all means ask for a transfer. Your work is highly regarded; there should be no difficulty in that. On the other hand, if you are prepared to put up with my lack of the social graces, I dare say we may rub along quite nicely.'

He smiled then, and she caught her breath, for he looked quite different—a man she would like to know, to be friends with. She said steadily, 'I would prefer to stay if you will allow that. You see, you're not a bit like Professor Smythe, but I'm sure once I've got used to you you'll find me satisfactory.' She added, 'What don't you like about me?'

'Did I say that I disliked you? Indeed I did not; I meant that you were not quite the secretary I would have employed had I been given the choice.'

'Why?'

'You're too young—and several other...' He paused. 'Shall we let it rest?' He stood up and held out a hand. 'Shall we shake on it?'

She shook hands and thought what a strange conversation they were having.

He was back behind his desk, turning over the papers before him.

'This case of agranulocytosis—Mrs Briggs has had typhoid and has been treated with chloramphenicol, the cause of her condition. I should like to see any old notes if she has been a patient previously. From her present notes you have seen that she remembers being here on two occasions but she can't remember when. Is that a hopeless task?'

'Probably. I'll let you have them as soon as possible. The path lab from the Royal Central phoned; they would like to speak to you when you are free.'

'Ah, yes. There's a patient there. Get hold of them and put them through to me, will you, Miss Beckworth?'

'I'm going to hunt for those notes,' she told him. 'I shall be in the records office until I find them.'

'Very well.' He didn't look up from his writing and she went to her own office, dialled the Royal Central and presently put the call through to his office. There was nothing on her desk that needed urgent attention, so she went through the hospital and down into the basement and, after a few words with the fussy woman in charge of the patients' records, set to work.

It was a difficult task but not entirely hopeless. Mrs Briggs was forty years old; her recollections of her previous visits were vague but positive. Say, anything between five and ten years ago... It was tiresome work and dusty and the fussy woman or her assistant should have given her a hand, although in all fairness she had to admit that they were being kept busy enough.

She longed for a cup of tea, and a glance at her watch told her that her teabreak was long past. Was she supposed to stay until the notes were found or could she go home at half-past five? she wondered.

It was almost five o'clock when her luck turned and, looking rather less than her pristine self, she went back to the professor's office.

He was on the telephone as she went in; she laid the folders down on his desk and, since he nodded without looking up, she went to her office and sat down at her own desk. While she had been away someone had tossed a variety of paperwork onto it. 'No tea,' muttered Julie, 'and this lot to polish off before I go home, and much thanks shall I get for it—'

'Ah, no, Miss Beckworth,' said the professor from somewhere behind her. 'Do not be so hard on me. You have found the notes, for which I thank you, and a dusty job it was too from the look of you.'

She turned round indignantly at that and he went on smoothly, 'A pot of tea would help, wouldn't it? And most of the stuff on your desk can wait until the morning.'

He leaned across her and picked up the phone. 'The canteen number?' he asked her, and when she gave it ordered with pleasant courtesy, and with a certainty that no one would object, a tray of tea for two and a plate of buttered toast.

She was very conscious of the vast size of him. She wondered, idiotically, if he had played rugger in his youth. Well, she conceded, he wasn't all that old—thirty-five, at the most forty... He had straightened up, towering over her, his gaze intent, almost as though he had read her thoughts and was amused by them. She looked at the clock and said in a brisk voice, 'I can get a good deal of this done this afternoon, sir. I'm quite willing to stay on for a while.'

'I said that tomorrow morning would do.' His voice was mild but dared her to argue. 'We will have our tea and you will leave at your usual time.'

She said 'Very well, sir' in a meek voice, although she didn't feel meek. Who did he think he was? Professor or no professor, she had no wish to be ordered about.

'You'll get used to me in time,' he observed, just as

though she had voiced the thought out loud. 'Here is the tea.'

The canteen server put the tray down on his desk; none of the canteen staff was particularly friendly with those who took their meals there; indeed, at times one wondered if they grudged handing over the plates of food, and the girl who had come in was not one of Julie's favourites—handing out, as she did, ill nature with meat and two veg. Now, miraculously, she was actually smiling. Not at Julie, of course, and when he thanked her politely she muttered, 'No trouble, sir; any time. I can always pop along with something.'

The professor sat down behind his desk. 'Come and pour out,' he suggested, 'and let us mull over tomorrow's schedule.' He handed her the toast and bit hugely into his. 'What an obliging girl.'

'Huh,' said Julie. 'She practically throws our dinners at us. But then, of course, you're a man.'

'Er—yes; presumably you think that makes a difference?'

'Of course it does.' Perhaps she wasn't being quite polite; she added 'sir'.

They had little to say to each other; indeed, he made a couple of phone calls while he polished off the toast, and when they had had second cups he said, 'Off you go, Miss Beckworth; I'll see you in the morning.'

Chapter 2

When Julie got home they were all waiting to hear how she had got on.

'At least he didn't keep you late,' observed her mother. 'Is he nice?' By which she meant was he good-looking, young and liable to fall in love with Julie?

'Abrupt, immersed in his work, likes things done at once, very nice with his patients—'

'Old?' Mrs Beckworth tried hard to sound casual.

'Getting on for forty, perhaps thirty-five; it's hard to tell.' Julie took pity on her mother. 'He's very good-looking, very large, and I imagine the nurses are all agog.'

'Not married?' asked her mother hopefully.

'I don't know, Mother, and I doubt if I ever shall; he's not chatty.'

'Sounds OK to me,' said Luscombe, 'even if he's foreign.'

Esme had joined the inquisition. 'He's Dutch; does he talk with a funny accent?'

'No accent at all—well, yes, perhaps you can hear that he's not English, but only because he speaks it so well, if you see what I mean.'

'A gent?' said Luscombe.

'Well, yes, and frightfully clever, I believe. I dare say that once we've got used to each other we shall get on very well.'

'What do you call him?' asked Esme.

'Professor or sir…'

'What does he call you?'

'Miss Beckworth.'

Esme hooted with laughter. 'Julie, that makes you sound like an elderly spinster. I bet he wears glasses…'

'As a matter of fact he does—for reading.'

'He sounds pretty stuffy,' said Esme. 'Can we have tea now that Julie's home?'

'On the table in two ticks,' said Luscombe, and went back to the kitchen to fetch the macaroni cheese—for tea for the Beckworths was that unfashionable meal, high tea—a mixture of supper and tea taken at the hour of half past six, starting with a cooked dish, going on to bread and butter and cheese or sandwiches, jam and scones, and accompanied by a large pot of tea.

Only on Sundays did they have afternoon tea, and supper at a later hour. And if there were guests—friends or members of the family—then a splendid dinner was conjured up by Luscombe; the silver was polished, the glasses sparkled and a splendid damask cloth that Mrs Beckworth cherished was brought out. They might be poor but no one needed to know that.

Now they sat around the table, enjoying Luscombe's good food, gossiping cheerfully, and if they still missed the scholarly man who had died so suddenly they kept that hidden. Sometimes, Julie reflected, three years seemed a long time, but her father was as clear in her mind as if he were living, and she knew that her mother and Esme felt the same. She had no doubt that the faithful Luscombe felt the same way, too.

She had hoped that after the professor's offer of tea and toast he would show a more friendly face, but she was to be disappointed. His 'Good morning, Miss Beckworth' returned her, figuratively speaking, to arm's length once more. Of course, after Professor Smythe's avuncular 'Hello, Julie' it was strange to be addressed as Miss Beckworth. Almost everyone in the hospital called her Julie; she hoped that he might realise that and follow suit.

He worked her hard, but since he worked just as hard, if not harder, himself she had no cause for complaint. Several days passed in uneasy politeness—cold on his part, puzzled on hers. She would get used to him, she told herself one afternoon, taking his rapid dictation, and glanced up to find him staring at her. 'Rather as though I was something dangerous and ready to explode,' she explained to her mother later.

'Probably deep in thought and miles away,' said Mrs Beckworth, and Julie had to agree.

There was no more tea and toast; he sent her home punctiliously at half past five each day and she supposed that he worked late at his desk clearing up the paperwork, for much of his day was spent on the wards or in consultation. He had a private practice too, and since he was absent during the early afternoons she supposed that he saw those patients then. A busy day, but hers was busy too.

Of course, she was cross-examined about him each time she went to the canteen, but she had nothing to tell—and even if she had had she was discreet and loyal and would not have told. Let the man keep his private life to himself, she thought.

Professor van der Driesma, half-aware of the interest in him at St Bravo's, ignored it. He was a haematologist first and last, and other interests paled beside his deep interest in his work and his patients. He did have other interests, of course: a charming little mews cottage behind a quiet, tree-lined street and another cottage near Henley, its little back garden running down to the river, and, in Holland, other homes and his family home.

He had friends too, any number of them, as well as his own family. His life was full and he had pushed the idea of marriage aside for the time being. No one—no woman—had stirred his heart since he had fallen in love as a very young man to be rejected for an older one, already wealthy and high in his profession. He had got over the love years ago—indeed he couldn't imagine now what he had seen in the girl—but her rejection had sown the seeds of a determination to excel at his work.

Now he had fulfilled that ambition, but in the meantime he had grown wary of the pretty girls whom his friends were forever introducing him to; he wanted more than a pretty girl—he wanted an intelligent companion, someone who knew how to run his home, someone who would fit in with his friends, know how to entertain them, would remove from him the petty burden of social life. She would need to be good-looking and elegant and dress well too, and bring up their children...

He paused there. There was no such woman, of course; he wanted perfection and there was, he decided cynically, no such thing in a woman; he would eventually have to make the best of it with the nearest to his ideal.

These thoughts, naturally enough, he kept to himself; no one meeting him at a dinner party or small social gathering would have guessed that behind his bland, handsome face he was hoping that he might meet the woman he wanted to marry. In the meantime there was always his work.

Which meant that there was work for Julie too; he kept her beautiful nose to the grindstone, but never thoughtlessly; she went home punctually each evening—something she had seldom done with Professor Smythe. He also saw to it that she had her coffee-break, her midday dinner and her cup of tea at three o'clock, but between these respites he worked her hard.

She didn't mind; indeed, she found it very much to her taste as, unlike his predecessor, he was a man of excellent memory, as tidy as any medical man was ever likely to be, and not given to idle talk. It would be nice, she reflected, watching his enormous back going through the door, if he dropped the occasional word other than some diabolical medical term that she couldn't spell. Still, they got on tolerably well, she supposed. Perhaps at a suitable occasion she might suggest that he stopped calling her Miss Beckworth... At Christmas, perhaps, when the entire hospital was swamped with the Christmas spirit.

It was during their second week of uneasy association that he told her that he would be going to Holland at the weekend. She wasn't surprised at that, for he had international renown, but she was surprised to find a quick flash of regret that he was going away; she supposed that she had got used to the silent figure at his desk or his disappearing for hours on end to return wanting something impossible at the drop of a hat. She said inanely, 'How nice—nice for you, sir.'

'I shall be working,' he told her austerely. 'And do not suppose that you will have time to do more than work either.'

'Why do you say that, Professor? Do you intend leaving me a desk piled high?' Her delightful bosom swelled with annoyance. 'I can assure you that I shall have plenty to do...'

'You misunderstand me, Miss Beckworth; you will be going with me. I have a series of lectures to give and I have been asked to visit two hospitals and attend a seminar. You will take any notes I require and type them up.'

She goggled at him. 'Will I?' She added coldly, 'And am I to arrange for our travel and where we are to stay and transport?'

He sat back at ease. 'No, no. That will all be attended to; all you will need will be a portable computer and your notebook and pencil. You will be collected from your home at nine o'clock on Saturday morning. I trust you will be ready at that time.'

'Oh, I'll be ready,' said Julie, and walked over to his desk to stand before it looking at him. 'It would have been nice to have been asked,' she observed with a snap. 'I do have a life beyond these walls, you know.'

With which telling words she walked into her own office and shut the door. There was a pile of work on her desk; she ignored it. She had been silly to lose her temper; it might cost her her job. But she wasn't going to apologise.

'I will not be ordered about; I wouldn't talk to Blotto in such a manner.' She had spoken out loud and the professor's answer took her by surprise.

'My dear Miss Beckworth, I have hurt your feelings. I do apologise; I had no intention of ruffling your temper.' A speech which did nothing to improve matters.

'That's all right,' said Julie, still coldly.

She was formulating a nasty remark about slave-drivers when he asked, 'Who or what is Blotto? Who, I presume, is treated with more courtesy than I show you.'

He had come round her desk and was sitting on its edge, upsetting the papers there. He was smiling at her too. She had great difficulty in not smiling back. 'Blotto is the family dog,' she told him, and looked away.

Professor van der Driesma was a kind man but he had so immersed himself in his work that he also wore an armour of indifference nicely mitigated by good manners. Now he set himself to restore Julie's good humour.

'I dare say that you travelled with Professor Smythe from time to time, so you will know what to take with you and the normal routine of such journeys…'

'I have been to Bristol, Birmingham and Edinburgh with Professor Smythe,' said Julie, still icily polite.

'Amsterdam, Leiden and Groningen, where we shall be going, are really not much farther away from London. I have to cram a good deal of work into four or five days; I must depend upon your support, which I find quite admirable.'

'I don't need to be buttered up,' said Julie, her temper as fiery as her hair. 'It's my job.'

'My dear Miss Beckworth, I shall forget that remark. I merely give praise where praise is due.' His voice was mild and he hid a smile. Julie really was a lovely girl but as prickly as a thorn-bush. Highly efficient too— everything that Professor Smythe had said of her; to have her ask for a transfer and leave him at the mercy of some chit of a girl… The idea was unthinkable. He observed casually, 'I shall, of course, be occupied for most of my days, but there will be time for you to do some sightseeing.'

It was tempting bait; a few days in another country, being a foreigner in another land—even with the professor for company it would be a nice change. Besides, she reminded herself, she had no choice; she worked for him and was expected to do as she was bid. She had, she supposed, behaved badly. She looked up at him. 'Of course I'll be ready to go with you, sir. I'm—I'm sorry I was a little taken aback; it was unexpected.'

He got off the desk. 'I am at times very forgetful,' he told her gravely. 'You had better bring a raincoat and an umbrella with you; it will probably rain. Let me have those notes as soon as possible, will you? I shall be up on the ward if I'm wanted.'

She would have to work like a maniac if she was to finish by half past five, she thought, but Julie sat for a few minutes, her head filled with the important problem of what clothes to take with her. Would she go out at all socially? She had few clothes, although those she had were elegant and timeless in style; blouses, she thought, the skirt she had on, the corduroy jacket that she'd bought only a few weeks ago, just in case it was needed, a dress... Her eyes lighted on the clock and she left her pleasant thoughts for some hard work.

She told her mother as soon as she got home and within minutes Esme and Luscombe had joined them to hear the news.

'Clothes?' said Mrs Beckworth at once. 'You ought to have one of those severe suits with padded shoulders; the women on TV wear them all the time; they look like businessmen.'

'I'm not a businessman, Mother, dear! And I'd hate to wear one. I've got that dark brown corduroy jacket and this skirt—a pleated green and brown check. I'll take a dress and a blouse for each day...'

'Take that smoky blue dress—the one you've had for years,' said Esme at once. 'It's so old it's fashionable again. Will you go out a lot—restaurants and dancing? Perhaps he'll take you to a nightclub.'

'The professor? I should imagine that wild horses wouldn't drag him into one. And of course he won't take me out. I'll have piles of work to do and he says he will be fully occupied each day.'

'You might meet a man,' observed Esme. 'You know—and he'll be keen on you and take you out in the evenings. The professor can't expect you to work all the time.'

'I rather fancy that's just what he does expect. But it'll be fun and I'll bring you all back something really Dutch. Blotto too.'

She had two days in which to get herself ready, which meant that each evening she was kept busy—washing her abundant hair, doing her nails, pressing the blouses, packing a case.

'Put in a woolly,' suggested her mother, peering over her shoulder. 'Two—that nice leaf-brown cardigan you had for Christmas last year and the green sweater.' She frowned. 'You're sure we can't afford one of those suits?'

'Positive. I'll do very well with what I've got, and if Professor van der Driesma doesn't approve that's just too bad. Anyway, he won't notice.'

In this she was mistaken; his polite, uninterested glance as she opened the door to him on Saturday morning took in every small detail. He had to concede that although she looked businesslike she also looked feminine; with a lovely face such as hers she should be able to find herself an eligible husband...

He gave her a 'good morning,' unsmiling, was charming to her mother when he was introduced, and smiled at Esme's eager, 'You'll give Julie time to send some postcards, won't you?' He picked up Julie's case and was brought to a halt by Esme. 'Don't you get tired of seeing all that blood? Isn't it very messy?'

Mrs Beckworth's shocked 'Esme' was ignored.

'Well, I'm only asking,' said Esme.

The professor put the case down. 'There is almost no blood,' he said apologetically. 'Just small samples in small tubes and, more importantly, the condition of the patient—whether they're pale or yellow or red in the face. How ill they feel, how they look.'

Esme nodded. 'I'm glad you explained. I'm going to be a doctor.'

'I have no doubt you'll do very well.' He smiled his sudden charming smile. 'We have to go, I'm afraid.'

Julie bent to say goodbye to Blotto, kissed her mother and sister, and kissed Luscombe on his leathery cheek. 'Take care of them, Luscombe.'

'Leave 'em to me, Miss Julie; 'ave a good time.'

She got into the car; they were all so sure that she was going to enjoy herself but she had her doubts.

The professor had nothing to say for some time; he crossed the river and sped down the motorway towards Dover. 'You are comfortable?' he wanted to know.

'Yes, thank you. I don't think one could be anything else in a car like this.'

It was an observation which elicited no response

from him. Was she going to spend four or five days in the company of a man who only addressed her when necessary? He addressed her now. 'You're very silent, Miss Beckworth.'

She drew a steadying breath; all the same there was peevishness in her voice. 'If you wished me to make conversation, Professor, I would have done my best.'

He laughed. 'I don't think I have ever met anyone quite like you. You fly—how do you say it?—off the handle without notice. At least it adds interest to life. I like your young sister.'

'Everyone likes her; she's such a dear girl and she says what she thinks...'

'It must run in the family!' Before she could utter he went on, 'She must miss her father.'

'Yes, we all do. He was a very special person...'

'You prefer not to talk about him?' His voice was kind.

'No. No, we talk about him a lot at home, but of course other people forget, or don't like to mention his name in case we get upset.'

'So—tell me something of him. Professor Smythe told me that he had a very large practice and his patients loved him.'

'Oh, they did, and he loved his work...' It was like a cork coming out of a bottle; she was in full flood, lost in happy reminiscences, and when she paused for breath the professor slipped in a quiet word or question and started her off again.

She was surprised to see that they were slowing as the outskirts of Dover slipped past them. 'I talk too much.'

'No, indeed not, Miss Beckworth; I have found it

most interesting to know more of your father. You have a knack of holding one's interest.'

She muttered a reply, wondering if he was being polite, and they didn't speak much until he had driven the car on board the hovercraft and settled her in a seat. He took the seat beside her, ordered coffee and sandwiches, and with a word of excuse opened his briefcase and took out some papers.

The coffee was excellent and she was hungry. When she had finished she said, 'I'm going to tidy myself,' in an unselfconscious manner.

He matched it with a casual, 'Yes, do that; once we land I don't want to stop more than I have to.'

He got up to let her pass and, squeezing past him, she reflected that it was like circumnavigating a large and very solid tree-trunk.

Back in her seat once more, she looked out of the window and wondered how long it would take to drive to Leiden, which was to be their first stop.

Shortly afterwards they landed. 'We'll stop for a sandwich presently,' the professor assured her, stuffed her into the car and got in and drove off.

'Bruges, Antwerp, cross into Holland at Breda and drive on to the Hague; Leiden is just beyond.'

That, apparently, was as much as he intended to tell her. They were out of France and into Belgium before she saw the map in the pocket on the door. They were on a motorway, and such towns as they passed they skirted, but presently she started looking at signposts and traced their journey on the map. The professor was driving fast but, she had to admit, with a casual assurance which made her feel quite safe, although it prevented her from seeing anything much. But when they reached Bruges he slowed down and said, to surprise her, 'This is a charming town; we'll drive through it so that you get an idea of its beauty.'

Which he did, obligingly pointing out anything of interest before rejoining the motorway once more. The traffic was heavy here and Antwerp, as they approached it, loomed across the horizon. Before they reached the city he turned off onto a ring road and rejoined the motorway to the north of the city. Obviously, she thought, he knew the way—well, of course he would since he went to and fro fairly frequently. A huge road sign informed her that they were forty-eight kilometres from Breda, and after some mental arithmetic she decided on thirty miles. At the rate they were going they would be there in less than half an hour.

Which they were, still on the motorway skirting the town, driving on towards the Moerdijk Bridge and then on towards Rotterdam. Before they reached the bridge the professor stopped by a roadside café, parked the car and ushered her inside. It was a small place, its tables half-filled. 'I'll be at that table by the window,' he told her; he nodded to a door beside the bar. 'Through there, don't be long—I'm hungry and I expect you are too.'

She was famished, breakfast had been a meal taken in another world, tea and dinner were as yet uncertain. She was back within five minutes.

'I've ordered for us both; I hope you'll enjoy my choice. I'm having coffee but they'll bring you tea—not quite as the English drink it, but at least it's tea.'

'Thank you, I'd love a cup. Are you making good time?'

'Yes. I hope to be at Leiden around teatime. You have a room close to the hospital. I shall want you tomorrow in the afternoon. In the morning I have several people to see so you will have time to look around. You may find the morning service at St Pieterskerk; it's a magnificent building.'

'I don't speak Dutch or understand it.'

'You don't need to—the service is similar to your own church, and if you need to ask the way practically everyone will understand you.'

'Then I'd like that.' The café owner had brought the coffee and, for her, a glass of hot water on a saucer with a teabag; he came back a moment later with two dishes on which reposed slices of bread covered with slices of ham and two fried eggs.

'This is an *uitsmijter*,' said the professor. 'If you don't care for it, say so, and I'll order something else.'

'It looks delicious.' She fell to; it not only looked good, it tasted good too, and, moreover, filled her empty insides up nicely. They ate without much talk; the professor was pleasant, thoughtful of her needs but not disposed to make idle conversation. Reasonable enough, she reflected, polishing off the last bits of ham; she had been wished on him and he didn't like her, although he concealed his dislike beneath good manners. At least he hadn't been able to fault her work...

They were back in the car within half an hour, heading towards Dordrecht and Rotterdam. As they left Dordrecht behind them the traffic became thicker, and as the outskirts of Rotterdam closed in on them she wondered how anyone ever found their way in the tangle of traffic, but it appeared to hold no terrors for her companion and presently they joined the long line of cars edging through the Maas Tunnel and then crossed the city and onto the motorway to den Haag. It bypassed the city, but here and there there were fields and copses which became more frequent as they reached the outskirts of Leiden.

As Professor van der Driesma drove through its heart Julie tried to see everything—it looked charming with its lovely old houses and bustling streets—but presently he turned into a wide street with a canal running through its centre. 'Rapenburg,' the professor told her. 'The university and medical school are on the right.'

Julie, outwardly calm, felt nervous. 'Will you be there?' she asked.

'No, I shall be at my house.'

She waited for more but it seemed that that was all she was to know. She persevered. 'Do you live here?'

'From time to time.' He wasn't going to say any more and presently he stopped before a narrow, tall house— one of a row of gabled houses just past the university buildings. 'I think you will be comfortable here.'

He got out, opened her door, got her case from the boot and thumped the knocker on the solid front door. The woman who opened it was tall and thin and dressed severely in black, but she had a pleasant face and kind smile.

The professor addressed her in Dutch before turning

to Julie. 'This is Mevrouw Schatt. She will show you your room and give you your supper presently.'

He spoke to Mevrouw Schatt again, this time in English. 'This is Miss Julie Beckworth, *mevrouw*. I know you'll take care of her.' He turned back to Julie. 'I will call for you here at one o'clock tomorrow. Bring your notebook with you. I'll tell you what I want you to do when we are there.'

'Where?'

He looked surprised. 'Did I not tell you? We shall be at the *aula* of the medical school—a discussion on various types of anaemia. Mostly questions and answers in English.'

Her 'very well, sir' sounded so meek that he gave her a suspicious look, which she returned with a limpid look from her green eyes.

He stood looking at her for a moment and she thought that he was going to say something else, but his 'Good evening, Miss Beckworth' was brisk. He shook Mevrouw Schatt's hand and exchanged a friendly remark. At least, Julie supposed that it was friendly; she couldn't understand a word.

'Come, miss,' said Mevrouw Schatt, and led the way up a steep flight of stairs and into a pleasant room overlooking the canal. It was rather full of furniture and the bed took up a great deal of space, but it was spotless and warm.

They smiled at each other and Mevrouw Schatt said, 'The bathroom, along this passage. If you want anything you ask, miss.' She turned to go. 'I make tea for you, if you will come down soon.'

Left alone, Julie tried the bed, looked out of the window and unpacked what she would need for the night. So far everything had gone smoothly. She only hoped that she would be able to deal with the work. Presently she went downstairs to sit in the living room and have tea with her hostess.

The room was charming, the furniture old and gleaming, and there was a thick carpet underfoot, and heavy velvet curtains at the long windows which overlooked the street. Mevrouw Schatt switched on several little table-lamps so that the room was visible to passers-by. 'It is the custom,' she explained. 'We are pleased to let others see how cosily we live.'

While she drank her tea and ate the little biscuits Julie nodded and smiled and replied suitably, and wondered what the professor was doing. If he had liked her, surely she would have stayed at his house? Would his wife object? She presumed that he had one, for he had never evinced any interest in any of the staff at the hospital, and, if not a wife, a housekeeper...

Professor van der Driesma had gone straight to the hospital and checked with his colleagues that the arrangements for the following afternoon were satisfactory. It was a pity that the seminar had to be on a Sunday, but he had a tight schedule; he very much doubted if he would have time to go to his home, but at least he could spend the night at his home here in Leiden.

He drove there now, past the university again, over the canal and into a narrow street beside the imposing library. It was quiet here and the houses, narrow and four-storeyed, with their variety of gables, were to outward appearances exactly as they had been built three hundred years ago. He drove to the end and got out, mounted the double steps to the front door with its ornate transom and put his key into the modern lock to be greeted by a deep-throated barking, and as he opened the door a big, shaggy dog hurled himself at him.

The professor bore the onslaught with equanimity. 'Jason, old fellow; it's good to see you again.'

He turned to speak to the elderly, stout woman who had followed the dog into the narrow hall. 'Siska—nice to be home, even if only for one night.' He put an arm round her plump shoulders.

'I have an excellent tea ready,' she told him. 'It is a shame that you must dine out this evening.' She added wistfully, 'Perhaps you will soon spend more time here. You are so often in England.' She went on, 'If you would marry—find yourself a good little wife.'

'I'll think about it, Siska, if I can find one.'

He had his tea with Jason for company, and then the pair of them went for a long walk along the Rapenburg which led them past Mevrouw Schatt's house. He could see Julie sitting in the softly lighted room; she had Mevrouw Schatt's cat on her knee and was laughing.

He stopped to watch her for a moment. A beautiful girl, he reflected, and an excellent secretary; he had been agreeably surprised at her unflurried manner during their journey from England; with no fidgetting or demands to stop on the way, she had been an undemanding companion who didn't expect to be entertained. He walked on, forgetting her as soon as he started to mull over the next day's activities.

He was dining with friends that evening. He had known Gijs van der Eekerk since their student days together. Gijs had married young—a pretty girl, Zalia, who had left him and their small daughter when Alicia had still been a baby. She had been killed in a car accident shortly afterwards and now, after six years, he had married again—an English girl. It was a very happy marriage from all accounts, with Alicia devoted to her stepmother Beatrice, who was expecting a baby in the summer.

He drove to a small village some ten miles from Leiden, stopped the car before a solid square house behind high iron railings and got out, opening the door for Jason. His welcome—and Jason's—was warm, and just for a moment he envied his old friend and his pretty wife and little daughter; they were so obviously in love and little Alicia was so happy. His evening was happy too; they spent an hour or so round the fire in the drawing room after dinner—Alicia had gone to bed—Jason and Fred, the van der Eekerk's great dog, heaped together before it.

On the way home the professor addressed Jason, sitting beside him. 'Do you suppose we shall ever find anyone like Beatrice? And if we do shall we snap her up?'

Jason, half-asleep, grumbled gently.

'You agree? Then we had better start looking.'

The next morning, however, such thoughts had no place in the professor's clever head; an early morning walk with Jason was followed by another visit to the hospital, this time to examine patients and give his opinion to his colleagues before going back to his home for lunch.

As for Julie, she had been up early, eaten her break-fast of rolls, slices of cheese, ham and currant bread, drunk a pot of coffee with them, and then, given di-rections by Mevrouw Schatt, had found her way to St Pieterskerk, where she stayed for the service—not un-derstanding a word, of course. The sermon had gone on for a very long time, but the organ had been mag-nificent and some of the hymns had sounded very like those at home.

She walked back slowly, looking at the quaint old houses, wishing that she had more time to explore, but the professor had said one o'clock and Mevrouw Schatt had told her that they would eat their lunch at noon.

They got on well together, she and her hostess, who was ready to answer Julie's string of questions about Leiden and its history. Her husband had been some-thing to do with the university, she explained, and she had lived there all her life. She had a great deal to say about everything, but not a word about Professor van der Driesma.

He came at exactly one o'clock, and Julie was ready and waiting for him.

He bade her good afternoon without a smile, passed the time of day with Mevrouw Schatt and asked Julie if she was ready.

'Yes, sir. What am I to do about my bag? Shall I take it with me or am I to fetch it later, before we leave?'

'We shan't leave until early tomorrow morning.' He glanced at his watch and ushered her with speed into the car. The drive was very short indeed, thought Julie; they could have walked in five minutes...

He drove across the forecourt of the hospital and under an arch at one side of the building, parked the car, opened her door and closed it behind her with a snap. 'Through here,' he said, indicating a door.

Julie stood where she was. 'Just a minute, Professor. I think there is something which must be said first.' Her voice shook with rage. 'You bring me here, drive me for miles, dump me, and now you expect me to go with you to some talk or other of which I know nothing. On top of that you alter your plans without bothering to tell me. I had my bag all packed...'

She paused for breath. 'You are a very inconsiderate and tiresome man.' She added coldly, 'Hadn't we better go in? It won't do for you to be late.'

He was standing there looking down at her indignant face. 'It seems that I owe you an apology, Miss Beckworth. I had not realised that you had suffered any discomfort during our journey. Since it is obvious that you feel the need to know exactly what I am doing hour by hour I will do my best to keep you informed. First, however, if you will allow it, we will proceed to the *aula*.'

Put in my place, thought Julie, fuming; he's made me sound like a fussy old woman. I hate him. Without a word she followed him through the door, along a narrow corridor and into the lecture hall, outwardly composed and seething under the composure.

Chapter 3

The *aula* was packed and they had to walk the length of it to reach the platform where a semicircle of learned-looking men were already sitting. Julie was given a chair beneath it and someone had considerately placed a desk lamp on a small table beside it. There was a tape recorder there too—just in case she couldn't keep up, she supposed. There was also a carafe of water and a glass—in case she felt faint? She smiled at the thought and then composed her features into suitable gravity as a stout, elderly man rose to his feet.

He made a lengthy speech in faultless English, most of it in dignified praise of Professor van der Driesma, who presently rose to his feet and began his lecture. His voice, Julie had to admit, after the rather plummy accents of the stout man, was a pleasure to listen to, and, thank heaven, deliberate enough for her to keep up. When he had finished and invited questions they came thick and fast. It was to be hoped that he wouldn't want the whole lot typed before they left in the morning.

There was an interval then, and someone brought her a cup of tea and a small, feather-light biscuit. She nibbled it slowly and longed for a second cup but it seemed that there weren't going to be any; there were groups of learned-looking men deep in talk and she supposed that for the time being at least there was nothing for her to do. Was she to sit there twiddling her thumbs until the professor came to fetch her or should she leave? It was less than five minutes' walk back to Mevrouw Schatt's house...

Professor van der Driesma detached himself from a group some way away from her and came unhurriedly towards her.

'We shall be having discussions for another hour or so, Miss Beckworth; I have asked someone to show you to a quiet room so that you can get your notes typed. I understand there is a very efficient computer there.' He turned as he spoke and a young man joined them. 'This is Bas Vliet; he'll show you where to go. I'll come for you when I'm ready.'

Julie offered a hand. Bas Vliet looked rather nice so she gave him a brilliant smile and he smiled back. She switched off the smile when she looked at the professor. Her 'Very well, sir' was uttered in a resigned voice which made him want to shake her. Anyone less like a downtrodden slave would be hard to meet, and here she was, the very picture of stoical servitude. Minx, thought the professor, and walked away.

'I dare say you have to work hard for the Prof,' said Bas Vliet sympathetically. 'He never spares himself and we lesser mortals can't always keep up.'

He opened a door and showed her into a small office. 'I hope there's everything you'll need here. If there's anything you want come and find me and I'll be glad to help.'

Julie thanked him prettily; at first glance there seemed to be everything she would need. She only hoped that the professor would remember that she was there and not go wandering off without her.

'I say, you won't mind if I say that I think you're very pretty?' said Bas. 'The Prof's a lucky man having someone like you working for him.'

Try telling him that, reflected Julie. 'Thank you,' she said demurely. 'I'd better get started...'

He went reluctantly, hoping that he would see her again.

Alone, Julie settled down to work. There was a great deal to get typed up but she was good at her job. All the same it was two hours later that she gathered the sheets together tidily, arranged them with her pen and notebook on the desk and then sat back.

It was almost six o'clock and she was hungry. She thought about supper—a substantial meal, she hoped, and several cups of coffee afterwards. This was a mistake, of course, because she got hungrier, so that when the professor strolled in half an hour later she said crossly, 'There you are. I've been finished for half an hour or more...'

His brows rose. 'You are anxious to return to Mevrouw Schatt?'

'I'm hungry,' said Julie.

'You had tea and a biscuit, surely?'

'Hours ago, and what use is wafer-thin biscuit to someone of my size?'

He said, poker-faced, 'Of no use at all,' and stared at her so fixedly that she blushed.

'We will go now,' he said at length, and held the door for her. 'Be ready to leave at eight o'clock in the morning. I have a lecture at half past nine and shall want you with me. Afterwards I have several patients to see. I shall want you there as I shall make observations for my own use which you will take down in English.' He added impatiently, 'Now, come along, Miss Beckworth.'

For all the world as though I had kept him waiting, fumed Julie silently.

He left her at Mevrouw Schatt's house after a brief conversation with that lady and an even briefer goodnight to herself, and she went thankfully to her room to tidy herself and then down to supper. Thank heaven the Dutch had their evening meal early, she thought, supping delicious soup, then savouring a pork chop with apple sauce and fluffy potatoes and making a contented finish with Dutch apple tart and cream.

Over coffee their desultory conversation merged into a lengthy gossip, while they still sat at the table, until Mevrouw Schatt said, 'You will have to be up early in the morning; you should go to bed, miss.'

'Julie—do call me Julie, please. Yes, I must, but I'll help you with the dishes first; that was a gorgeous meal.'

'You liked?' Mevrouw Schatt was pleased. 'I like to cook and I like also to see what I have cooked eaten with appetite.'

They washed up together in the small, old-fashioned kitchen, and presently Julie went to bed. She hadn't thought about the professor at all; she didn't give him a thought now, but put her bright head on the large, square pillow and went off to sleep.

The professor thumped the knocker at exactly eight o'clock, wished them both a civil good morning, put Julie's case in the boot and opened the car door. There was to be no hanging around... She bade Mevrouw Schatt goodbye and promised to write, unhappy that she had no time to buy flowers or a small thank-you gift, but plainly the professor had no intention of lingering. She got into the car and he closed the door on her at once.

'Are we late?' she asked as they drove away.

He glanced at his watch—an elegant, understated gold one on a leather strap. 'No. It is roughly twenty-six miles to Amsterdam. We shall be there in half an hour.'

An insignificant distance, the Bentley made light of it in rather less time.

There was a great deal of traffic on the motorway, which thickened as they passed Schiphol and went on towards the heart of the city. The streets were crowded now, with bicycles as well as cars and trams and buses and people. How they managed to avoid each other seemed a miracle; she decided not to watch the traffic but to look around her. They had left what she took to be an elegant residential area and were driving through narrow streets bordered by canals and narrow, gabled houses, turning away from the main streets.

They had been silent for a long time. She ventured to remark, 'I expect you know your way very well here, Professor?'

'Yes. The hospital is at the end of this street.'

A high wall separated it from the surrounding houses and from the outside at least it looked very old. 'There is an entrance on the other side,' said the professor, 'leading to one of the main streets.'

He was driving across the forecourt; she thought in a panic that she had no idea how long they were to be there or where she was to go.

'How long shall we be here and where am I to go?'

'Until the late afternoon, and you will come with me.'

It was like getting blood out of a stone. 'I wouldn't dream of going off on my own,' said Julie snappily.

He had stopped the car and turned to look at her. 'I would be extremely annoyed if you did, Miss Beckworth.' He added with a sigh, 'After all, I am responsible for you.'

'Oh, pooh,' said Julie, and tossed her bright head. 'You talk as if I were a child.'

His eyes held hers. 'I am very well aware that you are not a child. Come along now!'

The porter had seen them coming and picked up the phone, and by the time they were halfway across the vast entrance hall three persons were coming towards them: an elderly man with a beard and moustache and a jolly face, a younger man with a long, thin face and fair hair already receding from a high domed forehead, and a much younger man who looked awkward.

Everyone shook hands and Julie was introduced and forgot their names at once. They were obviously good friends of the professor, for there was a good deal of laughing and talk, and even the awkward young man joined in. A houseman, she supposed, a registrar and another professor.

'Coffee first,' boomed the older man. 'You will be glad of it I have no doubt, Miss Beckworth, for our good Simon will work you hard, I can assure you.'

He took her arm and led the way along a dark passage and into a rather grand room full of gentlemen with coffee-cups in their hands. They surged forward to greet the professor, who introduced her once more with a wave of the hand. 'My secretary, Miss Beckworth.' It was a signal for several of the younger men present to offer her cups of coffee, and presently the professor joined her. 'A sister will be here in a moment to show you where you can do your typing if you should have time to spare, and where you can put your jacket and so on.'

As long as there's a loo, thought Julie, following a placid-looking nurse down another dark passage. The room wasn't far away, and thank heaven there was a cloakroom next door. 'I will wait for you,' said the sister, and smiled. 'When the professor has finished his lecture I will fetch you from the lecture hall and show you where you can have your lunch.'

'You will? That's awfully kind.' Julie nipped smartly away, made sure that she had everything she needed with her and then rejoined her guide.

Most of the men had gone from the room when they returned but the professor was still there, deep in conversation with the elderly man who had met them. The young man was there too, hovering anxiously.

'Ready?' The professor was brisk. 'Come along, then.' He paused to say something to the sister, who smiled at him and made a quiet reply before he ushered Julie out of the room.

They all walked out of the passage and into a wide corridor and through a door at its end. There was a large lecture hall beyond; a sea of faces turned to look at them as they went in. Julie was ushered to a seat at the end of the front row and the others climbed onto the platform. She wondered if it was going to be the same lecture as the one he had given at Leiden; if so, that would make things easier for her.

It wasn't; it was all about haemorrhagic diseases— purpura and thrombocytopenia—and he was full of long medical words which taxed her intelligence and speed to their utmost. He had an awful lot to say about them too, and afterwards there were questions and answers. When he finally sat down she laid down her pencil with a shaking hand and heaved a sigh of relief.

There was a young woman sitting next to her. She turned to Julie now. 'You have noted every word?' she wanted to know. 'Is he not splendid? You must be proud to work for him. He is a brilliant man and much revered.'

The girl had an earnest face with lank hair and large spectacles.

'You're a doctor?' asked Julie politely.

'I am qualified, yes, but I have much to learn. I wish to be as clever as Professor van der Driesma; there is no one equal to him.'

She looked at Julie so accusingly that she made haste to agree. 'Oh, yes, he is a very clever man...' She paused because the girl had gone very red and was looking at someone behind Julie's shoulder.

The professor said quietly, 'There is someone come to take you to your lunch, Miss Beckworth.' And then to the girl he said, 'You enjoyed the lecture? I do hope so; it is a most interesting subject.'

'Yes, yes, Professor, I listened to every word. I have told your secretary what a brilliant man you are and she agrees with me...'

The professor covered a small sound with a cough. 'I am flattered. You are recently qualified?' he asked kindly. 'I wish you a successful future.'

They left the girl then and walked back along the corridor to where she saw the same sister waiting, but before they reached her he observed, 'There is no need to bolster my ego, Miss Beckworth; I feel sure that you consider that it is already grossly swollen.'

'Well, really,' said Julie. 'Whatever will you say next?'

'What is more to the point—what will you say, Miss Beckworth?'

She said suddenly, 'I do wish you would stop calling me Miss Beckworth; it makes me feel middle-aged and plain and dull...'

'Perhaps that is how I wish to think of you. Please be ready to accompany me to the wards at two o'clock. You will be fetched. You have all you need in the office?'

He said a word to the sister and went past them down the corridor. The sister said, 'If you will come with me? We have a dining room—a canteen, you call it?' She glanced at her watch. 'You have time to eat and then work before two o'clock.'

Julie walked beside her to the lifts and was taken down to the basement where she collected a bowl of soup, a salad, rolls, butter and cold meat and sat down with her guide, and all the time she wondered why the professor thought of her as plain and middle-aged. He must dislike me very much, she reflected; perhaps when they got back to St Bravo's she should apply for a transfer.

By two o'clock she had typed up more than half her notes and she had taken the precaution of going to the cloakroom to do her face and tidy her hair so that when the same sister came back she was ready. A good thing, for she was hurried along at a great rate through a warren of passages and in and out of lifts. 'We must not keep the professor waiting,' said her companion anxiously.

At the ward doors she was handed over to the ward sister, who smiled and nodded; there was no time to do more; the professor, wearing his glasses, a stethoscope slung round his shoulders and a preoccupied look, came into the ward with the three men who had met them when they had arrived.

He shook hands with Sister, saying something to

make her laugh, nodded to Julie, who gave him a wooden stare, and went to the first bed.

He spent several minutes talking to the young woman lying in it, which gave Julie time to study him at her leisure. He had, she conceded, a nice face—the word 'nice' covering a variety of things: good looks, the kind of nose which could be looked down with shattering effect and a thin mouth which could break into a charming smile. Despite the good looks, it was a man's face to be trusted. She wondered if one could trust someone who didn't like you and whom you didn't like either...

He looked up suddenly, staring at her across the bed, and she blushed, in a sudden panic that he had said something and she hadn't been listening. He hadn't, but after that she had no time to think about anything but the necessity of getting his comments down correctly. And since they were intersected by discussions in Dutch she had to keep her wits about her.

Altogether a tiring afternoon, she decided when finally he finished the round and went away with his companions and Sister. Leaving me here to get lost, I suppose, thought Julie, longing for a cup of tea—a whole pot of tea. She was roused from this gloomy thought by a tap on the arm. The same sister who had been her guide all day was there again.

'Tea?' she asked. 'In the sisters' sitting room; we shall be so pleased to see you.'

'Oh, I'd love that.' Julie beamed at her. 'But oughtn't I to let Professor van der Driesma know?'

'It is he who has arranged that you should have tea with us.'

'Really? Well, in that case, I'll come now, shall I?'

The nurses' home was attached to the hospital—a modern block built behind the main building—and the room she was ushered into was large and comfortable and fairly full of young women in uniform.

They welcomed her warmly, telling her their names, asking her if she had enjoyed her visit to the hospital, sitting her in one of the easy chairs, offering tea. 'With milk and sugar, just as Professor van der Driesma asked,' explained one pretty girl. '"English tea," he told us, "and there must be cake and not little biscuits!"'

'Oh, did he say that?' Julie felt guilty and mean—all her unkind thoughts of him not bothering about her and he had remembered about the biscuits. Oh, dear...!

She drank several cups of tea and ate the cake—*boterkoek*, a kind of madeira cake but buttery and without the lemon—and she answered the questions fired at her. They all spoke English, some better than others, and several of the girls there had been to England on holiday. An hour passed pleasantly until someone glanced at the clock and she was bustled away amid a chorus of goodbyes.

'The Professor must not be kept waiting' was followed by another chorus of *tot ziens*.

'That means see you soon,' said her guide, racing up and down passages very much in the same manner as the white rabbit in *Alice in Wonderland*.

Julie caught up with her in the lift. 'Are you all scared of the professor?' she asked.

'Scared? No, no. We like him very much, therefore

we do everything to please him. He is a good man and his heart is warm.'

Julie blinked. This was an aspect of him which she hadn't so far encountered. She must try and remember it next time he chilled her with an icy stare.

She collected her notebooks and typing, got her jacket and, urged on by her companion, went to the entrance. The professor was there, talking to the man with the beard, his hands in his pockets, looking as though he meant to stand there chatting for some time, but he glanced round as they reached him. 'Ready? You haven't forgotten anything?' He said something in Dutch to the sister and shook her hand before bidding the bearded gentleman goodbye, and then waited while the latter took Julie's hand and said that he hoped to see her again.

'You have seen nothing of our lovely city, Miss Beckworth; it is a pity that Simon has no time to take you sightseeing.'

Julie allowed her eyelashes to sweep her cheeks before glancing up at the whiskered face. 'Oh, but I'm here to work,' she said demurely. 'But I hope to come back one day and explore on my own.'

'My dear young lady, I am sure you would not be on your own for long.'

Julie smiled charmingly. 'Well, I dare say I would bring someone with me to keep me company.'

The professor coughed and she said quickly, 'I'm wasting time, I'm afraid. I must say goodbye—no, what is it you say? *Tot ziens*.'

The professor had opened the car door and she got

in, and after a brief conversation with his colleague he got in beside her.

'Where to?' asked Julie flippantly.

'Groningen. We shall be there for tomorrow and the greater part of the following day before we return to Leiden, where I have patients to see. You will lodge with Mevrouw Schatt again and we shall return to England on the day after that.'

'I expect you're tired,' said Julie sweetly. She wasn't surprised when he didn't answer her.

They were leaving Amsterdam behind when he said, 'Look at the map. We are going north-east to Groningen. The first town is Naarden, then Amersfoort; just past Harderwijk we will stop for a meal. A pity there is no time to use the less busy road; I'm afraid it must be motorway for the whole way.'

They had driven for little more than forty minutes when he turned off the motorway and took a side-road winding through woodlands. 'We have had a busy day,' he said. 'We deserve a leisurely dinner.' Then he drove between two stone pillars onto a drive which led to a hotel ringed around by trees and shrubs.

Julie peered around her; it looked a splendid place and she hoped that her clothes would live up to its magnificence. She was given no time to brood over this, however, but was swept in through its doors, pointed in the direction of the cloakroom and told that he would be waiting for her in the foyer.

He sounded impatient beneath the cool good manners and she whisked away, intent on making the best of things. The cloakroom was luxurious, full of mirrors and pale pink washbasins and with a shelf of toiletries. One could, she supposed, if one had time, shampoo one's hair, give oneself a manicure, try out a variety of lipsticks... It was tempting but the professor mustn't be kept waiting.

The restaurant was elegant and almost full, but the table the *maitre d'* led them to was in one of the wide windows with a view of the small lake half-hidden by trees. 'Oh, how very pretty! Do you come here often?'

'Occasionally. You would like a sherry while we order?'

His manner, she thought wistfully, was exactly the same as when he sat behind his desk dictating letters. 'Please.' She accepted the menu that she was offered and began to work her way through it. There was a great deal of it and the prices made her feel quite faint. Still, if he could afford it... On the other hand, out of consideration for his pocket she should choose those dishes which weren't quite so costly. Soup, she decided, and an omelette.

The professor's quiet voice cut into her pondering. 'The lobster mousseline with champagne sauce is an excellent starter, and how about duckling with orange sauce to follow? Merely a suggestion, of course.'

A suggestion that she was only too happy to agree to, and she sat quietly while he conferred with the wine waiter, looking around her. The women there were well-dressed and the men looked prosperous; it was nice to see how the other half lived.

The lobster was everything that the professor had said of it and she didn't know much about wines, but the white wine she was offered was delicious, pale and dry; she drank it sparingly and so did he. The duckling when it came was mouthwateringly crisp with its orange sauce, straw potatoes and baby sprouts.

While they ate they talked—by no means an animated conversation but easy, casual talk, with not a word about themselves or the day's work. Julie turned her attention to the toffee pudding with a light heart.

They didn't sit over their coffee; it was already dark and there were still, he informed her, more than eighty miles to drive. 'Another hour and a half's drive,' he observed, opening the car door for her.

It was too dark to see much of the countryside now, but as he slowed through the few villages on the motorway she craned her neck to see as much as possible. The road bypassed a big town too, brightly lighted and busy with local traffic. When they reached Assen, the professor said, 'Not long now. We will go straight to the hospital. You will sleep there and accompany me in the morning to the seminar. International.'

'Everyone will speak English, I hope?'

'Oh, yes, with a variety of accents.'

Groningen, when they reached it, looked charming under the streetlamps. The professor drove straight to the heart of the city, crossing first one square and then a second. 'All the main streets lead off from these two squares,' he explained. 'The hospital is down this side-street.'

It was a splendid building with a vast entrance hall, where she wasn't allowed to linger. The professor spoke to the porter and crossed to the row of lifts, taking her with him. 'My bag,' said Julie, hurrying to keep up.

'It will be taken to your room. Come along now, and I'll introduce you to the warden who will take care of you.'

'At what time do you want me to start work, Professor?' She was facing him in the lift. 'And how shall I know where to find you?'

'You will be fetched at half past eight. The seminar starts at nine with a coffee interval and a break for lunch. You will be shown where you can have a meal. We start again at two o'clock and finish around four. I hope to leave here not later than two o'clock on the day after tomorrow. Then you will spend the night with Mevrouw Schatt, and be free in the morning.'

The lift had stopped. 'Thank you, Professor; it's nice to know your plans. I'll be ready in the morning.'

He didn't answer but she hadn't expected him to. Why waste words when one or even none would do? He marched her along a corridor then over a covered bridge to a building behind the hospital and knocked on a door at the end of the passage. It was opened by an elderly woman in a sister's uniform who smiled at him and shook hands. 'Zuster Moerma, this is Miss Beckworth, my secretary; I know you'll look after her.'

Julie shook hands and then waited while the two of them engaged in a brief conversation in Dutch. That finished, the professor bade her goodnight, turned on his heel and went away.

Zuster Moerma watched him go. 'Such a kind man,' she observed. 'Now you will come with me, please, and I will show you your room. Someone will bring you a warm drink—tea, perhaps? You must be tired;

the professor works hard and he expects everyone else
to do the same.'

Julie's room was small, nicely furnished and pleasantly warm. She was bidden goodnight, assured that
breakfast would be brought to her at half past seven
next morning, that the bathroom was just across the
passage and that a tray of tea would be brought to her
in a few minutes.

Someone had brought her bag and computer up to
the room; she unpacked what she would need and put
the computer on the solid little table by the window.
She still had half an hour's typing to do. The professor, being the man he was, would probably ask for it
the moment he saw her in the morning.

The tea-tray came, borne by a cheerful girl in a print
dress and white pinny. Old-fashioned but nice, thought
Julie, and settled down to enjoy a cup. There were biscuits too—thin, crisp and sweet. She wasn't hungry but
she ate some of them before having a bath and settling
down at the table to finish her typing.

She was sleepy by the time she got into bed, and
closed her eyes at once with only a fleeting thought
of the professor. Probably buried under a pile of papers with those glasses on his nose, she thought, only
half-awake.

The same girl brought her breakfast in the morning.
Julie had been up since seven o'clock and had showered and dressed; now she sat down to enjoy the coffee
and rolls with the little dish of cheese and ham which
accompanied them, and, her meal over, she carefully

checked everything, packed her bag once more and put the computer into its case. She had no idea if she would have time to do any work before they left but doubtless the professor would tell her. He had, she conceded, been careful to keep her up to date with his plans.

Zuster Moerma came for her at half past eight exactly and led her back into the hospital. Julie, following on her heels, lost all sense of direction before long. The various staircases they went up and down all looked alike, as did the corridors. She could hear sounds of activity coming from the various doors they passed—the wards, she supposed.

The *aula* was reached finally; it was larger than in Leiden and filled to capacity with rows of serious-looking gentlemen. Professor van der Driesma was standing by the door as they reached it and bade them good morning, exchanged what Julie supposed were a few pleasantries with Zuster Moerma, then turned to Julie.

'They've given you a table under the platform so that you can hear easily. There will be a good deal of discussion.'

An understatement, thought Julie an hour later; there had been a great deal of discussion and she had had to keep her wits about her, and there was still another hour after the coffee-break. Much refreshed by the brimming mug that someone had brought her, she bent once more over her pad.

A nurse led her away for her lunch in the canteen. A pretty girl with fair hair and big blue eyes, with the unlikely name of Skutsje, which Julie was quite unable to pronounce correctly. She wasn't from Groningen but her home was in Friesland, just across the county border. 'I work here now,' she explained in awkward English, 'and it is very nice.'

Julie shared a table with her and several other nurses; all of them had a smattering of English, and plied her with questions over their bowls of soup and *Kaas broodjes,* and she wished that she could have seen more of them, but, anxious not to be late, she was led back to the *aula* to find the professor already there, talking to a small group of colleagues. He nodded to her as she went to her seat and presently came over to her.

'You have had lunch?' he wanted to know. 'When this session is finished you will have time to type up your notes, will you not? Tomorrow morning you will be free; I have consultations until lunchtime. I should like to leave here directly after that. Shall we meet in the entrance hall just before two o'clock?'

'Very well, Professor. You mean I can do as I like until then?'

'Certainly. I dare say you will want to look at the shops, and St Martiniskerk is well worth a visit. I'm sorry you have had no chance to look around Groningen today.'

'Well, I came to work, didn't I?' said Julie cheerfully. 'But I shall enjoy looking round tomorrow morning. I'll be in the hall on time.'

'Good.' He went away then and left her to settle herself down, ready for the afternoon's work. Various medical men were reading papers and she had to keep her mind on her work. There was a brief break for a cup of tea but then they were off again, and since they were from a variety of countries she was hard put to it to keep up with some of their accented English. She was glad that she had a tape recorder with her to fill in the gaps.

She didn't see the professor again but went away with Skutsje, who had come to fetch her to a small office where she could get on with her typing. That lasted till she was fetched once more to eat her supper—a cheerful meal with the nurses whom she had met at midday. Afterwards, despite their friendly offers to take her with them to watch TV in their sitting room, she went back to the office to finish her work.

It was quite late by the time she had typed the last of the notes; she tidied the pile of paper, collected her belongings and found her way back to the nurses' home where she showered and got into bed, to sleep at once. It had been a long and arduous day and she only hoped that she hadn't missed anything.

The morning was bright and crisply cold; she ate her breakfast while she was told where to go and what to see and presently left the hospital on her sightseeing tour, promising to be back for the midday meal. She went first to St Martiniskerk, admired the beautiful frescos, listened to the carillon and decided that she hadn't the time to climb the three hundred and twenty feet to the top of the Martini Tower.

A morning wasn't long enough, she decided, taking a quick look at the university and the gardens in the Prinsenhof before finding the shops so that she could buy presents to take home. She hadn't much money; she settled for illustrated books for her brothers, some chocolates for Esme, cigars for Luscombe and a small delft plate for her mother. Blotto would have to have biscuits.

That done, it was time for her to take herself back to the hospital and go to the canteen for soup and rolls and salad. Lunch was fun, with everyone talking at once, until she saw the time, regretfully said goodbye and hurried over to the home to get her things.

The warden met her. The porter had already taken everything, she was told, and then she was bidden a warm goodbye. She shook hands with the hope that she would come again some day and made her way to the entrance hall; it was ten minutes to the hour and she intended to be the first one there. There was no one in the hall and the porter in his box had his back to her. There was no sign of her bag and the computer either; she crossed to the big entrance door and looked out.

The professor was there, standing by his car, talking to a girl. Even at that distance Julie could see that she was strikingly good-looking and beautifully dressed. As she looked he put his arms around her shoulders and kissed her, and then, an arm in hers, walked her across the forecourt to a scarlet Mini. The girl got in and he bent once more to kiss her and then stood watching as she drove away.

Julie went back to where the lifts were without the porter seeing her, and a moment later the professor came into the hall; she started to walk towards him. 'I'm not late?' she asked as they met.

He was coolly polite. 'Exactly on time, Miss Beckworth.' She found it impossible to believe that he was the same man who had hugged the girl so closely.

Chapter 4

The professor drove straight to Mevrouw Schatt's house when they reached Leiden. 'I have an appointment shortly but I would be obliged if you will come to the hospital in about an hour's time. I have a number of letters to dictate. You can get them typed there and I will sign them before I leave the hospital.'

He stayed for a few minutes talking to Mevrouw Schatt before getting back into his car and driving away, and Julie went to her room and presently returned downstairs for a cup of tea and some of Mevrouw Schatt's *boterkoek*, while she told that lady of her visits to Amsterdam and Groningen. An hour wasn't long, though, and she got into her jacket once more and walked to the hospital. She was relieved that the porter expected her and summoned another porter to take her to Professor van der Driesma's office.

He was sitting behind a big desk, loaded down with papers, his specs on his nose, but he got up as she went in, asked her to sit down, hoped that she had had time for tea and began without more ado on his letters.

Most of them were straightforward, she was thankful to discover—courtesy thanks for this and that, arrangements to meet in London, agreements to consultations—only a handful were bristling with medical terms.

'Bring them here when you have finished, please, Miss Beckworth; I will see you back to Mevrouw Schatt's house then.'

'Please don't bother,' said Julie. 'It's only a few minutes' walk; you must have heaps of other things to do.'

'Indeed I have, but I must remind you that I am responsible for you, Miss Beckworth.'

Julie stood up and gathered up her pad and pencil and the little medical dictionary that she was never without. 'Oh, dear, so tiresome for you, Professor. I'll be as quick as I can.'

He got up to open the door for her and stood watching her walk away along the corridor. A pity that she didn't turn round to see him, and see the look on his face.

She went to the office that she had used before and wasted quite five minutes of her time thinking about him and the girl in the hospital courtyard. He had looked, even at a distance, loving, and for some reason the thought made her feel vaguely unhappy. She thrust it aside and switched on the computer. I ought to feel pleased that he's human like the rest of us, after all, she reflected.

She doubted that when she returned with his letters; the quick look he gave her as she laid them on his desk was coolly indifferent. As though he's looking at me over a high wall, thought Julie; if she hadn't seen him kissing that girl she wouldn't have believed it...

She looked at his downbent head as he signed his letters. Perhaps he was unhappy without her; perhaps for some reason they weren't able to marry; perhaps the girl was already married... Julie's imagination set off on a wild-goose chase of its own, to be interrupted by his quiet 'Miss Beckworth, if I might have your attention?'

She gave him a guilty look. 'Yes, yes, of course, Professor.'

'You have had no time to yourself while we have been in Holland; when we get back to London you might like to have a day to yourself before coming back to work?'

'Thank you, sir. I still have some notes to write up, though.'

He said indifferently, 'Just as you like. I expect you can arrange your work to suit yourself, but I shan't need you for the first day after our return.' He signed the last letter. 'You are ready? Let us go.'

He didn't wait at *mevrouw*'s house but saw her inside and drove off quickly. Siska and Jason would be waiting to welcome him home on the other side of Rapenburg.

They were expecting him; Siska had the door open as he got out of the car and Jason hurled himself at him.

The professor closed his front door behind him and thought how delightful it was to be home, and for the first time in many years he thought, too, how pleasant it would be if he had a wife waiting for him. Someone like Julie, who unfortunately had made it very plain from the beginning that she didn't like him.

He shrugged the thought aside, bent to caress his dog, listened to Siska's domestic gossip and went along to his study. There was time enough for him to catch up on his letters before dinner.

He took Jason for a walk later that evening but he didn't cross to the other side of the canal; he could see that the only light on at her house was an upstairs one and, in any case, what would be the point?

He was up early the next morning, taking Jason for his run then going over to the hospital for a brief examination of the patients whom he had gone to see previously. He would go back again to bid his colleagues goodbye before he left later in the day. Now he went back to his house to his study to telephone, and then into his drawing room to drink the coffee that Siska had ready from him.

The long windows overlooked the street, which was free from traffic and quiet in the autumn morning. Indeed, there was only one person in it—Julie, walking briskly towards the Rapenburg, probably on her way back from another visit to St Pieterskerk and the Persijnhofje—an almshouse founded by an ancestor of President Franklin Roosevelt—and doubtless on her way to another museum. It was a windy day and she had stopped to pin back her hair; on a sudden impulse he went to the house door and opened it and, as she drew level, her head bowed against the wind, went down the double steps.

'Good morning, Miss Beckworth. You're out early. Come in and have a cup of coffee?'

She gaped up at him. 'Oh, hello. I didn't expect… That is, are you staying in one of these houses?' She looked around her. 'Do they belong to the university?'

'Some of them do. Come inside; this wind is chilly.'

She went indoors with him and Siska, carrying the coffee-tray, came into the hall. The professor spoke to her, took Julie's jacket and then led the way into his drawing room, where Jason came to inspect her, rolling his yellow eyes and showing a splendid set of teeth.

Julie held out a fist and hoped that he wouldn't devour it, but he didn't; at a quiet word from the professor he butted his great head against it and leered at her in what could only be a friendly fashion. 'He's yours? You live here?' asked Julie.

'Yes, and yes. This is one of my homes, although I do spend a good deal of time in London.'

She looked around her; the room was large and high-ceilinged, its walls hung with mulberry-coloured paper. The floor was polished wood, covered by beautiful rugs, and the furniture was mahogany and tulip wood: a lovely William and Mary chest, a bureau of the same period, heavy with marquetry, a Dutch display cabinet, its shelves filled with silver and porcelain, and a sofa-table behind a vast couch. There were tripod tables too, each with its lamp, and here and there superb Meissen porcelain figures.

'What a very beautiful room,' said Julie.

'I'm glad you like it. Come and sit down and have your coffee.'

Julie sat down and drank her coffee from a paper-thin porcelain cup and nibbled little cinnamon biscuits, making polite conversation and feeling ill at ease. The professor behind his desk or lecturing in his quiet voice was one thing; drinking his coffee in his splendid house was quite another.

He responded to her rather vapid remarks with un-wonted gentleness and hidden amusement, egging her on gently to talk about her family and home so that she forgot her uncertainty towards him, again talking freely about her father.

She paused at length, suddenly shy and afraid that she had been rambling on and boring him. 'I must go,' she said. 'Mevrouw Schatt will be waiting for me. I'm sorry, I've wasted your morning; there must be so much you want to do when you're home…' She remembered something. 'I expect you have friends—and people you know in Groningen…'

'Indeed I have, for I was born there; my family live there, and people I have known for many years.'

She asked recklessly, 'So you don't want to go back there and—and settle down?'

'I imagine, Miss Beckworth, that you mean do I wish to marry and live there.' He studied her pink face before he went on. 'This is my true home; if and when I decide to marry, my wife will live here.'

Julie got to her feet. 'Yes, of course; I'm sorry, I wasn't prying. Thank you for the coffee.'

He went into the hall with her and picked up a jacket, calling something to his housekeeper. 'I'm going over to the hospital for half an hour. We may as well walk together.'

Jason went with them, keeping close to his master, the epitome of a well-mannered dog—curling his lip at a cat sitting on a windowsill, growling at a passing poodle on its lead, but obedient to the professor's quiet voice. They crossed the Rapenburg and paused outside Mevrouw Schatt's house.

'I will be here at two o'clock,' he reminded her. 'I wish to be back in London by the evening.'

Mevrouw Schatt had taken great pains with their meal: enormous pancakes filled with crisp bacon, swimming in syrup, a salad and something which looked and tasted like a blancmange and which she called *pudding*. There was a glass of milk too and, to finish, coffee. Julie, uncertain as to when she would have the next meal, enjoyed it all.

Mindful of the professor's wish to leave on time, she fetched her things from her room, gave Mevrouw Schatt the box of chocolates that she had bought that morning and got into her jacket. It had turned much colder during the last day or two and she stuffed a scarf and gloves into its pockets, made sure that her hair was bandbox-neat and sat down to wait. Not for long! The big car drew up silently outside the front door and the professor banged the knocker.

His conversation with Mevrouw Schatt was brief and

cordial; her bag and computer were put into the boot and she was invited to get into the car. Julie embraced Mevrouw Schatt, sorry to leave her kind hostess, and did as she was asked, sitting silently until they were clear of the town and on the motorway. 'Did Jason mind your leaving?' she asked at length.

'Yes, but I shall be coming over again very shortly. Not to work, though.'

To see that girl, thought Julie, and felt a sudden shaft of sadness at the thought.

Their journey back went smoothly. They stopped briefly in Ghent for tea and then drove on to Calais and a rather choppy crossing to Dover. Approaching London, Julie stared out at the dreary suburbs and wished herself back in Leiden, but when the professor observed idly, 'You will be glad to be home again, Miss Beckworth,' she was quick to agree.

'Although I enjoyed seeing something of Holland,' she told him, and went on awkwardly, 'thank you for arranging everything so well for me, sir.'

His reply was non-committal and most unsatisfactory. Their rare moments of pleasure in each other's society were already forgotten, she supposed.

He drove her straight home despite her protests. 'And take the day off tomorrow,' he told her. 'Any work you still have to do you can doubtless fit in later on.'

She murmured an assent; there *was* a backlog of work, despite her best efforts; she would go in early tomorrow morning and clear up what work was outstanding and then take the rest of the day off. He wouldn't know, for he had said that he wouldn't be needing her for a day. Doubtless he would take a day off too.

Rather cautiously, she asked him if he would like to come in for a cup of coffee when they reached her home. His refusal was polite and tinged with impatience, and she wasted no time in getting out of the car when he opened her door, took her bag and set it in the porch, before driving away with the remark that he would see her in a day's time. Luscombe opened the door as he drove away.

'Welcome home, Miss Julie—he's in a hurry, isn't he?'

'I expect he's going straight to the hospital, Luscombe.' She bent to pat Blotto. 'It's lovely to be home; where's Mother?'

'In the garden with Esme, sweeping up the leaves. They didn't expect you so early. Like a pot of tea? The kettle is on the boil.'

'I'd love one, Luscombe; I'll go and surprise them…'

'You do that, Miss Julie; we've had supper but I'll find something tasty for you—half an hour do?'

'Lovely—I'm famished. We seem to have been driving for ever; it seems later than it is.'

She went through the house and out into the garden. The light outside the kitchen door shone on her mother and sister, muffled against the chilly evening, busy with their rakes. They threw them down when they saw her.

'Julie, how lovely; you didn't say exactly when you'd be back on your card.' Her mother laughed. 'That's why we're here working in the dark. We wanted the garden to be spick and span when you got back.'

Esme had flung down her rake. 'Did he bring you back? The professor?'

'Yes, but he didn't want to stop. He's given me the day off tomorrow.'

'Quite right too,' said her mother. 'Were you kept very busy?'

'Yes, but I did manage to see Leiden and Groningen.'

They had all gone inside, and over the supper that Luscombe had conjured up she gave them an account of her few days in Holland.

'Liked it, did you?' asked Luscombe, leaning against the door with a dishcloth over one arm. 'Meet anyone nice, did you?'

'Any number of people, but only briefly; almost all the time I was either taking notes or typing them.'

'Well, you can have a nice, quiet day tomorrow,' observed Mrs Beckworth. She peered at her daughter thoughtfully. 'You didn't go out at all, I suppose? Or see much of Professor van der Driesma?'

'Only at the seminars and his ward rounds.' Julie paused. 'Oh, and he came out of his house as I went past it in Leiden and he asked me in for coffee.'

'He lives there? As well as here? He's married?'

'No, not as far as I know.' Julie sounded casual. 'I must go in to work in the morning. I'll go early—I've some audio typing to finish. A couple of hours will see to it and then I'll come home and we'll do something special—a film, perhaps? Or lunch out? I haven't spent a penny so I'll treat.'

'Let's go to a film,' begged Esme. 'It's ages since we went...'

'All right. We could go in the afternoon and have tea somewhere afterwards.' Julie went into the hall and fetched her bag. 'I didn't have time to do much shopping,' she explained, handing over her small gifts.

'You didn't ought,' said Luscombe, beaming at his box of cigars.

It was lovely being home, reflected Julie, and then frowned at the unbidden image of the professor's face which floated behind her eyelids. Why I should think about him, I don't know.

Probably because he was thinking about her. There was nothing romantic about his thoughts, however, rather a vague annoyance. He found her disturbing, prone to answer back—even though she was a first-rate worker, melting, as far as possible, into the background but always at hand. Despite this he was always aware of her.

She had, as it were, cast a spanner into the works of his life. He would probably have to get rid of her—nicely, of course. He had no intention of allowing any deep feelings to alter his life. He was no monk, but beyond mild flirtation with one or other of his women acquaintances he had remained heart-whole. Not that his heart was involved now, he reflected; he merely found her disturbing.

Julie was at her desk soon after eight o'clock; she had got up early, shared a cup of tea and some toast with Luscombe and caught a bus well before the rush hour started. She had her earphones on, transcribing the last of the tapes, when a hand fell on her shoulder; the other hand removed her headphones.

'I thought I had told you to take a day off, Miss Beckworth.' The professor's voice had a nasty edge to it.

'So you did, but you didn't say I wasn't to come into the office,' said Julie reasonably. 'I had quite a bit of work to finish, you know, and you know as well as I do that I'll never get a chance to fit it in once we're back here.'

She turned in her chair to look at him. 'I'll be finished in less than half an hour. I didn't think you would be here. Aren't you taking a day off too?'

Staring down at her lovely smiling face, the professor gave way to a sudden, ridiculous impulse.

'Yes, Miss Beckworth. Like you, I came in to finish some paperwork. But I have the rest of the day in which to do nothing. Shall we give ourselves a rest and spend the day in the country? I think that we both deserve it.'

'Me and you?' said Julie, not mincing her words. 'Well, I never… That is, thank you very much, Professor, but I promised that I'd take my mother and sister out.'

'Better still. Perhaps they would like to come too?'

A remark which disappointed her. She squashed the feeling at once. 'Well, I'm sure they'd like that very much. Where do you want to go?'

'Supposing we let your sister decide, or at least suggest somewhere?'

He's lonely, Julie thought suddenly. I dare say he's missing that girl and can't bear to be on his own. 'If I could have twenty minutes to finish this?'

'I'll be outside when you're ready.'

I must be mad, reflected Julie, making no effort to get on with her work. And what on earth are we going to talk about? They had driven miles in Holland exchanging barely a word between them...

He was waiting by the car when she left the hospital and as she came towards him he wondered if he had taken leave of his senses. Nothing of that showed on his face as he opened the car door for her to get in.

Mrs Beckworth opened the door as they reached it. 'Oh, good, you're back, Julie. Professor van der Driesma, come in; I'm just making coffee.' She gave him her hand and smiled up at him; whatever Julie said, Mrs Beckworth thought that he was a very nice man— that mild description covering her entire approval.

'Professor van der Driesma suggested that as he was free we might like to join him for a drive into the country.'

'Oh, how delightful.' Mrs Beckworth raised her voice. 'Esme, come here, love; something delightful...'

Esme came downstairs two at a time and landed up against the professor.

'Hello,' she said in a pleased voice. 'You're not going away again, are you? There are a lot of things I want to know.'

He smiled down at her. Why doesn't he smile at me like that? thought Julie.

'Are there? Perhaps I'll have time to answer them. We wondered, your sister and I, if you and your mother would like to come for a drive...?'

'With you? In your car? Oh, yes, yes. Where shall we go? And can we go now?'

'Coffee first,' said Mrs Beckworth, 'and you'll tidy yourself before you set foot outside the door, Esme.'

There was a general move towards the kitchen, where Luscombe was pouring coffee. He had, of course, been listening. 'Going off for the day?' he wanted to know. 'Suits me a treat; I'll pop over to my sister's if it's all the same to you, Mrs Beckworth.'

'Yes, do go, Luscombe. I don't know when we shall be back…' She looked at the professor, sitting opposite her at the kitchen table.

'Oh, after tea, if that suits you, Mrs Beckworth.' He turned to Esme, perched beside him. 'Where shall we go, Esme?'

'Brighton—oh, please say we can. Sally, my best friend, says it's super. The Lanes, all the shops and the Pavilion.'

'Why not? But we'll go the long way round to get there, shall we? We have all day. Supposing we go there in the afternoon and have tea there?'

Esme flung her arms round his neck and kissed him. 'Oh, you really are very nice,' she told him. 'May I sit with you so's I can ask you questions?'

'I shall be delighted.'

'Esme, you must allow Professor van der Driesma to decide where we are to go.' Mrs Beckworth sounded apologetic. 'I'm sorry, Professor, Esme's excited; we don't often get treats like this.'

'Nor do I, Mrs Beckworth, and I have a sixteen-year-old sister.'

'Have you? You must miss your family.'

'I do, although I don't see much of them whether I am here or in Holland.'

Julie had sat quietly drinking her coffee; now she said, 'Shall we go and get our things, Esme?' And when she and her mother and Esme had left the room the professor collected up the mugs and took them over to the sink.

'You worked for Dr Beckworth, of course,' he said to Luscombe. 'He was a good man and a splendid doctor.'

'Yer right there. Started 'ere when Miss Julie was a little nipper—general dogsbody, as you might say, till I took over the 'ousekeeping, like. The doctor would expect me to stay on and keep an eye on the ladies.'

'I'm sure he couldn't have picked a better man, Luscombe. Can we drop you off on our way?'

'Well, now, if you could spare ten minutes while I tidy meself a bit. I'd better take Blotto with me.'

'No need. He can come with us; there's plenty of room in the car. Where do you want to go, Luscombe?'

'The Whitechapel road, just this side of Fenchurch Street Station; me sister's got a fish and chip shop.'

'Splendid. I intend to cross the river; I can go over London Bridge.'

'You know your way around, then?' He glanced round the kitchen. 'Everything's shipshape.' He glanced at a peacefully sleeping dog. 'Sure you don't mind about Blotto?'

'Not in the least.' The professor turned to smile at Esme, her hair combed and plaited, in a pleated skirt and short jacket. 'Luscombe's coming as far as his sister's. We'll take Blotto with us, shall we?'

'Oh, please. We ought to have asked you; I'm sorry, but you see we weren't expecting you. Were you feeling rather lonely for your family in Holland?'

'I had no time to visit them. I'll be going back shortly, though.'

'Will they come and visit you at your house? Julie said you had a lovely old house near the hospital. Why don't you—?' She was interrupted by her mother's entry.

'Professor—oh, must I keep calling you that? What are we to do with Blotto? He'll have to go with Luscombe…'

'Call me Simon, Mrs Beckworth, and Blotto is coming with us.'

'I'll get his lead.' Esme flew away as Julie joined them, and a moment later so did Luscombe, in his best jacket and with his hair slicked down.

'You've got your key, Luscombe?' asked Mrs Beckworth. 'I've got mine. Don't hurry back; we'll be quite all right.'

'Right-o, Mrs Beckworth; I've locked up.'

The professor ushered his party out to the car and settled them with Luscombe in front and Blotto on Julie's knee. He was beginning to enjoy himself although he couldn't think why.

There was a small queue outside Luscombe's sister's shop and they turned as one to stare as he got out of the car. 'Made me day, you have, sir!' chortled Luscombe.

'Driving in a Bentley. Thanks a lot. Esme's going in front, is she?'

He helped her out and shut the door on her after she'd scrambled in. Then he stood waving as they drove off. A nice chap, thought Luscombe. ''E'd do very well for our Miss Julie.

The traffic was heavy; the professor crossed London Bridge and made his slow way south of the river, through Wandsworth, Kingston-upon-Thames and Chertsey, and then picked up speed going through Woking and Guildford, all the while listening to Esme's unceasing chatter, answering her questions with no sign of impatience.

Presently he said over his shoulder, 'There's a rather good pub at Midhurst; I thought we might stop there for lunch. He turned off the main road presently, taking the narrow country roads through charming country, and half an hour later stopped before the Angel Hotel, an old coaching inn skilfully restored.

Esme, peering at it, said, 'I say, this looks splendid and I'm famished.'

'Good. So am I,' said the professor. 'Let us go inside; I'll book a table and take Blotto for a run while you ladies tidy yourselves.'

In the ladies' Esme observed, 'He's sweet, isn't he? And so old-fashioned—I mean, the way he said "tidy yourselves"; anyone else would say going to the loo!'

'I would have felt very uncomfortable if he had said that,' said her mother, 'and I think he knew that. I only hope he's enjoying himself...'

Julie silently hoped the same thing.

They ate in the brasserie—tiny herb pancakes followed by beautifully grilled fish, finishing with creamy concoctions from the sweet trolley while the professor ate cheese and biscuits. Over coffee he said, 'How about going along the coast to Brighton? We can go to Chichester and take the A259 for the rest of the way; it's barely an hour's drive. We'd have plenty of time to go to the pier or wherever you would like to go before tea.'

He smiled round at them, his eyes lingering on Julie's quiet face. She had had little to say and he would have liked to have had her beside him as he drove. He dismissed the thought impatiently. She was encroaching on his well-ordered life; for the second time that day he decided to do something about it.

Strolling with Esme, while Blotto pottered briefly, he was taken by surprise with Esme's question: 'Do you like Julie, Simon?' She peered up at him. 'You always call her Miss Beckworth, don't you? And she doesn't talk about you—only if we ask. Don't you like each other?'

He chose his words carefully. 'Your sister is splendid at her job and a great help to me. We respect each other and that's very important when you work together.'

Esme opened her mouth to say more and closed it again; there had been a steely note in his pleasant voice which she dared not ignore. She said simply, 'She's very clever, you know. I don't mean typing and all that; she cooks almost as well as Luscombe and she sews beautifully. I'd like her to marry someone nice...'

'I'm sure she will; I'm surprised she isn't already married.'

'Well, she's had lots of chances, but she doesn't have much time to go out and, of course, a girl needs lots of pretty clothes to do that.'

The professor, with sisters of his own, agreed with that.

Once through Chichester and on the coast road, he set the car at a good pace, only slowing as they passed through the small seaside towns, so that Hove and Brighton were reached while the afternoon was still young.

They went to the Pavilion first; they inspected the entrance hall, the long gallery, the state apartments and lastly the kitchens. It was here that Julie found herself alone with the professor. Her mother and Esme had wandered off, leaving them in front of a vast row of copper saucepans on one of the walls of the huge place.

'I wonder how many cooks worked here?' said Julie for something to say.

He looked down at her with a faint smile. 'You have been here before?'

'No. It's—well, unusual. Have you?' And before he could reply she added, 'No, of course you haven't; it isn't the sort of place you would take a girl to, is it?'

'Why not?'

'Well, not the kind of girl you take out. I mean—' she was getting flustered '—she'd expect a super restaurant and dancing and black tie and all that. This isn't romantic...'

'Does one need to wear a black tie to be romantic? I would have thought that one could be romantic here in this kitchen if one felt that way inclined.' He sounded amused. 'Shall we find your mother and Esme? I dare say we have time to go to the pier.'

They spent half an hour there; Julie and Esme played the machines, winning small amounts of money on the fruit machines and losing it again, while her mother and the professor strolled round. Julie glanced at them once or twice; they appeared to be getting on very well. It was impossible to see whether he was really enjoying himself, though.

They went to the Lanes then, peering into the small shop windows. There was so much to see: jewellery, antiques, tiny boutiques with one exquisite garment flung over a chair in the window, and seaside shops open still, even though the season was over. They had tea here, in an olde-worlde tea shoppe, with waitresses in mobcaps and dainty little tables ringed with flimsy chairs. The professor set his large person down gingerly onto a chair which creaked and groaned under him.

They ate toasted teacakes and buttered toast and chocolate eclairs and ordered a second pot of tea. Julie, passing his cup for the second time, wondered uneasily just how much their outing was costing him. She should have refused his offer straight away, she reflected, and not mentioned her mother and sister; he had had no choice but to invite them too...

She wondered if he would be more friendly now—after all, her mother and Esme were on excellent terms with him, calling him Simon too. She had been careful not to call him anything for the whole day, and so, she noticed, had he avoided using her name.

They went back to the car finally and then drove

back to London, reaching it as dusk was turning to dark, and very much to her surprise he accepted her mother's offer of coffee. 'I'll take Blotto for a quick run,' he suggested. 'He should be tired out, but five minutes will do him no harm.'

Luscombe was back. 'Thought you might want a bite to eat,' he explainwifed. 'Kettle's on the boil and I've cut some sandwiches. 'Is nibs coming in, is 'e?'

'He's taken Blotto for a quick walk. Luscombe, that's good of you. Have you had your supper? Did you have a good day with your sister?'

'First-rate, Mrs Beckworth. That I should live to see the day I'd ride in a Bentley. Enjoy yourself, did you?'

'Lovely; we went all over the place and saw so much and had a gorgeous lunch. Had we better have coffee in the drawing room?'

'Not on my account, Mrs Beckworth.' The professor had come into the kitchen. He nodded to Luscombe. 'You had a good day too?' he asked.

'I'd say. Best fish and chips in town at my sister's.'

They sat around the table in the warm kitchen, all of them, and Luscombe cut more sandwiches and made more coffee. The talk was cheerful, with Esme and Luscombe doing most of it and Mrs Beckworth putting in a gentle word here and there and the professor joining in from time to time in his quiet voice. As for Julie, she joined in too, trying to ignore the nagging thought that next week she would be back at her desk with the professor in his office. Would this day's outing change things? Perhaps he would be more friendly now; perhaps he would stop calling her Miss Beckworth.

* * *

He wasn't there when she arrived on Monday, but there was a note on her desk. 'In path lab if wanted,' with his initials scrawled underneath. Julie opened the post, answered the phone, opened his diary and sat down to start her own work. She had been there for quite some time when the professor walked in, laid some papers on her desk and in an austere voice said, 'Good morning, Miss Beckworth.'

Julie sighed; they were back at square one again. She wished him good morning in a colourless voice, adding a snappy 'sir' and 'Dr MacFinn would like to see you if possible this morning.'

He was standing at her desk, looking at her, which she found unnerving. She poised her hands over her computer and gave him an enquiring look.

'I'll get these notes finished, sir.' She looked away quickly from his thoughtful stare, glad to have an excuse to turn away from his eyes.

Chapter 5

Julie saw very little of the professor after that first un-satisfactory conversation. She told herself that she was glad of it—something which she knew wasn't true; she wanted him to like her, to laugh and talk to her as he did with Esme and her mother. She wasn't a conceited girl; she was used to admiring glances and had fended off the tentative advances of several of the young housemen, but the professor's glances were strictly impersonal and he had shown no wish to add warmth to their relationship.

Why should he? she reasoned, when he had a girl waiting for him in Groningen. Or perhaps she wasn't waiting; perhaps they faced a hopeless future with only stolen meetings to keep their love alive. Julie, aware that she was allowing her thoughts to get too romantic, applied herself to her word processor once more.

It was during the morning that a call was put through to her desk.

'I can't contact Professor van der Driesma,' complained the operator. 'I can't get him on his phone. Will you take the call?'

Julie, glad of a diversion, lifted the receiver. The voice was a woman's—a young voice too. 'You are the secretary of Professor van der Driesma? I wish to speak to him, please.'

'He's not here for the moment. Will you hang on and I'll see if I can find him? Who shall I say?'

'Mevrouw van Graaf. I will wait.'

Julie heard the little chuckle as she put down the receiver. 'Drat the man,' said Julie, and went to check the phone on his desk. It hadn't been replaced; no wonder the operator hadn't got his desk. She put it back in its cradle and not very hopefully phoned his bleep. She was surprised when a minute or so later he phoned back.

'I hope it's urgent,' he told her testily before she could speak. 'I'm occupied.'

'Mevrouw van Graaf is on the phone for you, sir.'

He didn't answer at once, then said, 'Ask her for a number, will you? And tell her I'll ring her within half an hour.' He hung up then and she went back to her desk and picked up her own phone.

'Mevrouw van Graaf? The professor can't come to the phone for the moment; he has asked me to get your phone number and he will ring you during the next half-hour.'

'Very well; here is the number. I will wait.' There was a happy little laugh. 'I have waited for a long time and now I do not need to wait. I do not speak of the telephone, you understand…'

'Yes, I understand,' Julie said, and hung up. Something must have happened; Mevrouw van Graaf was free. Free to marry the professor. She didn't want to think about that; it was a good thing that she had so much work on her desk.

He came back presently. 'You have the number?' he asked.

Julie handed him the slip of paper and he went back to his office, leaving the door open. She would have to shut it; she had no intention of eavesdropping although she was longing to know what it was all about. But there was no need to shut the door for he spoke in his own language, although she understood the first word he uttered. *Lieveling*—darling—and an endearment which the Dutch didn't use lightly. Julie tapped away as though her life depended on it, not wishing to hear his voice; even speaking another language it sounded full of delight.

He talked for some time and a glance at the clock showed her that it was time for her to go to her dinner. She didn't like to go in case he needed her for something, so she sat there quietly, listening to the murmur of his voice and his laugh. He rang off presently and came to the open door.

'I have an Outpatients at one o'clock; I'll see you there, Miss Beckworth. There are a couple of tapes for you to type up; they're on my desk.'

'Very well, sir; I'm going to my dinner now.'

He glanced at the clock. 'Yes, yes, of course.' He

gave her an absent-minded nod and went away, pausing at the door to say, 'I'm on the ward if I should be wanted. Let them know, will you?'

Julie ate her dinner quickly and hurried back to her desk. Outpatients could sometimes run late and there would be no time for her to type up the tapes as well as the outpatients' notes; she could start on the tapes before one o'clock...

Outpatients was busy, and although it was already running late the professor remained unhurried, giving his full attention to each patient in turn; the nurses came and went for their tea but Sister stayed put at his elbow and so, perforce, did the two students.

Julie filled her notebook with her expert shorthand, sharpened her pencil and longed for her tea. She saw the last patient leave and closed her notebook smartly. It was past five o'clock but if the professor wanted the notes she would have to stay and type them—and the tapes weren't finished...

She was roused from her thoughts by his voice. 'Sister, I'm sure you are longing for a cup of tea; would you ring for someone to bring us a tray?' He looked across at Julie. 'And you, Miss Beckworth—it's been a long afternoon?'

She thanked him nicely, thinking that, for her at least, the afternoon wasn't over.

The tea came with a plate of biscuits, and over second cups he said, 'I will drop you off, Miss Beckworth, if you can be ready in half an hour?'

'I thought I'd stay and get these notes typed.'

'No need. I am going to Leeds tomorrow; you will have the day in which to finish any outstanding work.'

There was no point in arguing and Sister was sitting there listening. Julie said, 'Very well, sir,' in a neutral voice and presently went away to get on with the tapes. She didn't get them finished, of course; he had said half an hour and she knew by now that when he said something he meant it. She was ready, her desk tidied, work put away for the morning, when he came back to his office.

He had little to say as he drove her home and what he did say concerned his work and various instructions for her while he was away. He got out when they reached the house, opened her door, waited while she gained the front door, bade her goodnight and got back into his car and drove away.

A most unsatisfactory day, reflected Julie, going into the kitchen to see what Luscombe was cooking for supper.

'You look peaky, Miss Julie; 'ad a rotten day?'

'Yes, Luscombe; all go, if you know what I mean. I wish I could get a job miles away from any hospital, somewhere where people smiled and had time to pass the time of day...'

'Oh, you are low,' said Luscombe. ''Is nibs been tiresome, 'as 'e?'

'Not more than usual. Can I smell macaroni cheese? I'm famished.

'Ten minutes, Miss Julie. Your ma's in the sitting room and Esme's doing her homework.'

Julie went and talked to her mother then, glossing

over her unsatisfactory day before helping Esme with her homework, and it wasn't until they were sitting round the table that Mrs Beckworth asked, 'Did Simon say how much he had enjoyed his day out?'

Julie took a mouthful of macaroni cheese. 'He didn't mention it.'

Mrs Beckworth looked surprised. 'Didn't he? How very strange.'

And Esme chimed in, 'But he said he'd had a lovely time. He told me so.'

'He's had a busy day,' said Julie. 'And he's going to Leeds all day tomorrow, he said.'

'Have you quarrelled?' asked Esme.

'Of course not; we're both too busy—we hardly speak unless it's about the work.' Julie spoke so sharply that Esme, ready with more questions, swallowed them instead.

It was Luscombe who voiced his concern the next morning after she had gone to work. 'Miss Julie's got the 'ump,' he observed to Mrs Beckworth. 'Told me she'd like to find another job. It's my 'umble opinion that she and 'is nibs don't suit. On the other hand...'

'They have fallen in love?' suggested Mrs Beckworth.

'And don't know it, of course. 'Is nibs 'as more than likely got a girl already—someone in Holland; so he takes care to be extra stiff, if you see what I mean.'

Mrs Beckworth nodded. 'Yes, yes, Luscombe, but Julie doesn't seem to like him overmuch. When we were out together the other day she hardly spoke to him.'

'Got their lines crossed,' said Luscombe, peeling the

potatoes. ''E only 'as to say 'e's got a girl to make it all fair and square and Miss Julie can behave normal-like again. Me, I don't believe she don't like 'im, but she's got her head screwed on straight, 'asn't she? Not the sort to go crazy over a chap when he's already spoken for.'

'It's very worrying,' said Mrs Beckworth.

'It'll all come out in the wash,' said Luscombe.

Julie, laying piles of perfectly typed notes, memoranda and letters on his desk, wished that the professor were there, sitting with his spectacles perched on his nose, ignoring her for the most part and, truth to tell, unaware of her unless he required her services.

He wasn't expected back until the late evening, the head porter, who had a soft spot for her, told Julie when she arrived the next morning. Which meant that she could start on updating the files which Professor Smythe had stashed away in the filing cabinets and which should have gone to the records office long ago. She worked steadily at them all day and, since another hour or so's work on them would have the job done, decided to stay on after five-thirty and finish it.

She phoned home to say that she would be an hour or so late and then settled back to work. There would be no interruptions; the receptionist knew that the professor wasn't in the hospital and no one would phone or come to his office.

She worked steadily; there was more to do than she had expected but since she had started there seemed no point in not finishing. It was quiet in that part of the hospital where the professor had his office, and the sounds of traffic were muffled by the thin fog which had crept over the city. Julie, intent on getting finished, hardly noticed.

Someone opening the professor's door made her turn round. A man stood there, as surprised as she was, although his astonishment turned to a look of cunning that she didn't much care for. She got up and went through the door to the professor's office. 'You're visiting someone in the hospital?' she asked, and hoped that her voice wasn't wobbling too much. 'You've got lost—you need to go back along the passage and go up the stairs to the wards.'

The man laughed. 'Me? I'm not lost. You just sit quiet, like a good girl, and no one will hurt you.' He went past her and picked up her handbag from the desk.

'What do you think you are doing?' asked Julie angrily. 'Put that down at once. Get out of here...' She picked up the phone and had it snatched from her before she could utter a word into it. 'Now, now, that won't do. I told you to be good, didn't I?' He pushed her into the chair opposite the desk. 'You sit quiet or else...'

He began opening drawers in the professor's desk, sweeping papers onto the floor, pocketing some loose change lying there, and the Waterman pen that the professor used. There was a silver-framed photo in one of the drawers—Julie had never seen it before. He smashed the glass, threw the photo onto the desk and put the frame into his pocket. She could see that it was of a young woman and just for a moment she forgot her fright—so the professor kept a photo of his future wife tucked away in his desk like any lovesick young man. She smiled at the thought and then went white as the man came round the desk to her, grinning.

'Easy as kiss me hand,' he boasted. 'Walk in, I did, just like that, and that old codger in his little box doing his crossword didn't even see me. Now you'll tell me where there's some cash and, better still, I'll wait here while you fetch it.'

'I haven't the least idea where there's any money,' said Julie in a voice which didn't sound quite like hers. 'The cleaners will be along in a minute to collect the waste paper and turn off the lights. You're a fool to think you can get away with this. What are you doing here, anyway?'

'Thought I'd have a look around; didn't know I'd find a pretty girl—what yer doing with all this junk?' His eye roved over the computer and the answering machine, and he picked up the heavy paperweight on the desk. 'Let's smash 'em up...'

Julie's fright turned to rage; she darted from the chair that he had made her sit in, picked up the inkstand on the desk—a Victorian monstrosity of size and weight—and flung it at the man. Her aim was poor; it sailed past him and narrowly missed the professor as he opened the door, whistling past his ear to crash in the passage beyond.

The professor, not a swearing man, was surprised into uttering an oath of some richness—a welcome sound to Julie, doing her best to evade the man's clutches. 'Oh, hurry up, do!' she shouted. 'This fool's tearing the place to pieces.'

A needless remark as it turned out, for the professor had picked the man up by his coat collar and flung him into the chair that she had just left.

'Stay there,' he said in a flinty voice, and reached for the phone. As he dialed he glanced at Julie. 'You're all right, Miss Beckworth?'

She glared at him, conscious of enormous relief at the sight of him and at the same time furious with him for taking it for granted that she was all right. Of course she wasn't; she wanted to scream, indulge in a burst of tears and be cosseted with a cup of tea and a few kind words.

She said in a small voice stiff with dignity, 'Thank you, Professor, I am perfectly all right.'

He nodded at her, spoke into the phone and then sat her down in his chair, turning his attention to the man.

'Exactly why are you here?' he wanted to know. 'And how dare you frighten my secretary and make havoc of my office. I've called the police.'

The man peered up at him. 'Look, guv, I didn't mean no 'arm. Thought I'd find something to nick—it's easy to get into this place. Cor, I could've been in any of the wards but I thought I'd 'ave a peek round first...'

'Are you a thief by trade?' asked the professor. 'Or is this a one-off thing?'

The man looked sly. 'That's telling. Now, if you was to let me go... I 'aven't done no 'arm, only knocked a few things around...'

The professor's eyes studied the papers scattered on the floor and Julie's handbag flung onto the desk, its contents scattered too. He looked at Julie then, although he didn't say anything; only when the man started to get up did he say quietly, 'I shouldn't start anything if I were you; I shall knock you down.'

He was lounging against his desk, quite at his ease, and the three of them remained silent until presently there was the reassuring sound of the deliberate footsteps of the two police officers who came in. The elder man took one look at the man and said, 'Slim Sid. Up to your tricks again, are you?' He turned to the professor. 'Now, sir, if you will tell me what he's been up to.'

Two porters had followed the officers into the office. The professor sent them away and closed the door. 'I think Miss Beckworth can give you a better account than I, Officer. I—er—didn't get here until this man—Sid—had had time to cause this havoc. Miss Beckworth was coping with the situation with some spirit; she will tell you what occurred.'

He looked at Julie then and smiled; she hadn't known that a smile could wrap you round, make you feel safe and cherished and, despite the regrettable circumstances, happy. She sat up straight and gave a clear account of what had happened, and even if her voice was somewhat higher than usual and still a little wobbly she added no embellishments. When she had finished she added, 'I shouldn't have thrown the inkstand...'

The elder officer said comfortably, 'No, miss, but, in the circumstances, an understandable action—and you did miss him.'

Julie caught the professor's eye. She had very nearly hit him, hadn't she? Supposing she had? She might have killed him; the inkstand was as heavy as lead—perhaps it *was* lead; it would have bashed his head in...

She drew a sharp breath, feeling sick at the thought. To have ended his life like that... Her life would have ended too; she wouldn't have wanted to go on living without him.

This was neither the time nor the place to discover that she loved him; indeed, she couldn't have discovered it at a more inconvenient time, but there it was... She looked away from him quickly, thankful that the younger officer was asking her for her name and address.

'Just routine, miss,' he added soothingly. 'Slim Sid here is wanted for two break-ins already; since he's stolen nothing here it'll be taken into account but I doubt if he'll be charged.'

They went away presently with Sid, suitably handcuffed, between them. The professor went into the passage, picked up the inkstand, put it back on the desk and lifted the telephone, asking for tea to be brought to his office, and then stood looking at Julie.

'That was a warm welcome you gave me,' he observed mildly.

She burst into tears.

He sat down in the other chair, saying nothing while she sniffed and snorted, and when the tea came he took the tray from the porter and poured out a cup, put it in front of her on the desk and put a large, snowy handkerchief into her hand. 'Mop up,' he bade her, and he spoke very kindly. 'There's nothing like a good cry— much better than bottling it up. Drink your tea and tell me what happened. I only wish I had been here to prevent you being frightened like that.'

Julie gave a prodigious sniff. 'I nearly killed you…'

He took his sopping handkerchief from her. 'No, no, I'm made of sterner stuff. I must admit that I was taken aback.'

He had come to sit on the desk close to her chair; now he put a cup in her hand. 'Drink up and tell me exactly what happened.'

The tea was hot and sweet and very strong. 'I must look awful,' said Julie.

He studied her tear-stained face, the faint pink of her delightful nose, the puffy eyelids, her neat head of hair no longer all that neat.

'You look beautiful,' he told her.

She choked on her tea. He didn't mean it of course; he was saying that to make her feel better.

The professor watched her without appearing to do so. She had probably thought him an unfeeling monster for not offering instant sympathy when he had come into his office, but if he had she would have wept all over him—something she would have regretted later on; she hadn't shown weakness or fear of the intruder; to have burst into tears in front of him would have been something that she would have regretted afterwards. He had put her on her mettle and her report to the police had been sensible and clear.

She finished her tea, thanked him politely for it and collected the contents of her handbag. 'I'll just get these papers cleared up—I hadn't quite finished, I'm afraid.' She peeped at him. 'They're in a great muddle, I'm afraid.'

'They can stay as they are. I'll lock the door and tell

the porter that no one is to come in. They can be seen to in the morning.'

'You have a ward-round at eleven o'clock, sir.'

'Plenty of time before then,' he said comfortably. He picked up the phone and dialled a number. She turned sharply to look at him in surprise when he said, 'Mrs Beckworth? We have been delayed here—an unexpected upheaval. No, no, Julie's quite all right. I'm taking her back with me to have a meal and a rest; I'll drive her back later.'

He listened for a few moments. 'In a couple of hours, Mrs Beckworth,' he said, and then put the receiver down.

Julie was staring at him. 'We'll go and have a meal and I will drive you home presently.'

'There's no need. Really, just because I made a fool of myself, crying like a baby. If you don't mind I'll stay and clear up some of this mess and then go home.'

'I do mind. Get your jacket and we'll go.'

'Where?' asked Julie.

'My home. My manservant will have something ready; he expected me back this evening.' When she hesitated he said, 'I've driven down from Leeds and I've had a busy day. I'm hungry.'

There wasn't much point in arguing with him, and besides, she was hungry too. It was a friendly gesture on his part—the kind of gesture anyone might make in like circumstances. Probably he would be bored with her company even for a brief hour or so, but she would see where he lived, perhaps discover something of his life; he might even tell her about the girl that he had met in Groningen. If she knew when he was going to get married it might be easier to forget that she had fallen in love with him.

She had a lot to think about, she reflected, going with him to the car.

The streets were quieter now that the rush hour was over, the evening traffic not yet busy; he drove across the city and she saw presently that they were going through quiet streets of dignified houses with enclosed gardens and, here and there, trees.

The professor turned down a narrow lane beside a terrace of Regency houses and turned into the mews behind them. The cottages in it were charming, with flower boxes at their windows and pristine paintwork. He drove to the end and stopped outside the last cottage, got out and opened her door to usher her into a small lobby with a glass inner door.

This was opened as they went in by a middle-aged man, very dignified. He bade them good evening in a grave voice and the professor said, 'This is Blossom, who runs the place for me. Blossom, this is Miss Beckworth, whom I have brought home for a meal—she's had a rather trying experience at the hospital this evening.'

'Indeed, miss, I am sorry to hear it. There is a fire in the sitting room, sir. A glass of sherry, perhaps, for the young lady while I dish up?'

Her jacket tenderly borne away by Blossom, Julie was ushered into the sitting room which ran from the front of the cottage to the back, with windows at each end and a fireplace opposite the door. It was low-ceilinged, its walls hung with honey-coloured paper, and furnished with cosy armchairs, a lovely old corner-cupboard, a satinwood rent table under one window and small lamp-tables here and there. The lamps on them had been lighted and gave the room a most welcoming look.

'Come and sit by the fire,' suggested the professor, and pulled forward a chair covered in mulberry velvet, 'and take Blossom's advice.'

He went to a small table to pour the drinks. 'Dry, or something sweeter?'

'Dry, please.' Her eyes had lighted on a basket to one side of the fireplace. 'Oh, you have a cat...'

'Yes, and kittens; there should be two there.'

Julie got up to look. The cat opened an eye and studied her before closing it again, and she bent nearer. Two very small kittens were tucked between her paws.

'She's called Kitty—not very imaginative, I'm afraid, but Blossom assures me that she replies to that name.'

Julie sat down again and took the glass he offered. 'And the kittens?'

'They arrived shortly after she attached herself to us. A boy and a girl. I've had several offers of homes for them but I fancy that by the time they are old enough to leave their mother Blossom will refuse to part with them.'

He had gone to sit down opposite her and bent to stroke the cat. 'I must admit it is pleasant to come home to a welcome.'

'You miss Jason...'

'Indeed I do. I shall be going to Holland shortly and

hope to spend a few days with him.' He smiled. 'A holiday this time.'

Julie said in a steady voice, 'I am sure you will enjoy
that; you must miss your family and friends.'

'I have friends here as well.' An unsatisfactory answer, almost a snub. Justified, she reflected fairly; his
private life was no concern of hers.

She sipped her sherry and racked her brains for
something to say. Luckily Blossom came to tell them
that dinner was served and they crossed the little hall to
a small dining room at the front of the cottage. It held
a round table encircled by six Hepplewhite chairs, and
there was a small sideboard and a long-case clock, its
front of marquetry. The table, covered in white damask,
was set with silver and crystal glasses and the plates
were delft china. Did the professor dine in such state
each evening? she wondered, sampling the soup set before her. Tomato and orange—home-made, too.

The professor seemed determined to keep on friendly
terms, and indeed he was a perfect host, talking about
this and that as they ate their duckling with cherry sauce
and game chips, never mentioning the evening's unfor-
tunate event as he invited her to have a second helping
of Blossom's delicious hot almond fritters. Only when
they were once more in the sitting room drinking their
coffee did he ask her if she felt quite recovered. 'If you
wish there is no reason why you shouldn't have a day
at home tomorrow.'

She thought of the mess in his office. 'I'm quite all
right, really I am,' she told him. 'I'm ashamed of myself for being such a baby.'

'My dear girl, you behaved with exemplary calm; most women would have screeched the house down.'

'I was too scared to scream,' she told him.

'In future if you are working late you are to lock the door. You understand me, Miss Beckworth?' He sounded chillingly polite; the little flame of hope that he had decided to like her after all died. He had done his duty as he saw it; now she was Miss Beckworth again. It was ridiculous to imagine that she could possibly marry such a man; she put down her cup and saucer and observed in a voice devoid of expression that she would like to go home.

'It has been most kind of you,' said Julie, in a voice which sounded in her own ears to be far too gushing. The professor must have thought the same, for he glanced at her in faint surprise. 'I hope I haven't interrupted your evening.'

'No, no. I had nothing planned. I'll drive you home.'

They went into the hall and Blossom appeared, soft-footed and silent. 'I enjoyed dinner very much,' she told him. 'I wish I could cook like that; thank you, Blossom.'

He smiled then. 'A pleasure, Miss Beckworth. I trust you have fully recovered from your unpleasant experience?'

'Yes, thank you. Goodnight.'

The professor had stood by while she had talked; now he ushered her out to the car, got in beside her, and drove away, back through the city, away from the quiet streets and the gardens and trees until he turned into the gate of her home.

Julie made to get out, embarking on a rather muddled

speech of thanks to which he didn't listen but got out and opened her door and walked with her to the door of the house. Here she held out a hand. 'You've been most kind,' she began once again. 'Please don't wait—'

'I'm coming in,' said the professor.

The door was opened by Luscombe. 'There yer are, Miss Julie; come on in, both of you. Evening to you, Professor. Here's a turn-up for the book, eh?'

He closed the door behind them as Mrs Beckworth came out of the sitting room.

'Darling, whatever has happened? You're all right? Oh, of course you are; the professor's with you. Did you faint or feel ill? Come in and tell us what happened.'

Julie took off her jacket and they went into the sitting room to where Esme was sitting in her dressing gown with Blotto sprawled on her lap. She jumped up as they went in. 'I wouldn't go to bed until you came home, Julie; Simon, do tell us what happened.'

Julie went to pat Blotto and her mother waved the professor to a chair. Luscombe had followed them in and was standing by the door, all ears.

'Your sister was working late when a man got into the hospital and found his way to my office. He flung things around and threatened her. She was very brave; she threw an inkstand at him—'

'You hit him, Julie?' asked Esme, all agog.

'Well, no, and it only just missed the professor as he came into the room.'

'My dear Simon, you weren't hurt?' asked Mrs Beckworth anxiously.

'I? Not at all. I was lost in admiration for your daughter's presence of mind in throwing something at the man; it put him off his stroke completely.'

'Then what did you do?' asked Esme.

'The police came and took the man away; it seems he was known to them. We had a cup of tea and then a meal. You have a daughter to be proud of, Mrs Beckworth.'

Julie looked at her feet and Mrs Beckworth said, 'Thank you for looking after her so well, Simon. We're so grateful. Would you like a cup of coffee?'

'I won't stay, Mrs Beckworth, thank you; but I felt it necessary to explain what happened. Rest assured I'm going to make sure that it can never happen again.'

He bade them all goodnight, adding to Julie, 'Don't come in in the morning if you don't feel up to it.'

She mumbled an answer, not looking at him. Just because she had been silly and cried, there was no excuse to take a day off.

When he had gone Mrs Beckworth said, 'Now, darling, do tell us again what happened. I mean before Simon arrived. Was the man very nasty? He didn't hurt you?'

'No, but he flung things about—all the notes and files and case-sheets on the desk; he threw them all onto the floor. It'll take all day to get them straight. He wanted to break up the computer too. I couldn't reach the phone...'

'You were very brave, throwing something at him.'

'You always were a rotten shot,' said Esme. 'A good thing too; you might have knocked out Simon and I'd never have forgiven you.'

I wouldn't have forgiven myself either, reflected Julie.

Luscombe came in then, with a tray of tea. 'Nothing like a cuppa when you've 'ad a bit of a set-to,' he pointed out. He chuckled. 'I'd have liked to have seen the professor's face when he opened the door... I bet 'e was livid.'

Thinking about it, Julie realised that he had been very angry. Not noisily so; it had been a cold, fierce rage. No wonder the man hadn't attempted to get out of the chair that he had been thrown into. She hoped that the professor would never look at her like that.

Julie went to work early the next morning, intent on clearing up the mess before he got there, but early though she was he was earlier, crouched down on the floor, sorting out the scattered sheets.

'Oh, you're here already,' said Julie, and then added, 'Good morning, sir.'

He glanced up. 'Good morning, Miss Beckworth. What a very thorough job Slim Sid did. I am afraid he has torn several pages of notes. However, let us first of all get everything sorted out.'

He handed her a pile of folders, observing mildly, 'The floor is the best place.'

So she got on her knees and went to work. It was dull and tedious, and since he showed no signs of wanting to talk she kept silent. Before long the phone rang, and when she answered it it was an urgent request that he should go at once to the wards. Which left her alone with her thoughts.

Chapter 6

By the time the professor came back Julie had established some kind of order. There had been a good deal of sorting out to do and her normal day's work was already piled on her desk. She had paused briefly to open the post and lay the contents on his desk, find his diary and leave it open—it was crammed with appointments—and had dealt with several phone calls which hadn't been urgent.

He went past her into his own office without speaking and presently asked her to take some letters. As she sat down he looked at her over his spectacles. 'You are suffering no ill effects from your disturbed evening?' he wanted to know.

'None, sir.' She opened her notebook, pencil poised. After a quick look she bent her head, writing the date on her pad, taking her time over it, wishing that he would start dictating, because sitting there with him was a mixed blessing; it was pure happiness to be near him; on the other hand, the sooner he started dictating with his usual abruptness, apparently unaware of her as a person, the easier it would be for her to ignore her feelings.

The professor was, however, in no hurry. He was irritated that Julie was so frequently in his thoughts and yesterday he had, much against his will, told her that she was beautiful and been altogether too concerned about her. He had been so careful to hold her at arm's length when it was obvious that she didn't like him. Hopefully, she had been so upset that she had probably not been listening. He would have to be careful; he had no intention of allowing himself to fall in love with a girl who so disliked him.

He thought with relief of the few days' holiday he intended to take in Holland; to get away might bring him to his senses so that he could return to his austere, hard-working life.

He pushed his spectacles further up his handsome nose. 'The hospital director—you have his name and the hospital's in the letter—Stockholm. With regard to your invitation to lecture…'

Would he want her to go to Stockholm with him? Julie wondered, her pencil racing over the page. Perhaps not for such a brief visit to read a paper at a seminar there. She turned the page for a new letter and concentrated; this time it was full of long medical terms—she would have to check it all in her dictionary.

He went away presently and she made a cup of coffee before starting on her typing—the letters first and then printing out the spoilt sheets again and then getting down to the routine paperwork. The professor was still absent and she decided that she would miss her dinner. If there was a porter free he might bring her a sandwich from the canteen.

She rang through to the lodge, and since she was regarded as something of a heroine after last night's escapade a few minutes later one of the porters who had followed the police brought her a plate of sandwiches. 'Beef, miss, and a packet of biscuits. All right for coffee, are you?' When she thanked him, he said awkwardly, 'Wish I'd known about that fellow getting in here; I'd have put him to the right about. None the worse are you, miss?'

She assured him that she had never felt better. 'And I know you would have been the first to deal with him. I feel quite safe here. It was just chance that he managed to creep in.'

The professor returned just as she had taken a bite of sandwich. He eyed her coldly. 'Why have you not gone to your dinner, Miss Beckworth? Am I such a hard taskmaster?'

She said thickly through a mouthful of beef, 'No, no, sir, but the work's piling up and there's a lot of time wasted in the canteen, queueing for food.'

He looked surprised and then picked up the phone and asked for sandwiches and coffee to be sent to his office. Julie swallowed the last of the beef; it seemed that he was going to lunch at his desk too...

She was wrong; the porter, when he came with a tray

bearing a pot of coffee and sandwiches, was directed to put them on her desk, and when she turned a surprised face to him Professor van der Driesma said, 'They were for you, Miss Beckworth.'

The professor came through the door as the porter went away. Julie eyed the sandwiches with pleasure—egg and cress, ham, and a couple of leaves of lettuce on the side—very tasty. She said gratefully, 'Thank you, sir.'

He paused on his way out. 'I cannot allow you to waste away, Miss Beckworth.'

Her 'Well, really!' was lost on him as he closed the door gently behind him.

She drank a cup of delicious coffee and ate the sandwiches. What had he meant? Had it been an oblique reference to her size? She was a big girl but she had a splendid shape. Perhaps he preferred the beanpole type—or did he think that she was greedy? She ate another sandwich. 'Well, too bad!' said Julie, gobbling the last delicious morsel and pouring the last of the coffee. Though the canteen, if they knew that she was lunching off what was intended to be a light snack for a consultant, would be furious.

She started her work again, much refreshed, and by the time the professor came back, his head bent over the papers before him, she had finished her work. She took his letters in, waited to see if he needed her for anything else and went back to her office to start on the filing.

He had given her the briefest of glances and returned to his work again. I might just as well not be here, she reflected. Why does it all have to be so hopeless? Why

couldn't he have fallen in love with me? And why did
I have to fall in love with him? Useless questions she
couldn't answer. She finished her filing, bade him a
wooden goodnight and took herself off home.

Luscombe was in the kitchen when she went in. ''Arf
a mo', there's a cup of tea coming up,' he told her. ''Ad
a bad day?'

'Absolutely beastly.' She drank her tea and felt better,
so she was able to tell her mother that she wasn't in the
least tired and the day had been no busier than usual.

'Well, dear, that's a good thing. Do you remember
Peter Mortimer? He went to Australia—or was it New
Zealand?—last year. He's back home and phoned to see
if you'd have dinner with him this evening. You used
to be quite friendly…' Her mother looked hopeful. 'He
said he'd ring again.'

Which he did, exactly on cue. 'Remember me?' he
asked cheerfully. 'I'm here in town for a couple of days
before I go home. Will you have dinner with me this
evening and tell me all the gossip?'

She had liked him and he had more than liked her,
but she had almost forgotten what he looked like. He
sounded lonely and perhaps an evening out would restore her spirits. After all, what was the use of mooning
over a man who hardly looked at her, much less bothered to say anything other than good morning and good
evening? 'I'd like that,' she told him. 'Do you want me
to meet you somewhere?'

'I'll come for you. Seven o'clock be too early?'

'That's fine.' She ran off and went to tell her mother.

'How nice, dear. You have so little fun these days. I wonder where he'll take you?'

'No idea.' To discourage her mother's obvious hopes, she added, 'He's in town just for a day or two then he's going home.'

She put on a pretty silk jersey dress, its colour matching her hair, piled her hair in a complicated topknot and went to her mother's wardrobe to get the coat—a dark brown cashmere treasured from their better-off days and shared between them, used only on special occasions.

Esme was in the sitting room when she went downstairs. 'You look quite chic,' she observed. 'Take care of the coat, won't you? In a year or two I'll be able to borrow it too.'

'Such a useful garment,' said Mrs Beckworth. 'I shall need it for that committee meeting in a couple of days' time. You know the one—we drink weak tea and decide about the Christmas party for the rest home. Only they're all so dressy. I know I've worn the coat for several years, but no one can cavil at cashmere, can they?' She paused. 'There's the doorbell. You go, dear; Luscombe's busy in the kitchen.'

Peter Mortimer hadn't changed; he had a round, chubby face and bright blue eyes and no one took him seriously, although he was something successful in the advertising business. He came in and spent five minutes talking to Mrs Beckworth. Esme bombarded him with questions about Australia—only it turned out that it was New Zealand—but presently he suggested that they should go. 'I've got a table for eight o'clock and we're bound to get hung up crossing town.'

He was an easy companion, delighted to talk about his year away from England, and Julie was a good listener. The traffic was heavy but he was a good driver and patient. 'Not boring you?' he asked as he drew up outside the Café Royal. 'Pop inside while I get this chappie to park the car...'

Julie went into the foyer, left the coat in the cloak-room and hoped that he wouldn't be too long. He wasn't. 'Marvellous chap—tucked the car somewhere. Hope this place suits you?'

'Peter, it's heavenly. I haven't been out to dine for months.'

They were shown to their table and when they had sat down he asked, 'Why not?' He grinned. 'A gorgeous girl like you? I should have thought you'd have been out night after night, if not spoken for!'

'Well, I'm not. I know it sounds silly but I'm quite tired when I get home in the evenings and there's always something which has to be done. Don't think I'm grumbling; I've a good job and lots of friends, only I don't see any of them as often as I'd like to.' She looked around her at the opulent grill room with its gilded rococo and mirrors. 'This is quite something. Are you a millionaire or something?'

'Lord, no, but I'm doing quite nicely. I'm going back to New Zealand in a couple of weeks. Came over to see the parents, actually.' He looked suddenly bashful. 'I'm going to marry a girl—her father's a sheep farmer on the South Island; thought I'd better tell them about her. We'll marry after Christmas and come over here to see them.'

'Peter, how lovely! I hope you'll be very happy. Tell me about her...'

'Let's have a drink and decide what we'll eat—I've some photos of her...'

They had their drinks and decided what they would have—spinach soufflé, medallions of pork with ginger sauce—and, since Peter insisted that it was a kind of celebration—or a reunion if she'd rather—he ordered a bottle of champagne.

The soufflé eaten, he brought out the photos and they bent over them, their heads close together. 'She looks very pretty, Peter; she's dark, and her eyes are lovely.' Julie sat back while the waiter served her, and glanced round the room. The professor was sitting thirty yards away, staring at her.

He wasn't alone; the woman he was with had her back to Julie, but, from what she could see of it, it promised elegance. She had dark hair, cut short, a graceful neck and shoulders and when she turned her head, a perfect profile.

Julie managed a small, social smile and looked away quickly, not wanting to see if he would acknowledge it or not. Probably not, she thought peevishly, bending an apparently attentive head to hear Peter's description of life in New Zealand.

Who was the woman? she wondered. Of course, the professor was entitled to have as many girlfriends as he wanted, but what about the girl in Groningen? There had been no mistaking the way he had held her close and kissed her.

She had never thought of him as having a social life; to see him, sitting there in black tie, in one of the most fashionable restaurants in London, had surprised her. Just for a moment she wondered if he would say anything to her in the morning, but she dismissed the thought as Peter began a detailed description of the house he intended to buy for his bride.

When she contrived to peep towards the professor's table later it was to find that he and his companion had gone.

In the morning the professor was already at his desk when she got to her office. His good morning was affable. 'You had a pleasant evening, Miss Beckworth?' He sounded positively avuncular.

'Thank you, yes, very pleasant. Shall I ring the path lab for those results they promised for this morning?'

He didn't answer this. 'An old friend?' he asked.

'Oh, yes,' said Julie briskly. 'We've known each other for a very long time.' She wasn't sure how one simpered but it seemed an appropriate expression and she did her best.

The professor watched with secret amusement. 'I suppose we shall be losing you shortly,' he suggested. 'He didn't look the kind of man who would like his wife to work.'

Julie was thinking about the woman at the professor's table and wasn't listening with more than half an ear. 'He still has to get his house—of course, in that part of New Zealand there is plenty of space.'

'New Zealand? That's a long way away.'

'Twenty-four hours in a plane,' she told him, and added briskly, 'I'll phone the path lab…'

He watched her go to her office and pick up the phone, surprised to find that he didn't like the idea of her going to the other side of the world as another man's wife.

He gave an impatient sigh; she had somehow wormed her way into his mind and now his heart, and, what was worse, she was quite unaware of it. Well, he would never let her see that; a pity that after all these years he should be in danger of falling in love at last, and with the wrong girl. He opened his diary and studied its contents; a busy day lay ahead of him. He was too old for her, anyway.

That evening when he got home Blossom came to meet him. 'Mrs Venton telephoned, sir, not half an hour ago. Asked if you would ring her back. I did tell her that I didn't know how late you'd be.'

The professor paused on his way to his study. 'Ah, thank you, Blossom. Did she say why she wished me to ring her?'

'She mentioned a small dinner party with a few friends, sir.' Blossom coughed. 'The young lady whom you brought here recently, sir—I trust she is fully recovered from her nasty experience? I had the whole story from your head porter's wife while shopping at the supermarket.'

'Quite recovered, Blossom.'

'I am glad to hear it; a very nice young lady if I may say so, sir, and extremely pretty. Very well liked, I understand.' He slid past the professor and opened his study door for him. 'I lighted a small fire, sir; these evenings are chilly. Will you dine at your usual time?'

'Please.'

The professor went and sat at his desk, ignoring the papers on it, so still that Kitty in her basket by the fire left her sleeping kittens and climbed onto his knee. He stroked her gently while he thought about Julie. Despite her evasive answers to his questions he felt sure now that the man she had been with was no more than a friend. From where he had been sitting he had had an excellent view of the pair of them; they certainly hadn't behaved like people in love and yet he had had the distinct impression that that was what she would have liked him to think.

Since he was now quite certain in his mind that he loved her and intended, by hook or crook to marry her, he would have to find ways of getting to know her better, and that, he knew, would have to be a gradual process or she would be frightened off. First he must win her liking.

Blossom, coming to tell him that dinner was ready, wondered why he looked so thoughtful and at the same time so cheerful. Surely that Mrs Venton hadn't had that effect upon his master. A tiresome woman, thought Blossom, out to catch the professor, given the chance. Not that he would be an easy man to catch, but sooner or later someone would do just that.

Blossom, serving soup with the same perfection he would have shown at a dinner party for a dozen, thought of Julie again. She would do nicely.

It would have given him great peace of mind if he had known that the professor had come to the same conclusion, never mind his previous doubts.

Julie, unaware of these plans for her future, her feelings ruffled because the professor had shown no emotion when she had hinted that she might be going to New Zealand, went home in a bad temper, didn't eat her supper and flounced around the house doing a lot of unnecessary things like shaking up the cushions and opening and closing drawers and cupboards.

Her mother, placidly sewing name-tapes on Esme's new sports kit, watched her and said nothing; only later, when Julie had taken herself off to bed, did she remark to Luscombe worriedly, 'Julie doesn't seem quite herself. I do hope she's not sickening for something.'

Luscombe offered the warm drink he had thoughtfully prepared for her.

'In love, isn't she? I said so, didn't I? ''Ad a row, no doubt, with the professor...'

'When he's here he hardly speaks to her. I mean, she's his secretary.' A muddled statement which Luscombe had no difficulty in understanding.

'Goes to show—'e's smitten too. The pair of them 'as got crossed wires.'

On Monday the professor began his campaign to win Julie's attention, if not her affection, with caution. Nevertheless, she looked at him once or twice during the day; he had smiled at her several times, he had wished her a cheerful good morning and each time he came and went to and from his office he had a word to say; she could only conclude that he had had some good news of some sort. Perhaps that girl was coming to see him. He had told her that he would be going back to Holland shortly—the prospect of being at his home again might have put him in a good mood. She responded guardedly, carefully polite.

The professor, sitting at his desk watching Julie's charming back view as she typed, abandoned the notes he was preparing for a lecture and reviewed the situation; after three days there had been no obvious signs of Julie responding to his overtures of friendship. On the contrary, she was, if anything, decidedly tart. A lesser man might have been warned off, but the professor was made of sterner stuff. He brought his powerful brain to bear on the problem and reflected that he was enjoying himself.

The next day he told Julie that he would be going to Holland that evening. 'A few days' holiday,' he told her airily, 'and most conveniently Dr Walter's secretary is off sick, so you will be standing in for her. Perhaps you will look in here each morning and check through the post.'

Julie put the folder of papers down on his desk. However would she get through the days without him? To see his empty desk each morning and wonder what he was doing and with whom… 'How long will you be gone, sir?' she asked him.

He glanced up at her. 'A week—ten days. I'm not sure. I intend to see something of my family and friends and I want to spend a few days at least at my home. It rather depends on circumstances. George Wyatt—his registrar—will deal with anything which may crop up.'

'Very well, sir. If you should see Mevrouw Schatt give her my kind regards.'

'Of course.' He turned briskly to his desk. 'I see that in my diary you have a note reminding me to phone Mrs Venton. Perhaps you would be good enough to do that for me and tell her that I shall be away for the next week or so.'

'Very well. Is she the lady you were dining with at the Café Royal?'

He stared at her and she couldn't read the expression on his face.

'Since you ask—yes, Miss Beckworth.' He opened his eyes wide. 'Why do you ask?'

'Because I'm a nosy parker!' said Julie flippantly, and picked up the phone as it started to ring.

She rang Mrs Venton while he was on the wards and relayed his message in an impersonal voice.

'Who are you?' asked Mrs Venton rudely.

'Professor van der Driesma's secretary.'

'Where has he gone? You must know that. And when is he coming back?'

'I have no idea when he will be returning, Mrs Venton, and I have given you his message exactly as he gave it to me.'

'He's there now, isn't he?' Mrs Venton wasn't going to give up.

'No, Mrs Venton, he isn't here.'

'I don't believe you,' snapped Mrs Venton, and slammed down the receiver.

In an expressionless voice Julie reported the conversation when the professor returned. It was most unsatisfactory that all he did was grunt.

At five o'clock he looked up from his computer. 'That will be all for today, Miss Beckworth. Good evening.'

She tidied her desk and wished him goodbye and a pleasant holiday.

That night she had a good cry, thinking of him on his way to Holland. He'll probably come back married, she thought miserably. It was easy to account for his friendly manner now, he must have been happy...

The professor wasn't exactly happy, he realised that he would never be quite happy again unless he had Julie for his wife, but he was pleased enough with his careful planning. Absence makes the heart grow fonder, he reminded himself as he drove down to Dover, and if he wasn't distracted by the sight of Julie's beautiful face each day, he would be able to mull over the more likely schemes he had in mind.

It was very late by the time he reached his home in Leiden, but Siska and Jason gave him a warm welcome. He ate his supper while she told him all the latest news, took a delighted Jason for a walk and went to his bed, where he slept the dreamless sleep of a man who knew what he wanted to do and would do it.

* * *

To Mrs Beckworth's bright enquiry as to how the professor did, Julie, when she got home, replied briefly that she didn't know because he had gone away.

'Not for good?' Mrs Beckworth asked in a dismayed voice.

'No, no. He's going to Holland this evening for a holiday; he doesn't know how long he'll be away. I've been loaned to Dr Walters—his secretary's ill.'

'Oh, well, that will make a nice change, darling. Is he nice, this other doctor?'

'He's a medical consultant. He's all right in a dull kind of way.'

A not very satisfactory answer, thought her mother. 'Let's hope Simon has a nice break. I'm sure he deserves one.'

Julie mumbled a reply and went off to help Esme with her maths.

Dr Walters was pleased to see her in the morning. Miss Frisby, his own secretary, he explained, hadn't been feeling well for some days—something to do with her teeth. 'I'm afraid the filling and so forth has got rather neglected—she didn't feel up to it.'

Discovering the havoc in the filing cabinets, Julie concluded that Miss Frisby couldn't have been feeling up to it for weeks—even months. The muddle would keep her busy for hours, not to mention the routine work that she was expected to do as well. Perhaps if her teeth didn't improve Miss Frisby would resign. Julie knew her by sight—a washed-out girl with straggly hair and a loud and refined voice—but they had never said more than hello. They weren't likely to.

The post piled up on the professor's desk, and she quickly decided that she would have to go in to work an hour earlier each morning, so her days were busy. When she got home in the evening there was always plenty to keep her occupied—Esme to help with her homework, her mother to talk to and Luscombe to help around the house. Despite all this, the days dragged.

The professor had been gone for several days when Esme received a postcard from him. It was from Leiden, showing a view of the Rappenburg. He had written in his almost unreadable scrawl: 'I'll show you this one day. Ask your sister if she remembers it.'

Esme, proudly handing it round, said reflectively, 'He never calls you Julie, does he? Do you call him Simon?'

'Certainly not.' Julie hadn't meant to sound snappy, and she added quickly, 'That would never do—he's rather an important person at the hospital.'

Esme persisted. 'Yes, but when you're alone with him?'

'He's still my boss.'

'I wonder what he's doing?' mused Esme.

Julie wondered too, but she didn't say so.

Simon was sitting at the head of his table in the rather gloomy dining room of Huis Driesma. A large square house, its exterior belying its interior, redolent of a by-gone age, it stood in grounds bordered by water meadows on a lake fringed by trees and shrubs, fronting a narrow country road. Out of sight round a bend in the road was a small village, its cottages petering out as it wound away into a tranquil distance.

There were a number of people seated at the table: Simon's mother faced him at its foot, then his two brothers and their wives, and his youngest brother, still a medical student, sat beside the youngest of all of them—a girl of almost seventeen.

The conversation had been animated, for although they were a close family they lived at some distance from each other, and for them all to be together was seldom possible. The house was Simon's, inherited from his father, and until he should marry his mother lived there with his sister and—whenever he could get away from the hospital—his younger brother, Hugo.

His mother was saying now, 'I wish you would marry, Simon; it is time you took over this house. I know you have a charming house in Leiden, but you should spend more time here. Weekends, perhaps? I know you have your work at St Bravo's, but travelling is so easy these days…'

Celeste, the baby of the family, chimed in. 'You must meet any number of girls. What about all the nurses, or are you too lofty for them?'

'They are all so pretty and young and already spoken for,' said Simon lightly.

'When I phoned your secretary answered. Is she as pretty as her voice?' asked the younger of his sisters-in-law. She laughed. 'I didn't say who I was—at least, I said I was Mevrouw van Graaf. I thought you might not like her to know about your family… Hospitals are gossipy places, aren't they?'

The professor sat back in his chair and said placidly, 'She is even prettier than her voice. I hope you will all meet her some day, for I intend to marry her!' He looked down the table at his mother. 'You will like her, Mama.'

His mother smiled. She was a handsome woman whose dignified appearance concealed a gentle nature. 'If you love her, my dear, then I shall too. Will you bring her here to meet us all?'

'I hope to, but not just yet.' He smiled. 'I believe that she doesn't like me very much.'

There was a ripple of laughter. 'Simon, what do you mean? Why doesn't she like you? Have you been horrid to her?' This from his youngest sister.

'No, no. I have behaved with great correctness towards her. Somehow we started off on the wrong foot—and she has a sharp tongue.'

'Just what you need,' said Celeste. 'I'm going to like her very much. What is her name?'

'Julie—Julie Beckworth. She has green eyes and bronze hair, very long and thick, and she is what the English call a fine figure of a woman.'

'All curves?' asked Celeste.

'All curves,' agreed Simon.

Dinner over, they gathered in the drawing room on the other side of the wide hall. It was a splendid room, the polished wood floor covered with lovely rugs, their colours muted by age. The windows were tall and narrow, draped in old rose brocade, and the same colour covered the comfortable chairs scattered around. There were vast cabinets against the walls and a very beautiful long-case clock between the windows.

Arranged here and there there were lamp-tables, as well as a sofa-table behind the enormous sofa facing the stone fireplace. A fire was burning briskly and Jason, asleep before it, roused himself to go to his master, although an elderly labrador, his mother's dog, merely wagged her tail and went back to sleep.

'You'll be able to stay for a few days?' asked his mother. 'It was such a quick visit when you were last here.'

'Two days. I must go back to Leiden for a few days…'

'Does Julie know when you're going back?' asked Hugo.

'No. I'm not absolutely sure myself.'

Jan, who looked after the house with his wife, Bep, brought in the coffee and they sat talking until late. It was midnight before they all dispersed to their rooms.

Simon, strolling round the garden in the chilly night while the dogs had a last run, wished very much that he had Julie with him. He wanted to show her his old home and he wanted her to meet his mother and his family, but he would have to be patient.

The dogs settled in the kitchen, he went up the oak staircase at the back of the hall and along the wide corridor to his room. As he passed his mother's door she opened it.

'Simon, dear, I'm so very happy for you. I was beginning to think that you would never find her—your ideal woman—but now that you have I shall welcome her with open arms.'

He bent to kiss her cheek. 'Father would have approved of her, my dear.'

* * *

He went back to Leiden two days later, to Siska, waiting for him with a splendid supper and anxious to hear the news from Huis Driesma. 'I hope I'll be seeing you again soon,' she observed. 'I'm that happy about the young lady—took to her at once, I did.'

The professor, hardly able to wait before he should see Julie again, nevertheless delayed his departure so that he might meet several of his friends and colleagues at the hospital. But three evenings later he drove down to the Hoek, boarded a ferry and sailed for England.

It was cold, misty and overcast when the ferry docked at Harwich. He drove up to London and let himself in to his cottage. Blossom might be getting on a bit, but his hearing was excellent—he was in the hall almost before the professor had shut the door.

'Welcome back, sir.' He uttered the words with grave pleasure. 'Breakfast or an early lunch? You probably fared indifferently on board the ferry.'

'Breakfast would be nice, Blossom.' The professor glanced at his watch. 'I'll miss lunch, but I'll dine here this evening. I'll have a shower while you cook.'

The temptation to go straight to St Bravo's and see Julie was very great, but first he must get his affairs in order. Having eaten a splendid breakfast, he got into his car and drove to his consulting rooms.

Mrs Cross, his receptionist, was there at her desk. 'Oh, good you're back,' she observed. 'I wasn't sure when you would be back—you didn't say.' She cast him a reproachful look. 'But I've booked several appointments for tomorrow, starting at four o'clock. I said I'd phone if you weren't back today.'

'Splendid, Mrs Cross. Anything in the post that I should know about?'

'Plenty. Can you spare the time now, or will you be in tomorrow morning?'

'I'll see to them now. If you bring your notebook I'll give you the answers and you can get them out of the way.'

The afternoon was well advanced by the time he had finished dictating. He drank a cup of tea with Mrs Cross and then drove to the hospital. The late afternoon traffic was building up and it took much longer than usual. Perhaps Julie would already have gone home...

It wasn't quite five o'clock as he opened his office door. She was kneeling on the floor, sorting a pile of papers into neat heaps. The overhead light shone on her hair, turning it to russet streaked with bronze, and he paused for a moment to relish the sight.

As he closed the door she turned her head, and he wished that her face wasn't in shadow. He had wanted to see how she looked when she saw him.

'I didn't expect you,' said Julie. 'I'm not nearly ready with all this.' She sounded cross, and he thought ruefully that it wasn't quite the greeting he had hoped for.

'Well, now I am here,' he said placidly, 'supposing I give you a hand?'

Chapter 7

The professor squatted down beside her but she didn't look up. His hands, large and well-shaped, sorting the papers, sent her insides fluttering with the sheer delight of seeing them—to look at him would have been fatal. Her own hands were shaking—something which he noticed at once with satisfaction, although he reminded himself ruefully that she might be shaking with rage at his sudden return.

He asked politely, 'You have been kept busy? Is Miss Frisby not yet back?'

Julie said in an indignant voice, 'Not for another two days…'

'You had difficulty coping with her work?' he asked gently.

'Difficulty? Difficulty?' Julie slapped a pile of papers with some force. She drew a deep breath. 'Her teeth must have been giving her a great deal of trouble.'

The professor suppressed a grin. 'You have reduced chaos to a tidy state?'

'Yes. Do I have to stay there until she returns, now you're back?'

'Certainly not. I shall probably erupt into a maelstrom of work which won't leave you a moment for anyone else. What are all these papers?'

'Referred notes from patients you have been asked to examine. Some of them are from other hospitals. I've classed them as far as possible.'

She got to her feet and he did the same, towering over her. 'Your post is on your desk, sir. I've dealt with the routine stuff and your private mail is on your blotter. You may wish to take it home with you.'

He glanced at his watch. 'Get your coat; I'll drive you home.'

'Thank you, but there is no need...'

'I don't think need comes into it. Get your coat, Miss Beckworth.'

'I have just said—' began Julie, and stopped when she caught his eye.

'Julie,' said the professor, in a voice which she didn't care to ignore. Besides, he had called her Julie. A slip of the tongue, or deliberately said to persuade her?

She fetched her coat, and when he opened the door went past him without looking at him. He must have had a splendid time in Holland, she reflected, and most certainly he must have seen the girl from Groningen. Perhaps the way now lay clear for them to marry. She closed her eyes for a second at the thought and tripped over the doormat.

The professor scooped her up neatly and stood her back on her feet. The temptation not to let her go was so fierce that he was compelled to release her briskly, an act which unfortunately she misinterpreted.

Her lovely face was a mask of haughtiness as she got into the car—something he chose to ignore, talking cheerfully of nothing in particular as he drove the short distance, and when she asked him in a quelling voice if he would like to come in, her stony face daring him to do so, he remarked that he would be delighted.

The warmth of Mrs Beckworth's and Esme's welcome more than made up for Julie's coldness. He was offered coffee and Luscombe produced an apple cake he had just taken from the oven.

'Glad ter be back 'ome?' he enquired chattily. 'Not but what you've an 'ome in foreign parts. Still, I dare say you've friends in London?'

'Us,' said Esme. 'We're friends, aren't we?'

'Of course you are,' declared the professor. 'And that reminds me—I have tickets for *La Bohème*—Saturday evening. I would be delighted if you would be my guests?'

Esme flung herself at him. 'Oh, yes—yes, please. Opera—and it's that marvellous singer.' She turned to her mother. 'Mother, say yes, do please…'

'That's very kind of you, Simon. It would be a wonderful treat.' Mrs Beckworth looked as delighted as Esme.

Julie didn't say anything at all.

'Shall we dress up?' asked Esme, filling an awkward pause.

'Er—well, something pretty…' The professor, so fluent when it came to unpronounceable medical terms, was at a loss.

'Will you be wearing a dinner jacket?' asked Mrs Beckworth. 'We none of us have anything very fashionable, I'm afraid.'

The professor looked at Julie. 'When I saw you at the Café Royale you were wearing something silky and green—that would be exactly right.'

'That old thing,' declared Esme. 'Julie's had it for years. It suits her, though.'

'That's most helpful, Simon,' said her mother. 'We wouldn't want to embarrass you.'

'I'm quite sure that would be impossible, Mrs Beckworth. May I fetch you shortly after seven o'clock?'

He went soon afterwards, bending to receive Esme's kiss, shaking hands with Mrs Beckworth and wishing Luscombe a friendly goodnight, but giving Julie no more than a casual nod, with the reminder that he would see her in the morning.

Esme was on the point of remarking upon this, but before she could utter her mother said, 'We must settle this clothes question. Esme, finish your homework; we'll talk over our supper. Yes, I'm sure Julie will help you with your essay while I talk to Luscombe…'

In the kitchen she sat down at the table where her old and devoted servant was making a salad. 'Toasted cheese,' he told her. ''Is nibs popping in like that didn't give me no time for anything else.'

'Well, yes, we weren't expecting him. It's very kind of him to invite us out. If you would like to have Saturday afternoon and evening off, Luscombe, we shan't be back till late. I think we'd better have a kind of high tea before we go, and we can get that for ourselves.'

'OK, Mrs Beckworth. There's a film I'd like ter see—I could go to the matinee and 'ave tea at my sister's.' He was cutting bread. ''Is nibs didn't so much as look at Miss Julie. 'E's smitten, all right, and so's she, bless 'er. 'E'd better love 'er dearly, or I'll wring 'is neck for 'im!'

Mrs Beckworth acknowledged this generous offer in the spirit with which it had been given. 'We would be lost without you, Luscombe. Ever since the doctor died you've been our faithful friend.'

'And 'appy to be so, Mrs Beckworth.' He put the bread under the grill. ''Is nibs is right for our Julie. All we need's a bit of patience while they discover it for themselves. At cross purposes, they are, aren't they?'

'Yes, Luscombe, I do believe you're right. We'll just have to wait and see.'

Over supper the important question as to what they should wear dominated the conversation. Julie, secretly surprised that the professor had noticed what she had been wearing, agreed that the green jersey would do. Her mother had what she called her 'good black', which was instantly vetoed as being too dull. 'There's that grey silk you had for your silver wedding,' she said thoughtfully. 'If I alter the neck there's that bit of lace in the trunk in the attic—I could turn it into a jabot.'

Esme was rather more of a problem. There were four

days before Saturday, and nothing in Esme's cupboard which would suit the occasion.

'There's that sapphire-blue velvet cloak you had from Granny, Mother,' Julie said. 'There's enough material in it to make a pinafore dress for Esme. If you get a pattern I could cut it out tomorrow and run it up on the machine. You'll need a blouse, Esme—have I got anything? There's that white short-sleeved one of mine— I can take it in everywhere and add a blue bow at the neck. If it doesn't turn out we can rush out on Saturday afternoon and find something.'

The professor, pursuing his own plans, took care to be away from his desk as much as possible during the next few days. It meant that he had to work late after Julie had gone home, but it also meant that save for dictating his letters he needed to see little of her. True, she accompanied him on his ward-rounds, but so did half a dozen other people; there was no fear of being alone with her.

It wasn't until Julie was on the point of leaving on Friday that he said casually, 'I'll see you tomorrow evening—I did say shortly after seven, did I not?'

'Yes, Professor. We'll be ready,' Julie replied, and added, 'We're looking forward to it.'

She went home then, intent on finishing Esme's outfit—which had turned out surprisingly well. The blue suited her, and although they all knew it had originally been an old cloak no one else did, and the blouse, taken in drastically, was mostly concealed under the pinafore.

* * *

On Saturday evening, dressed and ready, they inspected each other carefully. Mrs Beckworth looked charming—the jabot had made all the difference and she was wearing her amethyst brooch. Esme preened herself in childish delight, and Julie, in the green dress, hoped that the professor wouldn't find them too unfashionable.

He arrived punctually, complimented them on their appearance, and helped Mrs Beckworth into the cashmere coat.

'We share the coat,' Esme told him chattily. 'It's Mother's but Julie wears it too, and just as soon as I'm big enough I shall be allowed to borrow it as well.'

Not a muscle of the professor's face moved; he ignored Mrs Beckworth's small distressed sound and Julie's sharp breath.

'You'll be a charming young lady in no time,' he observed. 'I like the blue thing you are wearing.'

'You'll never guess—' began Esme.

She was brought to a halt by Julie's urgent, 'Esme, no.' And Luscombe, coming into the hall to see them off, proved a welcome diversion...

Much later, lying in bed, too busy with her thoughts to sleep, Julie mulled over the evening. It had been wonderful; the Opera House had been magnificent, the audience sparkling and colourful, and the singing magnificent too—more than that, it had been breathtakingly dramatic. As the curtain had come down on the last act Julie had wanted to weep at the sadness. She hadn't been able to speak, only to shake her head and smile when the professor had asked her if she had enjoyed it.

He had driven them to the Savoy Grill Room and given them supper, and Esme, she remembered thankfully, had behaved beautifully—although her eyes had been sparkling with excitement and it had been obvious that she was longing to stare around her and make remarks. Her mother had said little, but Julie hadn't seen her look so happy for a long time.

She, herself, knew that there would never be another evening like it; it was something she would treasure for the rest of her life, something to remember when the professor became once more coldly impersonal and addressed her as Miss Beckworth.

She closed her eyes at last on the happy reflection that the blue velvet pinafore dress had been a great success; even though the seams and finish wouldn't bear close inspection, no one would have guessed...

The professor hadn't guessed but he had suspected—a suspicion confirmed by Esme, that outspoken child, who, finding herself alone with him for a few moments, had confided that it had been made out of her granny's old evening cloak.

'It took Julie three days—she's ever so good at cutting out and we've a very old machine, but it doesn't work very well. It's best not to look inside and inspect the stitches, but it's nice, isn't it?'

'It's charming,' he had assured her gently. 'And no one would have any idea that it wasn't brand-new from one of the best shops.'

A remark which had encouraged her to tell him about her mother's lace jabot…

It was a relief that the next day was Sunday. It gave Julie time to remind herself that just because the professor had invited them out to such a splendid evening it didn't mean that he felt any friendlier towards her. He was behaving very strangely too. She was never quite sure of him—one minute coolly disinterested, bent only on the work in hand, the next asking friendly questions about her mother and Esme.

The professor, on the other hand, was well pleased with the evening.

Late though it was by the time he had let himself into his little house, Blossom had still been up.

'A pleasant evening, I trust, sir?' Under his severe exterior Blossom hid a soft heart and a real fondness for his master. 'Mrs Venton telephoned to remind you that you are lunching at her house tomorrow. I am to tell you that Professor Smythe and his wife will be there.'

The professor, his head full of Julie and the way she had looked during the last act of *La Bohème*, had given an absent-minded nod. Even the mention of Professor Smythe, old friend and respected colleague though he was, had roused no interest in him just at that moment. Later, of course, when he had disciplined his thoughts to be sensible, he would look forward to seeing him again.

When they did meet the next day, over drinks at Audrey Venton's house, they were given little chance to talk.

Mrs Venton was a woman who liked to be the centre of interest. She was well aware that she was attractive, well dressed and an amusing companion, and she expected everyone else to think the same. She also expected to monopolise the conversation.

The professor, who had from time to time taken her out to dine, discovered that he no longer had any interest in her. Lunch was a lengthy meal, and when the Smythes got up to leave he made the excuse that he had to call in at the hospital and left with them.

'Perhaps we could have an evening out soon?' asked Audrey.

'I'm afraid not—there are the students' exams coming up. They'll keep me busy for some time—marking the papers.'

'I'll phone you...'

'A delightful lunch,' he told her smoothly, and remembered the Beckworths' kitchen, with a cake on the table and everyone drinking mugs of coffee. The conversation might not be scintillating but it was spontaneous and sometimes amusing, and everyone listened to everyone else...

Seeing Professor Smythe and his wife into their car outside, he put his head through the open window. 'Will you dine with me one evening soon? Just the three of us? We had no chance to talk.'

'We'd love that,' said Mary Smythe. 'I'll bring my book or my knitting and you two can discuss whatever it is you want to discuss. How do you get on with that dear creature, Julie, Simon?'

'She's a splendid worker...'

'Had you noticed that she was beautiful too?'

'Yes—she isn't easily ignored, is she?'

His elderly friend asked, 'How did she get on in Holland? Never got into a flap with me, but of course we never went across the channel.'

'Took it in her stride—worked like a beaver.'

'Good. Aren't you glad that I bequeathed her to you?'

'Indeed I am.' He smiled suddenly. 'You have no idea how glad!' He withdrew his head, saying, 'I'll give you a ring about dinner.'

He stood on the pavement and watched Professor Smythe drive away. He in his turn was watched by Audrey Venton from behind the drawing room curtains. She was clever enough to know that what little interest he had had in her had gone completely, and she wondered why.

As for the professor, he went back home, finished an article for a medical journal and then sat back to think about Julie. He was quite capable of making her fall in love with him, but he had no intention of doing that—love, if there was any love, would have to come naturally from her. All it required, he concluded, was monumental patience. Although, of course, if fate cared to intervene in some way, he would be grateful.

Fate did intervene.

The fire alarm sounded just after five o'clock on Monday, while Julie, requested by the professor to find the old notes of a long dead patient, was patiently going through the racks of dusty folders housed in a vast bare room just under the hospital roof. There were no windows—only a skylight, never opened—so she had to work by the aid of the strip lighting above the racks. There was another girl there too, one of the clerks attached to the records office, standing at the end of the room, close to the door. She gave a squawk of fright at the sound, dumped her papers and made for the door.

'Quick, there's a fire. We'll all be burnt alive.' The squawk became a scream. 'And all those stairs...'

'Only one flight,' said Julie. 'Probably it's only a small fire in the kitchens. You run on; I'm just coming.'

She kept her voice calm although her insides were quaking as she put back the folders she had taken from the rack—and at the same time she saw the folder the professor wanted. She tucked it under her arm and started towards the door.

It was slammed shut before she reached it. The girl, in her hurry, had forgotten to slip the lock. There was no key on the inside of the door, which was a solid affair, fitting snugly into the wall. Julie turned the handle in the vain hope that a miracle would happen, but it didn't. The door was shut and she was on the wrong side of it.

She wasted a few minutes shouting, even though she knew that no one was likely to hear her—nor would she be missed. The professor would expect her to make her way to the assembly point for the staff and there was no reason to suppose that the nursing staff would miss her.

'A pretty kettle of fish,' said Julie, and cheered herself with the thought that the girl who had fled so hastily would remember that she had slammed the door shut. The attic was too remote for her to hear much, but faintly she caught the sound of the fire engines and then, faint but ominous, a crackling sound.

Something had to be done, and she looked around her.

There was a small solid table and chair for the convenience of those checking the folders. She dragged the table under the skylight and climbed onto it. Even by stretching her arms above her head she couldn't reach it. She got down again and began to pile folders onto the table. When she had stacked a goodly pile she climbed up again, and this time she could reach the skylight. The iron catch had rusted off and it was jammed.

She got down again and carried the chair over to the table, balanced it on the piles of folders and climbed back on. The chair was light, she ought to be able to smash the skylight… She remembered the notes the professor had wanted, and got down again to fetch them. She climbed back as quickly as possible—the little puff of smoke finding its way through a minute crack in the door warned her to waste no time.

All the same, she paused for a moment—if smoke could get through cracks in the door maybe if she waited until it collapsed in the fire she could escape down the stairs… Second thoughts revealed the futility of such a scheme; she climbed carefully, dragging the chair after her and, since she was a practical girl, with the professor's folder tucked under one arm.

She raised the chair above her head, wobbling uncertainly on the pile of folders, but it was awkward lifting the chair and the prod she gave the skylight was no more than a tap. She lowered the chair, and at the same time the lights went out.

It was evening outside by now, and raining. She stared up into the dark outside, so frightened now that she couldn't think.

The sound of the skylight being opened almost sent her off balance.

'Hello,' said the professor from the dark above her, and shone a torch onto her upturned face, suddenly lightened by a glorious smile.

'Oh, Simon,' said Julie.

She couldn't see his face clearly, couldn't see his slow, wide smile. He said cheerfully, 'I see you've started to escape. Good. Now, this may be a bit tricky— I'm going to have to heave you out. The moment you can reach the edge of the skylight get a grip of it so that I can shift my hold a bit.'

She said idiotically, 'I've found those notes you wanted.' And went on, 'Couldn't you open the door, and then I could come through? I'm awfully heavy!'

'Too much smoke. I'm awfully heavy too; I dare say we'll manage very well between us. Only do exactly as I say.'

'Yes, I'm ready.'

'Lift your arms and don't whatever you do fall off the table. I shall probably hurt you; I rely on you not to burst into tears or have hysterics.'

Julie said crossly, 'What do you take me for?' and lifted her arms.

He began to haul her up, inch by inch. The iron grip on her arms was almost more than she could bear—if he were to drop her... She went stiff with fright.

'Relax,' said the professor calmly, and went on heaving, his powerful arms straining. It seemed like a very long time before he said, 'Now try and get hold of the sides and hold on very tightly. I'm going to move my hands.'

Julie let out a squeaky gasp and did as she had been told, and then she squeaked again as his hands slid from her arms and held her in a crushing grip.

'Now heave yourself up a bit. I've got you safe and I'm heaving too. You're almost out.'

It took a few more anxious minutes before she tumbled out in an untidy heap. 'Don't move,' said the professor, and flung a great arm across her. 'There's a slope here. We'll lie still for a moment and get our breath.'

Julie reflected that standing up would be difficult—moving of any kind would be impossible. She had no breath and she ached all over. She lay thankfully under the shelter of his arm and felt his heart thudding mightily against her.

Presently she gasped, 'Thank you very much—you saved my life. How did you know I was there?'

'Well, I asked you to come here, didn't I?' He gave a rumble of laughter. 'I can't afford to lose my secretary, can I?'

A remark which brought tears to her eyes. She gave a sniff and told herself that it was the kind of remark that she might have expected.

'Why are you crying?'

'I'm not...'

'It's a good thing it's dark—we must look a fine pair, spreadeagled on the tiles. Now, the next thing to do is to attract attention. There's a low parapet round the roof, and we have to slide down to it. Slowly, hanging on to everything handy as we go. Ready?'

He kept his arm around her and began to edge his way down. 'You won't fall; I have you safe.'

It was a tricky business, and hard on the knees and hands, but finally they reached the narrow gutter and felt the parapet against their feet.

'Keep perfectly still. I'm going to stand up.'

The professor rose to his splendid height, put two fingers in his mouth and whistled. He repeated the car-piercing noise until he heard a shout from the ground below, and a moment later a searchlight almost blinded him.

He sat down then, content to wait until they were rescued, putting a hand on Julie's shoulder. 'Stay as you are,' he told her. 'We'll be home and dry in a very short time. Have you stopped crying?'

'Yes. I am sorry.'

He patted her shoulder. 'You have been a dear brave girl, Julie.' He gave a chuckle. 'We're wet, aren't we?'

She nodded in the dark. 'Is it a bad fire?'

'The medical wing.'

'That's under here.'

'Everyone has been got out.'

'Not us…'

'Very soon now. I'm quite happy here, aren't you?'

'Yes. I don't think I've ever felt so happy. What's that noise?'

'The fire brigade's ladder.'

A cheerful voice from the other side of the parapet accosted them.

'Getting a bit wet, are you? I'll have one at a time…'

'I'm not going without you,' said Julie.

'Yes, you are, and don't do anything on your own.'

'Young lady, is it?' The fireman shone his torch. 'Best to lift her in without turning her.'

Two pairs of hands shovelled her gently over the parapet and onto the ladder. She kept her eyes shut; if she opened them she would scream. 'Don't be long,' she mumbled to the professor, and was borne to the ground, feeling sick.

'Oops-a-daisy,' said the fireman cheerfully. 'We're on the ground, missy! I'll go back up for the gentleman.'

'He's a professor,' said Julie, and added, 'thank you very much.'

She was whisked away then, trundled in a chair to Casualty, on the other side of the hospital, where she was clucked over by the dragon in charge, divested of her sodden clothes and cleaned up and plastered where plaster was needed.

'Lucky girl,' said the dragon, 'nothing serious— a few cuts and scratches. Was it Professor van der Driesma who got you out? A man of many parts. That silly girl, panicking and slamming the door—didn't tell a soul either. Only he went round looking for you and she plucked up courage to tell him. Silly with fright, poor girl.'

She took her phone from her pocket as it bleeped. 'She's fine, sir—a few bruises and cuts. Nothing a good sleep won't cure.' She listened for a moment. 'I'll send her home now. A good hot bath and bed.' She listened again and laughed, then turned back to Julie. 'You're to go home. I'll parcel up your clothes and you can go in that blanket. I'll get an ambulance.'

'He's all right—the professor?'

'Sounded normal enough to me. Giving a helping hand, he said.' The dragon eyed her thoughtfully. 'Those bruises on your arms are going to be painful—how did he get you out?'

'Through the skylight. He pulled me out.'

'Very resourceful. You're not exactly a wisp of a girl, are you?'

'No. I told him I was heavy but he wouldn't listen…'

'Well, no, I don't imagine he would. Lie there while I get that ambulance.'

Julie, swathed in a grey blanket, was driven home—away from the chaos of the hospital. The fire was under control now, but there was a good deal of smoke and great pools of water.

'A nasty fire,' said the ambulance driver. 'Lucky no one was hurt, though I dare say it shook up some of the patients. As soon as they've been checked, we'll be ferrying them over to New City and St Andrew's…'

He stopped the ambulance then, and her mother came running out.

'Half a mo', love. I'll carry the young lady in—she can't walk without her shoes.'

'Oh, yes, of course.' Mrs Beckworth opened the door wide and Julie was carried into the sitting room and laid on the sofa.

'A cup of tea?' her mother asked the driver. 'I know you can't stay, but there's one ready in the kitchen…'

'If it's made…'

Julie thanked him and sat up as Esme came racing downstairs. 'Whatever happened?' she wanted to know. 'Simon phoned and said you were being sent home for a rest. He said there's been a fire.' She eyed Julie. 'Why are you wearing a blanket?'

'I've no clothes. We had to lie on the roof, and it's raining.'

Mrs Beckworth came and sat down on the edge of the sofa. 'Esme, go to the kitchen and get a mug of tea for Julie. She'll tell us what's happened when she's rested.'

'I'll tell you now,' said Julie. 'I'm quite all right—only a bit scratched and bruised.' She took the mug Esme offered and Luscombe, ushering the driver out, followed her in.

'Gave us a fright, Miss Julie—and there's the phone…' He went to answer it. 'It's 'is nibs. Wants you, Mrs Beckworth,' he reported.

The professor's voice was almost placid. 'Julie's home? Good. She needs a warm bath and bed. I don't want her to come in tomorrow—let her have a lazy day.'

'Yes—yes, all right, Simon. You can't tell me what happened now—I expect you're very busy. She'll tell us presently.'

'She's a brave girl. I must go.'

He rang off, and Mrs Beckworth went back to sit by her daughter.

'That was Simon, dear. Just wanted to make sure you were safely home and to say you're not to go to work tomorrow.'

'He saved my life,' said Julie. 'He pulled me through a skylight. He must have hurt himself.'

'He sounded all right, love. Why a skylight?'

Julie finished her tea and Luscombe came back with a plate of thin bread and butter and the teapot. 'I'll explain,' she said.

It took some time but no one interrupted, and when, at length, she had finished, Luscombe said, ''E's a bit of all right, isn't he? I'm going to put a hot water bottle in your bed, Miss Julie, and when you've had your bath I'll bring up a drop of hot milk and a spot of brandy.'

He went away and Mrs Beckworth said, 'Darling, you've had an awful time—thank heaven Simon found you. You could have been...' She choked on the word. 'We can never repay him.'

'I can think of all sorts of ways,' said Esme. 'I'll go and run a bath—and you'd better have Blotto with you tonight for company.'

So Julie, still wrapped in the blanket, went upstairs presently and got into a bath, and her mother exclaimed in horror at her bruised arms.

'They look worse than they are,' said Julie untruthfully. 'I expect he's bruised too.'

Tucked up in bed, drowsy with the brandy and milk, and with Blotto pressed close to her, Julie slept.

The professor, letting himself into his house at three o'clock in the morning, was met by Blossom. 'A fine time to come home, if I may say so, sir! I trust you've suffered no hurt and that the fire is now under control. I gather from your telephone call that no one was injured.'

He sounded disapproving, but he had a fire burning brightly in the study and a tray with coffee and sandwiches ready on the desk. He fetched the whisky and a glass and poured a generous measure.

The professor sat down tiredly. 'Thanks for staying up, Blossom. I'll go to bed presently. Everything's under control at the hospital. I'll go in as usual if you'll give me a call around eight o'clock. Goodnight.'

Blossom, dignified in his plaid dressing gown, went to the door. 'I must say that I am relieved that you are none the worse, sir. Goodnight!'

The professor drank his whisky, swallowed the coffee and sandwiches and stretched aching muscles, thinking of Julie. Safe in her bed, he hoped, and sleeping. Upon reflection he concluded that he had rather enjoyed himself on the roof. He hoped that the next time he had his arms around Julie it would be in a rather more appropriate situation.

Presently he went to his bed, his tired muscles eased by a long hot shower. When he woke later and went down to his breakfast there was nothing about his elegant appearance to suggest that he led other than a pleasant life and an uneventful one.

Julie woke late and Luscombe brought her breakfast in bed. 'Had a good sleep, Miss Julie? Your ma's on her way up and I'm off to the shops—chops for supper tonight, and I'll make a macaroni cheese for lunch.'

'You're an angel, Luscombe, but I feel fine. I'm going to get up presently.'

The bruises looked rather awful in the morning light,

and the scratches and little cuts and grazes were sore, but they didn't seem to matter. Her mother sat on the side of the bed while she ate and Esme, on her way to school, came to see how she was and gobble up the last slice of toast. 'If Simon comes give him my love,' she said airily, and clattered downstairs and banged the front door.

'Of course he won't come,' said Julie to her mother. 'I'm going to get up.'

The secret wish that he would come she kept hidden; he had no reason to do so. Tomorrow she would go back to work and he would be the professor again, not Simon, holding her fast on that awful roof.

'Now I'm home for the day,' she declared, 'I'll make myself useful.' And when her mother protested, she said, 'I'm going to polish the silver.'

'Your hands, darling...'

'I'll wear gloves.' She sat down at the dining room table with the spoons and forks, and the small pieces of silver that her mother treasured, and started work.

Chapter 8

Julie didn't hear the professor arrive; her mother had seen him drive up from the sitting room window and had opened the door to him before he could knock. It wasn't until Julie turned round, suddenly aware that she was being looked at, that she saw him standing in the doorway watching her.

'Hello, Julie,' said the professor, and crossed the room to take her hands in his and remove the rubber gloves she was wearing. He examined them in turn. 'Did they give you an ATS jab?' he asked.

'I think so, but I'm not quite sure. I was being sick…'

He pushed the spoons and forks to one side and sat down on the table.

'I'd like to take a look at your arms.'

Julie took off her cardigan and rolled up the sleeves

of her blouse. The bruises were a vivid purple, blue and green, the marks of his fingers very clear. He examined them very gently, observing, 'They are going to hurt for a few days, I'm afraid. I'm sorry.'

'Yes, but you got me out—the bruises don't matter. Did did it hurt you pulling me up? Your muscles must be so tired.'

'A little stiff.' He gave her a gentle smile and she was suddenly shy.

'I'll never be able to thank you enough...' she began, 'I—'

Her mother's voice from the door stopped her from saying something she might have regretted. 'There's coffee in the kitchen—you won't mind having it there, Simon?'

They sat around the kitchen table, the professor, her mother, Luscombe and Julie, drinking their coffee and eating the fairy cakes her mother had made, and the talk was cheerful and easy—and if Julie was rather silent, no one mentioned it.

Presently the professor got up to go. He shook Mrs Beckworth's hand, clapped Luscombe on the shoulder, told Julie that if she felt like it she could return to work in the morning and bent and kissed her cheek, leaving her with a very pink face. Her mother pretended not to notice and walked out to the car with him.

I mustn't interfere, reflected Mrs Beckworth, but spoke her thought out loud. 'Do you like Julie, Simon?'

He smiled down at her. 'Like her? I love her, Mrs Beckworth. I'm in love with her and I intend to marry her. I believe that she loves me, only there is something that won't allow her to show her feelings. I have no idea what it can be but I have plenty of patience—I'll wait until she is ready.'

'I didn't mean to ask,' said Mrs Beckworth. 'Interfering, you know. Only I'd said it before I could stop myself.'

'You will be a delightful mother-in-law,' said the professor, and got into his car. 'And you will like my mother.'

She watched him drive away and went back to the kitchen. Julie wasn't there.

'Gone back to that polishing,' said Luscombe. 'How's the lie of the land?'

'Just what you and I hope for, Luscombe. But all in good time.'

Her faithful old friend and servant nodded his head. 'That's OK, by me, ma'am—as long as the end's a happy one.'

'I'm quite sure it will be.'

The professor was deep in discussion with one of the medical consultants when Julie arrived back the next morning. He wished her good morning in an impersonal voice and resumed his talk and presently he went away, which gave her time to assume the mantle of the perfect secretary and sort out the post, find the right page in his diary and fetch the patients' notes he had listed.

It was mid-morning before she saw him again, when he returned to read through his post and dictate his letters. Not once did he mention the terrifying happenings on the roof. She went to her dinner eventually, where she was surrounded by eager acquaintances anxious to hear exactly what had happened.

'Weren't you terrified?' someone asked.

'Yes. I never want to feel like that again.'

'I bet you were glad to see Professor van der Driesma's face peering down at you.' The speaker was a pale-faced girl given to spiteful remarks. 'He must be as stout as an ox—you're no lightweight, Julie.'

A cheerful voice chimed in. 'I wouldn't mind being rescued by someone like the Prof. I don't suppose he swore once...'

'No, he didn't—anyway, it would have been a waste of breath, and he needed all he'd got. As Joyce said, I'm no lightweight.' Julie studied the cottage pie on her plate. 'Just how much damage has been done? Does anyone know?'

'Well, it's not as bad as it might have been. The whole wing is gutted, but the rest of the place escaped damage. The secretaries have had to move across to the surgical side, somewhere in the basement, and a lot of equipment went up in smoke. It could be worse.'

When she got back to her office the professor was at his desk. 'I'm going over to the New City,' he told her. 'There are several patients bedded there that I must check. If I'm not back, go home as usual.' He glanced up at her, pushing his spectacles up his handsome nose. 'Arms all right?'

'Yes, thank you, sir. You have a consultation in Manchester tomorrow at two o'clock.'

'I'll be in to go through the post with you before I go. I should be back here some time in the evening.'

He turned back to his desk, once more immersed in

his work, and she went to her desk and began to type the letters he had dictated.

If it hadn't been for the pain in her arms and the almost healed scratches, the night of the fire might have been a figment of her imagination. He had kissed her too—not that it had meant anything. Probably given in the same spirit as he would pat a dog or stroke a cat, and already forgotten. She shook her head angrily to dispel her thoughts, and applied herself to her typing.

The professor went presently, wishing her a bland good afternoon, and she was left to thump her machine with unnecessary vigour. She was finished by five o'clock and ready to go home, but she lingered briefly, tidying her desk and then his, careful not to move any of the papers. His diary was open still and she glanced at it and saw his scrawl at the bottom of the page: 'Phone Groningen'.

'And why not?' she asked herself out loud. 'It's a perfectly natural thing to wish to speak to the girl you're going to marry.'

Perhaps he would make a joke of his rescue of herself, make light of it.

Julie took herself off home and spent the evening helping Esme with her homework and cutting up the windfalls from the old apple tree in the garden, so that Luscombe could make apple jelly. He liked to do that for himself actually, but it was obvious to his fatherly eye that she needed to be occupied. She went to bed early, pleading a headache, and wept herself to sleep.

She greeted him coolly in the morning, made sure with her usual efficiency that he had everything he needed with him, and when he had gone settled down to clear her desk. She was on the point of going to her dinner when one of the junior registrars came in—a pleasant young man she had met on several occasions. He had some papers for the professor and handed them over and then lingered to talk.

'Going to the hospital dance with anyone?' he asked diffidently.

'No.' She smiled at him as she laid the papers on the professor's desk.

'Then would you go with me? I'm no great shakes as a dancer, but I dare say we could amble round the floor.'

Why not? thought Julie. I'll have to start all over again making a life for myself. 'Thank you. I'd like to go with you. It's a week tomorrow, isn't it? Shall I meet you here?'

'Would you? If I wait in the entrance hall for you— around half past eight?'

'Yes, that suits me very well. I may have to leave before the end—you wouldn't mind?'

'No, no of course not. I look forward to it. Probably won't see you again before the dance—but you'll be there?'

She assured him that she would. She hadn't gone the previous year because Esme had had the measles. She had no idea if the professor intended to go. 'Not that it is of the slightest concern to me,' said Julie aloud, and went away to eat her dinner.

She had nothing to wear and little more than a week in which to solve that problem. She and her mother, with occasional unhelpful advice from Esme, combed through their wardrobes and then the trunks in the attic. They laid out the results on her mother's bed, and from them contrived a suitable ensemble. A grey chiffon dress, so out of date that it was fashionable again, high-heeled sandals, which pinched a bit but were just right with the dress, and a little brocade jacket which concealed the rather out-of-date cut of the dress's bodice. With minor alterations it would do very well.

'And of course you can have the coat,' said Mrs Beckworth. 'Is he nice, this young man who is taking you?'

'One of the junior registrars—Oliver Mann.'

'Does Simon go to these dances?'

'I've no idea. I suppose he'll have to put in an appearance—to dance with consultants' wives and the senior staff.'

Mrs Beckworth, glancing at her daughter's face, refrained from asking more questions.

The professor appeared to be his usual rather aloof self, intent on his work and giving her more than enough to do, but on the evening before the dance, as Julie was getting ready to go home, he looked up from his desk.

'Are you going to the dance?' he asked.

'Yes.' She returned his stare. 'With Oliver Mann— he's a junior—'

'Yes, I know who he is.' His usual bland voice sounded harsh. 'I hope you have a very pleasant evening.'

She very much wanted to ask him if he would be there, but that might look as though she expected him to dance with her. She wished him goodnight and went home to try on the grey dress once more.

The hospital dance was an annual affair and everyone went—from the most junior of the student nurses to the hospital governors—if their circumstances permitted. Julie, dressed and wrapped in the coat, her stylish sandals already nipping her toes, got into the taxi her mother had insisted upon her having.

The entrance hall at St Bravo's was thronged, but Oliver was looking out for her, and once she had left her coat in the improvised cloakroom they made their way to the hospital lecture hall—a vast place, decorated now with streamers and balloons. The dancing had started some time ago and they joined the crowds on the dance floor.

Julie, looking around her, was thankful for the crush. Her dress, compared with most of those around her, wouldn't stand up to close scrutiny. Oliver didn't notice that, though. He told her awkwardly that she looked nice, and swung her into an old-fashioned foxtrot.

He had been quite right—he wasn't a good dancer. He had no sense of rhythm and every now and then he trod on her feet…

The music stopped and he said enthusiastically, 'That was great. I hope the next dance is a slow one—you know, the kind where you can stay in the one place all the time.'

And which would be a good deal kinder to her feet, reflected Julie.

The next dance was a waltz, an 'excuse-me', and

they had circled the room once before someone tapped Oliver on the shoulder and she found herself looking at the vast expanse of the professor's white shirt front.

She glanced up briefly. 'I didn't think you'd be here.'

'Of course I'm here, so that I may dance dutifully with all the right ladies.'

So it was a duty dance! thought Julie peevishly. She might have known it. She said with a snap, 'Well, at least this duty dance doesn't have to last too long. Hopefully someone will come along and relieve you of one of them at least.'

'Tut-tut, you are too quick with your guesses.' He looked down at her and wondered with a flash of tenderness from where she had unearthed her dress. Not a made-over cloak, but definitely not *haute couture*. Whatever it was, she looked beautiful in it—but then she would make a potato sack look elegant.

He ignored the tap on his shoulder from one of the radiographers and swung her into a corner of the room. 'You are enjoying yourself?'

'Very much. Oliver is rather nice, you know,' she improvised quickly. 'We've known each other for some time.'

'Indeed.' The professor, who didn't believe a word of that, sounded no more than polite, and she rushed on quickly.

'He's from Leeds, and hopes to get a job there when he's finished here. From what I hear, it's a rather nice city. I'm sure I should like it.'

The professor didn't allow himself a smile—not even

a twitch of the lip. 'You wouldn't mind living so far away from your family?' he enquired politely.

What had she started? thought Julie, and plunged even deeper into deception. 'Oh, no! One can always drive to and fro,' she added airily.

'Indeed one can.' He was all affability. 'And when are we to be given the glad news—wedding bells and so on?'

If Oliver were to come now she would die. 'Oh, there's nothing definite.'

'I'm glad to hear that. I hope you will stay until I leave.'

'Leave? Leave? You're going back to Holland, of course.' She had gone quite pale.

'Not entirely—merely altering the balance of my work. I'll still have a consultant's post here, but I shall undertake much less work here and more in Holland.'

She said, unable to help herself, 'You're going to get married?'

'It's high time I did, isn't it?' He spoke lightly, and when one of the medical students tapped him on the shoulder he handed her over with nothing more than smiling thanks.

After that Julie danced and laughed and talked, and now and again caught a glimpse of the professor dancing with his colleagues' wives and then with the pretty theatre sister and the even prettier Outpatients sister.

She and Oliver shared a table with several others, but the delicacies laid out for their consumption were dust and ashes in her mouth. She danced again after supper, for she danced well and was in demand as a partner, but she longed for the evening to end.

It was after midnight when she saw her chance and told Oliver that she was leaving. When he protested, and then said that he would see her home, she told him lightly that a taxi would be waiting for her. 'It's been a lovely evening, Oliver, and thank you for inviting me. You go back and do your duty on the dance floor. There's that nice staff nurse from Casualty casting eyes at you...'

'You don't mind? I mean, I'll take you home with pleasure...'

'I'll be there in ten minutes, and I mustn't keep the cab waiting.' Out of the corner of her eye she had seen the professor looking at her from across the floor, which prompted her to kiss Oliver's cheek before she slipped away.

It took a few minutes to find her coat. The attendant—one of the servers from the canteen—was sleepy and impatient, but once it was found Julie nipped smartly towards the hospital doors. She didn't relish her solitary walk home and she hoped there might be a late bus or a real taxi, but she didn't care. Anything was better than staying there watching the professor smiling down at his partners...

It was dark, very dark, and the bright lights streaming from the hospital seemed to make it darker. She paused for a moment and put out a hand to push the doors open.

There was no mistaking the long-fingered elegant

hand which came over her shoulder, gave her her hand back and opened the door.

'It isn't raining,' said the professor breezily. 'The car's close by.'

He bustled her across the courtyard and into the Bentley, and it was only when he had got in beside her that she found her breath.

'This is quite unnecessary, Professor,' said Julie coldly.

'My dear girl, you're behaving foolishly—trotting off home in the middle of the night in this neighbourhood. That's what you intended to do, wasn't it? What fairy tale did you spin to young Oliver?'

'I'm not a child—' began Julie.

'Something which I have discovered for myself. And for which I am thankful.'

Julie sat bubbling over with temper, at the same time aware of heartfelt relief. Only a fool would traipse the streets at that hour of the night, and only her disappointment over the evening had overridden her caution. She had been silly to feel disappointed too; there was no reason why the professor should even have nodded to her, let alone danced with her...

The professor had nothing to say either, and he had stopped outside her front door before she could decide whether to speak.

'Is there someone waiting up for you?' he wanted to know.

'No. I have a key. Thank you for bringing me. I hope I haven't spoilt your evening.'

He turned to look at her. 'The answer to that is so complicated that I'll say no more. Give me your key.'

She handed it over meekly; there were times when it was wise not to argue with him.

'Stay there while I unlock the door.' He got out, opened the door and switched on the hall light, came back and helped her out, then waited while she went indoors. She had to say something, thought Julie desperately.

She turned to face him. 'I'm sorry I've been silly. Thank you for bringing me home. Goodnight.'

She looked very beautiful, standing there with the dim light from the hall shining behind her. The professor resisted a strong urge to take her in his arms and kiss her, but he sensed that she was in no mood to be kissed. He bade her a cheerful goodnight, adding the rider that he would see her on Monday morning, and when she had gone inside, shut the door, got back into his car and returned to the hospital.

There was still an hour or more before the dance would end, and the more senior the member of the staff the more obligatory it was to remain until the very last note from the band.

The first person he saw when he entered the hall was Oliver, looking worried.

'Anything wrong?' asked the professor.

'No, sir—at least, I came here with Julie—you know, your secretary—and she told me she'd be leaving before the end and that she had a taxi coming for her.' His youthful brow furrowed. 'I should have made sure that it was there.'

'It was.' The professor, who only lied when it was absolutely necessary, considered that it was necessary now. 'Julie got in and was driven away. I wished her goodnight and she answered me.'

The relief in Oliver's face was very evident. He gave the professor a disarming smile. 'I say, sir, thanks awfully. I was a bit worried.'

The professor told him kindly to go and dance, and felt old. Too old for Julie? He had no chance to pursue the thought as the senior medical consultant's wife had tapped him on the arm.

'You should be dancing, Simon. You must know that half the nurses here are hoping you will do just that.'

'You're flattering me. I've a better idea...' He whirled her away while she laughingly protested.

Presently she said, 'Clive wants to talk to you—you'd better come to dinner one evening. I'm not supposed to know, of course, but you're thinking of making your headquarters in Leiden, aren't you? You'll still work here?'

'Oh, yes. But more or less on a part-time basis.'

'You have that charming little house here, though. Won't you miss it?'

'I shall be to and fro quite frequently—it will still be my home while I'm over here.'

'What a restless way to live, Simon. You ought to marry.'

'And live here permanently?'

She looked up at his face; its expression gave nothing away. 'No, I don't think you would do that. I think your roots are in Holland, even though you choose to work here too.'

He smiled suddenly. 'Yes, they are. None the less, I hope to go on working at St Bravo's for a long time yet.'

'Oh, good.' The music stopped and they stood together on the edge of the dance floor. 'But I should like to see you married, Simon. Men need someone to look after them.'

'Don't let Blossom hear you say that!'

She laughed. 'He always looks so grumpy, but I think that secretly he would chop his right arm off for you.'

'Heaven forbid. But he looks after me splendidly when I'm over here.'

Simon danced until the band played a final encore, and then waited patiently with the senior hospital staff while the nurses and housemen said their goodnights and went off to their beds. There were a further five minutes or so while everyone agreed that the evening had been a success before they, too, went home.

The professor went quietly into his house, but not so quietly that Blossom didn't hear him—appearing silently on the narrow staircase, cosily clad in his dressing gown.

'Here's a fine time to come home,' he observed tartly. 'There's coffee on the Aga. Shall I fetch you a cup, sir?'

'I'll fetch it for myself, Blossom. Do go back to bed, there's a good fellow.'

Blossom turned on his heels, his duty done. 'Had a good time? Was that nice young lady there?'

'Miss Beckworth? Yes, she was.' The professor paused on his way to the kitchen. 'You liked her, Blossom?'

'Indeed I did. Danced with her, did you?'

'Yes.' For a moment the professor savoured his memories. 'Goodnight, Blossom.'

He went down to Henley in the morning, and wandered from room to room in his cottage there. Even in the winter it was pretty—small and old, and furnished with simple tables and chairs. His mother had come over to England when he had bought it and chosen curtains and covers, and Blossom had equipped the kitchen to suit his fancy. Simon wondered if Julie would like it as much as he did, with its pocket handkerchief of a garden bordering the Thames and the flowerbeds and the plum tree.

It was a haven of peace after his busy week at the hospital, and presently he went to the garden and began digging over the empty bed at its end, where Blossom had suggested that a herb garden might flourish. He worked for some time and then took himself off to the local pub for bread and cheese and beer and the friendly talk in the bar. He went back eventually, and finished his digging, then made himself a pot of tea and locked the little place up once more.

He would bring Julie to see it very soon, he reflected, driving back to London, and to make sure that she came he would invite her mother and Esme too.

Blossom had the day off, but he had left soup on the Aga and a cold supper ready in the dining room. And later, his meal over, the professor went to his study and began to write an article for the *Lancet*. He worked until he heard Blossom's key in the door and then, after his loyal servant had gone to his bed, he sat, his work forgotten, and thought of Julie.

Julie was thinking of him, her feelings mixed. She was going to feel awkward on Monday morning and she hoped that he would make no reference to her stupid behaviour. She had told her mother that the dance had been delightful, that she had danced every dance, that the dress had been perfectly all right, and, when pressed, had offered the information that the professor had brought her home.

'You danced with him?' asked her mother, artfully casual.

'Yes—once. There were an awful lot of people there—you know, governors and their wives and daughters. Some of their dresses were lovely.'

It was a red herring which her mother ignored. 'I expect Simon looked very handsome...'

'Well, yes. I mean, men always look elegant in black tie, don't they?'

'I hope he comes to see us soon,' chimed in Esme. 'I found a book in the library all about diabetes—really gruesome—and I want to ask him about it. Do you suppose he'll know?'

'I'd be very surprised if he doesn't,' said Julie. She added carelessly, and with well-hidden pain, 'He's going to spend more time in Holland, by the way. He'll still work at St Bravo's, but on a part-time basis.'

'He's going away?' Esme was upset. 'That means I'll not see him again.'

'He's not going yet—at least, I don't think so. It's just

that instead of working part of the time in Holland and most of the time here, he's changing it round.'

'I wonder why?' asked Mrs Beckworth.

Julie didn't answer.

She need not have worried about Monday. The professor was already at his desk when she got to work, glasses on his nose, his desk littered with patients' notes. His good morning was absent-minded and he didn't look up for more than a moment when he asked her to let him have the post as quickly as possible.

Whatever her feelings were, Julie knew her job; ten minutes later she laid the letters on his desk, sorted into important and trivial, and waited with her notebook and pencil while he read them. Presently he said, 'I'll leave you to see to these,' and handed back the pile of unimportant letters he had wasted little time over. 'I'll dictate these now.'

When he had finished—and how he managed never to be at a loss for a word in someone else's language always surprised her—he got up.

'I'm going to Birmingham. I should be back some time this evening. If I'm not in in the morning do whatever you think fit.'

He had gone while she was still telling him in a meek voice that she would do her best.

He wasn't there the next morning. She sorted the post, arranged his diary just so, made sure that his desk was exactly as he liked it and started on her own work. The phone never ceased to ring—various wards and departments wanted him and the path lab wanted him to phone the minute he returned. His registrar dealt with most of the queries she passed on to him, and when she asked him rather worriedly if the professor would be in that day, said in a non-commital voice that he supposed so.

She got on with her work—filling in various forms so that all he would have to do was sign them, making appointments, and all the while wondering where he was.

He was in her mother's kitchen, drinking the coffee Luscombe had made.

'I'm playing truant,' he explained, 'and I mustn't stay. But I wanted to ask you and Esme and Julie if you would like to come down to my cottage at Henley next Sunday. It's a pretty little place and delightfully quiet.'

'Oh, yes,' breathed Mrs Beckworth happily. 'We'd love to. Esme's dying to see you again—something about diabetes. It was diabetes, wasn't it, Luscombe?'

''S'right. Something to do with some islands, she said.'

'Ah, yes—they call some special cells the islets of Langerhans. I'm not an authority, I'm afraid, but I'll do my best to answer her.' He got up. 'I must go. Thank you for the coffee and I'll hope to see you on Sunday— about ten o'clock? Is that too early?'

'I'll see the ladies are ready,' Luscombe assured him, and went out to the car with him. 'A day out'll do Miss Julie good. A bit down in the dumps, she is.' Luscombe met the professor's eye. 'She's not happy, sir.'

'I know, Luscombe. But will you trust me to make her happy when the time's right?'

Luscombe grinned. 'That I will, sir.'

* * *

Back in his office, the professor contemplated the pleasing sight of Julie's downbent head, her colourful hair highlighted by the wintry sun edging its way through the small window of her office. He had wished her a brisk good morning and received an equally brisk reply, although she had gone a bit pink. She had bent over the computer again with a decided air of being busy, and he reflected that now was hardly the moment to invite her to join her mother and Esme on Sunday. Time enough for that; he was a man who could wait.

He waited until Friday afternoon, at the end of a tiresome day for Julie. She had finished finally, tidied her desk, made sure that everything was as it should be, and asked if there was anything else he wanted done.

'Thank you, no.'

She went to get her coat from the hook on the wall. 'I'll see you on Monday, sir.'

'Monday? Ah—it quite slipped my mind—we've had a busy week, haven't we?' He gave her a guileless look. 'Your mother and Esme are coming down to my cottage on Sunday. I hope you will come with them.'

She stared at him, her mouth open. 'Your cottage? Have you got another one? And Mother didn't mention it.'

'Oh, dear. Perhaps she thought that I would tell you. It seems that Esme has a great many questions to ask me... You will come?'

Her mother and Esme wouldn't go without her, and it would be unkind to deprive them of a pleasant outing. Besides, she wanted to see this cottage. She said reluctantly, 'Very well—since everything is arranged.'

'Splendid. I am sure you will like it—it is by the river at Henley. I'll call for you around ten o'clock.' He saw her hesitate, and added in a matter-of-fact voice, 'It's a place I shall miss when I go back to Holland.'

She thought fleetingly of the girl in Groningen, but he was going away wasn't he? He would forget them all once he was back in Holland, even if he came back from time to time. She had never given the girl cause to feel uneasy anyway...

She said soberly, 'I shall enjoy seeing your cottage, sir. Goodnight.'

That evening she asked her mother if she had forgotten to tell her about their outing. 'Professor van der Driesma didn't say a word to me; it was a surprise.'

'Oh, darling, how silly of me. I thought he would have said something to you and it quite slipped my mind—besides, I said nothing because I thought if Esme knew about it it might interfere with her schoolwork. She's so keen on all this medicine...'

Julie, her mind full of the prospect of a day with Simon, hardly listened to this excuse.

They were ready when he arrived on Sunday morning, warmly clad since it had turned cold and grey and threatened rain or even snow, and Blotto—securely attached to his lead and begged to be a good boy—uttered little yelps of pleasure, sensing that the day ahead would be something special.

Luscombe saw them into the car, exchanged the time

of day with the professor and waved them off, before going back into the house to enjoy a quiet day on his own.

The professor had invited Mrs Beckworth to sit beside him, and Julie and Esme, with Blotto between them, were ushered into the back of the car. 'You shall sit beside me when we come home,' he promised Esme as he got in and drove off.

He crossed the city, the streets quite empty of traffic, joined the M4 at Chiswick and made short work of the journey to Maidenhead—taking a minor road for the last few miles to Henley-on-Thames.

The cottage, when they reached it, looked enchanting. It was near the bridge over the Thames, not far from where the Royal Regatta ended its course. It was a dull morning and very quiet. The professor parked the car and helped Mrs Beckworth out.

She stood for a moment, looking at the charming little place. 'It's perfect,' she told him. 'The kind of home one longs for.'

Esme had rushed through the gate to circle the cottage, peering in at the windows. 'Oh, Simon, may we go inside? Don't you wish you lived here all the time? You could, you know—drive up and down to the hospital each day...'

He opened the door and ushered them inside. 'Make yourselves at home while I fetch in the food. Does Blotto need a run?'

Esme went with him, and Julie and her mother stood in the tiny hall, looking around them and then at each other. 'He's already got that dear little mews house,' said Julie. 'And a house in Leiden…'

'I'm sure he deserves all of them,' said her mother. She pushed open a door. 'What's in here?'

Chapter 9

Julie and her mother were standing in the kitchen, admiring its perfection, when the professor and Esme came in—arms laden and Blotto prancing between them. They put everything on the kitchen table and he said, 'Shall we have coffee first, or a tour of inspection?'

'I'll make the coffee—I can always go round later,' said Julie. 'And shall I unpack whatever is in these boxes?'

'Will you? I left the food to Blossom. I hope there's enough…'

'For at least a dozen,' observed Julie, and opened the first box. Blossom prided himself on doing things properly; there was a Thermos of coffee, cream in a carton, the right kind of sugar and little biscuits. She arranged these on the table, found four mugs, then opened the other boxes.

Soup to be warmed up, and cold chicken, potato salad and a green salad, crisp and colourful, game chips and little balls of forcemeat. There were jellies in pots, thick cream, some chocolate mousse with orange, and caramel puddings packed separately, a selection of cheeses, pats of butter and an assortment of savoury biscuits. She stowed everything neatly into the fridge and peeped into the last box. Teacakes, more butter, tiny sandwiches, a fruit cake. Blossom was indeed a treasure.

The others came back presently, and they sat around the table while her mother and Esme exclaimed over the delights of the cottage. 'It's quite perfect,' declared Mrs Beckworth. 'How could you want to live anywhere else than here? It must be glorious in the summer.'

'Have you a boat?' asked Esme. 'Do you row?'

'Yes, there's a skiff moored at the bottom of the garden. We'll go and look at it presently, if you like.' He passed his mug for more coffee. 'But first Julie must see the cottage…'

He took her presently into the sitting room and stood while she wandered round looking at the pictures and picking up the delicate china and silver lying on the lamp-tables. 'Come upstairs,' he invited. 'But take a look at my study first. It's small, but ample for my needs.'

As indeed it was—furnished with a desk and a big chair, and with rows of books on shelves. It was deliciously warm from the central heating. As they went back into the hall Simon said, 'There's a minute cloakroom under the stairs.' He opened a little door to disclose it. It was small, but it had everything in it, as far as she could see, that was needed.

Upstairs there was a small square landing with four doors. The three bedrooms were furnished in pastel colours with white carpetting underfoot and Regency furniture, and the fourth door opened into the bathroom—surprisingly large and containing every comfort. It was a perfect little paradise and she said so.

'I can understand how much you must like coming here,' she told him as they went down the narrow stairs. For the moment she had forgotten her awkwardness with him, delighting in the little place, picturing him there on his own. Well, not for long, she reminded herself, and he watched her happy face cloud over and wondered why.

'Come and see the garden,' he suggested, and they all went outside and inspected the bare flowerbeds and admired the plum tree even though there wasn't a leaf on it.

'In the summer,' sighed Mrs Beckworth, 'I can just imagine everything growing—all those roses. Do you do the pruning yourself?'

They talked gardening for some time and then went indoors to set lunch on the table and warm the soup. The professor opened a little trap door in a corner of the kitchen and disappeared into his cellar to return with two bottles of Australian Chardonnay under one arm. They all had a glass while the soup was warming, and Julie popped the small crusty rolls into the oven to warm too.

She had been reluctant to come; there was no point in making her unhappiness and hurt worse than they already were, but now she forgot that for the moment. The wine was delicious, the little room was cosy, and just to be there with the professor sitting on the other side of the table was heaven.

As they ate and drank the talk was light-hearted with no awkward gaps—the professor, a seasoned host, saw to that. And presently, after they had drunk the delicious coffee Blossom had brewed in yet another Thermos, they tidied away the remains of their lunch and went for a walk beside the river, with Esme racing ahead with Blotto on his lead and Julie between her mother and Simon.

She hadn't much to say but the other two kept up a rambling conversation—the river, the pleasures of living away from London, the weather, the best places in which to take a holiday. She was astonished at the professor's capacity for small talk, and at how easy and friendly he was away from the hospital—easy with her mother and Esme, she reflected, but not with her. She was still Miss Beckworth, even if occasionally he addressed her as Julie.

They stayed out until dusk began to creep upon them, and then went back to tea—a leisurely meal, with Esme asking her endless questions and the professor good-naturedly answering them.

'When can I start training to be a doctor?' demanded Esme.

'If you work hard and get your A levels, when you are eighteen. It's hard work and goes on for years…'

'How long did you take to be a real doctor—I mean like a registrar?'

'Well, four years in Leiden, and then I came over to Cambridge and went to a teaching hospital in London—almost eight years.'

'You have Dutch degrees?' asked Mrs Beckworth. 'You must be awfully clever.'

'No, no. I'm lucky enough to have found the work I want to do and to have been given the opportunity to do it.'

In a little while they packed up, loaded everything into the boot and drove back to London.

The shabby streets around Julie's home were in cruel contrast to the cottage by the Thames, but Luscombe was waiting for them with a bright fire in the sitting room and the offer of coffee. The professor, when pressed to stay, refused.

'There is nothing I would enjoy more,' he assured Mrs Beckworth, and stole a quick glance at Julie, 'but I have an engagement this evening.' He took Mrs Beckworth's hand. 'Thank you all for coming today. It was most enjoyable.'

She smiled up at him. 'We've all had a lovely time— thank you for asking us. We'll see you again before you go off to Holland?'

'Yes, it will be some weeks yet. I've a good deal of work to clear up here.'

He submitted to Esme's kiss, laid a gentle hand on Julie's shoulder and went away.

'I don't want him to go,' said Esme. 'I wish he was my brother or uncle or something.'

Julie silently agreed. Only she wished him to be something other than that.

Monday was much as usual; there he was at his desk, spectacles on his nose, writing furiously in a scrawl she would be obliged to decipher presently.

His good morning was genial but he went back to writing at once, leaving her to see to the post, answer the phone and fill his appointments book. It wasn't until the evening, as she was tidying her desk preparatory to going home, that he looked up, through the open door to where she was reaching for her coat.

'I'll drive you home,' he told her. 'It's a wretched evening.'

She came to the doorway. 'There's absolutely no need, thank you, Professor.'

'Need doesn't come into it. I should like to drive you home.'

She twiddled the buttons on her coat. 'I'd much rather not, if you don't mind.'

He stared across the room at her. 'I do mind. Do you dislike me so much? Julie?'

'Dislike you? Of course I don't dislike you.' She paused and then rushed on, 'It's because I like you that I don't want to come.'

'Oh, indeed?' He settled back in his chair. 'Could you explain that?'

'Yes, perhaps I'd better—and it doesn't matter because you're going away, aren't you? You see, I mustn't like you too much. It wouldn't be fair to her...'

'Her?' His voice was very soft.

'Yes—I saw you in Groningen, outside the hospital. I wasn't spying or anything, I just happened to be there...'

'Go on...'

'It was so evident that you loved—that you loved each other, and she's so pretty. I'm sure you love her dearly, but you're away from her for a lot of the time and sometimes you must feel tempted.' She looked down at her shoes. 'And—and...'

The professor, a man with iron self-control, allowed it to slip. He left his desk and folded her into his arms and kissed her. He had been wanting to kiss her for a long time now, and he made the most of his chances.

Julie didn't try to stop him; it was his bleep that did that. He let her go reluctantly and picked up the phone. He listened, then said, 'I'll come at once,' and strode to the door. 'Tomorrow,' he said, and gave her a smile to melt her bones.

She went home then, in a blissful dream which lasted until she got off the crowded bus and opened the door of her home, when good sense suddenly took over, leaving her dismayed and furiously angry with herself. How could she have been such a fool? To point out to him in that priggish way that he must feel tempted and then allow him to kiss her—perhaps he had taken it as an invitation on her part. Well, she would put that right— first thing in the morning.

She spent the evening rehearsing what she would say when she saw him, answering her mother's remarks at random and getting Esme's maths all wrong, and the next morning, after a wakeful night and no breakfast to speak of, she marched into his office full of good resolves.

The professor was telephoning, which was a drawback, and his good morning was exactly as usual—uttered in a voice devoid of expression. She went to her office, leaving the door open, took off her coat and arranged her desk, and the moment he had put down the phone and before she let her courage slide from her completely she went and stood in front of him.

'About yesterday,' she began. 'I should like to forget about it completely. That's if you don't mind.' He had looked up as she had spoken, and the expression on his face puzzled her. All the same, she went on, 'You'll be going soon, so it won't be…that is, there's no need for it to be awkward. I thought I'd like to clear the air before we—well, we might find it a bit awkward.' She added earnestly, 'You don't mind that I've said something about it?'

He looked at her over his spectacles. 'No, I don't mind, Julie. By all means forget it.' He sounded more remote than usual, and she supposed that she should be pleased about that. He looked at her, unsmiling, 'Let me have the post as soon as possible, will you?'

She spent the rest of the day worrying that perhaps she need not have said anything—he must think her a conceited creature to have imagined that a kiss was so important. Well, it had been for her. Her heart raced at the mere thought of it.

The day, like any other, wound to a close and she went home presently.

The professor went home too, to sit in his chair deep in thought.

'Your dinner is ready,' Blossom told him, faintly accusing. 'Didn't hear me the first time, I suppose. Got too much on your brain, sir.'

'I do have a problem, Blossom, but I'm happy to say that I've solved it. Something smells delicious.' As he seated himself at the table and Blossom ladled the soup he said, 'I may be going over to Holland very shortly. Just for a few days.'

'It'll be Christmas in a week or two.'

'Yes, yes. This isn't work. I'm going to Groningen to see my family. I shall be taking Miss Beckworth with me.'

Blossom allowed himself to smile. 'Well, now, that is a bit of good news, sir.'

'Let us rather say that I hope it will be good news.'

'A spirited young lady, if I may say so,' said Blossom, who, being an old and faithful servant said what he liked. 'Took to her at once, I did.'

'Which augurs well for the future.'

It seemed to Julie that during the next day the professor was very occupied. Moreover, the various departments and wards were constantly phoning him, and twice he had asked her to get a Dutch number for him and then, infuriatingly, had spent a long time speaking in Dutch to someone in Holland. Arranging to meet his future wife? she wondered. Discussing their wedding? Planning a holiday together?

Turning the knife in the wound hurt, but she couldn't help herself. She tried not to think of the months ahead without much success. They would be without him. If he intended to work at the hospital from time to time only then she wouldn't be needed by him; she would be transferred to another consultant and would probably never work for him again. Or see him. The quicker she got used to the idea the better!

The following morning when she arrived for work there was no sign of the professor. She saw to the post, arranged things to his liking on his desk and sat down in front of her computer. There was, thank heaven, a good deal of work to get through.

It was almost her dinner time when he walked into his office, and sat down at his desk. 'Anything urgent?' he wanted to know, and glanced through the letters she had arranged so neatly. 'No? Good. I shall be going to Holland in two days' time. I shall want you to go with me.'

He gave her a brief glance. 'There is nothing that can't be dealt with today and tomorrow. Will you ring my receptionist at the consulting rooms and ask her to deal with the appointments? She'll know what to do. Get hold of the path lab for me too, will you? I'll be on the ward if I'm wanted.'

He was at the door before she spoke. 'How long shall we be away, sir?'

'Three or four days—maybe less, certainly not more. There's too much to deal with at this end. We'll go as before, with the car.' He added gravely, 'You had better borrow the coat. It may be cold!'

Beyond that he had nothing further to say. She supposed that it was a seminar or a series of lectures, and she hoped that she would be staying with Mevrouw Schatt again. That was why he had made those telephone calls—to arrange to meet the girl. She went to her dinner and pushed beef casserole around the plate, joining in the chatter of the others with unusual animation.

Her mother took her news with a placid observation.

'That will be a nice change for you, dear. Sitting in an office all day must be so dull.'

Not when Simon's there, reflected Julie. 'Would you mind if I borrowed the coat? It might be cold.'

'Of course, love, and hadn't you better have some kind of a hat?' Mrs Beckworth pondered for a moment. 'There's that brown velvet that I had last winter—if you turned it back to front, with the brim turned up...'

They were both clever with their fingers, and the hat, brushed, pulled and poked into shape, sat very nicely on Julie's bright hair.

'Three or four days,' she observed. 'If I travel in a blouse and skirt and a thin sweater and take one dress that should do. Perhaps another blouse—and undies, of course.'

'You're not likely to go out?' asked her mother hopefully.

'No. When I'm not taking notes I have to get them typed up whenever I've time.'

It wasn't until the afternoon before they were to go that the professor told her that he would collect her at nine o'clock the next morning. 'We shall travel as before,' was all he said.

When he came for her, Julie, elegant in the cashmere coat and the made-over hat, bade her mother and Esme goodbye, assured Luscombe that she would take care and, after an exchange of civilities on the part of the professor; her mother, Esme and Luscombe, was ushered into the car.

Three, perhaps four days, she told herself. I must

make the most of them. Only she hoped that she wouldn't see the girl again, and she must remember to be an efficient secretary and nothing more.

The journey was a repetition of the previous one: they boarded the Hovercraft at Dover, ate their sandwiches and drank coffee while the professor buried his commanding nose in his papers and once on shore wasted no time in small talk but drove steadily. They did not stop at the café they had eaten in before but crossed the Moerdijk Bridge and, after a mile or two, drew up before a restaurant, all plate glass windows with a row of flags waving in the wind.

'Off you go,' he told her. 'Over in that right-hand corner. I'll be here—I can spare half an hour.'

When she joined him there was a glass of sherry on the table, and he held a glass of tonic water in his hand. 'It will warm you up,' he said. He had stood up and then sat down opposite her again. '*Echte* soup,' he observed. 'Also very warming at this time of year. And an omelette to follow. I hope you don't mind me ordering, but we have quite a way to go still.'

That surprised her, for she had thought that Leiden wasn't all that distance.

'We're going to Leiden?' she asked. Really, it was time she was told a few details.

'Leiden? Briefly, to collect Jason. We're going to Groningen.'

She should have expected that. She supped her soup, drank her sherry and made short work of the omelette, then told him that she was ready when he was.

He was driving fast now, his hands light on the

wheel, his face, when she peeped at it, placid. They were slowing through Leiden before she realised that they were there, and he drew up before his house.

'You would like to go indoors?' he asked, opening her door.

She nodded thankfully, wondering when the journey would end—Groningen seemed a long way off. He opened his door and Jason came bounding to meet them followed by Siska, who beckoned Julie to go upstairs and then turned her attention to the professor. They were still talking when she came down again, but the housekeeper shook her hand and smiled and opened the door. No time was to be lost, it seemed.

Julie longed for a cup of tea; it would make things seem more normal. She had the feeling that the day wasn't going as she expected.

With Jason breathing great happy gusts from the back seat they set off again. It had been a clear cold day, and now, although it was almost dark, there was a multitude of stars and half a moon creeping up the horizon.

Julie, lapped in warmth and the pleasant smell of good leather mingled with dog, decided sensibly to wait and see what was to happen. The professor had little to say and had offered no further information—presumably he took it for granted that she expected to go to the hospital.

He was travelling fast again, never recklessly, but overtaking everything on the road. Presently he asked, 'You are warm enough?'

'Yes, thank you.'

'I don't intend to stop again now we are back on the motorway.'

He didn't say much after that, and she made no effort at conversation. He was probably conning over a lecture, or thinking about the girl, and Julie had her own thoughts.

She was surprised when they flashed past a sign to Groningen—ten kilometres away. The time had passed quickly, and even as she thought it she saw the lights of the city ahead of them, clear in the flat landscape. Then he turned away from the motorway, along a narrow country road leading away into the dark fields around them.

'Is this a short cut?'

'It is the way to my home.'

'But you live in Leiden and London. Aren't we to go to the hospital?'

'No.' He drove on steadily, and Julie sat trying to think of something sensible to say. If they weren't going to the hospital but to his home—another home—why was that?

'I think you should explain.'

'Certainly, but not just yet.'

There were lights ahead of them and a very small village, and presently he drove through its short street and back into the empty country again. But not for long. Soon he turned the car between great gateposts and stopped before his home.

Julie sat where she was. The glimpse she had had of the house had rather taken her breath. It looked like an ancestral home and, sensible girl though she was, she wasn't sure what to expect now. The professor opened her door and helped her out, and let Jason out as well, and the three of them mounted the steps to the great front door. It was thrown open as they reached it and the girl standing there flung herself at the professor. He gave her a hug and disentangled himself.

'Julie, this is my sister Celeste,' he said. It was the girl Julie had seen in Groningen.

Julie went pale and then pink and took Celeste's hand, but her eyes were on his. 'Why didn't you tell me?' she asked.

'If you remember, I was interrupted.' He smiled. 'And in the morning you expressed a wish not to say anything more about it.' He turned to his sister. 'Are we all here?'

'Yes.' She switched to Dutch. 'She's gorgeous, Simon, we're all thrilled to bits. Have you quarrelled?'

'No. No. But I think for this evening we will remain sociable and nothing more. So no awkward questions, *lieveling*.'

'Ah, here is Bep to take your coat, Julie.' He saw her look. 'No, don't ask questions now. Let us have a pleasant dinner—I am sure you must be tired. Tomorrow is time enough…'

'For what?' She had the feeling that she was in a dream; she said so. 'It's like a dream.'

'Dreams come true, Julie.' And that was all he would say.

Hours later, lying snug in bed, convinced that she would never sleep, Julie tried to sort her muddled thoughts.

She had been swept into an enormous room full of people—well, not full, but five could be a crowd when you weren't expecting them—and they had welcomed her with smiling warmth just as if they had known about her. She had been given sherry and had presently crossed the hall to a dining room with dark-panelled walls and a table decked with white damask and a great deal of silver and crystal. She had sat next to Simon and eaten a delicious meal and taken part in a conversation not one word of which she could remember. Simon had had little to say to her, but he had been there, close by.

She had been taken to her room later by Celeste—a charming room, with a four-poster bed and dainty Regency furniture—and kissed goodnight and told to sleep well. Simon, she remembered sleepily, had opened the door for them and had smiled down at her in a way which had made her heart lurch...

She slept then, and didn't wake until a cheerful girl came in with a little tray of tea. There was a note folded between the teapot and the milk jug. The professor's familiar scrawl invited her to get up and come downstairs.

He was waiting for her in the hall, sitting in an enormous chair with Jason beside him. He got up and crossed to where she was hesitating on the last stair and took her hand. He led her to the back of the hall and opened a door there.

'Haven't you guessed, Julie?' he asked her. He turned her round to face him and put his hands on her shoulders.

'Perhaps just a little, but not until last night. I was afraid to.' She studied his tie. 'Why have we come here?

I mean, I can see that you wanted me to meet Celeste—did you think I wouldn't believe you?'

'No. No, my darling. But you were cross, were you not? It didn't seem quite the right moment, and I wanted you here in my home, away from the hospital.'

'Oh, well—I'm here now,' said Julie, and looked up at him. She smiled and his hands let go of her shoulders, and she was caught close in his arms.

'I thought you didn't like me,' she muttered into his jacket. 'As a person, that is; I tried to be a very good secretary, because I hoped that if I was you'd notice me.'

'Dear heart, I have never stopped noticing you since the first moment I saw you. I shall continue to notice you until the end of time. I shall love you too, just as I love you now. Could we marry soon, do you suppose? We have wasted so much time.'

He kissed her then, and really there was no need to answer, but presently she asked, 'Your family—Mother...?'

'My family know all about you, my love, and I phoned your mother last night.'

'Were you so sure?'

'Yes. And now be quiet, my dearest love, for I'm going to kiss you again.'

Julie smiled and didn't say a word!

* * * * *

THE DOUBTFUL MARRIAGE

Chapter 1

The waiting-room was full and smelled of wet rain-coats and old Mr Stokes's eucalyptus cough lozenges; he had chronic bronchitis and treated himself with a variety of cures from the chemist until he finally gave in and went to the doctor. He sat glowering at the people around him, his eyes on the green light over the surgery door; he was next in.

But when the light changed it flickered on and off, a signal for the girl sitting behind the desk in the corner to go into the surgery. She got up without haste to obey the summons, aware that Uncle Thomas wanted her to see to Mrs Spinks's varicose ulcer. She smiled at him as she went in; smiled, too, at his patient and urged that lady to the curtained-off cubicle behind his desk. Mrs Spinks eased her stout person on to the chair and extended her leg on to the stool provided for her.

'Busy this morning,' she commented. 'We keep you on the go, don't we, love?'

The girl was bending over her leg, dealing with it with kind, gentle hands. She was a very pretty young woman, with chestnut hair piled on top of her head, large brown eyes, a straight nose and a generous mouth. She was wearing a white overall with a blue belt buckled in silver and when she stood up it was apparent that she was tall and splendidly shaped.

She said in a pleasant voice, 'Oh, I think the doctor and I wouldn't know what to do with ourselves. When are you to come back, Mrs Spinks?'

She helped her to her feet and ushered her out through the door behind them, tidied the cubicle and went back into the surgery where her uncle was dealing with Mr Stokes. There was nothing for her there; Mr Stokes was barely half-way through his testy list of grievances while her uncle listened patiently, as he always did.

In the waiting-room a dozen pair of eyes watched her as she crossed to the desk again. The doctor's niece had been living in the village since she was a little girl; they all knew her well. A nice young lady she had grown into, they considered, and one of them as it were, despite her years at the London hospital where she had gone for her training. High time she was married; she and the squire's only son had been courting for the last year or two, and even though he was away from home a good deal that was time enough for them to get to know each other. At least, that was what the ladies of the village said. They held old-fashioned views about such matters—a year or so to get acquainted, another year's engagement and then a proper wedding in church with the banns called and bridesmaids. Anything less wasn't seemly.

Matilda smiled impartially upon them all, sifted through the patients' cards and counted heads. If Mr Stokes didn't finish his grumbling pretty smartly, morning surgery was going to be very behindhand, and that meant that her uncle's morning round would be even later, which would lead inevitably to gobbled sandwiches and a cup of coffee before afternoon surgery. That did him no good at all; he worked too hard and long hours, and just lately she had begun to worry about him. He wasn't a young man and was all she had in the world; he had been father and mother to her since the day she had gone to live with him after her parents had been killed in a car accident.

Mr Stokes came out, still muttering, and she ushered the next patient in.

Finally the waiting-room was empty and she poked her head round the surgery door. 'Coffee in the sitting-room, Uncle. I'll clear up while you're on your round.'

He was sitting at his desk not doing anything, a tired, elderly man, short and stout and almost bald, with a cheerful, chubby face and bright blue eyes.

'A busy morning, Tilly.' He got up slowly. 'Another couple of months and it will be spring and we'll have nothing to do.'

'That'll be the day! But it will ease off soon—January and February are always busy, aren't they?' She urged him gently to the door. 'Let's have that coffee before it gets cold. Would you like me to drive? I can clear up in ten minutes.'

'Certainly not—almost all the visits are in the village anyway. You've got the list? There may be a call from Mrs Jenkins—the baby is due.'

They sat down on either side of the log fire and Tilly poured the coffee. The room was comfortable, albeit shabby, but the silver on the old-fashioned sideboard shone and the furniture was well polished. As she put down the coffee-pot, an elderly grey-haired woman came in.

'I'm off to the butchers,' she observed. 'A couple of lamb chops, Miss Matilda, and a nice steak and kidney pudding for tomorrow?'

'Sounds splendid, Emma. I'll give you a hand as soon as I've tidied the surgery.' As Emma trotted off, she added, 'I don't know how we'd manage without Emma, Uncle. I can't imagine life without her.' Which wasn't surprising, for Emma had been housekeeping for her uncle when she had gone to live with him.

She filled his coffee cup again and sat back, her feet tucked under her, planning what she would do in the garden once the weather had warmed up a little.

'How would it be...' she began, to be interrupted by her uncle.

'I forgot to tell you, I've had a letter from someone who was at St Judd's when I was there—oh, it must be ten years ago. He was my houseman for a time—a splendid fellow and very clever. We've kept up a casual friendship since then but we haven't met—he's a Dutchman and has a practice in Holland, I believe, though he comes over to England fairly frequently. He's in London now and wanted to know if he might call and see me. I phoned him last night and asked him for the weekend.'

It was her uncle's free weekend and Matilda had cherished one or two ideas as to what they would do with it. Now they were to be burdened by some elderly foreigner who would expect a continental breakfast and want coffee instead of tea. Matilda, who in all her twenty-six years had never set foot outside Great Britain, tended to think of Europeans as all being cast in the same mould.

She said hastily, 'That'll be nice for you, Uncle. I'll get a room ready. When do you expect him?'

'Tomorrow, after lunch. Friday's clinic shouldn't be too full—there's not much booked so far, is there?—and I'll be free after that. You can entertain him if I get tied up.' He added a shade anxiously, 'He's a nice chap.'

'I'll make some scones,' said Matilda. The steak and kidney pudding would never do; on the other hand she could slip down to the butchers and get more steak... Calabrese and carrots, mused Matilda silently, and creamed potatoes; there was enough rhubarb forced under the old bucket at the end of the garden to make a pie. They could have beef on Saturday instead of Sunday; perhaps he would go on Sunday morning. 'Does he know this part of the country, Uncle?'

'I don't believe so. It'll make a nice change from London.'

She was left on her own presently to get one of the

bedrooms in the roomy old house ready for the guest and go to the kitchen and tell Emma.

'Dutch?' questioned Emma, and sniffed. 'A foreign gentleman; probably have faddy ways with him.'

'Well, he oughtn't to be too bad,' mused Tilly, 'if he comes over to London fairly often, and Uncle said he does. I'll go and pull some leeks, shall I?' She pulled on an old jacket hanging behind the kitchen door. 'I'll get a few apples in at the same time—we might have an apple crumble...'

When she got back she saw to the waiting-room and the surgery, made sure that the room was ready for her uncle's guest and went down to the kitchen to help with lunch.

It was after morning surgery on the following day that the phone rang. It was Mr Jenkins, sounding agitated.

'It's the missus, started the baby and getting a bit worked up.'

It was Mrs Jenkins's fourth; Uncle Thomas wouldn't be back for half an hour at least and the Jenkins's farm was outside the village. Moreover, it seemed to Tilly that Mr Jenkins sounded as worked up as his wife.

'The doctor's out,' she said soothingly. 'I'll jump on my bike and come and have a look, shall I? I'll leave a message for Uncle; he shouldn't be long.' She heard Mr Jenkins's heavy sigh of relief as she hung up.

She warned Emma to let her uncle know as soon as he came in, fetched her midwifery bag, put on the elderly coat once more and cycled through the village to the farm.

A far cry from the clinically clean delivery rooms of the hospital, she thought, going into the cluttered warm kitchen. Mr Jenkins was hovering over a boiling kettle on the stove, under the impression that, since this was the common practice on the films in similar circumstances, it was the correct thing to do.

'Hello,' said Tilly cheerfully. 'Upstairs in bed, is she?'

He nodded. 'Carrying on, too. Good thing the kids have gone over to Granny's.'

'I'll go up, shall I?' Tilly went up the wooden staircase at the end of the passage and knocked on the half-open door at the top. Mrs Jenkins was sitting on the bed, looking apprehensive.

She looked more cheerful when she saw Tilly, who put her bag down and sat down beside her, put a comforting arm round her and asked pertinent questions in a calm voice.

Presently she said, 'Well, I don't suppose it'll be long—shall I have a look? And how about getting into bed?'

The bouncing baby boy bawling his head off with satisfying vigour arrived with commendable speed. The doctor, arriving some ten minutes later, pronounced him to be in splendid health, declared his satisfaction as to Mrs Jenkins's well-being, observed that he might leave Tilly to make her patient comfortable, and left again to see the last of his patients.

It was almost one o'clock by the time Tilly had seen to Mrs Jenkins, bathed the baby, shared a pot of tea with the proud parents and got back on her bike. Mrs Jenkins's sister would be arriving very shortly and she would be in good hands.

'See you this evening,' called Tilly, and shot off down the lane.

She was a bit dishevelled by the time she reached home; there was a fierce wind blowing, and a fine, cold rain falling, and she had had to cycle into it. She propped the bike against the wall outside the kitchen door and hurried into the house, kicking off her shoes as she went and unbuttoning her coat. There was no one in the kitchen; she went through to the hall and opened her uncle's study door, still struggling with the coat. Her uncle was standing by his desk, and sitting in the big leather chair by the fire was a man. He got to his feet as she went in, an extremely tall man, broad-shouldered and heavily built. Somewhere in the thirties, she guessed fleetingly, and handsome, with lint fair hair and heavy-lidded blue eyes. Surely not their visitor?

But he was.

'Ah, Matilda, there you are.' Her uncle beamed at her, oblivious of her untidy person. 'Here is our guest, as you see, Rauwerd van Kempler.'

She said, 'How do you do,' in her quiet voice and had her hand engulfed in his large firm grasp. He greeted her pleasantly and she thought peevishly that he might have come at a more convenient time.

The peevishness sparked into temper at his bland, 'I'm afraid I have arrived at an awkward time.' His glance took in her shoeless feet and her damp face and her hair all over the place.

'Not at all,' said Tilly coolly. 'I got tied up with the Jenkins's baby.' She looked at her uncle. 'I hope you haven't been waiting for me to have lunch?'

'Well, dear, we had a good deal to talk about, you know, over a drink.' Her uncle studied her carefully. 'I expect you'd like to tidy yourself—I'll pour you a glass of sherry while you're doing it.'

Tilly, aware that the Dutchman was studying her as carefully as Uncle Thomas, took herself out of the room.

Very deliberately she did her hair and her face and changed into a skirt and sweater. On the way to the study she went to the kitchen to see if Emma needed any help. She didn't, so Tilly joined the two men, accepted the sherry and made polite conversation about the weather. Her uncle looked at her once or twice, puzzled by her aloofness; she was puzzled by it herself.

Dr van Kempler had an easy way which made conversation simple, and he had good manners; it was obvious that he and her uncle had a lot in common and plenty to talk about, but he was careful to keep the talk general and when Uncle Thomas began to reminisce, headed him off with unobtrusive ease.

The two of them went off to the study when they had had their coffee, leaving her to clear the table and help Emma with the washing up. She agreed that their visitor seemed a nice enough man. Nice wasn't the right word, she mused silently; a milk-and-water word which had no bearing upon his good looks and vast proportions. She would like to get to know him better, a wish instantly suppressed as disloyal to Leslie, who would be home for the weekend and expect her up at the Manor, ready for one of their lengthy walks in which he delighted whenever he was home. He was a rising young barrister, working hard in London, and they didn't see much of each other. They had known each other for years now and she couldn't remember when the idea of marrying him first entered her head. She supposed it was his mother who had planted it there—a rather intimidating matron who saw in Tilly a girl who could be moulded into the kind of wife she wanted to have for her son. Not quite the same background, she pointed out to her husband, but Dr Groves had a good solid country practice and a delightful house, set in grounds of an acre or two, most conveniently running alongside one of the boundaries of the Manor grounds. Nothing could be more suitable. She was proud of Leslie's work as a barrister; at the same time she was terrified that he would meet some quite unsuitable girl in London and marry her out of hand. Tilly, known to her since childhood, was eminently preferable.

Tilly had more or less accepted the situation. She liked Leslie, was fond of him without loving him; if she regretted giving up her hospital career in order to help her uncle she had never said so. She owed him a lot and he hadn't been well for some time; she was able to take some of his work on to her own shoulders and, although she didn't think about it very often, she supposed that she would continue to do so until he retired and she married Leslie. She was a fortunate girl, she knew that, but at the same time there was the disturbing thought, buried deep, that something was missing from her life: romance; and being a normal pretty girl, she wanted that. It was something she wouldn't get from Leslie; he would be a good husband and once they had settled down she would forget the romantic world she dreamed of. She was old enough to know better, she chided herself briskly, and, indeed, she wasn't quite sure what she wished for.

She went down to the village presently; supper would need to be augmented by a few extras. It was still raining and very windy as she went round the side of the house to the front drive. The doctor's car was standing there: a Rolls-Royce in a discreet dark blue, and she stopped to admire it. Undoubtedly a successful man, their guest.

The doctor, watching her admire his car from the study window, admired her.

Mrs Binns, in the village shop, already knew as much about Dr Groves's guest as Tilly. The village was very small but there were scattered farms all around it and, although many of the villagers went into nearby Haddenham to shop, Mrs Binns was still the acknowledged source of local gossip.

'So 'e's 'ere, Miss Matilda, and an 'andsome gent from what I hear.' She sliced bacon briskly. 'Nice bit of company for the doctor. Speaks English, does 'e?'

'Very well, Mrs Binns. I'd better have some cheese…'

'Mr Leslie coming this weekend?'

'Yes. I hope it will stop raining.'

People were more interesting than the weather from Mrs Binns's point of view. 'He'll be glad to get 'ome, I'll be bound. Named the day yet, 'ave you, Miss Matilda?'

'Well, no.' Matilda sought for something harmless

to say which Mrs Binns wouldn't be able to construe into something quite different. 'We're both so busy,' she said finally.

Which was true enough, but, when all was said and done, no reason for not getting engaged.

She started back up the lane and met Dr van Kempler. He said cheerfully, 'Hello, I've come to carry your basket. Is there a longer way back or do you mind the rain?'

'Not a bit. We can go down Penny Lane and round Rush Bottom. It'll be muddy…' She glanced down at her companion's highly polished shoes.

'They'll clean,' he assured her laconically. 'What do you do in your spare time, Matilda?'

'Walk, garden, play tennis in the summer. Go to Thame or Oxford to shop.'

'Never to London to go to a play or have an evening out?' He glanced at her from under heavy lids. 'Your uncle mentioned your…fiancé, is he?'

'Not yet. He is a barrister and he'd rather spend his weekends here than in London.' She got over the stile to Rush Bottom. It was her turn to ask questions. 'Are you married, Dr van Kempler?'

'No, though I hope to be within the next months. Life is easier for a doctor if he has a wife.'

She was tempted to ask him if that was his reason for marrying, but she didn't know him well enough and, although she thought he was friendly, she sensed that he could be quite the reverse if he were annoyed. He didn't want to talk about himself; he began to talk about her work as practice nurse with her uncle. That lasted until they got back to the house.

She was in his company only briefly after that; there was the evening visit to Mrs Jenkins before she phoned the district nurse in Haddenham who would take over for the weekend. When she got back, Emma, normally so unflappable, was fussing over the supper. 'Such a nice young man,' she enthused. 'I must do me best.'

'You always do, Emma,' Tilly assured her, and then, 'He's not all that young, you know.' She paused over the egg custard she was beating gently over the pan of hot water. 'All of thirty-five—older than that...'

'In 'is prime,' declared Emma.

Her uncle had no surgery in the morning. After breakfast he and his guest disappeared into his study, leaving Tilly free to clear the table, make the beds and tidy the house, having done which she got into her newest tweed skirt and quilted jacket, tied a scarf over her dark locks and walked through the village to the Manor.

Leslie always drove himself down late on Friday evening, too late to see her; besides, as he had pointed out so reasonably, he needed a good night's sleep after his busy week in town. He would be waiting for her and they would decide where they would walk, and afterwards he would go with her to her uncle's house, spend five minutes talking to him and then go home to his lunch. It was a routine which never varied and she had accepted it, just as she had accepted Sunday's habitual visit to morning church and then drinks at the Manor afterwards. Sometimes she wished for a day driving with Leslie, just the two of them, but he had pointed out that his mother had come to depend on his weekly visits, so she had said nothing more.

He was in the sitting-room, glancing through the papers, when she reached the Manor and for some reason his, 'Hello, old girl,' annoyed her very much. Normally she was an even-tempered girl and sensible; better a sincere greeting shorn of glamour than a romantic one meaning nothing.

She paid a dutiful visit to his mother and they had their walk, he talking about his week and she listening. He was still explaining a particularly interesting case when they reached her uncle's house, to find him and the Dutch doctor sitting in the drawing-room, deep in discussion. They got to their feet as Tilly and Leslie went in and the doctor introduced Leslie to his guest and offered him a drink. It irked Tilly considerably that Leslie should refuse and, worse, give her a careless pat on the shoulder and a ''Bye, old girl,' as he took his leave. With a heightened colour she gave the Dutchman a defiant look and met a bland face which gave nothing away; all the same she was sure that he was amused.

She wouldn't be seeing Leslie until the next morning; he was taking his mother over to Henley to see old friends and would stay there to dine, something which she had to explain to her uncle at lunch.

'Pity you couldn't go, too. Better still, have a day out together…'

Tilly, serving the custard, said calmly, 'I dare say we shall when the weather's better.'

'Well, if you've nothing else to do, you can go with Rauwerd to Oxford. He has a mind to renew his acquaintance with the colleges.'

Dr van Kempler came to her rescue very nicely. 'I'd

be delighted if you would,' he said. 'I didn't mention it because I supposed that you would be spending the day with—er—Leslie, but I should enjoy it much more if I had a companion.'

'Oh, well, then I'll come.' Tilly smiled at him. 'Were you there?'

'Yes, years ago. There was a splendid tea-room in the High Street...'

'It's still there.'

'Then perhaps we might have tea there?'

The afternoon was a success. The rain didn't bother the doctor. They walked down High Street to Magdalen Bridge and looked at the river, stopped to stare at Tom Tower, peered around Magdalen College, studied Radcliffe Camera, the Sheldonian Theatre and the Rotunda and then had their tea in a tea-room which the doctor swore hadn't altered so much as by a teaspoon since he was there. They walked back presently to where he had parked the car and drove home. He was nicer than she had at first thought, mused Tilly, sitting back in the comfort of the Rolls, and it had been pleasant to spend an afternoon well away from the village. A pity that she and Leslie couldn't take time to do that sometimes... She dismissed the thought as disloyal.

The doctor wasn't going until after tea on Sunday; Tilly got up early, made a trifle for lunch so that Emma would be free to see to the main course, whisked together a sponge cake as light as air, helped to get breakfast and went to church, Uncle Thomas on one side, Dr van Kempler on the other. Their pew was on the opposite side of the aisle to the Manor pew; she caught

Leslie's eye and gave him a warm smile, and when the service was over joined him in the porch.

Mrs Waring, waiting with him, had to be introduced and said at once in her slightly overbearing manner, 'You must come up for a drink. You, too, Thomas— you are so seldom free.'

There was a path through the churchyard which led to the Manor grounds, and Mrs Waring led the way with the two doctors, leaving Tilly and Leslie to follow.

For some reason which Tilly couldn't quite understand she didn't enjoy herself; everything was exactly as it always was on a Sunday morning, with Mrs Waring dominating the conversation while they sat around in the rather grand drawing-room sipping the rather dry sherry Tilly had never really enjoyed. Dr van Kempler had behaved with the ease and unselfconscious poise of someone to whom good manners are as natural as breathing, yet behind that bland face she was sure that he was laughing, not at them, she conceded, but at some private joke of his own.

The talk followed a well-worn routine: Mrs Waring's opinion on world affairs, a severe criticism of the week's work done or mismanaged by the government and a detailed résumé of the village life since the previous Sunday. When she paused for breath her husband muttered, 'Quite so, my dear,' and everyone murmured, for there was no chance to speak. It surprised Tilly when, having come to the end of her diatribe, Mrs Waring began to question Dr van Kempler. Was he married? Where did he live? Exactly what work did he do?

She had met her match. The Dutchman answered

her politely and told her nothing at all. Tilly, who had her ears stretched to hear his replies, was disappointed. Mrs Waring tapped him playfully on an exquisitely tailored sleeve. 'You naughty man,' she declared, 'you're not telling us anything.'

'I have nothing to tell,' he assured her with grave courtesy, 'and I much prefer to hear of your English village life.'

'Well, yes, I flatter myself that I take an active part in it. What do you think of our two young people? I cannot wait for Matilda to become my daughter.'

'You will indeed be most fortunate.' His voice was as bland as his face.

Tilly blushed and looked at her shoes. It was a relief when Uncle Thomas declared that they must be off home otherwise Emma would have their lunch spoilt.

After lunch she saw little of the doctor. He spent the afternoon with her uncle and after tea got into his splendid car and drove away. His goodbyes had been brief but warm to her uncle and equally brief but considerably cooler towards herself.

She watched the car disappear down the lane with mixed feelings: regret that she couldn't get to know him better, and relief that she never would. He wasn't only the handsomest man that she had ever set eyes on; she was sure he was someone she instinctively trusted, even though she was still not sure if she liked him.

The house seemed empty once he had gone. She listened to her uncle contentedly reflecting on his weekend, but when she asked where the doctor lived and what exactly he did, he was vague.

'You should have asked him,' he pointed out. 'I dare say we'll be seeing more of him; he's often in England these days and we still have a great deal to say to each other. He has become successful—modest about it, too.' He chuckled. 'Didn't give much away to Mrs Waring, did he?'

For that matter, mused Tilly, getting ready for bed later that evening, he hadn't given much away to her, either. He was as much a stranger as when she had encountered him. Yet not a stranger; it puzzled her that she felt as though she had known him for a lifetime.

'What nonsense,' said Tilly loudly and jumped into bed.

There was precious little time to think about him during the next few days. Mrs Jenkins and the infant Jenkins, both flourishing, still needed visiting, there were several bed-ridden patients who required attention once if not twice daily, and morning and evening surgeries were overflowing by reason of the particularly nasty virus 'flu which had reached the village. The days went fast and by the end of the week she and her uncle were tired out.

The weekend was a succession of anxious phone calls from people who had stubbornly gone on working through the week and then decided to call in the doctor on Friday evening, and morning surgery on Saturday was no better. There was no question of Sunday church; Tilly drove her uncle from one patient to the next through rain and sleet and hail and high winds. They had a brief respite until the early evening, when Tilly went to visit a couple of elderly patients in the village and her uncle was called out to a farm some miles away.

She was back before him, helping Emma with supper, ready with a hot drink for him when he got in.

He sat down in his chair by the fire and she thought how ill he looked.

'Coffee with a spot of whisky in it. You look all in, Uncle.'

She sped away. When she got back she took one look at him motionless in his chair. She put the tray down on the table and felt for a pulse which was no longer there. He had always told her that he hoped to die in harness, and he had.

Everyone who could walk, and quite a few who couldn't but had cajoled friends and family to push wheelchairs, came to the funeral. Tilly, stunned by the suddenness of it all, found that their concern for her uncle's death almost shattered the calm she had forced upon herself. Everyone had been so kind and Leslie had come from London to attend the funeral. Mrs Waring had begged her to go and stay at the Manor house but this she refused to do; for one thing she couldn't leave Emma on her own and for another, Mrs Waring, though full of good intentions, was overpowering.

'Of course, you and Leslie can marry now,' she pointed out with brisk kindness. 'You can live in your uncle's house and Leslie can commute each day; nothing could be more convenient.' A remark which, well-meaning though it was, set Tilly's teeth on edge.

She was aware of disappointment that there had been

no letter or message from Dr van Kempler. There had been a notice in *The Times* and the *Telegraph* as well as a short item in the *Lancet*. Once or twice she caught herself wishing that she had him there; she needed someone to talk to and somehow, when Leslie came, it was impossible to talk to him. She wanted to talk about Uncle Thomas and she sensed that he was avoiding that.

He had spoken of their marriage, echoing his mother's suggestions, and Tilly, who above all wanted to be loved and cherished and allowed to cry on his shoulder, felt lost. To his rather colourless suggestion that they should marry quietly within the next month or so she returned a vague answer. It was too soon to think of marrying; she had to get used to being without Uncle Thomas and she didn't mind living alone in his house for the time being. She had said that defiantly to Leslie and his mother, sitting on each side of her giving her sound advice. When she said it she had no idea that she wasn't going to have the chance to do that anyway.

Uncle Thomas's sister came to the funeral and with her came her son and his wife. Tilly had only a fleeting acquaintance with her aunt and almost none with her cousin and his wife. They uttered all the very conventional phrases, behaved exactly as they should and were a little too effusive towards the Warings, and, when the last of the doctor's friends and patients had gone, followed Tilly and the family solicitor into the doctor's study.

Half an hour later they led the way out again. Her aunt had the smug look of someone who had found a ten pound note in an empty purse and her cousin Her-

bert had an air of self-righteous satisfaction which he
made no effort to conceal now the funeral was over. He
moved pompously across the hall and into the sitting-
room where he sat down in his uncle's chair.

Tilly eyed him with sternly held-back feelings. He
wasn't in the least like her dear Uncle Thomas: of only
average height, with a waistline already going to seed
despite his thirty or so years; portly was the word which
crossed her mind, and overbearingly conceited. He
smoothed his thinning dark hair back from his forehead and gave her a superior smile.

'Well, well, that's been a surprise to you, I dare say,
Matilda.' He glanced at his wife, Jane, a rather timid
colourless young woman. 'We shall have to make room
for our cousin, won't we, my dear? I would be the last
person to disregard the wishes of Uncle Thomas.'

He looked around him complacently. 'This is a
comfortably sized house. There is no reason why you
shouldn't stay here, Matilda, even keep your room until
you marry Leslie Waring.' He added, 'I could do with
a cup of tea—such a very busy day…'

Tilly said tonelessly, 'I'll get it,' and went out of the
room to the kitchen where she found Emma crying over
a plate of cakes. 'Oh, Miss Tilly, whatever came over
your uncle? The dear man couldn't have thought…'

Tilly put the kettle on. 'Well, yes, he did, and I'm
sure he thought he was doing the right thing. He hasn't
seen Herbert for years; he wasn't to know what he's
like.' She shuddered. 'I'm to stay here until I marry and
when I do, Emma, you're coming with me.'

'Of course I will, Miss Tilly. Me stay 'ere with that

nasty man? You and Mr Waring find a nice 'ouse and I'll look after it for you.'

She wiped her nice elderly face and put the cakes on the tea tray. 'I dare say it won't take too long.'

'Well, no. I'd told Mrs Waring that I didn't want to get married for a month or two, but now things are altered...'

Her aunt and Herbert and Jane were driving back to Cheltenham that evening. He had work to do, Herbert had told her pompously, but he would write and tell her their plans within the next few days. He owned a small factory on the outskirts of the town which he supposed he could run just as well from the house he had inherited as his own smaller, modern one in Cheltenham. 'If that isn't satisfactory I can sell this place—it should fetch a good price.'

Tilly didn't say anything—what would be the good? Uncle Thomas had so obviously meant it to stay in the family and for Herbert to provide a home for her for as long as she would need one. She bade them a polite goodbye and went thankfully to help clear away the tea things and then phone Leslie.

To her disappointment he had already gone back to London. 'He won't be back until the weekend, my dear,' his mother told her. 'Why not give him a ring? I expect you want to tell him about the will—so very satisfactory that you can settle on a date for the wedding now.'

Tilly held her tongue; everyone would know sooner or later but she wanted Leslie to be the first. She would phone him in the morning; better still, she would drive up to town and see him.

She dressed carefully in the morning, taking pains with her face and hair and wearing a suit Leslie had said that he liked. It was still early when she left and she was at his rooms soon after ten o'clock. His clerk was reluctant to accept her wish to see Mr Waring without delay.

'It's most important,' said Tilly and smiled at him with charm, so that he picked up the receiver to announce her.

Leslie looked different—she supposed it was his sober suit and manner to go with it—but he greeted her warmly enough. 'Sit down, Tilly—I've fifteen minutes or so before I go to court. Have you decided to marry me after all? I thought you would once you heard your uncle's will.'

There was no sense in beating about the bush. She said quickly, not mincing matters, 'He left the house to my cousin Herbert, with the wish that I make it my home until I marry.'

The sudden frown on Leslie's face frightened her a little. 'You mean to say that your uncle has left you nothing?'

'Five hundred pounds. He made the request that Herbert would pay me a fitting allowance...'

'Can the will be overset? I'll see your solicitor. Why, you're penniless.'

Tilly stared at him. 'That makes a difference to our plans?' she asked, and knew without a doubt that it did.

Chapter 2

Leslie looked at his wristwatch. 'I must go. This is something which we must discuss quietly. I'll come home as usual tomorrow and we can talk everything over with my mother and father.'

'I haven't told them as I didn't think there was any need to. After all, they have been urging us to get married now that Uncle is dead.' Tilly's voice was calm but inside she shook and trembled with uncertainty. She had expected Leslie to reassure her, tell her that she had no need to worry, that he would take care of her future. Now she wasn't sure of that.

Leslie looked uncomfortable. 'Look, old girl, we'll sort things out tomorrow.' He got up and came round his desk and kissed her cheek. 'Not to worry.'

But of course she worried, all the way back home

and for the rest of the day. The house seemed so empty, the surgery and the waiting-room empty, too, waiting until Monday when the medical centre in Haddenham were to send over one of their members to take morning surgery until such time as a new doctor came to the village or things were reorganised and a small surgery was set up and run by the Haddenham doctors. In any case, thought Tilly, she would never be needed any more. Not that that would matter if she married Leslie. For the first time she put her nebulous thoughts into words. 'Leslie might not want to marry me now.'

She had a phone call from Mrs Waring the next morning; would she go over for dinner that evening? Leslie hoped to be home rather earlier than usual, and they had a lot to discuss. There was a letter from Herbert, too; he and Jane and her aunt would be coming down and would go over the house and make any changes needed at the beginning of the week. Jane and his mother would move in very shortly, he wrote, and he would commute until such time as the sale of his own house was dealt with. The letter ended with the observation that she was probably looking for a nursing post.

She put the letter tidily back into its envelope. It wasn't something she could ignore; it was only too clear that that was what she was expected to do. Unless Leslie married her out of hand...

Something it was only too obvious he didn't intend to do.

His, 'Hello, old girl,' was as friendly as it always had been and his parents greeted her just as they had always done for years, yet there was an air of uneasiness hang-

ing over the dinner-table and a deliberate avoidance of
personal topics. It was only when they were drinking
their coffee in the drawing-room that the uneasiness
became distinctly evident.

'I hear,' said Mrs Waring, at her most majestic, 'that
your uncle's will was unexpected. Leslie tells me that
there is no way of contesting it.'

Tilly glanced at Leslie. So he had spoken about it
with his parents, had he? He didn't look at her, which
was just as well, for her gaze was fierce.

'It has always been our dearest wish,' went on Mrs
Waring in a false voice, 'that you and dear Leslie should
marry—your uncle's property matched with ours, the
house was ideal for a young couple to set up home;
besides, we have known you for so many years. You
would have been most suitable.' She sighed so deeply
that her corsets creaked. 'It grieves us very much that
this cannot be. You must see for yourself, my dear, that
our plans are no longer practical. We are not wealthy;
Leslie needs to marry someone with money of her own,
someone who can—er—share the expenses of married
life while he makes a career for himself. Luckily there
is no official engagement.'

Tilly put down her coffee cup, carefully, because
her hands were shaking. 'You have put it very clearly,
Mrs Waring. Now I should like to hear what Leslie has
to say. After all, it's his life you are talking about, isn't
it?' She paused. 'And mine.'

She looked at Leslie, who gave her a weak smile and
looked away. 'Well, old girl, you can see for yourself…
Where would we live? I can't afford a decent place in

town. Besides, I'd need money—you can't get to the top of the ladder without it…meeting the right people and entertaining…' He met Tilly's eye and stopped.

'I can see very well,' said Tilly in an icy little voice, 'and I am so thankful that the engagement isn't official. If it were I would break it here and now. A pity I have no ring, for I would fling it in your face, Leslie.'

She got to her feet and whisked herself out of the room, snatched her coat from the hall and ran out of the house.

She couldn't get home fast enough; she half ran, tears streaming down her cheeks, rage bubbling and boiling inside her. It was fortunate that it was a dark evening and there was no one around in the village to see her racing along like a virago.

Emma took one look at her face, fetched the sherry from the dining-room cupboard, stood over her while she drank it, and then listened patiently.

'Well, love, I'd say you're well rid of him. If a man can't stand up against 'is ma, he'll make a poor husband. As to what you're going ter do, get a job, Miss Tilly. I'm all right 'ere—yer uncle saw ter that, bless 'is dear 'eart. But don't you go staying 'ere with that cousin of yours—no good will come of it, mark my words.'

Tilly went to church on the Sunday morning, her chin well up, sang the hymns loudly and defiantly, wished the occupants of the Manor pew a chilling good morning and went home to compose a letter to the principal nursing officer of her training school. She hadn't worked in a hospital for some years now, but she had been in the running for a sister's post when she left; she could hardly expect that, but there might possibly be a staff nurse's job going.

Two days later Herbert, Jane and her aunt arrived without warning. Herbert sat back in her uncle's chair, looking smug. 'It seemed a good idea if Mother and Jane should get used to the idea of living here. I'll come at weekends, of course. The house in Cheltenham is up for sale with most of the furniture—I'll get the stuff we shall want to have here sent down when I have time to arrange it. I'm a busy man.'

Tilly said tartly, 'Too busy to let us know that you were coming? And even if you were, surely Jane could have telephoned?'

'I deal with all the domestic arrangements.' He smoothed his hair back and half closed his eyes. 'Jane isn't strong.'

Jane, thought Tilly, was as strong as the next girl, only her strength was being syphoned off her by her great bully of a husband.

Herbert waved a hand, presumably in dismissal. Tilly stayed right where she was sitting. 'So who does the housekeeping?' she asked sweetly.

'Oh, Mother, I suppose, though you might carry on for a day or two until she's found her way around.'

'I might and then I might not,' said Tilly. 'You have been at great pains to remind me that this is no longer my home—I'm here on sufferance, aren't I? You haven't considered me at all; why should I consider you? I'm sure Aunt Nora will manage beautifully.'

She took herself off to the kitchen, shutting the door on Herbert's outraged face. There was a lot of coming and going—Aunt Nora and Jane finding their way around, thought Tilly waspishly. She went to find Emma crying into the potatoes which she was peeling.

Over a cup of tea they faced the future. Tilly would have liked a good cry but she couldn't; Emma had to be comforted and given some kind of hope.

'Has the postman been? There may be a letter from the hospital—I wrote for a job. As soon as I'm settled Emma, I'll find a flat and we'll set up house. Just hang on here, Emma dear, and I promise everything will be all right. There's the postman now.'

There was a letter. Tilly read it quickly and then a second time. There was no job for her; regretfully, there was the full quota of nurses and no way of adding to it, but had Tilly thought of applying for a job at one of the geriatric hospitals? They were frequently under-staffed; there was no doubt that she would find a post at one of them.

It was a disappointment, but it was good advice, too. Tilly got the *Nursing Times* from her room and sat down there and then and applied to three of the most likely hospitals wanting nursing staff. Then, while Emma was seeing to lunch, she went down to the post office and posted them. She met Mrs Waring on the way back and wished her a polite good day and that lady made as if to stop and talk.

'I'm in a great hurry,' said Tilly brightly. 'My cousin and his wife have arrived unexpectedly.'

'Moving in already?' asked Mrs Waring in a shocked voice. 'Tilly, what are you going to do? Leslie's so upset.'

Tilly went a little pale. 'Is he? Goodbye, Mrs Waring.'

She smiled in Mrs Waring's general direction and raced off home. If Leslie was upset, he knew what to do…

Only he didn't do it. He neither telephoned her nor wrote, which made life with Jane and her aunt just that much harder to bear. So that when there was a letter from a north London hospital asking her if she would attend an interview with a view to a staff nurse's post in a female geriatric ward, she replied promptly and two days later presented herself at the grim portals of a huge Victorian edifice, very ornate on the outside and distressingly bare within.

She followed the porter along a corridor painted in margarine-yellow and spinach-green, waited while he tapped at its end on a door and then went in. She hadn't much liked the look of the place so far; now she felt the same way about the woman sitting behind the desk, a thin, acidulated face topping a bony body encased in stern navy blue.

'Miss Groves?' The voice was as thin as its owner.

'Yes,' said Tilly, determinedly cheerful. 'How do you do?'

'I am the Principal Nursing Officer.' The lady had beady eyes and no make-up. 'I see from your letter that you are seeking work as a staff nurse. A pity that you have not worked in a hospital for a while. However, your references are quite in order and we are willing to give you a trial. The ward to which you will be assigned has forty patients. I hope you don't mind hard work.'

'No. Would I be the only staff nurse?'

The beady eyes snapped at her. 'There are part-time

staff, Miss Groves. We take a quota of student nurses for a short period of geriatric nursing—they come from various general hospitals—and we also have nursing auxiliaries.' She paused, but Tilly didn't speak, so she went on, 'You will do day duty, with the usual four hours off duty and two days free in the week. It may be necessary from time to time to rearrange your days off. You will be paid the salary laid down by the NHS, monthly in arrears, and your contract may be terminated at the end of the month by either of us. After that you will sign a contract for one year.'

'I should like to see the ward,' suggested Tilly, and smiled.

She got no smile in return, only a look of faint surprise.

'Yes, well, that can be arranged.'

In answer to a phone call, a dumpy little woman in a checked uniform joined them. 'Sister Down,' said the Principal Nursing Officer, 'my deputy.' She turned the pages of some report or other on the desk and picked up her pen. 'Be good enough to let me know at your earliest convenience if you are accepting the post, Miss Groves.' She nodded a severe dismissal.

The hospital was left over from Victorian days and as far as Tilly could see no one had done much about it since then. She followed the dumpy sister along a number of depressing corridors, up a wide flight of stone stairs and into a long narrow ward. It was no good, decided Tilly, gazing at the long rows of beds down each side of it, each with its locker on one side and on the other side its occupant sitting in a chair. Like a recurring nightmare, she thought as they traversed the highly polished floor between the beds to the open door at the end. It led to the ward sister's office, and that lady was sitting at her desk, filling in charts.

She greeted Tilly unsmilingly. 'The new staff nurse? I could do with some help. How soon can you come?'

She looked worn to the bone, thought Tilly, not surprising when one considered the forty old ladies sitting like statues. There were two nursing auxiliaries making a bed at the far end of the ward and a ward orderly pushing a trolley of empty mugs towards another door. Tilly didn't know what made her change her mind; perhaps an urge to change the dreary scene around her. Music, she mused, and the old ladies grouped together so that they could talk to each other, and a TV...

'As soon as you want me,' she said briskly.

She didn't tell her aunt or Jane, but confided in Emma, who had mixed feelings about it.

'Supposing you don't like it?' she wanted to know. 'It sounds a nasty ol' place ter me.'

'Well, it's not ideal,' agreed Tilly, 'but it's a start, Emma, and I can't stay here.' Her lovely eyes took fire. 'Aunt has changed all the furniture round in the drawing-room and she says an open fire is wasteful there, so there is a horrid little electric fire in there instead. And she says Herbert wants all the books out of Uncle's study because he is going to use it as an office. So you see, Emma, the quicker I settle in to a job the better. I've a little money,' she didn't say how little, 'and I'll go flat hunting as soon as possible. It's not the best part of London but there'll be something.'

She spoke hopefully, because Emma looked glum. 'You do realise that it will be in a street and probably no garden? You'll miss the village, Emma.'

'I'll miss you more, Miss Tilly.'

Leslie came to see her on the following evening, and without thinking she invited him into the drawing-room. She had nothing to say to him, but good manners prevailed. She was brought up short by her aunt, sitting there with Jane.

She wished Leslie a stiff good evening and raised her eyebrows at Tilly.

'Will you take Mr Waring somewhere else, Matilda? Jane and I were discussing a family matter.' She smiled in a wintry fashion. 'I'm sure it is hard for you to get used to the idea that you can't have the run of the house any more, so we'll say no more about it.'

Tilly clamped her teeth tight on the explosive retort she longed to utter, ushered Leslie out into the hall and said in a voice shaking with rage. 'Come into the kitchen, Leslie. I can't think why you've come, but since you're here we can at least sit down there.'

'That woman,' began Leslie. 'She's... She was rude, to me as well as you.'

Not quite the happiest of remarks to make, but Tilly let it pass.

She sat down at the kitchen table and Emma gathered up a tray and went to set the table in the dining-room. No one spoke. Tilly had nothing to say and presumably Leslie didn't know how to begin.

'You can't stay here,' he said at length. 'You're going to be treated like an interloper—it's your home.'

'Not any more.'

'Well, your uncle meant it to be; surely your cousin knows that?'

'Herbert is under no legal obligation,' Tilly observed.

Leslie stirred uncomfortably. 'I feel…' he began, and tried again. 'If circumstances had been different… Tilly, I do regret that I am unable to marry you.'

She got up. 'Well, don't.' She kept her voice cheerful. 'I wouldn't marry you if you were the last man on earth, Leslie. Besides, I've got a job in London; I shall be leaving in a few days.'

She watched the relief on his face. 'Oh, that is good news. May I tell Mother? She will be so relieved.'

He went awkwardly to the door. 'No hard feelings, Tilly?'

She opened the door and stood looking at him. 'If you ask a silly question you'll get a silly answer,' she told him.

When he had gone she sat down again and had a good cry; she was a sensible girl, but just at that moment life had got on top of her.

Herbert arrived the next day, stalking pompously through the house, ordering this to be done and that to be done and very annoyed when neither Tilly nor Emma took any notice of his commands.

'I expect co-operation,' he told her loftily when he asked her to move a chair from one room to another.

'If you wish any of the heavy furniture to be moved, then I suggest you do it yourself, Herbert. After all, you are a man, aren't you?' Tilly said it in a placid voice which stopped him doing more than gobble like a turkey cock. It was an opportunity to tell him that she would be leaving; she had had a letter from the hospital asking her to report for duty in two days' time—a Monday. It didn't give her much time to pack up but, if she didn't manage it all, Emma could finish it for her and send the rest on.

When it came to actually leaving, it was a wrench. The nice old house had been her home for almost all of her life and she had been very happy there. Besides, there was Emma. She promised to write each week and to set about finding somewhere to live just as soon as possible.

The nurses' home at the hospital was as gloomy as its surroundings. Tilly was shown to a room on the top floor with a view of chimney pots and one or two plane trees struggling to stay alive. At least they would provide some green later on to relieve the predominant red brick. The room was of a good size, furnished with a spartan bed, a built-in dressing-table and a wardrobe with a small handbasin in one corner. There was no colour scheme but the quilt on the bed was a much washed pale blue. There was a uniform laid out on it, blue and white checks, short-sleeved and skimpily cut. With it was a paper cap for her to make up. She stood looking at it, remembering the delicately goffered muslin trifle she had worn when she had qualified, and the neat blue cotton dress and starched apron.

She was to go to the office as soon as she had unpacked and changed into her uniform. The Principal Nursing Officer was there to bid her a severe good afternoon and speed her on her way to the ward. 'Sister Evans is waiting for you, Staff Nurse.'

It was barely three o'clock but the monumental task of getting forty old ladies back into their beds had already begun. As far as she could see, Tilly could count only four nurses on the ward, and one of those was Sister, who, when she saw her, left the elderly lady she was dealing with and came to meet her.

She nodded in greeting and wasted no time. 'I'm off duty at five o'clock, Staff Nurse. I'll take you through the Kardex and show you where the medicines are kept. You do a round after supper at seven o'clock. Supper is at six o'clock; ten patients have to be fed. You'll have Mrs Dougall on with you—she's very reliable and knows where everything is kept. There's a BP round directly after tea. The trolley's due now, but you'll get a few calls before the night staff come on at eight.' Sister Evans smiled suddenly and Tilly saw that she was tired and doing her best to be friendly.

'You'll be able to manage? I'm having days off—I've not had any for two weeks. The student nurses aren't due to come for another two weeks and one of the part-time nurses has left. There'll be one in tomorrow after dinner, so that you can have the afternoon off.' She was sitting at the desk, pulling the Kardex towards her. 'I'm very sorry you're being thrown in at the deep end.'

Tilly stifled a desire to turn and run. 'That's all right, Sister, I'll manage. This Mrs Dougall, is she trained?'

'No, but she's been here for five years, longer than any of us, and she's good with the old ladies.' She nodded towards a chair. 'We'll go through the Kardex…'

The rest of the day and the two which followed it were like a nightmare. Mrs Dougall was a tower of strength, making beds, changing them, heaving old ladies in and out of their chairs, a mine of information. When she wasn't on duty Tilly had to manage with the three other nursing auxiliaries, whose easy-going ways tried Tilly's temper very much. They were kind enough, but they had been there long enough to regard the patients as puppets to be got up, fed and put back to bed. Which wasn't the case at all. At least half of them could have been at home if there had been someone to look after them; the patient despair in their eyes almost broke Tilly's soft heart. It was always the same tale—daughter or son or niece didn't want them, because that would mean that they would have to stay at home to look after them. Tilly was of the opinion that a good number of the old ladies were perfectly capable of looking after themselves with a little assistance, but the enforced idleness and the hours of sitting in a chair staring at the patients opposite had dulled their energy and blunted their hopes. However strongly she felt about it, there wasn't very much that she could do. She suspected that a new principal nursing officer might alter things; it was lack of staff and the adhering to the treatment used several decades earlier which were the stumbling blocks. The geriatric wards in her own training school had been light and airy, decorated in pastel shades, and the patients had been encouraged to take an interest in life.

Sister Evans looked ten years younger when she came back on duty.

'You coped?' she asked, and added, 'I see that you

did. We'll be able to have days off each week now, thank heaven.'

At Tilly's look of enquiry she said, 'No staff, you see. They won't stay because Miss Watts won't allow us to change the treatment. She ought to retire—she's not well—but she won't. I'd have left months ago but my fiancé is in Canada and I'm going out to him as soon as he is settled.' She looked at Tilly. 'You're not engaged or anything like that?'

'No, Sister.'

'Well you ought to be, you're pretty enough. If you get the chance,' went on Sister Evans, 'don't let a sense of duty stop you from leaving. As soon as Miss Watts retires all the things you need doing will be done.' She opened the Kardex. 'Now we'd better go through this…'

The week crawled its slow way to Sunday and on Monday Tilly had her days off. She wanted very much to go to her uncle's house but that wouldn't be possible; she wouldn't be welcome. She had written to Emma in the week and mentioned that she would have two days off a week and explained why she wouldn't be returning to her old home. To her delight Emma had written back; why didn't Miss Tilly go to Emma's sister who lived at Southend-on-Sea and did bed and breakfast? The fresh air would do her good.

Tilly had never been to Southend-on-Sea and certainly not in early March, but it would be somewhere to go and she longed to get away from the hospital and its sombre surroundings. She phoned Mrs Spencer, and found her way to Liverpool Street Station early on Monday morning. It was an hour's journey and the scenery didn't look very promising, but the air was cold and fresh as she left the station and asked the way to South-church Avenue. Mrs Spencer lived in one of the streets off it, not ten minutes from the Marine Parade.

The house was narrow and on three floors, in a row of similar houses, each with a bay window framing a table set for a meal and a sign offering Bed and Break-fast. In the summer it would be teeming with life, but now there was no one to be seen, only a milk float and a boy on a bicycle.

Tilly knocked on the front door and it was flung open by a slightly younger version of Emma.

'Come in, my dear,' invited Mrs Spencer, 'and glad I am to see you. Emma wrote and I'm sure I'll make you comfy whenever you like to come. Come and see yer room, love.'

It was at the top of the house, clean and neat, and, provided she stood on tiptoe, it gave her a view of the estuary.

'Now, bed and breakfast, Emma said, but it's no trouble to do yer an evening meal. There's not much open at this time of the year and the 'otels is expensive. There's a sitting-room and the telly downstairs and yer can come and go as yer please.'

The kind creature bustled round the room, twitch-ing the bedspread to perfection, closing a window. 'Me 'usband works at the 'ospital—'e's a porter there.' She retreated to the door. 'I dare say you could do with a cuppa. I got a map downstairs so that you can see where to go for the shops, or there's a good walk along the cliffs to Westcliff if you want a breath of fresh air.'

Half an hour later Tilly set out, warmed by her welcome and the tea and armed with detailed instructions as to the best way to get around the town. It was a grey morning but dry; she walked briskly into the wind with the estuary on one side of her and the well-laid-out gardens with the houses beyond on the other. By the time she reached Westcliff she was glowing and hungry. There were no cafés open along the cliff road so she turned away from the sea and found her way to Hamlet Court Road where she found a coffee bar and she had coffee and sandwiches. Then, since Mrs Spencer had warned her that it was nothing but main roads and shops when away from the cliffs, she walked back the way she had come, found a small café in the High Street and had a leisurely tea, bought herself a paperback and went back to Mrs Spencer's.

Supper was at half-past six when Mr Spencer got back home; sausages and mash and winter greens and apple pie with cups of tea to follow. It was a pleasant meal with plenty to talk about, what with Mr Spencer retailing his day's work and Mrs Spencer's careful probing into Tilly's circumstances. 'Emma didn't tell me nothing,' she assured Tilly, 'only of course we knew that you worked for your uncle...' She smiled at Tilly so kindly that she found herself telling her all about it, even Leslie. But she made light of it and, when she could, edged the talk back to Emma.

It was a fine clear morning when she woke and after breakfast she helped with the washing-up, made her bed and went out. This time she walked to Shoeburyness, in the other direction, found a small café for her coffee and sandwiches and started to walk back again. She hadn't realised that it was so far—all of five miles—and half-way back she caught a bus which took her to the High Street. Since she had time on her hands she looked at the shops before going back to Mrs Spencer's. It was poached egg on haddock for supper, treacle tart and more tea. She ate everything with a good appetite and went to bed early. She was on duty at one o'clock the next day and she would have to catch a train about ten o'clock.

It had been a lovely break, she reflected on the train as it bore her to London, and Mrs Spencer had been so kind. She was to go whenever she wanted to, 'though in the summer it's a bit crowded—you might not like it overmuch, love. Kids about and all them teenagers with their radios, but it'll stay quiet like this until Easter, so you come when you want to.'

She would, but not for the next week; she would spend her two days going to the local house agents and looking over flats.

Going back on duty was awful but the awfulness was mitigated by Sister Evans's real pleasure at seeing her again. They had been busy, she said, but she had felt a bit under the weather and would have her days off on Saturday and Sunday and have a good rest.

Tilly, once Sister had gone off duty for the afternoon, went round the beds, stopping to chat while she tidied up, fetched and carried, and coaxed various old ladies to drink their tea. Some of them wanted to talk and to hear what she had been doing with her free days and she lingered to tell them; contact with the outside world for some of them was seldom and most of them knew Southend-on-Sea.

The later part of the afternoon was taken up with the Senior Registrar's visit. He was pleasant towards the patients but a little bored, too, and not to be wondered at since he had been looking after several of them for months, if not years.

'There are one or two temps,' Tilly pointed out, 'And a number of headaches.'

"Flu? Let me know if they persist. Settling down, are you?"

'Yes, thank you.'

He nodded. 'This isn't quite your scene, is it?'

She had no answer to that so it was just as well that he went away.

By the end of the week a number of old ladies were feeling poorly.

'I said it was 'flu.' The registrar was writing up antibiotics. 'You'll need more staff if it gets much worse.'

Two extra nurses were sent, resentful of having to work on a geriatric ward instead of the more interesting surgical wing, but it meant that Sister Evans could have her weekend off. She had been looking progressively paler and more exhausted and Tilly went on duty earlier on the Friday evening so that she could go off duty promptly.

'I'll do the same for you, Staff,' said Sister gratefully. 'You've got days off on Tuesday and Wednesday.'

However, Sister Evans wasn't on duty when Tilly got on to the ward on Monday morning. Instead there was a message to say that she was ill and Staff Nurse

Groves would have to manage. The Principal Nursing Officer's cold voice over the phone reminded her that she had two extra nurses.

'We are all working under a great strain,' added that lady. 'You must adapt yourself, Staff Nurse.'

Which meant, in fact, being on duty for most of the day, for various of the old ladies added their symptoms to those already being nursed in their beds, so that the work was doubled, the medicine round became a major chore and the report, usually a quickly written mixture of 'no change', or 'good day', now needed to be written at length.

By the end of the week Tilly was looking very much the worse for wear; hurried meals, brief spells of off duty, and the effort of keeping a cheerful comforting face on things were taking their toll. The last straw was the Principal Nursing Officer informing her that Sister Evans was to have a further week's sick leave and that Tilly could not have her days off until she was back.

Tilly tackled the Registrar when he came on to the Ward later that day. 'Forty old ladies, more than half of them ill—there's me, Staff Nurse Willis who comes in three times a week from two o'clock until six, and there is Mrs Dougall, two auxiliaries and the two extra I've been lent. With off duty and days off I'm lucky to have more than two on at a time. You must do something about it.'

He didn't want to know. He was a good doctor, but overworked, and there were acutely ill patients on the medical side. He said unwillingly, 'I'll see what I can do.'

He wasn't very successful. Not only was she refused

any extra help, but she was sent to the office where she was told that at the end of the month her services would no longer be required. 'You are not suitable for the post,' said the Principal Nursing Officer, 'although I am sure that you have done your best.'

Matilda, since she had been given the sack already, felt that she could speak her mind. 'What you mean is that my ideas of nursing geriatric patients don't fit in with yours. They are human, you know, they still think and talk and take an interest in the things going on about them, but you haven't moved with the times, you treat them as though they were workhouse patients, sitting in rows until they die of boredom.' She was so carried away that she actually shook an admonitory finger at the incensed lady sitting behind the desk. 'Many more staff, a little painting and decorating, organised occupational therapy, a chance for the more active patients to walk around...'

'You will leave at the end of the month, Staff Nurse.'

'Yes, I will. I shall also write to the local MP, the Regional Nursing Board, and anyone else I can think of. The geriatric unit is an absolute disgrace and you should be ashamed of yourself!'

She got herself out of the office, shaking with rage and presently with fright. Probably she would be struck off, or whatever they did to staff nurses who dared to argue with their superiors.

Off duty was quite out of the question. It wasn't Staff Nurse Willis's day to come in and though Mrs Dougall was perfectly capable of running the ward she wasn't allowed to. Tilly plunged into a round of chores with brief respites for meals and at the end of a long day, sat down to write the report. The one nurse she had on duty had gone to her supper, so Tilly took her Kardex into the ward and sat at the table where she could see everyone. The old ladies were quiet now, dozing away the first early hours of the evening, and she wrote busily, making her tired brain remember the day's happenings. She was almost finished when the door at the far end of the ward opened and Dr van Kempler came in.

Chapter 3

Matilda, her mouth slightly open, watched him make his unhurried way towards her. When he reached the table he stood quietly looking at her, his look so intent that she put a hand up to her hair and said stupidly, 'I'm a bit untidy; I've had a very busy day...'

'I only heard this morning.' He had ignored her remark; she might never have made it. 'I came at once. I'm so sorry—he was a good man. Why are you here, looking—' he paused '—so tired? And why are you working in this place? Why have you left your home?'

'Questions, questions,' said Tilly peevishly. 'I've no time to answer them. There's the report to finish and the night staff will be here in ten minutes.'

'In that case, once you have dealt with it, we will go somewhere quiet and you shall answer them.'

He drew up a chair and sat down and when Tilly said, 'You can't do that,' he said calmly,

'A friend of mine is on the committee here. I arranged to come and see you; some gorgon on the telephone did her best to prevent me.'

'The Principal Nursing Officer. She has given me the sack.'

'Yes? That's good.'

There was a flutter of movement as the night nurses came on to the ward; two auxiliaries, and one of those would only stay until the patients had been settled for the night.

'I'll stay here while you give the report,' said Dr van Kempler. He spoke with a quiet authority which took it for granted that she would do just that; so she did, with all her usual calm, her quiet voice omitting nothing, while at the back of her head there was a rising tide of disbelief. She had imagined it all: doctors who weren't attached to hospitals didn't just walk on to wards and sit down coolly as though they had a right to do so. She got to the end of the report and stole a look out of the open office door. He was still there, sitting relaxed like a man at his own fireside.

She went with the nurse to take a final look at the ill patients and found him walking beside her as she left the ward. At the head of the staircase he said, 'I'll be at the front entrance—is fifteen minutes long enough for you?'

She pushed back a dark curl. 'I'm tired...'

'We will go somewhere quiet.' The smile he gave her was very kind.

It would be a waste of time arguing with him. She nodded and turned away to go to the nurses' home.

She looked a fright. She cast one look in the mirror on the dressing-table and tore out of her uniform. She had showered, got into a tweed suit, done the best she had time for with her face and hair, and pushed her tired feet into high heels. It had been a grey day and it was dark now; she hoped she would be warm enough as she hurried down to the front entrance.

Dr van Kempler was lounging against a Grecian pillar bearing the bust of some long-dead gentleman with side whiskers and a stern mouth. He reached the door as she did and opened it with a cheerful, 'You were quick—the car is here.'

Her tired head seethed with questions but it was too much bother to utter them. She sat in blissful comfort while he drove away from the hospital and the rows of small, dull streets until they reached Oxford Street. He turned off at St Giles's Circus and presently stopped at Neal Street Restaurant, smallish and quiet, somewhere, she thought gratefully, where her suit wouldn't look too out of place.

They had a table in a corner and the doctor spoke for the first time. 'What would you like to drink while we choose, Matilda?'

She sipped her sherry and studied the menu, aware that she was hungry.

'Did you have lunch?' he asked casually.

'Well, a sandwich...'

'Iced melon?' he suggested. 'And how about *sole véronique* to follow?'

The food was delicious and beyond a modicum of conversation the doctor spoke little, leaving her to enjoy the fish and the splendid dish of vegetables which went with it—new potatoes, broccoli and artichoke hearts. A hot soufflé covered in chocolate sauce followed and it wasn't until she had finished these and the coffee had been put on the table that he sat back and said quietly, 'Now, from the beginning, Matilda.'

The hock had loosened her tongue. Besides, it was marvellous to be able to talk to someone; someone who would listen, she felt instinctively, and who had known Uncle Thomas well.

It was fairly difficult to begin, but once she had started, words came easily. She laid the whole sorry story before him in a matter-of-fact voice and when she had finished she asked him, 'More coffee? I'm afraid it's not very hot now.'

He ordered another pot with a gently raised hand. 'Thank you for telling me. I have to go back to Holland,' he didn't tell her that he was flying back, leaving his car in London, 'but something shall be done, I promise you.'

'You are coming back?' She had no idea that she sounded so anxious, and his bland face and heavy-lidded eyes told her nothing.

'Oh, yes.' She took comfort from his smile.

'How did you know where I was?' she asked.

'I telephoned your uncle. Someone—your aunt?— told me what had happened. They were not very forth-coming, so I drove down and saw Emma.' He caught

her questioning look. 'Very early in the morning, before anyone was about. She told me where you were.'

'You went to a lot of trouble.' She studied his quiet
face.

'Your uncle was my friend. I'm going to take you
back now.' His eyes searched her face. 'You're all right?'

She nodded. 'I'm very grateful—just to talk…'

He nodded and smiled, the kind smile which changed
his rather austere face.

He saw her into the hospital, lifted his hand in casual
farewell and drove away, leaving her deflated. She remembered as she undressed that she hadn't asked him
why he was bothering about her. Perhaps he felt an
obligation towards Uncle Thomas. In which case, she
thought sleepily, *I must make it clear that he need not
be. I'm quite able to look after myself.*

She was far too busy with the old ladies to give herself any thought at all. The sad state of affairs they
were in couldn't last for ever, she comforted herself,
as, gamely seconded by Mrs Dougall, she plunged into
yet another day's work. She was tired and she had a
dull headache and everything took twice as long as it
should have done; from the other side of the bed they
were making Mrs Dougall said flatly, 'You've got the
'flu, Staff Nurse.'

'I'm a bit tired, that's all. I think we're over the worst
of it; another week and we'll be back to normal, hopefully. If only we had more nurses…'

Her headache got worse as the day wore on. She
had gone off duty for a couple of hours in the afternoon while the part-time staff took over, and she had

slept heavily, waking unrefreshed. Filling in the Kardex, waiting for the night staff, she decided not to go to supper; Panadol and bed made more sense.

She felt worse in the morning but there was nothing for it but to go on duty; there would be only three of them—herself, Mrs Dougall and another nursing auxiliary. She had just finished taking the report from the night nurse when Mrs Dougall answered the phone.

'You're wanted in the office, Staff,' she said, and added *sotto voce,* 'and don't let her flatten you.' She cast an anxious eye over Tilly's white face. 'You don't look fit to be here—it's a crying shame.'

Tilly went carefully out of the ward and down the stairs, holding her head very carefully still because it ached so atrociously. At the office door she took a deep breath, knocked and went in.

The Principal Nursing Officer wasn't there; there was a stout balding man sitting at her desk and beside him a thin man with a clever face. Standing a little apart was Dr van Kempler.

He stepped forward, took the door handle from her and shut the door, and offered her a chair, but he didn't speak. It was the man behind the desk who addressed her.

'Staff Nurse Groves, we owe you both an apology and an explanation.' He paused and looked carefully at her. 'You are very pale—that is no wonder. I must tell you on behalf of the whole hospital committee that we are very distressed to have been made aware of the situation here. It will be put right immediately. We have already arranged for agency nurses to supplement the staff; the Principal Nursing Officer has—er—gone on extended sick leave. I may say that we are happy to have secured the services of a most capable lady in her place. Things will be put right as soon as possible. I am told that you were dismissed—quite unfairly. We shall be only too happy to retain your services; you can rest assured that you will have no further fault to find with the administration.'

He had a sonorous voice; it went through Tilly's throbbing head like a sledgehammer. She caught a word here and there and when she looked at him he was all fuzzy round the edges. She frowned in her efforts to understand what he was saying. And what was Dr van Kempler doing, standing there? She turned her head to look at him and winced with pain. Perhaps if she shut her eyes for a minute...

Dimly she heard Dr van Kempler speak. ''Flu, and I'm not surprised. I'll take her home. I think you can take it from me that she won't be coming back.' He nodded at the thin man. 'Thanks for all the help, Dick.'

'Only too glad to have helped. And our thanks for bringing this state of affairs to light, Rauwerd. Keep in touch...'

Dr van Kempler nodded again, scooped Matilda up as though she had been a bundle of straw, and carried her, apparently without effort, through the hall and out of the entrance. The surprised porter who had opened the door followed him outside and opened the car door as well. The doctor arranged Matilda tidily in the front seat. 'Will you see someone about packing up Miss Groves's things and sending them to my house?' He

scribbled in his notebook. 'Here is the address. Thanks.'
A coin or two changed hands. 'As soon as possible.'

Matilda collected her wool-gathering wits. 'Nurses'
home,' she muttered urgently, and then, remembering
her manners, 'So sorry…'

The doctor didn't answer that but got into the car
and drove off, away from the hospital, leaving the dull
streets behind and finally stopping in a narrow elegant street close to Grosvenor Square. His house was
the end one of a terrace, a small Regency cottage with
spotless paintwork and shining windows. Its handsome
front door opened as he drew up and Emma came down
the steps.

'Have you got Miss Matilda there, sir?' she asked
anxiously. 'Is she all right?'

He got out without haste. 'She's here, Emma. She has
'flu—she must go straight to bed. Is the room ready?'

'Oh, yes.' Emma trotted round the car and peered in
at Matilda, who gazed back at her in a bemused way.
Really, the strangest things were happening. It was a
pity that she couldn't be bothered to think about them.

'Emma,' she said, 'why are you here and where am I?'

'Don't talk now,' advised the doctor, and since he
sounded a little testy, she didn't. In any case, it was
too much effort.

Thinking about it afterwards, she was vague as to
what had happened. She was aware of Emma fussing
round her, of being carried upstairs and of another elderly face peering down at her and voices talking quietly. She wasn't sure who got her into bed, only that
its cool comfort was bliss. Someone gave her a drink,

offered pills and then more drink and told her to go to sleep.

When she woke, the dull day was dwindling into dusk and her headache was bearable. She turned her head just to make sure and saw the doctor; he was sitting near her bed. He had a folder of papers on his knees and was writing, but he looked up as she moved and got up and came over to the bed.

'Feeling a little better?' And, when she nodded, 'No, don't talk—time enough to do that later. Emma will freshen you up and give you a drink and you'll go to sleep again.' He poured some water from the carafe on the table beside the bed. 'Take these now.'

She felt hot and cross, and when he left the room tears of tiredness and temper trickled down her cheeks. Emma, bearing a tray on which was a jug of lemonade, properly made from her own recipe, wiped her cheeks for her, washed her face and hands, then combed her hair and coaxed her to drink.

'There, there, my lamb, you'll feel better in the morning. Just you close your eyes now.'

'That's all very well,' said Matilda peevishly, 'but why are you here, Emma, and where are we?'

'Why, the doctor fetched me, sensible man that he is, and this is his house. Now do go to sleep, Miss Tilly.'

'I don't want to,' said Tilly a little wildly, 'not until someone's explained.'

Her hand was taken in a firm cool grasp. 'You have a high temperature,' said Dr van Kempler, sounding exactly like a doctor should when dealing with a recalcitrant patient. 'You will go to sleep now; tomorrow you will feel more yourself and you may ask all the questions you wish.'

He didn't let go of her hand, but sat down on the bed. 'I shall stay here until you are asleep,' he observed calmly.

'Oh, well, in that case,' mumbled Matilda and closed her eyes.

Incredibly, it was morning when she woke again. She lifted her head cautiously from the pillow and found her headache a mere echo of what it had been. She sat up in bed and looked around her. Emma was asleep in a big armchair, wrapped in a dressing-gown and with a blanket tucked around her. There was a small table by her with a shaded reading lamp on it; by its light and the glimmer of light around the curtains, Matilda inspected the room. It was of a fair size and very elegantly furnished with Regency period pieces, the curtains were old-rose watered silk with swathed pelmets and the bedspread matched them. Eaten up with curiosity, Matilda got rather gingerly out of bed. A peep from the window might give her some clue as to where she was. She crept across the carpeted floor and twitched the curtains very gently aside. It was still very early but the sky was clear and there was the promise of sun before long. She looked down on to a small garden, having high walls and paved round a small ornamental pool; there were flower beds around it and neatly trimmed grass. She studied it all slowly and craned her neck to see directly below the window, to encounter the doctor's up-turned face.

It gave her quite a shock. She got back into bed,

feeling guilty, and wondered about him. He had been in a thick sweater and slacks and there had been a dog with him, a very large and woolly German Shepherd dog, who had looked at her with the same intentness as his master.

It was a good thing that Emma woke up then, enquired anxiously how she felt and bustled away to get tea, waving aside Matilda's pleas to be told where she was and why. 'You'll be told soon enough, now you're better, love,' said Emma, pulling back curtains and folding a blanket.

She closed her eyes the better to think and then opened them at the gentle tap on the door. The doctor came to the bed and picked up her arm and took her pulse and remarked pleasantly, 'You're better.'

'That's a very large dog,' said Matilda.

'Dickens. We had just returned from our morning walk.' The blue eyes studied her. 'You are, of course, dying of curiosity.'

'Yes, oh yes, I am. How did I get here and where am I anyway, and how did Emma get here and how did you know…'

He smiled slowly. 'You are better, aren't you?' He got up from where he had been sitting on the edge of the bed and took Emma's tray from her as she came through the door. 'If we perhaps have our tea together while I answer your questions?'

He glanced at Emma, who smiled at him and said, 'I'll get dressed, doctor, if it's all the same to you.'

He poured their tea, put another pillow behind Matilda and offered her a cup. 'Emma has been a splendid source of information,' he told her, 'but I'm sure she could not know the whole, I hope that you will tell me exactly what has happened. But you have questions of your own.'

She was feeling herself better with every passing minute. 'Where am I?'

'At my house.' He added the address. 'I brought you here yesterday morning. Your things came yesterday afternoon; Emma has unpacked them.'

'But there was no need for that. It was very kind of you to look after me, but I'm quite able to go back to the nurses' home.'

'But you are not going back,' said Dr van Kempler baldly. 'You will remain here.'

She gaped at him. 'Stay here? Of course I shan't—I must get back on duty.' She frowned suddenly. 'Oh, I was sacked, wasn't I? I'd forgotten.' She finished her tea. 'Those men in the office with you. I didn't feel very well; I'm not sure what they were talking about.'

'They were offering you an apology and an explanation, Matilda. It seems that no one had realised that the Principal Nursing Officer was on the verge of a nervous breakdown and quite unfit for her task.'

'How did you know?'

He shrugged. 'I made it my business to find out. I told you that I knew someone on the hospital committee.'

'Emma—how on earth did Emma get here?'

'I fetched her and she won't be going back.'

'You fetched her? But didn't Herbert object?'

The doctor's smile came and went. 'Er, yes, he did. But of course he had no say in the matter.'

Matilda looked at him sitting there. He really was vast; she quite saw that Herbert wouldn't have stood a chance. His blustering would have gone unheeded and the sheer size of the doctor would have reduced him to reluctant agreement.

'Emma's pleased,' she said.

'I understand so.' He poured more tea and she took the cup, frowning while he watched her.

'But where will she go? And you said I wasn't going back to the hospital. Where am I going?'

'Ah, yes. Well, supposing we discuss that presently. I think that now you must have your breakfast and sleep again for a while. You may get up after lunch if you feel like it, but I must warn you that you are going to feel off colour for a few days.' He put down his cup and saucer. 'I must change and go to the hospital.'

'Which one?'

He mentioned a famous teaching hospital and she said, puzzled, 'But Uncle Thomas said you lived in Holland?'

'I do, but I frequently work over here. When you are better I'd like to hear about your uncle.'

He picked up the tray and went to the door. 'Do as Emma tells you,' he warned and he left her.

She ate her breakfast presently and, although she had no intention of doing so, went sound asleep until Emma came back with a light lunch.

'Now I'll get up—I may, you know.'

'Yes, love. Just for a jiffy while I make your bed.'

'I'll stay up for tea,' said Matilda and walked on cotton-wool legs to the chair. It was barely a dozen steps away but she was absurdly glad to sit in it. When teatime came she was only too glad to get back into her bed.

It was a quiet house and the traffic in the street was infrequent. Once or twice she heard Dickens bark and twice footsteps going past her door. She drank her tea, took the pills Emma offered and went to sleep again.

She woke to find the doctor's face looming above her. A tide of self-pity engulfed her and for no reason at all she burst into tears.

He sat down on the bed and gathered her close, waiting patiently until she had sniffed and choked herself to a standstill, offered her a handkerchief, shook up her pillows and settled her against them.

Matilda drew a few shuddering breaths, aware that although she felt ill she no longer felt depressed. She pushed a cloud of hair away from her pale, red-eyed face and said in a watery voice, 'I'm sorry. I can't think why I did that. I'm quite all right now.'

'I did warn you,' he said cheerfully, 'but of course no one ever listens to the doctor in his own house.' He took his sopping handkerchief from her grasp and got up. 'I'm going to give you something to make you sleep soundly. Emma will bring you some soup presently and settle you for the night, and I promise you that in the morning you will feel almost your old self.'

'I can get up?'

'For an hour or so, but don't get dressed. I'll see you presently.'

He came back when she had eaten her soup and been washed and tidied to settle for the night. He watched her swallow the pills he gave her, wished her goodnight and went away again. She would have liked him to stay and talk, but he was in a dinner jacket ready to go out so she had said no more than goodnight. The pills were very effective; she had no time to do more than wonder where he was going and who with before she was asleep.

The doctor had been quite right; she felt quite her usual self when she woke in the morning, although she had the sense to know that if she got up and did too much she wouldn't feel too good. Emma brought her her tea and a visitor as well, Mrs Cribbs, a small mouselike woman with a gentle voice: the doctor's housekeeper.

'Me and Cribbs are so pleased that you're better, miss. You did have a nasty turn and no mistake.'

She slipped away, leaving Emma to explain that she and her husband ran the doctor's house for him. 'Not that he's here all that much—a week here and there and sometimes only a couple of nights—but it's handy for him to have a home to go to when he's finished with his lectures and such.'

She trotted round the room, setting it to right. 'In Vienna, 'e is, for a couple of days. Then back 'ere for a week before 'e goes back to Holland.'

Matilda sat up straight. 'But Emma, we can't stay here. He said we would discuss it and now he's gone away.'

'Yes, love, I was ter tell you that 'e'll talk about it when 'e gets back and you're not ter go out for a day or two, not until this east wind's stopped blowing.'

'He did, did he? He's being very bossy. Emma, we could go to your sister at Southend.'

'The wind'll be worse there,' said Emma. 'Now you have a nice warm bath and I'll bring up your breakfast.'

Matilda dressed after breakfast and went downstairs and was met by a portly middle-aged man who introduced himself as Cribbs, begged her to sit in the living-room and offered coffee. With the coffee came Mrs Cribbs. 'Maybe you'd like to see over the house, miss? The doctor said I was to ask you, just so you will know your way around.'

So Matilda passed a pleasant hour being shown the dining-room, very elegantly furnished in the Chippendale style, the pretty living-room, all pinky-beige and chestnut-brown and flowers everywhere, and the kitchen at the back of the house, which was a good deal larger than she had expected. There was another room on the ground floor; Mrs Cribbs opened the door and allowed her to peep in—the doctor's study, not to be entered unless invited. It was furnished with a large desk and a chair roomy enough to accommodate the doctor's vast frame and its walls were lined with books. The desk was littered with papers and books and Matilda had a strong urge to tidy it.

Upstairs there were three large bedrooms, besides her own, as well as two bathrooms. The main bedroom was at the back of the house with a small balcony overlooking the garden and its own bathroom and dressing-room. It was a beautiful room, all pale pastel colours with rosewood furniture and swathed brocade pelmets above the windows. Matilda sank her feet into the soft pile of the carpet. 'It looks ready to sleep in,' she observed.

'So it is, more or less, miss. I asked the doctor, very respectful, if he was thinking of marrying and he said, "Well, no, Mrs Cribbs, I can't say that I am at the moment, but it's as well to be ready, isn't it?" I dare say he's got some young lady in mind—Dutch, maybe?'

There was a small staircase leading to the floor above. 'Our flat,' explained Mrs Cribbs proudly. 'Me and Cribbs live here all the year round, caretaking as it were, seeing that everything is ready when the doctor comes—sometimes at a few hours' notice. Me and Cribbs are very happy here; we wouldn't work for anyone else but the doctor; a right good man he is.'

Emma echoed these sentiments later when she brought Matilda's lunch to the dining-room. When Matilda protested that she could quite well eat her meals in the kitchen with everyone else she was treated to a pained silence, followed by a brief homily from her old friend on the subject of knowing her place in the world and doing exactly what the doctor ordered. 'And that was that you was to have yer meals here or in the bedroom. And quite right, too.'

Matilda agreed meekly. It seemed a bit silly to her but presumably he had a reason for it and it was obvious that Emma had no intention of doing differently. She was more tired than she realised; it didn't take much persuasion on Emma's part for her to get on to her bed and snooze until teatime. After tea there was television to watch and the papers to read and a whole shelf of books to examine. She went happily to bed and had her supper on a tray, feeling a fraud but unable to deny that she was tired out.

She did better the next day. It was still cold outside and Emma wouldn't let her go out but there was plenty to do indoors. There was a small grand piano in the drawing-room, a vast apartment on a half-landing at the back of the hall which Matilda had found rather over-powering when she had been shown it by Mrs Cribbs, but, once inside, sitting at the piano, playing a little of this and that, she began to like the room. True, it was a bit splendid for her taste, but she supposed that if one had guests it would be a splendid background for party clothes; and there was a magnificent fireplace—Adam she thought, but she wasn't quite sure. While she was playing, Cribbs came in and put a match to the logs. She protested at that but he assured her gravely that the room was a good deal more pleasant with a fire burning. 'And the fire is always lighted when the room is occupied, miss.'

'I shouldn't have come, why didn't someone tell me? I'm sorry, Cribbs.'

He looked shocked. 'The doctor said that you were to regard the house as your home, miss, and if I might say so it is a pleasure to have you with us.'

So Matilda spent the afternoon remembering odd snatches of music and enjoying every minute of it, and from time to time she got up and wandered round the room, looking at the portraits on the walls. The doctor must have had a vast number of ancestors, all rather stern, she decided. She preferred the landscapes and a group of delightful miniatures, ladies with smooth oval faces and ringlets, and one or two children's heads, too angelic to be true.

She had her tea and went back to the piano, her hands idling over the keys. It would be nice to see the doctor again, if only to thank him for his hospitality and bid him goodbye. She and Emma could go to a small hotel while she did a round of the agencies and got a job at one of the hospitals. She had some money, enough to keep them for a few weeks. Tomorrow, she promised herself, she would plan something so that when the doctor returned she would have a definite plan for her future. The thought unsettled her so she began another tour of the room, taking a second look at the paintings on its walls. One particular canvas was well worth another look: a group of a family with a stern-faced gentleman in its centre, a mid-Victorian from his dress, his hand on the back of the chair upon which his wife sat, a very pretty young woman in the lavish satins of that period, and presumably happy from the beaming smile upon her face. They were surrounded by children of various ages and a dog or two.

'You all look happy enough; I suppose Papa wasn't as stern as he looks,' observed Matilda to the empty room.

Only it wasn't empty. Rauwerd van Kempler said, with the hint of a laugh, 'My great-great-grandfather, an eminent physician of his day, a devoted husband and a doting father. Great-great-grandmother was English; so for that matter is my grandmother.'

He stood there, smiling at her. 'You're better. Have you been bored?'

'Not in the least, thank you. I—I hope you don't mind; I've been playing the piano. I didn't know that you were coming back today.'

'Oh, I come and go,' he told her airily.

'Vienna, Emma said...'

The blue eyes stared down at her. 'Very wintry there.'

For some reason she felt vexed with him. She said austerely, 'I'm glad you're back Dr van Kempler. I am quite well again.' She drew a breath and embarked on the thank you speech she had thought over. 'I'm very grateful for your hospitality, it was very kind of you. I know you were Uncle Thomas's friend—I expect any friend would do the same...'

'Possibly. I must confess to having other reasons as well as that of a remembered friendship.'

She prided herself on her common sense. She said matter-of-factly, 'Oh, I expect you know of a job for me. I must confess that I'd hate to go back to that place, though I'm sorry for the old ladies.'

'There will be changes made; they will, I hope, have a much happier life. No, I don't know of a job for you, Matilda.' He strolled over to the fireplace and kicked a log into place, then turned to face her.

'I should like us to be married, and before you say anything, perhaps you will listen to me.'

He need not have said that; she was bereft of words. He studied her astonished face for a moment. 'You don't dislike me?'

She shook her head.

'Good, I am thirty-four, Matilda, I have a good prac- tice with three partners, I travel a good deal, lecturing, examining, sitting on boards. I have a home in Hol- land and this house inherited from my grandmother. I have no financial worries, many friends and a busy life.

I have for some time considered taking a wife—perhaps now that I am older I have a wish to come home to someone at the end of the day. I think that you might be that someone. I shall not insult your intelligence by saying that I love you. I have been in love—what man hasn't at my age?—but never loved, and there is a difference. I'm not in love with you, either. I like you enormously, I admire you, I enjoy your company, I believe that you will fit into my life-style and that I can make you happy, but I'm not prepared for any romance—we can have a working relationship and, I hope, a sound friendship. Perhaps later we can live as man and wife, but only if and when we both want that.' He smiled slowly. 'I've surprised you, but you're a sensible girl; think about it and let me know some time.' He glanced at his watch. 'I have to go out. I'm free tomorrow afternoon. Shall we go for a walk and talk about it?'

Matilda said slowly, 'I really don't know...'

He said briskly, 'Of course you don't. You've not had time to think about it, have you?' He crossed the room and put his hands on her shoulders and kissed her cheek gently. 'Till tomorrow, Matilda.'

She stood without moving after he had gone. He had called her a sensible girl; she only hoped that her senses would return to her in time for her to give him his answer on the following day. A refusal politely put.

Chapter 4

Contrary to her expectations, Matilda slept well and got up the next morning already composing a graceful refusal to the doctor's astonishing offer. She added to it, altered it, scrapped the whole thing and made up a new one before the day was half over. She had it off by heart by teatime and then forgot the whole thing when he walked into the drawing-room where she was curled up by the fire half asleep.

His hello was genial as he sat down in the chair on the opposite side of the fireplace. 'A little late for a walk, but we can talk here.'

She was struggling to remember the bare bones of what she had intended to say. 'There's really nothing to talk about,' she managed.

He chose to misunderstand her. 'Oh, good, I knew you'd be sensible.'

'I'm not being sensible,' she snapped. 'I really don't wish to marry you. It's—it's a preposterous idea; it couldn't possibly work...'

He settled back more comfortably into his chair. 'No? Tell me why not?'

The arguments she had marshalled all day so carefully melted away. She mumbled crossly, 'Well, I thought of a great many reasons.'

'All of them either romantic or illogical.' He smiled suddenly and she only just stopped herself in time from smiling back. 'Oh, they are real enough, but they hardly apply, do they? I'm not offering romance and all my reasons for marrying you are logical, aren't they?' He paused. 'Matilda, I wouldn't have proposed to you if I hadn't been certain that we could live together amicably.'

She said a little wildly. 'I want to marry for love.'

'I imagine that we all do. But love isn't always a flash of lightning; it can grow slowly from friendship and respect and regard.' He smiled again very kindly. 'Tell me, Matilda, did you—do you—love Leslie Waring?'

His voice was as kind as his smile and she paused to think so that she could give him an honest answer. 'Well, no—I sort of slipped into thinking that I did, if you see what I mean. We got on well and didn't quarrel and it would have been so nice for Uncle Thomas, and Mrs Waring seemed to like me.'

'None of them, if I might say so, good reasons for marrying.'

She said with a sudden flare of anger, 'Well, you tell me what they should be.'

'We will make an exception of love; that is a bonus in a happy marriage. Liking, respect, a shared interest in similar things, a similar background, an ability to laugh together and at each other, loyalty   they all add up to a happy marriage, even without your romantic ideas about falling in love—and that, my dear Matilda, isn't the same thing as loving. One can fall in love and out again—I'm sure we've both done that—but to fall in love and to love at the same time is, for those fortunate enough to do it, the crown of life.'

She eyed him in amazement. 'My goodness, you've given it some thought, haven't you?'

'Indeed I have.' His blue eyes gleamed. 'Logical thought.' When she didn't speak, he said, 'Will you marry me, Matilda? I believe that we may have a pleasant life together, even if unromantic. You will never be bored; I'm a busy man and I shall expect your help in many ways.' He smiled. 'Consider the alternatives and think about it. I've had a difficult day; I'll take a nap while you weigh up the pros and cons.'

He closed his eyes and there was no mistaking the fact that within a couple of minutes he was snoring very gently. Matilda sat and looked at him, thoughts running in all directions like frightened mice running from a cat. She called them to order and sensibly bent her reflections into a serious vein. He had, for him, had a lot to say and there was no doubt that it had been to the point. There had been no protestations of affection, let alone love; on the other hand, she felt certain that as long as she was a good wife he would be a good husband. He had harped on the unromantic aspect and she regretted that, for she was a romantic girl, and to marry a man who regarded her as a good friend and nothing more was lowering to say the least, but he was honest about it, and, she reminded herself, it wasn't as though she were in love with him. But she liked him…

'Well?' asked the doctor without opening his eyes.

Of all the strange proposals, she thought pettishly and said coldly, 'I have a great many questions before I can even consider an answer.'

'Fire away.'

'Where would we live? What is to happen to Emma? Are you C of E? Do you have a family? Would you wish me to go on working after we are married?'

He raised a large, well-kept hand. 'Shall we deal with these first? I live in Leiden—there is a medical school there—in an old house with a quite nice garden. The town is old and charming and there is a good deal of social life. I have a wide circle of friends; they will be your friends, too. Emma, if she will, can make her home with us. I have a housekeeper who will be glad of help and the companionship of someone of her own age. Yes, I am the Dutch equivalent of C of E. My mother and father live near Hilversum, not too far away, and I have three sisters and two brothers. I'm the eldest. And, lastly, I most definitely do not wish you to continue working after we are married.'

'I haven't said…' began Matilda.

'I am merely answering your questions, Matilda,' he told her smoothly.

She brooded for a moment on the alternatives life had to offer. A job at some hospital—the best she could hope for was a Staff Nurse's post while she caught up with modern methods and new drugs. A small flat with Emma to share it, enough money to live on, but only just, and the chance that she might meet someone who would want to marry her; not a very big chance, for she was, under her calm front, a shy girl and she had got out of the way of accepting the invitations of housemen because there was always Leslie. Besides, she had to admit to being a bit strait-laced, due no doubt to living with Uncle Thomas and Leslie's easy-going attitude; he had known her for years and any glamour in the relationship had long been rubbed off.

She drew a deep breath. 'All right, I'll marry you!' she said. 'I'm not sure if it's the right thing to do. If I were really honest I'd say no and find work and make a success of it, but if I marry you I'll do my best to be a good wife, only I do think you're getting the worst of the bargain.'

'Allow me to be the best judge of that, Matilda. Now, are we to settle on some plans for our marriage? Supposing we marry by special licence? Somewhere quiet—I'll make the arrangements if you agree to that. We can leave for Holland after the wedding. Have you any family you would like to have with you?'

She shook her head. 'No, Uncle Thomas was all I had.'

'Then shall we ask the rector to give you away? He was a friend of your uncle's, wasn't he?' He went on easily, 'I expect you want to buy clothes, and then it might be a good idea if you and Emma spent a few days with her sister at Southend. I'll be going to Manchester tomorrow for several days and if you feel up to it you could do your shopping. When I get back I'll drive you both down to Southend—the sea air will do you good.'

'For how long?' She felt that she was being rushed along towards a future she had hardly had time to contemplate.

'Oh, until a couple of days before the wedding. I shall be in Holland until then. My mother and father will want to come over to meet you; I think you will like them.'

He saw her rather blank look and added kindly, 'I'm rushing you along, aren't I? But there is really no point in waiting, is there? Do you suppose Emma will agree to come to Holland?'

'I think so; she hasn't anywhere to go here. My cousin only kept her because he was afraid of what people might say—she worked for Uncle Thomas for years and I don't think she ever expected to leave him.'

'Well, you talk to her, my dear. If she did dislike the idea we could find her a small flat near her sister and pension her off, but I think she'll want to stay with you.'

He got up and strolled across to the drinks set out on the sofa table. 'Will you have a sherry or do you prefer something else?'

He poured her drink and gave it to her. 'Have you enough money to buy all you need?' He sounded so matter-of-fact that she answered without hesitation, 'I think so, thank you. Uncle left me a little money— enough to get some clothes and something for Emma.'

She added reflectively, 'It won't be a dressy affair, will it, our wedding?'

'Er, no, and you can get anything else you want when we get to Holland.'

She supposed that if they had been an ordinary couple, marrying for love and perfectly at ease with each other, they could have discussed little problems concerning money and what they would live on, but beyond the vague notion that the doctor appeared to be in comfortable circumstances she hadn't a clue as to his life and didn't like to ask.

He watched her, aware of her thoughts and smiling a little. 'I shouldn't worry, Tilly,' he said quietly, 'we shall have plenty of time to discuss things later on—leave everything to me.'

Something she was only too glad to do.

She woke up the next morning to find Emma there with her early morning tea and the doctor leaning over the foot of the bed, watching her. His 'good morning' was genial and brisk. 'I'm just off,' he told her. 'I've fixed things with Emma's sister—Emma will tell you presently. Cribbs will drive you down in a couple of days; I won't be back. Take a taxi to the shops and back again and please don't overdo things.'

Matilda peered at him through her wealth of hair. 'Shan't I see you before you go to Holland?'

'It rather depends.' He didn't say on what. 'I'll keep in touch.'

He came round the bed and bent and kissed her cheek and was gone, leaving her indignant. 'Well, I never did!'

she said explosively to Emma. 'Arranging everything like that without saying a word. I've a good mind to...'

'Now, now, Miss Tilly,' said Emma placidly. 'No need to get worked up. You be glad that you're marrying a man who sees to everything for yer comfort. Proper gent, 'e is.' She trotted to the door. 'You drink your tea and after breakfast we'll do that shopping. Termorrer, too; I must have a new 'at.'

Matilda hopped out of bed and looked out of the window. The garden, rather bleak in the wintry morning, was empty. 'Where's Dickens?' she asked Emma's retreating back.

'Gorn with his master—very devoted 'e is. Always lived 'ere with Mr Cribbs but the doctor says 'e's to go with us when we go to Holland. 'E says 'e won't be coming over quite so often when 'e's married.'

Matilda drank her tea and wondered why, but being a practical girl she didn't waste too much time about that but found paper and pencil and made a list of clothes. Most of her wardrobe was suitable for a GP's wife—and she supposed that he was a GP, with lecturing on the side, as it were—but she would have to have something to be married in: shoes, a couple of pretty dresses, more undies. She pruned the list to fit the contents of her balance at the bank, had a bath and dressed and, accompanied by Emma, got into the taxi Cribbs had waiting for them. Fenwick's would do, she had decided; pretty clothes, but not too wildly expensive.

It didn't take all that time to find what she wanted: palest pink crêpe and to go over it a darker, dimmer pink tweed coat. 'I need a hat,' she told the nice girl serving her. 'It's a wedding outfit,' and blushed when the girl's eyes slid to her left hand, looking for the ring which wasn't there.

The three of them went along to the hat department and found a velvet trifle which matched perfectly. 'You will look nice,' enthused the assistant. 'Your husband is going to like that.'

Matilda wondered if he would; he might not even notice what she was wearing. She put her gloves on over her ringless hand and paid the bill.

Emma, a country woman born and bred, didn't fancy any of the big stores. She settled for a majestic hat in plum-coloured felt which they found in a small shop off Oxford Street and, since they were both thirsty and a little tired, they had coffee before Matilda went in search of undies. It was almost lunchtime by then. She hailed a taxi and they went back to the doctor's house very pleased with themselves, already making plans to go again the next day.

She was getting into bed when the telephone on the bedside table rang. 'In bed?' asked the doctor.

'I was just getting in. We've had a lovely day shopping.'

'My name's Rauwerd. Have you finished your buying?'

'Not quite; we're going tomorrow morning.' She hesitated. 'Thank you for arranging everything, it was kind of you. Have you had a busy day?'

'Yes. You will be gone by the time I get back, but I'll find the time to come and see you in Southend before I go over to Holland. Sleep well, Tilly.' He rang off.

She found two pretty dresses the next day and, since there was still some money left, she bought a couple of sweaters and a silk blouse as well as a handbag and gloves for Emma. When they got back there was the packing to do. They wouldn't need much; she repacked almost all her things into her biggest suitcase and put it in the wardrobe, hung her wedding finery there as well, and declared herself ready to leave in the morning. Although she told herself that it didn't matter at all, she was decidedly disappointed when Rauwerd didn't telephone her.

They travelled to Southend in a Rover, a car, Cribbs told her, which was kept in London in case the doctor didn't drive himself over from Holland and which he and Mrs Cribbs were free to use when they wished. He was a chatty man, but Matilda couldn't get him to talk about his employer and after one or two discreet questions she gave up. She was a fool, she told herself worriedly, plunging head-first into matrimony. Indeed, by the time they had reached the end of their journey she was in a state of near panic. But that quickly subsided once she was in the company of Mrs Spencer and Emma; their matter-of-fact acceptance of the situation made it seem perfectly normal so that she ate her lunch, went for a brisk walk along the promenade before tea and went to bed directly after supper to sleep soundlessly.

The following evening the doctor telephoned. His calm voice dispersed any remnants of her doubts. He was going over to Holland on the following day, he told her, and he would be down in the morning to see her.

He hadn't said exactly when; Matilda was up be-
times, ate a hasty breakfast and then mooned around,
ignoring Emma's sensible observation that it was all
of an hour's drive from London and it was still only
nine o'clock.

Half an hour later he arrived, accepted the coffee
Mrs Spencer offered him, passed the time of day with
Emma and then suggested a walk with Matilda. 'I must
leave at midday,' he said casually. 'I've still one or two
things to see to.'

So Matilda got her coat and a scarf to tie round her
head and they started off into the teeth of a strong cold
wind. Presently he took her arm.

'I've settled everything for our wedding,' he told her.
'I shall be back in ten days' time and we shall marry
two days later. I'll come for you and Emma—I'll let
you know what time. Are you quite happy here, Tilly?'

'Oh, yes, thank you. Aren't you coming back before—we—we get married?'

'Probably I shall have to, but don't count on seeing me.' He stopped and turned her round so that the
wind was at her back. 'I have something for you.' He
put a hand into his pocket and took out a small box and
opened it: a ring, a sapphire surrounded with diamonds
set in gold. 'I hope it fits. It can be changed.'

It fitted. A good omen? Matilda took heart from that.
She thanked him nicely but without gush, a little sad
that they hadn't chosen it together.

'I should have liked to have had you with me,' said
Rauwerd, unerringly reading her thoughts, 'but I tried
to choose something we would both like.'

'It's beautiful, and I'm sure I'd have chosen it if we'd been together.'

He turned her round and they began to walk into the wind again. It wasn't possible to talk much; they turned back presently, blown along by the gale, and outside Mrs Spencer's house he flung a friendly arm around her. 'You look delightful.' And indeed she did, her eyes sparkling, her cheeks pink from their walk, and her hair whipped from its pins. He bent and kissed her cheek, the kiss of an old friend, nothing more. 'I'll not come in, I'm late already.' He opened the door and pushed her gently inside. '*Tot ziens,* Tilly.'

He had gone before she could answer.

She would ask him the next time they met what *Tot ziens* meant. He had been casual about seeing her again, but she had the rest of their life together to ask him questions.

A week went by, Matilda, fully recovered from the 'flu, looked prettier than ever. She missed Uncle Thomas, but that was a sorrow she kept to herself, and already in those few weeks she had taught herself not to think about her former home. The future mattered, and she intended to make a success of it. The days went by uneventfully, a kind of half-way house between her past and her future. She read and knitted and walked miles and gossiped gently with Emma and her sister and thought about Rauwerd.

There were four days left before the wedding when he came again, and then only briefly. He had returned to fetch Dickens back to Holland, he told her, but he would be back in two days' time and would drive down to take her back to his house. He looked tired; all the same he walked her along the esplanade in the spring sunshine, not saying much, listening to her quiet talk, and when he went after an hour or so he said, 'You're a restful girl, Tilly—did anyone ever tell you that?'

He gave her a casual kiss and got into his car and drove off. It seemed to her that, pleasant though their relationship was, it was unlikely to be more than that, but she must never forget that she had been chosen by him to be his wife; not for the usual reasons, it was true, but it was satisfying to be wanted.

She and Emma were ready when he came to fetch them two days later. It was still early and the road was fairly empty so that the Rolls ate up the miles. They were almost at their journey's end when Rauwerd observed casually that his mother and father were at his home, a remark which had the effect of throwing her into a panic.

All to no purpose, as it turned out. At the end of the day, lying in her comfortable bed in the elegant room she had previously slept in, she mulled over the last few hours. Rauwerd's parents hadn't been at all what she had expected. They had been waiting in his drawing-room when they arrived, his father older than she had imagined, upright and as tall as his son, and his mother—she was tall, too; a fine figure of a woman, her uncle would have said—still good-looking in a severe way, although she had been kindness itself to Matilda. Thinking about it, Matilda decided that they liked her, just as she liked them; another good omen, she told herself.

They hadn't bothered her with a lot of questions,

either, nor expressed the least surprise at their son's sudden decision to marry. Of course, he might have told them everything that was to be told, but somehow she doubted that. Tomorrow the best man and his wife would be arriving to lunch: a lifelong friend and his English wife. Matilda curled up in her bed and wondered what she should wear and she was still pleasantly occupied with this when she fell asleep.

Doubts as to whether the best man and his wife would like her rather clouded her morning, to be instantly dispelled when they arrived. Sybren Werdmer ter Sane was a large man, as large as the bridegroom. He engulfed Matilda's hand in his and twinkled down at her in a reassuring manner which put her at her ease, and as for his wife Rose—she was small and unassuming with magnificent brown eyes and a happy face. She was beautifully dressed, but then Sybren was an eminent surgeon in Amsterdam; she was also quite plainly the most important thing in her husband's life. Matilda suppressed a pang of envy as she led her upstairs to their room to tidy herself.

'Such fun,' said Rose. 'Rauwerd told us all about you, of course. He said you were very pretty and of course, you are. We shall be able to see each other—that's if you'd like to?' she added shyly.

'Oh, please. I don't know a thing about Holland or about Rauwerd's work. It'll be a bit strange...'

'It's very like England and all the people you will meet speak English. Besides, Rauwerd will see that you have a good Dutch teacher.' Rose was sitting at her dressing-table, piling her mousy hair into a neat top-

knot. 'Sybren and Rauwerd were at Leiden together—
he is little Sybren's godfather.'

'You've got a baby? How lovely! How old is he?'

'Six months and a bit. He's with his Granny and
Grandpa and Nanny while we're here. He's gorgeous.'
Rose patted the last strands into place and got up.
'Aren't you excited? We had a quiet wedding, too, but
there was a huge party afterwards. Where are you going
for your honeymoon?'

'Well, we have to go straight back to Leiden. I expect we'll go somewhere when Rauwerd's not so busy.'
She gave Rose a bright smile. 'Let's go down if you're
ready.'

Later that night, Rose, sitting up in bed watching
her husband emptying his pockets on to the dressing-
chest, said thoughtfully, 'They don't seem very in love,
darling; more like old friends who haven't seen each
other for a long time. Do you think they will be happy?'

Her husband cast her a loving look. 'Yes, darling,
I do. Perhaps not for a while, but neither of them are
young and silly; they'll work at it and make a success
of it. She is a nice girl and Rauwerd is one of the best.'

'Then why are they getting married?'

'I can think of a dozen reasons, all good.'

'When I know Matilda better, I shall ask her,' said
Rose.

The sun shone in the morning, Matilda, getting
into her wedding finery, peered out of the window and
watched Rauwerd and Sybren strolling round the garden. From the back they looked rather alike in their

sober grey suits and with their hair fair and silvery. Someone called them from the house and Matilda withdrew her head smartly, but not before Rauwerd had seen her and given her a casual wave.

They were to be married at a small church a bare five minutes' drive away. Matilda, waiting nervously in the drawing-room with the rector after everyone else had gone, swallowed down panic behind a calm face. There had been no time for that until now; when she had gone downstairs to meet the others there had been a good deal of cheerful talk and her future mother-in-law had taken a velvet case from her handbag and begged her to open it.

'All the wives have it in turn, and now it's for you, Matilda, my dear,' she had said kindly. 'Will you wear it?'

A brooch, rose diamonds, any number of them in an old-fashioned setting of gold. It sparkled and shone and Mevrouw van Kempler said gently, 'Let me put it on for you, dear, and wish you all the happiness in the world.'

Rose had given her a present, too, to be opened later, she whispered, and so had the rector. Emma's present was packed: a dozen of the finest lawn hankies, housed in a quilted sachet which had been her sister's gift. There had been nothing from the Warings or her aunt and Herbert. Rauwerd had put the notice of their marriage in the *Telegraph* and she had hoped that they might have sent a card. It was a little frightening not to have family or friends; perhaps, she thought hopefully, she would find both in Holland.

She followed the rector out to the car and, when they

arrived at the church, walked steadily beside him up the aisle to where Rauwerd was waiting.

She walked just as steadily down the aisle, her arm tucked into Rauwerd's, twenty minutes later. The plain gold ring on her finger proclaimed her to be married but she didn't feel any different. Indeed, she was suddenly very scared. Perhaps Rauwerd guessed what she felt, for he gave her hand a gentle reassuring squeeze and, when she looked at him, smiled at her with an equally gentle smile, so kind that she felt tears pricking her eyes. She wasn't scared any more; everything would be all right. She liked him now, even if she hadn't when they had first met, and she respected him, and that was surely more important between husband and wife? She smiled back at him and got into the Rolls beside him and was driven back to her new home.

There was a luncheon party, of course. Mrs Cribbs had excelled herself with lobster patties, caviar, tiny sausages on sticks, chicken vol-au-vents and smoked trout, followed by *crêpes de volaille florentine,* a variety of salads and *asperges polonaise,* and finally the wedding cake, cut with due ceremony and washed down with champagne. Presently it was time for Matilda to change into a jersey dress to wear under the new tweed coat and to pack the last of her things. She was taking a final critical look at herself when there was a tap on the door.

'Ready?' asked Rauwerd. 'You do look nice, Tilly. They are all waiting to say goodbye.'

She collected her gloves and handbag and went

downstairs with him, feeling shy, to be instantly engulfed in a round of embracing and kissing.

'We shall see you very soon, my dear,' Rauwerd's mother told her. 'We travel back tomorrow.' His father hugged her close and kissed her cheek. 'I couldn't have chosen a lovelier bride myself,' he told her gallantly.

Rose and Sybren were staying for a few days and going to fly back. 'I'll give you a ring as soon as we get home,' promised Rose and stood back to allow Emma to say goodbye. Not for long, for she was to travel to Holland with Rose and Sybren.

'Just you be 'appy, the pair of yer,' whispered Emma.

They drove to Dover and went by hovercraft over to Calais. It was all new to Matilda. The Rolls ate up the two hundred-odd miles they had to go, along the coast to Bruges, skirting Antwerp, and then on to Breda, stopping for tea before they reached Dordrecht. Here Rauwerd left the motorways, taking a route which took them to Schoonhoven, Gouda, and then, avoiding Alpen aan de Rijn, Boskoop and finally Leiden.

Rauwerd had bypassed the towns and cities, so that Matilda had her first real glimpse of an old Dutch town as he slowed to go into its centre.

She had been careful not to chatter, but now she exclaimed, 'Oh, look—all those old houses and the gables, and what is that little castle built up on that mound?'

'That is the Burcht—eleventh century, with a fort overlooking the old and new Rhine. We're turning off here, before we reach it. This is the Rapenburg Canal; the university and the museums and laboratories are here.' After a moment he added, 'And this is where our home is.'

She could have hugged him for that 'our'.

He turned the Rolls into a narrow street lined with tall old houses, three and four storeys high, their massive front doors reached by double stone steps guarded by wrought iron palings. He stopped at the first house, its high stone wall abutting on to Rapenburg, its elegant front facing the tree-lined street.

Rauwerd got out and came round the bonnet to open Matilda's door. He took her hand and went with her up the steps to where a stout elderly man was waiting at the open door. Rauwerd said something to him in Dutch and added, 'Matilda, this is Jan. He has been in the family for a very long time and looks after me; he will be only too delighted to look after you as well. His wife does the housekeeping; her name is Bep.'

Jan bent his portly frame in a bow. 'Welcome, Mevrouw—we are delighted.'

His English was heavily accented but it cheered her enormously. She shook hands and, urged by Rauwerd, went into the house. The hall was lofty and narrow, the ceiling hung with pendant bosses, the walls panelled in some dark silk and hung with oil paintings. There was a marble-topped console table against one wall and a long case clock with floral marquetry on the opposite wall; the floor was black and white tiles. Exactly like an old Dutch interior on a museum wall, thought Matilda, as she allowed herself to be led forward to where Bep was waiting, small and stout as her husband and with just as warm a welcome. Rauwerd said something to her and she smiled and slipped through a door at the back of the hall while Jan opened the double doors facing the clock. The room was long and wide and as lofty as the hall. The windows overlooking the street were draped in a rich plum-coloured velvet with elaborate pelmets, a colour repeated in the brocade of the chairs and sofas each side of the hearth. A lovely room, with a magnificent plaster ceiling, the walls lined with glass-fronted display cabinets.

Rauwerd, standing beside her, watched her face as she turned to him, to be interrupted by the re-opening of the door and the entry of Dickens. He was a well-behaved dog but his greeting was none the less ebullient. By the time they had made much of him, Bep was back, waiting to take Matilda to her room. But before she went Rauwerd caught her by the hand.

'Welcome to our home, Tilly,' he said and bent and kissed her cheek.

She stared up at his quiet face. 'It is a very beautiful one,' she told him seriously. 'We'll be happy here.'

There was a faintly anxious question in her voice and he said at once, 'Of course we shall.' He smiled reassuringly. 'Don't be too long; Bep has a meal ready for us.'

Chapter 5

The staircase was at right angles to the hall, its oak treads curving round to the narrow gallery above. The gallery had several doors leading from it and a corridor leading to the back of the house, which hadn't looked large from the outside; but now that she was inside, Matilda came to the conclusion that she had been mistaken about that. The doors were mahogany crowned by carved wreaths of fruit and flowers. Bep opened one of them and ushered Matilda into a large room at the front of the house.

The furniture was of yew, the bedhead beautifully decorated with marquetry to match the sofa-table between the tall windows, and the tallboy against one of its walls. There was a thick carpet underfoot and the long curtains of old-rose matched the bedspread. A magnificent room, with its enamelled wall sconces, the gilded triple mirror on the sofa-table and the two small easy chairs on either side of a lamp-table. Just right for a midnight gossip, thought Matilda, and stifled a giggle at the very idea. The giggle had been nervous; she called upon her common sense and followed Bep across the room to the door in the far wall. A bathroom, fitted with every conceivable luxury, and leading to another room. This would be Rauwerd's she guessed: a little austere, its windows at the side of the house overlooking the Rapenburg Canal. There was a door in that room, too; she opened it and peeped out. The gallery led to a narrow passage with more doors; it would take her a month of Sundays to find her way around. She went back to her bedroom and, when Bep left her, did her face and hair and presently went downstairs.

Rauwerd was sitting on the bottom stair, reading a newspaper. He got up as she reached him and smiled at her. 'Over here,' he said. 'It's a funny old house but you'll soon find your way around.'

The dining-room was on the opposite side of the hall, with windows overlooking the street as well as the Rapenburg. It wasn't as large as the drawing-room and was furnished in the rather heavy Beidermeier style. But somehow it suited the room, with its patterned crimson wallpaper and matching curtains. The table was oval and the cloth upon it was starched linen, set with heavy silver and sparkling glass. There was a beautiful old Delft bowl full of hyacinths at its centre and crystal wall sconces shed light on it.

'You have a very beautiful home here,' said Matilda, doing her best not to sound overawed.

'I'm glad you like it, Tilly. It's very old, as you can see, and I'm told the very devil to keep clean, but I love it. If you are not too tired, we'll go on a tour of inspection presently.'

Their dinner was delicious, although, thinking about it later, Matilda wasn't at all sure what they ate. Certainly they had drunk champagne, so that by the time they started on their tour of the house, she was feeling decidedly cock-a-hoop.

They wandered slowly from room to room. There was a small sitting-room behind the drawing-room, opening on to a veranda leading to the garden, which was long and narrow and walled with rose-coloured bricks. Back in the house, she was allowed to peep into the study before going upstairs.

'Bep will show you the kitchen,' explained Rauwerd. 'She and Jan will be having their supper.' He paused on the gallery. 'You've seen your own room, of course, and the bathroom. My room's beyond that. There are two more rooms on that side, with a bathroom and two rooms opposite.'

He led her round, waiting patiently while she paused before a picture or admired the furniture, and then climbed another staircase tucked away at the end of a short passage. 'Bep and Jan have their flat there.'

There was a door at the head of the staircase and he opened it to reveal a short passage with a door on either side. 'They're here.' He waved an arm. 'Emma shall have the room on this side.' He opened the door and showed her a large room, nicely furnished. 'There's a bathroom through there and I expect you and Bep can contrive to make everything comfortable for her.'

'She'll love it,' declared Matilda. They were in the back passage. 'What's that?'

A narrow steep staircase at the end. 'The attics— two of them. We loved them when we were children.' He added abruptly, 'If you've seen all you want to, shall we go down again? Is there anything you want before you go to bed?'

She felt a pang of disappointment; she would have liked to have sat down quietly somewhere and talked. She said composedly, 'Nothing, thank you. It's been a long day, hasn't it?'

She skipped down in front of him and when they reached the gallery opened her door. She gave him a bright smile and asked cheerfully, 'What time is breakfast?'

'Half-past seven, but you can have it when you like.'

She kept the smile there. 'I'm used to getting up early. Goodnight, Rauwerd.'

Not a very good start, she reflected as she got to bed, but perhaps they were both feeling awkward. Not that she could imagine Rauwerd feeling awkward for any reason at all. Perhaps he was regretting their marriage already. She dismissed the idea as silly. She was tired; it had indeed been a long day—her wedding day.

In the morning everything was all right. Somehow, sitting opposite him, eating breakfast together, it seemed as though they had been doing just that for years; not talking much but content with each other's company. Indeed, from Rauwerd's manner, they might have been married a decade at least.

She debated within herself as to whether that was a good thing or not. It would certainly make for a placid, undemanding relationship; on the other hand it would be nice to stir up a little interest. Nothing much, just enough for him to look at her twice.

She was roused from her thoughts by Rauwerd's pleasant voice. 'You are very far away, Tilly...' There was a faint question there and hastily she assured him that she had merely been wool gathering.

'There is such a lot to think about—it's rather like a dream.'

'Let us hope that the reality will be as nice. I have to go to the hospital this morning and I have some patients to see this afternoon, I won't be home for lunch. Will you be happy here? Bep's longing to take you all over the house again and I dare say you want to unpack. I should be home by four o'clock or thereabouts and perhaps we can discuss several matters.'

'What matters?'

'Oh, lessons—for you. The quicker you learn to speak Dutch the better. You can drive? Good, then you must have a car. Now that I have a wife we can entertain from time to time, and there are various functions at the hospital and medical school you will attend with me, so you'll need clothes.'

He got up and paused by her chair. 'It's all strange for you, isn't it? But you're sensible and you will soon have friends.'

'And you,' said Matilda rather tartly.

'Yes, yes, of course. I have no doubt that we shall settle down very well together.'

He laid a hand on her shoulder for a moment. 'I must be off.'

She sat for some minutes after he had gone, frowning, considering what he had said. Perhaps it would be best to wait until he came home; it would be nice to know something more about their social life. In the meantime she would try and learn something of her wifely duties.

Bep was delighted to show her the contents of the linen cupboards, the china pantry and the baize-lined drawers containing the table silver. The morning passed in a flash and after lunch Matilda toured the garden with Dickens. It wasn't large, but it had been laid out with imagination and she spent an hour poring over labels and poking her nose around the beds. She went indoors presently and sat by the fire with the dog beside her while she tried to make out the headlines of the newspapers. She was engrossed in this when Rauwerd got home.

He paused in the doorway, for she made a charming picture curled up in an armchair by the hearth with Dickens pressed close to her, and with her pretty nose buried in the paper. Dickens rushed to meet him and she folded the paper neatly and got up. 'I'll ask Bep for tea,' she said and smiled a little shyly.

'I saw Jan as I came in; he's bringing it now. Have you been bored?'

He sat down opposite her and Dickens lay at his feet.

'Bored? Heavens, no. Bep showed me everything— you know, the linen and the silver and the kitchen. And after lunch Dickens and I went into the garden and I've been trying to read the newspaper ever since.'

'I'm very sorry I wasn't free to spend the day with you. My partners and their wives have invited us to dinner—they want to celebrate our wedding—and I accepted for us both. In two days' time. I expect you may like to get a new dress for the occasion? Which reminds me—I've opened an account for you at my bank and paid in your quarter's allowance. Let me know if you run out of money.'

Jan came in with the tea and he sat silent while she poured it out but presently she said, 'Thank you, Rauwerd. Yes, I'll need a dress, I think. Are they very smart, your partners' wives?'

'Nicely dressed,' he observed. 'They are easy to get on with. Jacob Thonus and Beatrix — he's the senior of the three—they have three children. Then there is Pieter van Storr and Marie—they have a boy and a girl, then Gus and Gerda Swijstra—he joined us two years ago. The dinner is to be held at Jacob's house in Leiden and they are all looking forward to meeting you. But don't worry about not speaking Dutch, they all speak English.'

He passed his cup for more tea. 'If you would like it, I will arrange for you to start Dutch lessons with a retired Professor of English; he's elderly but a splendid teacher. He lives on the other side of the canal and perhaps you would like to go to his house. He's rather crippled with arthritis and he doesn't get around much.'

'I'd like that. Will it take me long to learn Dutch?'

He reassured her. 'No, you're an intelligent girl and besides you will have the day-to-day running of the household and the shopping, which will be excellent practice for you.' He put his cup down and got to his feet. 'I must do some work and take Dickens for his walk. I'll see you at dinner, my dear.'

He strolled to the door. 'By the way, I've ordered a car for you.'

She should have been delighted; instead she felt forlorn. A walk with Dickens would have been very pleasant, and they could have talked. But he didn't seem to want her company, although he was kind and considerate and generous. Perhaps it would be better once he had got used to having a wife.

She went shopping for a dress the next day. There were some delightful boutiques in Leiden and she spent some time searching for what she wanted. She found it finally: amber crêpe, finely pleated and deceptively simple. It took almost all the money she had but it would be, she decided, just right.

Rauwerd came home to lunch, and they talked about nothing much until he asked, 'Did you go shopping?'

'Yes. I found a dress, too. There are some nice shops...'

'Let me know if you run out of money.'

'Well, I haven't used any of yours yet. I had a little of my own.'

He said evenly, 'You are my wife, Matilda. I expect you to use the allowance I have arranged for you.' He glanced at the clock. 'I must go. Private patients until five o'clock. I've sent Emma her ticket—she will be coming next week. We'll meet her, shall we?'

He laid a large hand on her shoulder and went to the door. 'I'll not be back until some time after six o'clock.'

Matilda dreaded the dinner party. She was dressed far too early; Rauwerd was just arriving when she went downstairs. If she had but known, she had never looked lovelier; the rich colour of the dress suited her and apprehension had lent colour to her cheeks and a sparkle to her eyes. Rauwerd, pausing in the doorway, took a long look at her. 'Charming,' he said softly. 'I'll be fifteen minutes.'

He came down presently, wearing another of his sober, beautifully cut suits and helped her into her coat and then put his hand in a pocket.

'I almost forgot. You must forgive me, my dear.' He fastened a choker of pearls around her neck. 'A belated wedding gift.'

She put up a hand to feel their creamy smoothness. 'Thank you, Rauwerd.'

And was quite nonplussed when he added, 'They've been in the family for a very long time.'

Her dread had been unnecessary; Jacob Thenus and his wife were ready to welcome her with open arms. Jacob was thickset, with a round face, bright eyes and an endearing smile, and Beatrix was a small fairylike creature, who kissed Matilda with warmth. 'Isn't it nice,' she observed, 'now we're all married? Come and meet the others.'

Pieter van Storr and Marie were a little older, tall and strongly built and just as warm in their greeting, and Gus and Gerda Swijstra were a young and lively couple whom she liked at once.

Jacob lived in Leiden, too, in an old house on the outskirts of the town, and he and Beatrix had gone to a good

deal of trouble to make a success of their dinner party.
And it was a success. Matilda, watching Rauwerd, saw
that he was on excellent terms with his partners, an observation borne out by Gerda as they chatted over drinks.

'He is nice, your Rauwerd,' she said. 'He is the boss,
but we're all friends. We are so happy that he is married, now we shall no longer have to find pretty girls
for him when there is a party. He has found his own for
himself.' She beamed at Matilda. 'You find it all a little strange, I expect, but not for long. Leiden is a most
friendly part and there is much to do.'

Someone had gone to a lot of trouble over dinner:
lobster soup, morsels of fish in a delicious sauce, champagne sorbets and beef tournedos, followed by a magnificent dessert which, Beatrix explained, had been
made especially in honour of the newly married pair.
There was champagne, too, and speeches and a great
deal of laughing and cheerful talk. Matilda went to bed
that night feeling that she had made some friends, and
the thought was comforting.

What was even more comforting was Rauwerd's suggestion that, since he could spare an hour or so on the
following morning, they might go to den Haag and do
some shopping. 'For you will get asked out to coffee
and tea,' he told her, 'as well as dinner parties to which
we shall be invited.'

Before they set out the next day he gave her a cheque
book. 'And if you find yourself short of money just ask
to have whatever it is charged to me,' he told her casually.

'Are you very rich?' asked Matilda.

'Well, yes.' He smiled down at her. 'But let us go and make me a little poorer, shall we?'

She had a heavenly time. Rauwerd took her to Lange Voorhout and Noordeinde and waited with patience while she shopped. The sum he had mentioned as her quarterly allowance had left her open-mouthed, but the desire to spend was irresistible. She wasn't a foolish spender but she had the sense to know that she was quite inadequately dressed as the wife of an eminent and wealthy doctor. She didn't dither; she knew what she needed and bought it while Rauwerd sat quietly in a number of boutiques and nodded his approval. When at length she professed herself satisfied he bore her off to tea and rich cream cakes at a teashop in Lange Voorhout and, as they left, observed regretfully that he would be out that evening.

'You won't mind dining alone?' he asked. 'I shall be very late in.'

She assured him that she didn't mind at all and wondered silently what could possibly occupy him at the hospital so late in the day. Although they had been on excellent terms all the day she couldn't bring herself to ask.

Back at the house he unloaded all her parcels and band boxes. 'I'll see you at breakfast,' he observed casually. 'Goodnight, Tilly.'

'A lovely day,' she told herself, going up to her room, stifling loneliness; and to pass the time before dinner, she tried on all her new clothes.

She went to bed soon after dinner, for the house seemed very silent. Dickens had gone with Rauwerd, and Jan and Bep, after making sure that she lacked for nothing, had retired to the kitchen to their own supper. She had a bath, lying in the hot water, reading until the water cooled, and at last getting into bed, to lie awake until she heard Rauwerd's quiet footfall just before midnight.

At breakfast she asked, 'Were you very busy at the hospital last night?'

He gave her a cool stare. 'I wasn't at the hospital, Matilda. Would you like to visit my parents this weekend? We could go over on Sunday morning for coffee. I have to go out after lunch so we had better have it here. I'm free on Saturday; if you care to we'll drive around so that you can see something of Holland.'

She thanked him nicely and wondered where he was going on Sunday afternoon. She was behaving like a suspicious wife, she reflected.

She was too sensible to waste time on idle conjecture. She found plenty to occupy her during the following day and on Saturday morning, dressed in one of the new outfits—a pleasing speckled tweed suit—went down to breakfast anticipating a very pleasant day.

So it was. Rauwerd drove her north to the Frisian Lakes, gave her coffee in Sneek, allowed her half an hour in which to glimpse the little town, then went on to Leeuwarden and north to the coast of Groningen. Here they lunched off enormous pancakes at Nenkemaborg Castle, after exploring its interior. They returned along country roads, narrow and often built in brick, but affording Matilda a good look at rural Holland. They stopped for tea at a small wayside café and then drove home through an early evening grown suddenly gloomy.

The weather might be depressing but Matilda hadn't felt so happy for a long time. Rauwerd, who had seemed so remote, revealed himself to be an amusing companion, easy to talk to and willing to answer her endless questions. She got out of the car with regret; the day had gone too quickly and now she supposed Rauwerd would go to his study…

He joined her in the hall as Jan shut the street door. 'You've had a dull time for a bride, Matilda. Shall we go out to dinner and dance afterwards?'

She beamed her delight. 'Oh, Rauwerd, how lovely. I'd like that.' She frowned. 'But I ordered dinner…'

He glanced at his watch. 'I doubt if Bep has started on it yet.' He spoke to Jan who smiled and nodded and went away in the direction of the kitchen. 'Wear that pink dress you bought the other day.'

He took her to den Haag, to the Saur Restaurant, where they dined off lobster thermidor and drank champagne, and later he drove to Scheveningen and they danced. He danced well with casual perfection, saying little, and Matilda was content that he did. The evening was proving a delight and she didn't want it to end; indeed, it was the small hours before they returned home.

'A lovely evening, Rauwerd,' she told him as they went indoors. 'Thank you…' She would have said more but his coolly polite, 'I'm glad you enjoyed it, Matilda,' took the words from her. She wished him a quiet goodnight and went to bed, vaguely unhappy, and not quite sure why.

He was his usual calm and friendly self at breakfast and during the drive to Hilversum. The elder van Kemplers lived in a square house with a steep roof, painted white and with green shutters to its windows. It stood in a large garden beautifully landscaped, a mile or so outside one of the many villages around the town.

'Have your family always lived here?' asked Matilda.

'Yes. A van Kempler built it early in the eighteenth century, and its been added to and modernised from time to time. You like it?'

'It looks charming.' She got out of the car feeling nervous. His family had been kind to her on their wedding day but they might have had second thoughts since then.

They hadn't. She was welcomed warmly, swept into a vast drawing-room and plied with coffee and small crisp biscuits while Mevrouw van Kempler chatted about nothing much. But presently she began to talk about the family: Rauwerd, the eldest...

'Six children,' she observed contentedly. 'The other boys are away—they'll be home shortly; both married, as are his sisters. Rauwerd has taken longer than the others to find himself a bride.' She beamed at Matilda and patted her hand. 'And such a dear girl, too. His father and I are so pleased, my dear. He works so hard, he needs a wife and children to slow him down a little.'

Matilda murmured and to her own annoyance blushed, something which Mevrouw van Kempler noted with pleasure.

It was too chilly a day to go into the garden; Matilda was taken on a tour of the vast conservatory at the back of the house instead, walking with her father-in-law, able, to her relief, to carry on quite a sensible conversation about the variety of plants growing there. She liked the elderly man, so like his eldest son, yet so much easier to talk to.

Before they left, Rauwerd, sitting with his mother, called across to her, 'My dear, we would like Mother and Father to come to dinner one evening, wouldn't we? I'm free on Thursday after lunch, shall it be then?'

His manner towards her made her feel very married. She agreed smilingly and hoped that his parents wouldn't guess at the real state of affairs, for she liked them too much to hurt them.

They went back home for lunch and soon afterwards Rauwerd left home saying that he hoped to be back for dinner but he would ring her if he found it impossible.

She almost bit her tongue off in her efforts not to ask him where he was going. She said serenely, 'Very well, Rauwerd,' and returned his intent look with a smile, aware that he was expecting her to question him.

Dickens didn't go with him. Matilda spent the evening watching a television programme she couldn't understand, then walked Dickens in the garden. When Rauwerd phoned, as she had guessed he would, she assured him that she was having a pleasant evening, had her dinner and went to bed very early.

Not, however, to sleep; not until long after midnight when she heard the car and presently Rauwerd's quiet footsteps going past her door.

She forbore, with the greatest effort, from mentioning the previous evening over their breakfast, but remarked brightly that it was a fine morning and she intended to explore the town.

He would be home for lunch, he told her, and would she phone Rose and ask her and Sybren for dinner on Thursday? 'They are friends of my parents. I have to go to Amsterdam on Friday—I should like to bring back an old friend to dinner; we'll need someone to make a fourth, and I'll ask Professor Vouters—I was his registrar years ago and we've not lost touch, although he's retired now. You'll like him.'

It was only after he had gone that Matilda remembered that he hadn't said anything about the old friend in Amsterdam.

She had a long talk with Rose on the phone. They were going to be friends, she felt sure of that, and Rose's sensible reassurances about the pitfalls Matilda was likely to encounter made life seem suddenly rather fun.

'Little Sybren's cut a tooth,' said Rose. 'We're so pleased with him. Wait till you have a baby; they're such fun. What are you going to wear on Thursday?'

Matilda went to see Bep in the kitchen and, with Jan to translate, discussed the dinner parties. It took the best part of half an hour to decide on the two menus and at the end of it, Bep asked her if she would buy flowers for the house.

The florists were bursting with early spring flowers as well as great bunches of hothouse roses and carnations. She bore a great armful back to the house and spent the rest of the morning happily arranging them. Setting the last vase just so in the drawing-room, she felt a pleasant little glow; she was beginning to feel

like a housewife. Once she had mastered sufficient
Dutch she would be able to order the groceries and see
the butcher and the greengrocer and inspect the cupboards…and Emma would arrive on Sunday. She told
herself that she didn't feel lonely or strange any more.
Which wasn't quite true.

She was nervous about the dinner parties but she
need not have been, at least for the first one. No one
could have been kinder than Rauwerd's mother and father, and Rose and Sybren treated her with the ease of
long friendship, even though they hardly knew her. The
evening was a success; she wore a patterned crêpe dress
and the pearl choker, and the dinner was excellent. Listening to Rauwerd laughing and talking with Sybren
and his father, she found herself wishing that he could
talk and laugh like that with her. He treated her with
charming manners and thoughtfulness but with a re-
serve which made an invisible barrier between them.
Something which would improve with time, she told
herself.

'A penny for them?' said Rose.

'It's all a bit strange,' began Matilda.

'Don't let it get you down. I spent the first few weeks
wondering if I should have married Sybren or not even
though I'm crazy about him. It's just getting used to
them being important and horribly rich and quite sure
of themselves. Don't worry, it won't last. Sybren's the
most modest of men when it comes to his fame, and
Rauwerd's the same. They take money for granted, and
being venerated by students and all that.' She beamed
at Matilda. 'I'm so happy, I can't believe it. You are,

too, only all this—' she waved a hand round the lovely room '—takes a bit of getting used to. You're coming to dine with us as soon as we can fix a date. Rauwerd has to go to Brussels this week, hasn't he? So it'll have to be the week after.'

Mevrouw van Kempler joined them then, which saved Matilda answering.

Confident that the second dinner party would be as successful as the first one, Matilda put the finishing touches to the table, put on another new dress, silvery green this time with long tight sleeves and a round low neckline which set off the pearls to perfection. Going down to the drawing-room in her new kid slippers, she felt a surge of confidence as she opened the drawing-room door.

Rauwerd was there, sitting in his chair, laughing at something the woman sitting in her chair opposite had said. He got up as she paused in the doorway, and said easily, 'Ah, my dear, there you are. We got here earlier than we had expected. This is Nikky van Wijk, who lives in Amsterdam.'

The woman had got up and he touched her on the arm. 'Nikky, my wife, Matilda.'

She wasn't very young—mid-thirties perhaps—but she was strikingly handsome with silver-blonde hair, cool blue eyes and regular features. She smiled charmingly as she took Matilda's hand, but her eyes didn't smile.

Matilda disliked her on sight.

'I'll leave you to get to know each other,' said Rauwerd smoothly, 'while I change.'

'You've known Rauwerd a long time?' asked Nikky, still smiling.

'Not long,' said Matilda politely.

Nikky waited for her to say something else and, when she didn't, observed, 'We've known each other for years, but of course you know that already. It's nice of you not to mind that he's spent so much time with me.' She shrugged prettily. 'I'm a fool over business. I don't know what I'd do without Rauwerd to help me— and we have so much to talk about.'

'I expect so; you're much the same age, are you not?' Matilda, by no means a catty girl, sharpened her claws.

The blue eyes became very cold indeed. 'Rauwerd is thirty-three...'

'Thirty-four,' corrected Matilda gently.

'I'm a good deal younger,' began Nikky and was interrupted by Rauwerd's return. Hard on his heels came Professor Vouters, a dear old man she took an instant liking to. The conversation became general over their drinks and presently they went in to have dinner: clear asparagus soup, crayfish in a rich cream sauce flavoured with anchovy, a lemon sorbet before the pork fillets cooked in a madeira sauce and finally a fresh fruit salad and whipped cream.

Professor Vouters sat back with a sigh. 'A delicious meal, Matilda—I may call you that? Rauwerd has chosen himself an excellent wife and a very beautiful one.' He raised his glass to her. 'You and I must become friends. You must have time to spare while Rauwerd works, and I, alas, have more time on my hands than I would wish. You must come and visit me and I will show you our famous Hortus Botanicus gardens. There are also a number of museums, but perhaps you do not care for those?'

He sounded so wistful that she assured him that she did.

They talked over their coffee and presently Professor Vouters got up to go. It seemed that he lived very close by; all the same as Matilda wished him goodnight a silent Jan appeared to escort him into the street and the few hundred yards to his flat.

'He must be eighty,' remarked Nikky lightly from her seat by the fire. 'Time he went into a home.'

Matilda was pleased to see the look of annoyance on Rauwerd's face. 'Certainly not! His brain is as clear as yours or mine—clearer, probably.'

'I forgot that he was one of your fans, Rauwerd!' She sat up gracefully. 'I've had a lovely evening, but I should get back.' She smiled at Matilda. 'You don't mind if Rauwerd runs me home? Silly little me can't drive a car.'

She turned to Rauwerd. 'And while you are there, will you spare five minutes to look over that tiresome paper I had from the *notaris?*'

'A little late,' observed Rauwerd blandly.

'Not really. Good gracious, we've been up later than this before now. And it will save you coming tomorrow—you'll be going to Brussels…'

Just as though I weren't here, fumed Matilda silently, and smiled a little too brightly. Matters were getting out of hand; a little talk might clear the air—that was, she thought sourly, if he could spare the time between seeing to Nikky's affairs and going to Brussels!

She bade her guest goodnight in a serene voice and expressed the hope that they might meet again very soon, aware that Rauwerd was looking at her in his disconcertingly direct way. She bade him goodnight, too, and wished she hadn't when she saw Nikky's nasty little smile.

Perhaps, being such an old friend, Nikky knew all about their marriage. She dismissed the thought as unworthy of Rauwerd.

It was absurd to imagine that she was jealous. All the same, she lay awake until she heard the car return.

At breakfast Rauwerd told her that he would be in Brussels for the whole of the day. 'I should get back in the evening,' he told her, 'but don't wait dinner for me.'

She said coldly, 'Yes, Rose and your friend Nikky told me that you would be there. Would you like a meal left for you?'

'Coffee, perhaps, and some sandwiches.' He added silkily, 'I should have told you, but I'm not used to having a wife.'

Matilda buttered a roll. 'No. Emma gets here tomorrow, doesn't she?'

'I hadn't forgotten. We'll meet her at Schiphol. The plane gets in at five o'clock.'

He gathered up his post and got to his feet. 'I'll be home about ten o'clock.' He stood looking at her. 'Months ago I accepted an invitation to a seminar in Las Palmas. Would you like to go with me? I could manage a week's holiday added on to the week's seminar.'

He strolled to the door. 'Think about it,' he suggested, 'and let me know this evening.'

She could have told him then and there. Of course she would go, and not just because it would be marvellous to spend two weeks in the sun. Las Palmas was a long way from Leiden; it was also a long way from Amsterdam and Nikky.

Chapter 6

Matilda began her morning's routine: the flowers, shopping with Bep at her elbow to help with the difficult bits and then a walk with Dickens who, of course, had had to stay at home. Once these tasks were done, she had leisure to sit down and think about the trip to Las Palmas. Rauwerd hadn't told her when it would be but she would need clothes. She found paper and pen and made a list, a pleasant occupation which kept her occupied until lunchtime.

She had an unexpected visit from Rauwerd's mother in the afternoon. 'I should have telephoned you, my dear,' said that lady, 'but I had a sudden impulse to come and see you and have a chat. We so enjoyed ourselves the other evening and I am so glad that you have Rose Werdmer ter Sane for a friend. She is a dear girl.' She settled herself comfortably and said that yes, she would indeed stay for tea. 'Rauwerd will be home?' she asked.

'No, he is in Brussels. But he will be back later on this evening.'

'He's a busy man, what with his practice and the hospital beds he has. And now this lecturing. You feel lonely, Matilda?'

'Well, no. You see, everything is strange to me; I go shopping with Bep and take Dickens for a walk when he hasn't gone with Rauwerd; and I like doing the flowers—and in a house as large as this one, that takes some time. I am now to start Dutch lessons, too…'

She poured the tea and they sipped it in pleasant friendliness. 'We had Professor Vouters to dinner yesterday—I liked him—and a friend of Rauwerd's, Nikky van Wijk.'

Mevrouw van Kempler bit into a wafer-thin biscuit. 'Ah, yes, a striking-looking woman, I always think.'

'Oh, very, and so beautifully dressed. I've always envied that kind of silvery fair hair.'

'Out of a bottle,' said Mevrouw van Kempler, surprisingly.

Matilda stifled a giggle and then said soberly, 'I mean to like her because she is such an old friend of Rauwerd's. I think she's very clever and that is nice for him. I mean, he is clever, too, isn't he?'

'Oh, very,' agreed his mother, 'but not with everything, my dear.'

There didn't seem to be anything to say to that. Matilda said chattily, 'He is going to Las Palmas and

I'm to go with him. I've never been there; it will be lovely…'

'Ah, yes. When do you go?'

'I don't know; he forgot to say.' She added hastily, 'He's so very busy.'

Mevrouw van Kempler said, 'H'm,' and then, 'I must be going, my dear.'

Matilda accompanied her outside to the street where she had parked a rather elderly Rover. She kissed Matilda briefly before she got into the car and drove away a great deal too fast.

Matilda was about to sit down to her solitary dinner that evening when Rose telephoned them to invite them to dinner on the following Saturday. 'Just the four of us,' she explained, 'so that you can get to know us a bit better. Eight o'clock—we'll expect you unless something crops up.'

Rauwerd got home just before ten o'clock. He looked tired and she hurried to get the coffee and sandwiches Bep had left ready in the kitchen. He was surprised when she came into the room with the tray. 'Where is Bep? Or Jan?'

'I told them to go to bed—they have a long day, you know. I was wondering what there would be for Emma to do when she comes, but she's just what is needed—another pair of hands.'

She poured his coffee and handed him the plate of sandwiches.

'Should we have some more staff? Aren't there two maids who come in each day?'

'Yes, but they go at six o'clock and they don't come

at all on Sundays. That is where Emma is going to fill a gap. They'll be glad of some help and she'll be so pleased to have a job.' She went and sat down opposite him. 'Did you have a successful day?'

He nodded. And that was to be all, she realised.

'Rose has asked us to dinner next Saturday—just us and them. She said to let her know if you couldn't make it.'

'I should be free. I try to keep the weekends open, though I don't always succeed. Do you want to do anything tomorrow other than fetching Emma?'

'No, thank you.'

'Then we'll go to morning church and have a lazy day until we leave for Schiphol. I forgot to tell you that I've asked your teacher to come for drinks before lunch tomorrow—you can get to know each other. He'd like to start this week, if that's all right with you.'

'I'll be glad to start.' She poured more coffee. 'Rauwerd, this trip to Las Palmas, when will it be?'

'Two weeks' time. You'll need clothes. We shall fly over and stay until the seminar is over, then have a week off.'

'I shall enjoy that. Will it be warm there?'

'Pleasantly so, I hope. But take something warm to wear if we go into the mountains.'

He sounded faintly bored, and she made haste to change the conversation. 'Your mother came to tea. It was very pleasant.'

'I'm glad.'

He didn't want to talk any more. She said goodnight

quietly and went up to bed, stifling her hurt because he didn't need her company.

They breakfasted together, exchanging platitudes, and presently walked along the canal to church. Even though she couldn't understand a word of it, Matilda found it comforting, and some of the hymn tunes were familiar. After the service there were various friends and acquaintances of Rauwerd's to meet. They went back to give her teacher a drink and then to lunch and have a quiet hour or so sitting in the drawing-room. There were no Sunday papers in Holland, but there were books and magazines in plenty. They sat there, she quiet as a mouse, reading a book she had no interest in because Rauwerd was immersed in a sheaf of papers and quite obviously didn't want to be disturbed.

Schiphol was barely half an hour's drive away. They had tea a little earlier than usual and got into the car. Rauwerd had little to say, which made it difficult for Matilda to voice something she felt had to be said.

'It's very kind of you to have Emma,' she began. 'I'm very grateful and I know that she is, too.'

'My dear girl, you said yourself that she will fill a gap in the household. I am the one to be grateful and I'm sure that Jan and Bep will be.'

'Oh, I do hope they'll like each other.'

She need not have worried. Emma, still nervous from the flight, so happy to see Matilda again, became, in some miraculous way, a member of the household the moment she set foot inside the front door. She was borne away by Bep to have her tea and then followed Matilda upstairs to her room.

'Why, Miss Tilly, it's luxury! Look at that chair and the TV and a bathroom all to myself.' A few difficult tears trickled down her cheeks. 'I never thought it'd end like this—you so 'appy and this lovely 'ouse and me in the lap of luxury. I only 'opes I'll earn me keep.'

Matilda flung a comforting arm about her shoulders. 'Of course you will, Emma. Bep and Jan need you; there is so much you can do to help and they are both elderly, you know. It means that they can take things a little more easily. There are two daily maids so there is no hard work but there's masses of silver and glass and furniture to be polished. You're just what is needed.'

She left Emma to unpack and went to tidy herself for dinner. When she went downstairs Rauwerd was on the phone in the hall. She hurried past him, unwilling to eavesdrop, but she couldn't help hearing him say with clear deliberation, 'No, Nikky, I can't manage this evening and I'm pretty busy during the week. Get your *notaris* to deal with it and let me know if you have any difficulties.'

He followed Matilda into the drawing-room. 'Nikky is the most unbusinesslike woman I have ever met.' He went to pour the drinks. 'But I've no intention of puzzling over stocks and shares this evening. I prefer to be by my own fireside.'

He turned to look at her and she switched the peevish frown on her face to an expression of casual interest. She hoped that she had done it smartly enough. 'I should think that stocks and shares are very complicated things; I wouldn't know one from the other.'

'No, perhaps not, Tilly, but I fancy you would make

it your business to find out. You're self-reliant, or do I mean self-sufficient?'

'Neither of them sound like me.' And because he was staring at her so hard she plunged into talk. 'Emma is so happy. She's not at all worried about being in another country; I dare say she'll pick up more Dutch in a week than I shall in six months.'

Rauwerd laughed. 'Not if old Professor Tacx has anything to do with it. What did you think of him? We must have him to dinner one evening.'

'I liked him, though he seemed a bit fierce.'

'Just his manner. He'll make you work hard.'

'Well, the sooner I can speak and understand Dutch the better. I shall do my best.'

They dined unhurriedly, carrying on a desultory conversation which for some reason Matilda found reassuring, perhaps because it made her feel so secure and married. But her new-found content received a jolt as they sat over their coffee.

'I have been waiting for you to ask about Nikky.' Rauwerd's voice was bland and faintly amused.

Matilda took a big sip of coffee and scalded her tongue. 'Why?' she asked baldly. 'You told me that she was an old friend. I have no intention of prying.' She went on matter-of-factly, 'It isn't as if I were in—in love with you and wanted to know everything about you.' And, when he didn't say anything, 'I'm quite content. That sounds selfish, but I don't mean it to be. What I'm trying to say is that you have no need to worry about me. I don't expect you to change your life just because you married me...'

He raised his eyebrows. 'No? Should I feel flattered, I wonder, or downcast at the idea of making so little impression upon you?'

She blushed. 'You know I don't mean that. You said before you married me that we would get on well together—that's what you want, isn't it?'

He said slowly. 'Yes. That's what I wanted, Matilda.' He got up from his chair. 'I've some telephoning to do. Why don't you arrange to meet Rose and do your shopping together? I'll have to be in Amsterdam tomorrow, you can drive there with me and I'll pick you up on my way home.'

'That sounds a marvellous idea. I'll telephone her in the morning.' She picked up the knitting lying on the table beside her. 'I'll go and make sure that Emma is all right. I dare say she'd like a gossip; she must be feeling a bit strange. Then I'll go to bed, so I'll say goodnight.'

She gave him a friendly nod and smile; if he didn't want her company then she would be the last person to let him know that she minded.

Emma was in her room, arranging her bits and pieces just so. Far from feeling strange she appeared to have settled in without a qualm; she liked Jan and Bep and, with Jan's translating, had already agreed to take over several chores from Bep. 'Ever so 'appy, I am, love,' she told Matilda. 'I reckon we're two lucky ones, you with that lovely man for a 'usband and me falling on me feet, and all thanks to 'im.'

Matilda agreed with her, wished her goodnight and went to her own bed. She had, she reminded herself, a great deal to be thankful for. She lay awake a long time, planning her clothes for the forthcoming trip. But her last thought was of Rauwerd.

Rose was delighted to go shopping. She took Matilda to Maison de Bonneterie and the two of them spent a delightful hour or so choosing an outfit suitable for Las Palmas in the spring. Having money to spend made it much easier, of course, but Matilda refused to be carried away by the more exotic garments on display and settled for a cotton jersey dress and matching long coat, several cotton dresses in bright colours, and two crêpe evening dresses which would take up no room in her luggage and wouldn't crush either. She did allow herself to be extravagant over swimsuits and their accompanying cover-ups; surely while Rauwerd was at his seminar she would be able to spend hours on a beach somewhere or, failing that, in the hotel swimming-pool.

The two of them took a taxi back to Rose's home, a lovely old house in a narrow street tucked away from the city centre. They had lunch, played with little Sybren, examined Matilda's purchases and gossiped until Sybren arrived at the same time as the tea-tray was brought in and, hard on his heels, Rauwerd.

Rose had flown into Sybren's arms the moment he arrived and Matilda hoped that the casual, 'Hello, Tilly' would pass unnoticed when Rauwerd joined them. He made things easier by leaning down and kissing her cheek—a gesture without warmth, and not to be compared with Sybren's fierce hug for his small wife, but at least it was something.

They spent an hour—a happy one—before leaving,

with the promise that they would return on Saturday for dinner.

'Finished your shopping?' Rauwerd wanted to know as he drove back.

'Yes, thank you. I don't need to take many clothes, do I? You'll be busy for the first week, won't you?'

'Only until seven or thereabouts in the evening. I shall need to relax then—dinner, dancing.' He added airily, 'And I thought we might hire a car and see something of the island.'

At least two more evening dresses, she reflected, and perhaps more cotton tops and skirts. She said, speaking her thoughts out loud, 'I'm not very happy in slacks.'

His firm mouth curved into a smile. 'Then skirts, my dear, although I should have thought that slacks were invented for legs like yours.'

A compliment. The first he had ever paid her. She would go to that chic little boutique in Leiden and invest in a couple of pairs—pastel colours; they would go well with the floral tops she had already bought.

She said quietly, 'Thank you. Have you been there?'

'A couple of times. I think you will like it.'

She bought the slacks the next day and then went for her first Dutch lesson. Professor Tacx was a dear old thing although she quickly discovered that he was going to be a hard taskmaster. Her brain addled with Dutch verbs, she went back home with enough work to keep her busy for the rest of the week, only she would have to get it done before then for she was to have another lesson on Friday.

At dinner that evening Rauwerd asked, 'Lesson go well?'

'Oh, yes, I enjoyed it. How long will it take before I can speak Dutch?'

'Some months, but you'll be able to understand it before then and make yourself understood. Shopping and so forth. I must remember to speak Dutch to you and, of course, you can practise on Bep and Jan.'

'Should Emma have lessons?'

'She'll pick up all she needs just being with Bep and Jan. Lessons would only bother her. Our grammar is quite different and I doubt if she will want to read Dutch; there are plenty of paperbacks and papers in English. Tell me what she enjoys reading and I'll arrange for it to be sent.'

'That's kind of you. She seems quite at home already.'

'Good. And you, Matilda? Do you feel at home?'

She raised serious eyes to him. 'Yes, Rauwerd. I love this house and I like your parents very much. I only hope that I'll be a help to you— giving dinner parties and entertaining your friends.'

'Ah, yes. When we get back we must give a small party, don't you think? And there will be the Spring Ball at the medical school and several evening functions to attend, here and in den Haag.'

'I had a note from Beatrix Thenus asking me to go to coffee on Thursday. She wants to talk to me about joining a fund-raising scheme—something to do with children...'

He glanced across the table at her. 'Yes? I imagine

you will be asked to attend similar functions as well as innumerable charitable organisations.'

'You would like me to join them?'

'My dear, you must do as you please. They are mostly worthwhile and I can't imagine that you will want to fritter away your days. I'm involved in several schemes to do with children; it would be nice if you shared my interest.'

'I'd like that.' She was eager to hear more but his laconic, 'Good. Shall we have coffee in the drawing-room?' stopped her from asking any more questions.

The week came to its end with another lesson from Professor Tacx and a delightful dinner with Rose and Sybren. The next week went as smoothly, with more lessons, packing for their trip and an almost imperceptible taking over of the household reins. She was careful not to trespass on Bep's domain in the kitchen and the house, but she began to deal with bills and accounts, spent time with Bep learning the price of things and what to buy, and she went to the cellars with Jan and inspected their contents under his knowledgeable eye. She wasn't likely to be called upon to choose wine, but she was abysmally ignorant on such matters.

Any qualms she might have had about Emma settling down were quickly put at rest; Emma declared herself to be completely at home and content. There were tasks enough in the old house; beautiful furniture to polish, the linen cupboards to keep tidy, smalls to wash, clothes to press. She had never been so happy, she assured Matilda. Ignorance of the language didn't bother her in the least; she trotted off to the shops with

Bep, and in her free time took herself off to the town to explore on her own. She and Bep also shared an enthusiasm for knitting and she was already busy on a pullover for Rauwerd, a thank you present for his kindness.

Matilda had searched the bookshops for information about Las Palmas, and by the time they were due to leave she had worked her way through several guidebooks and a brochure or two, so that she wasn't completely ignorant about the city and the island. She wore the coat and dress in which to travel and was conscious of Rauwerd's approval as they got into the car.

They drove to Schiphol not saying much, with Jan sitting in the back so that he might drive the car back to Leiden, and once at the airport they went aboard immediately. How quickly one got used to comfort and ease, reflected Matilda, settling into her first-class seat. It was a mid-morning flight and the plane was only half full. She looked from the porthole as they took off and then, since Rauwerd had opened his briefcase and taken out a sheaf of papers, buried her pretty nose in one of the magazines he had bought her.

When their lunch was served he put his work away. 'The nice part about you, Matilda,' he observed, 'is that I don't have to worry about ruffling your feelings if I need to do some work. You like flying?'

Her feelings, if he did not know it, were ruffled, but she said matter-of-factly, 'I'm not sure. Uncle and I, when we went on holiday, which wasn't often, used to take the car and tour around Britain.'

He looked surprised. 'This is your first flight? My

dear girl, if I had known I wouldn't have occupied myself with these notes.'

He sounded concerned and she said quickly, 'Oh, that's all right, I'm not nervous.'

He talked as they ate lunch and she felt relaxed and soothed. He could be a delightful companion when he wanted to be, and very amusing, too.

'We are staying at a rather nice hotel, not very near the shops or the beach, but there is a car waiting for us. It's called the Santa Catalina and, since I'd rather you didn't go out on your own, it won't matter that it's a little way out of the centre of the city.'

She received this high-handed arrangement of her days silently and he went on, 'I'll be at the conference and various meetings each morning, back at the hotel for lunch and then back at three o'clock until about seven in the evening. Everything closes in the afternoons but we can swim or drive around the island. There is plenty of night-life...'

'Clubs and things?' asked Matilda doubtfully.

He smiled. 'They abound. I dare say we shall be content with a visit to one of the bars on Las Canteras beach and perhaps some dancing. The hotel is very comfortable but quiet, but there is nothing to stop us driving to Maspalomas—Sybren was telling me of a good hotel there where we can dance or visit the casino.'

Perhaps not high-handed after all. 'That sounds fun,' she said.

'For our second week I thought we might go to Tenerife. I've booked at the Botanico in Puerto de la Cruz; there's a dance floor and cabaret and it's in a small park. I think you'll like it. We'll have a car there, too, and explore.'

It all sounded marvellous; by the time the plane landed Matilda was happy and excited.

The car was waiting at the airport and Rauwerd drove the fourteen miles into the city and on to their hotel. Matilda was instantly impressed; it was built in the Spanish style and lay well away from the road, surrounded by trees and a rather pretty garden. Once inside she could see that it was pleasantly and comfortably furnished. Their rooms were on the first floor and were large and airy and overlooked a small park. Altogether charming, she decided, and told Rauwerd so when he came into her room.

'I've asked for some tea to be sent up,' he told her, 'and when you've unpacked we might go for a short run in the car so that you can get your bearings. Unless you are tired.'

'Tired! It would be criminal to be tired—just look at those trees...' She craned her neck over the balcony. 'And geraniums, hundreds of them.'

After tea they drove through the busy city and along the coast road to Arucas, a charming little town of white-walled houses, dominated by a modern cathedral. They returned along a winding road which brought them back to Las Palmas, humming with evening traffic, had a drink in the bar and then went to change for dinner.

A delightful evening, decided Matilda, laying her sleepy head on the pillow later that night.

The evenings which followed it were just as delightful. True, she found the days lonely; there was a limit to the amount of sunbathing and swimming in the hotel pool she could enjoy. By the time Rauwerd returned in the evening, she was more than glad to see him, for lunch, although they ate it together, was usually a hurried meal, for, contrary to custom, the members at the conference had decided to do without a siesta. But even though she was tempted, she stayed at the hotel and was rewarded for this by evenings spent driving to Maspalomas to dance or to stroll along the esplanade to one of the numerous bars, or to try their luck at the casino.

On the last day, after Rauwerd had got back from his final conference, he took her into the city and wandered around the shops, waiting patiently while she bought embroidery, leather handbags for Emma and Bep, and exquisitely stitched handkerchiefs for the maids, and when she admired a beautifully made silver bracelet, he bought it for her and clasped it around her wrist.

She thanked him a little shyly. 'It's been a lovely week,' she told him and he nodded.

'Next week will be even better', he observed.

They went by hydrofoil to Tenerife, transferred to the car waiting at the quay, and drove to the hotel. Puerto de la Cruz captured Matilda's fancy at once and the hotel, a short distance from the centre of the town, appeared delightful. It was surrounded by a large garden with banana plantations beyond it, and was close to the botanical gardens. Inside it was as superbly comfortable as one could wish for. She was surprised to find that they had a suite, their rooms opening on to a sitting-room whose doors gave on to a patio and a swimming pool.

'Just for us?' Matilda wanted to know.

'Yes.' He was watching her happy face. 'You like it?'

'It's super. What did you say was the name of this hotel?'

'Botanico—it's close to the botanical gardens.'

'Is the pool heated?'

'Yes. Shall we have a swim before dinner?'

She wasn't a good swimmer but she felt safe enough, for the pool wasn't large and, besides, Rauwerd was there. She left him still ploughing strongly through the clear water and went to dress. The patterned chiffon, she decided, and debated whether she should buy another evening gown; the guests in the bigger hotels dressed for the evening and she had only the two crêpe dresses besides.

The chiffon did her justice; she did her face carefully, brushed her hair until it shone and went into the sitting-room. Rauwerd was already there. 'Shall I ring for drinks or shall we go down to the bar?' he asked.

She felt suddenly shy of him. 'Oh, the bar.' She spoke too quickly and he gave her a hard stare before opening the door. She caught the tail end of it and wondered if he was annoyed, but the smile which followed the stare was bland, so she decided that she had been mistaken.

The evening was delightful; they dined and danced and presently wished each other goodnight. If every day was going to be like this one, Matilda told herself, then the week was going to be a success; she had felt at ease with him as well as so much enjoying his company. She got into bed, eager for the morning so that she would be with him again.

They had agreed to swim before breakfast and he was already in the pool when she lowered herself cautiously into the shallow end. But once in, she found the water exactly right and the morning sun, shining from a blue sky, was warm on her as she swam sedately backwards and forwards.

'Why not try something else?' asked Rauwerd, loitering along beside her. 'The crawl, perhaps? I'll stay beside you.'

She splashed and splattered her way to and fro and finally she gave up. 'I don't think I'm built for it,' she observed, 'and I hate to get underwater.'

His eyes flickered over her shapely person. 'Perhaps not,' he agreed gravely while his eyes gleamed beneath their lids. 'Shall we have breakfast on the balcony? I'll order it while you are dressing. Orange juice and croissants and coffee?'

They spent the day pottering round the shops and having another swim at the lido on the promenade before lunching out of doors at a nearby restaurant. In the afternoon they went back to the shops along the seafront because Matilda had seen a dress she had rather liked in the window of one of the chic boutiques there.

'Buy it,' said Rauwerd lazily, 'I like you in pink.'

The dress, very pale pink voile with a tiny bodice and yards of stole to match it, was a perfect fit. At the elegant jeweller's shop next door Rauwerd bought her pink coral earrings to go with it.

Another lovely day, mused Matilda, sliding into bed hours later. The dress had been a success and they had danced for hours. She sighed with a half-understood happiness and went instantly to sleep.

They would take the car in the afternoon, said Rauwerd over breakfast the next morning, and go north through the mountains to Bajamar. 'It's a small seaside resort, not particularly pretty, but to get to it one must drive along a magnificent road with some splendid views. We'll stop at the Pico del Inglés and you will be able to see for yourself.'

They went to the lido again after breakfast and had an early lunch at the hotel. It was still a bright day but as they drove north they could see dark clouds above the mountains ahead of them.

'I'll take you to the African market tomorrow morning,' said Rauwerd. 'This place we're coming to is San Andrés—a fishing village.'

They didn't go right into the village but turned sharply and began to climb, presently leaving the scattering of houses behind them. The road was rather frightening, cut into the sides of the mountains looming all around them with a steep gorge on one side of it and towering sombre rock on the other. It wound up and up in a continuous bend and from time to time made a U-turn so tight that the car seemed to hang over the edge of the road as Rauwerd pulled it round. The higher they drove, the more awesome were their surroundings, with clouds dipping and swirling through the giant pines and beech trees, cutting them off from the outside world.

'You're not enjoying it?' said Rauwerd presently.

'Oh, yes, it's magnificent... Well, perhaps not quite. How did you know?'

'Your hands, so tightly clasped; besides, I can feel you stiffen at every bend.'

She said quickly, anxious to reassure him, 'It's really an experience—I wouldn't have missed it for the world.'

He gave a short laugh. 'All the same, you're scared. I'm sorry.'

'No, no, not that. You're here.' She spoke simply. 'With anyone else I would be, though. I'm overawed; it's so lonely, it could be the end of the world.' And, to make sure that he didn't think that she was complaining, 'It's a marvellous road…'

'Yes. Well used, too, though there is not much on it today.'

He took another U-turn and she remembered not to clasp her hands, only to grip them hard and let out a startled breath as he braked hard at the end of an S-bend to avoid two cars ahead of them, tangled together on the road. They must have met head on, for the back wheels of one of them were hanging over the edge of the ravine and the bonnet of the second car was crushed against the rock of the mountain side.

Rauwerd slid to a halt. His calm, 'Dear me,' soothed Matilda into instant obedience when he said, 'Take that red scarf of yours, my dear, and go back to the bend and hang it on to a handy branch—anything, just as long as it can be seen.'

He turned to study the road ahead of them. The road wound round the mountain in a wide sweep; any car coming that way would be able to see them.

'Off you go and take care.' He leaned across to open her door and kissed her hard. 'I'm going to have a look.'

Matilda got out of the car aware, over and above the horrors of the moment, of his kiss. She found a branch, tied the scarf—a new one she had bought only that morning—and hurried back, to stop short at the sight of Rauwerd, head and shoulders through the window of the car teetering so dangerously on the edge of the road.

'Don't come any nearer, Tilly.' His voice sounded loud and calm and she did as she was told, watching him with her heart in her mouth as he took the wheel and slowly pushed the car away from the edge. He emerged then, dusting his hands, breathing rather hard.

'We must get that man out—thank heaven you're a big strong girl.' He ignored her indignant glance. 'He is unconscious. There are two in the other car, but I think he is the more urgent.'

He had the door open and was heaving gently at the man behind the wheel. Matilda didn't wait to be told what to do; she could see for herself. They laid him gently on the side of the road and she fetched a rug from their car and put it under his head.

'The others first,' said Rauwerd and wrenched the second car's door open. The woman in the back was easily lifted clear but the driver took a good deal longer. He looked in a bad way, his breathing shallow and his colour ashen.

'Undo his shirt,' said Rauwerd and, 'Just as I thought, his lung is pierced—look at that bruise. See what you can do about it, Tilly.'

Just as though I had a dressing trolley handy, thought Matilda, and ripped off the hem of the flowered cotton skirt she was wearing. It was first aid of the crudest kind but at least it stopped the bleeding and his pulse when she took it was regular, even if it was weak.

She crossed the road to where Rauwerd was bending over the woman. 'Broken arm, concussion, a nasty cut from glass.'

She tore another strip from her skirt and used it to good effect.

'I need a sling,' said Rauwerd.

There was a Gucci scarf still in its elegant packet; she had bought it for Rose. She went to the car and fetched it and offered it silently.

'I'll buy you a dozen,' said Rauwerd.

The second man was a more serious matter; his chest was already showing massive bruising, he was cold and clammy and his pulse was a mere thread. Over and above that he had a broken leg. Rauwerd straightened it as best he could and tied it to the sound one with the man's leather belt while Tilly found cushions and more rugs.

Rauwerd got to his feet. 'I'm going to drive back until I find a phone—there was a house a few miles back. It'll be light for some hours yet and I'll leave you the torch.'

'You're going to leave me here?' Indignation and fright made her voice squeaky.

'I must, Tilly, dear. I can't let you drive, you couldn't on this road.'

She swallowed panic. 'You won't be long?'

'Not a second longer than I must be. If anyone comes along, stop them and make them stay, too.'

'Make them stay—how?'

He grinned. 'You are a beautiful girl—they'll stay.'

He bent and kissed her cheek. 'Take care,' he told her and got into the car, reversed carefully round the bend and, after what seemed an age, turned it. Moments later she saw the car going dangerously fast along the road curving round the next ravine.

There wasn't much she could do but she did it faithfully—pulses and breathing to check and colour to watch. After an hour she sighed with relief to find them all still alive.

It was another half-hour before she was able to see the car intermittently as it climbed the steep curving road below her, then a further ten minutes before Rauwerd pulled up gently beside her and got out.

The wish to fling herself at him and burst into tears was overwhelming but she fought it hard.

'That's my girl. How are they? There is a police car and an ambulance on their way from Bandama—there's a first-aid clinic there and they can be sent on to Santa Cruz as soon as they have been examined.' He patted her shoulders and went to look at the three prone figures.

The police were there five minutes later; she heard the siren long before she saw the blue light flashing along the road ahead of them. They didn't waste much time in talk but set to, with Rauwerd helping them to move the wrecked cars to the side of the road. They had just finished when the ambulance arrived.

It took time to load the three patients into it; first it had to turn round, for it would have to return the way it had come from Bandama. When it was at last on its way, there were questions to be answered for the police, taking twice as long because every word had to be translated by Rauwerd. But they finished at last, shook hands all round, and, in their turn, drove back the way they had come.

It was quiet once more and the mist had turned the afternoon into twilight evening. Rauwerd walked back to the bend and fetched her scarf and then stood holding it, smiling at her. She had a nice safe feeling seeing him standing there. It was strange to think that when they had first met she had thought she disliked him. She stared back at him, her lovely mouth slightly open with the sudden surprise of knowing that she was in love with him.

Chapter 7

Matilda felt like someone who had taken a step which wasn't there at the bottom of a staircase. With difficulty she closed her mouth but she couldn't stop the colour leaving her cheeks; emotion had washed over her leaving her with her bones changed to water, and she almost choked with her efforts not to voice her feelings.

Rauwerd was watching her closely, no longer smiling. 'Are you all right?' he wanted to know. 'Come and sit in the car.' He came and took her arm and the touch of his hand started her shaking. 'We'll drive on to Bajamar and find you a stiff drink. You were marvellous, Tilly.' He glanced down at her ruined skirt, smiling a little.

'Well, I am a nurse,' she mumbled. 'It's only that it was so sudden. I'm quite all right now.'

She was still trembling, but not because of the accident. This nonsense must stop! she told herself silently as he started the car and drove on once more.

The road was just as bad but it could be no worse than the last hour or two; she averted her eyes from the ravines below and after a few miles heaved a sigh of relief as trees closed in on them on either side and the cloud blotted out the awe-inspiring views.

They began to go downhill and presently the road wound itself gently down to green fields and rows of tomatoes and potatoes and wild flowers rioting at the roadside. She could see the sea now and a cluster of white-walled and red-roofed houses—Bajamar, a disappointingly ordinary little town with one or two hotels, a row of shops facing the sea, and a series of pools corralled from the ocean. Rauwerd stopped before the row of shops, all of them still open, and ushered Matilda into a coffee shop at the end of the row. It was pleasant inside, full of customers, but there was an empty table in a corner. He sat her down at it and ordered tea for her and coffee for himself. He ordered two brandies, too, and made her drink hers at once. That, and the hot, milkless tea, stopped her trembling and sent the colour back into her cheeks. She had had time, during the drive down the mountains, to pull herself together.

Rauwerd ordered more tea for her. 'That's better. It was quite an experience, wasn't it?'

Common sense had taken over once more. She said steadily, 'Yes, I shall never forget it.' She wasn't thinking of the accident.

They sat for half an hour, during which time Rauwerd

carried on a placid flow of small talk, and presently she was able to get into the car beside him, carefully not looking at him, although it was difficult for her to keep her eyes off his large, capable hands on the wheel.

He drove back another way. They had driven through Santa Cruz on their way to the mountains; now he followed the coast south for a few miles before joining the main road at Tacoronte and so along the coast still to Puerto de la Cruz. Back at the hotel he recommended that she should take a bath and, if she felt like it, a nap before changing for dinner and she complied, grateful for the chance to have time to herself in which to think.

She lay in tepid, fragrant water and tried to see into the future. Ten minutes' hard thinking convinced her that this wasn't at all a wise thing to do. It was going to be a difficult enough task living with Rauwerd on the friendly casual basis he took for granted, taking no part in his life other than running his household and playing hostess to his friends. Which brought her to another worry: Nikky. She hadn't liked her in the first place; now she seethed at the mere thought of her. She would have to form a plan of campaign if she intended to be happy ever after, and that meant Rauwerd falling in love with her...

He had shown no romantic interest in her so far; pleasure in her company perhaps, but no more than that. She would have to change, become more like Nikky—lose weight for a start; Nikky had almost no curves. Matilda studied her own charming person with a frowning eye. And a new hairstyle. There was a beauty salon in Leiden; she would go there and have a facial and make-up. She would have to diet and perhaps have sessions of those slimming techniques she had never thought much of. She couldn't do much about it until they got back to Leiden, only eat less...

She wore the pink with the stole again, ate a splendid dinner, quite forgetful of her resolve to slim drastically, and danced until one o'clock in the morning. Rauwerd was his usual calm self, although a little withdrawn, which was just as well for it reminded her that from his point of view, at least, nothing had changed. Even if her whole world had been turned upside down, she must never let him see it.

He took her to the African market after breakfast the next morning; they strolled from stall to stall, looking at the cheeses and fruit and the fish and flowers, and then they went to the lido and swam and sat in the sun with fruit drinks. They were both nicely tanned; Matilda was beginning to look like a magnificent gypsy and Rauwerd's hair had become pale gilt.

They sat for an hour doing nothing after lunch, in the cool of their sitting-room, and then, after an early cup of tea, he drove her to Icod de los Vinos to see the Dragon Tree. 'It's reputed to be three thousand years old,' he told her, 'and it certainly looks it.'

They got out of the car and sat in its shade until a busload of tourists sent them on their way again. They were much nearer Pico del Tiede now but Rauwerd turned away from it. Instead he drove back the way they had come and turned off to La Orotava, where he parked the car and took her wandering up and down its steep streets to admire the lovely old houses and pleasing buildings and presently to sit outside in Calle San Francisco, the most interesting street of them all, and to drink small cups of dark, rich coffee in a café. Later they went back to their hotel, driving through the lovely Orotava Valley, bright with flowers and every kind of tree and bush. The road was a series of S-bends, but the scenery wasn't sombre or frightening and Matilda loved every moment of it.

She told Rauwerd so when they got back to the hotel, lifting a happy face to his, carefree of anything but the delight of the moment. 'Oh, it was gorgeous,' she told him. 'What shall we do tomorrow?'

He smiled down at her and then bent and kissed her cheek. 'I'm glad you enjoyed it, my dear. Supposing we drive right round the island? We can take our swimming things and stop somewhere quiet for lunch.'

They danced again after dinner. Such a pity, grieved Matilda silently, that when they got back to Leiden she would spend her evenings endlessly alone or entertaining his friends—Nikky... She shuddered at the very thought of her and his arm tightened round her. 'You're cold? You feel all right?'

She assured him that she had never felt better, speaking into the crisp whiteness of his shirt front, afraid to meet his eyes.

It was remarkable, she reflected as she got ready for bed, how well she had taken herself in hand. No one would ever guess that she was besotted over her husband, least of all her husband. She derived a wry satisfaction from the thoughts and then burst into tears.

The drive round the island took almost all day, for

they loitered to admire the views, wander round the cathedral at La Laguna, and drink coffee in a pavement café before following the road down the east coast, stopping again at Candelaria so that Matilda might marvel at the black sand and the statues of Guanches lining the sea front. The country began to change, its vivid greenness giving way to dry earth, although the coastline was enchanting. They didn't stop at El Medano—obviously it was a budding tourist centre—but went on to the Costa del Silencia, with its rocky coast and peace and quiet. They had lunch at the charming little hotel there, then found a small cove, nicely sheltered from the sun, and presently they swam.

When they drove on later they didn't stop at Los Cristianos but paused to drink their tea in Los Gigantes before making their way back to the hotel. A lovely day rounded off with a delightful evening.

The last day came too soon and they decided to go to the lido once more and do nothing but lie in the sun and swim. They had explored the island thoroughly and wandered round the shops and now next day they would fly back to Holland and she would be lucky if she saw Rauwerd for more than an hour or so each day. They wandered down to the pool and found long chairs, and Matilda, in a vivid bikini, veiled by a thin matching wrap, her dark hair crowned by a large straw hat, was unaware of the stares of the men around her.

Rauwerd settled himself beside her, chuckling. 'I'm not surprised that you are collecting leers from all sides, Tilly—you look good enough to eat, which is more than I can say for those around us. I've never seen so much bare flesh so unwisely exposed, and I'm not speaking as a medical man.' He turned over on his back and looked sideways at her.

'Have I ever told you that you're a beautiful young woman?'

She was glad of the wide brim of her sunhat; it screened her face nicely from his stare. She said quietly, 'No, you haven't and I'm not—it's just the blue sky and the sun and a very expensive beach outfit...' She went on slowly, 'I'm the same girl as I always was, only dressed differently.'

'Not quite the same girl,' he reminded her. 'You're married now.' He spoke silkily and she bit back the retort which sprung to her lips. It would never do to destroy the still shaky foundations of a deeper friendship between them. She rolled over and smiled widely at him.

'I like being married and I've loved our holiday. I hope we'll be able to do it again some time!'

He said lazily, 'I'm a busy man, but we'll see what we can do.'

'Have you enjoyed it, too?'

His eyes were half shut. 'Oh, indeed, yes.' And then, 'Shall we swim?'

It was raining at Schiphol when, well on schedule, they landed, and Holland looked flat and uninteresting after the mountains of the Canary Islands, but once in Leiden Matilda forgot all that. Jan had met them at the airport with a wide smile, but that was nothing compared with the warmth of their welcome home: Bep and

Emma waiting on the doorstep and the two daily maids hovering in the background. Matilda tidied herself and hurried downstairs to join Rauwerd in the drawing-room, to find the tea tray already there and him immersed in a great pile of letters.

She poured the tea and he accepted his cup with a vague nod, so that she went to sit opposite him, as still as a mouse, sipping from her own cup. It was with a sinking heart that she realised that he had become immediately immersed in his correspondence. She drank a second cup of tea and, since he seemed unaware of her, went upstairs to her room and unpacked her things, while Emma fussed gently around, collecting things for cleaning and the laundry. That didn't take long; Emma went away presently and Matilda sat down before her dressing-table, did her face and her hair and then changed into a pretty dress. It was almost time for dinner; surely Rauwerd would have finished his post by now. She was half way down the staircase when she heard his voice; she couldn't understand what he was saying but she heard him exclaim 'Nikky' in a laughing voice and then *'Tot straks'*, and that meant, near enough, presently.

She went on down the stairs and her heart went down into her pretty slippers as she went; Nikky had seemed far away and forgotten while they had been on holiday, but of course that wasn't the case; she had been there all the time, ready to pounce the moment they got back to Leiden. She went into the dining-room, outwardly serene, inwardly seething.

Rauwerd was standing by the window, looking into

the street. 'Ah, there you are, my dear. Will you forgive me if I leave you to dine alone? Something has come up which needs dealing with at once.'

'The hospital?' asked Matilda mildly.

'Nikky. She has become so used to me helping her when she gets into difficulties about something; I can't let her down.' He poured their drinks and handed her a glass of sherry. 'Nice to be home, isn't it?'

'Delightful,' said Matilda evenly. 'Don't let me keep you if you want to leave right away. I'll just go to the kitchen and tell Bep to do something about dinner.' She flashed him a brilliant smile, put down her untouched sherry and left him there.

Bep was puzzled and put out. She had planned a splendid meal for their homecoming and when Matilda told her that the doctor wouldn't be there to eat it, she almost burst into tears.

'But I shall enjoy it,' declared Matilda stoutly, 'and I'm famished. Perhaps you would leave sandwiches for the doctor? I don't know when he will be back; very late I expect.'

She was crossing the hall as he opened the front door. 'Have a nice evening,' she said flippantly. 'It'll make a welcome change for you.' She swept into the drawing-room and shut the door on his surprised face.

Matilda had plenty of time to think the situation over. She had dined in solitary state, eating something of everything so as not to upset Bep and then, after a suitable interval, going up to her room. But not to sleep. She settled into one of the comfortable chairs and, clearing her head of rage, envy and near panic, made plans for a future which, at the moment, didn't look too rosy. Obviously she had been living in cloud cuckoo land, so she must forget the two weeks that they had just spent together. Rauwerd had wanted a wife to run his house, and come home to, someone who would cope with the social side of his life without bothering him so that he could get on with his work. And Nikky, said a small voice, interrupting her thoughts. So she would have to be just that. She might not have his love but she was his wife; she would do all the things expected of her: entertaining, get to know all the right people at the medical school, join all the committees she was asked to, take an interest in local charities, be a good daughter-in-law, and, when he wanted her company, comply willingly.

'Mid-Victorian,' said Matilda loudly to the empty room. 'Only I'm not sitting back and taking it lying down, even if it takes me a lifetime.' He liked her; she was sure of that. He enjoyed her company, they liked doing the same things and they shared a sense of humour; the only thing missing was his love.

She got ready for bed and closed her eyes resolutely. She would begin how she intended to go on; she would go to sleep and not lie awake wondering when he would be home. She didn't hear him come in hours later and make his way to his room.

After breakfast she was friendly and suitably quiet while he read his letters, answered his brief remarks with a few placid ones of her own and wished him a pleasant day when he got up to go.

'I'll be home for lunch.'

He told her as he went and she said with just the right touch of warmth, 'Oh, good.'

She had post of her own. An invitation to coffee at the medical director's house—a friendly little note from his wife apologising for the short notice but saying that she was anxious that Matilda should meet a few people already known to Rauwerd. There was a letter from Rose, too, asking her to go to lunch in a couple of days' time, and another invitation from a local charity. There was a telephone call after breakfast from Rauwerd's mother asking if they were free to go and see them the following Sunday. Matilda said that she would have to ask Rauwerd, but if he were free, she was sure that they would be delighted.

Quite a good beginning, she decided; the busier her days were, the better. Rauwerd had wanted a wife to come home to, but there wasn't much point in that if he was going to turn tail and rush off to Nikky at the drop of a hat. She must contrive to be away from home from time to time.

She went to the kitchen and consulted with Bep, had a chat with Emma, took the shopping list she was offered and walked to the shops. The list was a short one; she was back with time to spare before setting out for the medical director's house on the other side of the canal.

It was a large, old-fashioned house set in a pleasant garden and close to the medical school. Matilda was ushered into a large drawing-room filled with ladies of all ages. She had expected half-a-dozen fellow visitors and she paused in the doorway, feeling shy. Mevrouw van Kalk surged towards her, a large elderly woman with a kind face, and shook her hand.

'My dear Mevrouw van Kempler, I am so delighted to meet you, come and be introduced—you know Rauwerd's partners' wives, do you not? Here is Mevrouw Troost, our Senior Medical Officer's wife, and this is...'

The introductions took a long time but once they were over Matilda began to enjoy herself. They were kind, all of them, putting her at her ease and swamping her with invitations to coffee and tea in their own homes. Presently the talk turned to the Spring Ball.

'You will, of course, be coming?' said Mevrouw van Kalk. 'It is a splendid affair and it will be so nice to see Rauwerd partnering his wife at last. We were all beginning to think that he was going to remain a bachelor for the rest of his days.'

Matilda smiled and nodded and answered questions and talked for a while with Beatrix and Marie and Gerda, inviting them to tea. 'Friday?' she wanted to know. 'I have a Dutch lesson in the morning so I shall be able to practise on you all.'

She walked back home and found Rauwerd already there.

'Oh, hello.' She greeted him cheerfully, while her heart thudded against her ribs at the sight of him. 'I'm sorry I wasn't at home. You're early. I've been having a coffee with Mevrouw van Kalk and I met ever so many wives—it'll take me weeks to work off all the invitations to coffee and tea. It was great fun, too. I must work hard at my Dutch. I've a lesson tomorrow. I'll just go and tidy before lunch.'

She skipped away rather breathless, without giving him a chance to get in a word edgeways. But at lunch she asked after his morning, expressed the wish that he would have a good afternoon and mentioned that Rose wanted her to have lunch. 'So you won't mind if I go to Amsterdam?' she asked matter-of-factly. 'Mevrouw van Kalk says there is a splendid train service.'

'Jan will drive you; you can phone when you are ready to come back. Taking revenge, Tilly?' He spoke quietly, watching her unsmiling.

It was wonderful how easy it was to conceal one's feelings when one really wanted to. She opened her eyes wide. 'Revenge, Rauwerd? What do you mean? If you don't want me to go to Amsterdam, then I won't.' She gave him a questioning smile.

'By all means go to see Rose. I can't take Dickens with me this afternoon. Would you mind taking him for a walk later on? He is obedient, but perhaps you'd better keep him on a lead.'

'Oh, good, I'd love to. We'll go to the end of Rapenburg and up the other side. Will that be long enough?' She refilled his coffee cup. 'Your mother would like us to visit them on Sunday. I said I'd ask you and ring her back.'

'Lunch? Yes, I'll be free, though I may have to go out on Sunday evening.'

Matilda's insides came to a halt. Nikky again. She said pleasantly, 'Oh, then I'll let her know, shall I?' And then, 'You have so many friends, Rauwerd, and they all have wives; I'm sure I'll never be at a loss for something to do.'

He gave her another keen glance. 'I am glad you are happy, Matilda.'

He got up to go and rather surprisingly dropped a kiss on her cheek as he went.

He was home by five o'clock, a circumstance which gave Matilda great satisfaction, unhappily short-lived, for after less than half an hour's desultory talk he observed that he had several phone calls to make and he went off to his study. Matilda closed the Dutch grammar she had been worrying over with something of a snap and wandered upstairs; it was early to change her dress but she had no intention of sitting there waiting for him to return. She mooned around, discarding first one dress and then another, and finally settled on a silvery grey woollen crêpe, very demure, very becoming and wickedly expensive. The dress called for extra care with her face and hair and it wanted but ten minutes to dinner time by the time she went back to the drawing-room. Rauwerd was there, sitting in his chair and surprisingly doing nothing. He got up when she went in and poured her a drink.

'That's a pretty dress,' he commented, and then, 'I must go out after dinner... I'm so sorry.'

'You don't have to be sorry,' said Matilda matter-of-factly. 'I quite understand.'

He raised his eyebrows and although his face was grave she had the impression that he was secretly amused. 'Do you? So I don't need to explain?'

'Heavens, no. After all, you explained everything very clearly before we married.' She gave him a sweet smile and tossed off her sherry.

Over dinner they discussed giving a dinner party; the partners and their wives, of course, Rose and Sybren, Professor Tacx and, it went without saying, Nikky.

'Next week?' suggested Rauwerd. 'Tuesday? Will you write the notes and I'll get them posted tomorrow? Don't forget it's the Spring Ball at the end of next week, an annual event of some splendour. Get yourself a new ball gown, Tilly; get Jan to drive you to den Haag. A pity your car hasn't been delivered yet.'

She made a pleasant rejoinder, poured his coffee and said equally pleasantly, 'If I'm to write those notes, I'd better begin straight away. I can do them in English? Good, then I'll go into the sitting-room. I'll say goodnight, Rauwerd.'

She had slipped through the door before he could get to his feet.

The days slid by; everyone accepted for the dinner party and she went to den Haag and spent a good deal of money on a new dress for the ball—satin, the colour of clotted cream, with a wide skirt pleated into a narrow waist and a cunningly cut bodice which showed off her splendid figure to its fullest advantage. She bought matching slippers and a marabou wrap, too, bore them back to the house and didn't mention it to Rauwerd. Hanging the dress in the wardrobe she reflected that normally she would have rushed home and showed Rauwerd the lot, but she doubted sadly if he would be interested.

There was no good wallowing in self-pity. She plunged into the preparations for the dinner party, shared her breakfasts with Rauwerd and took care to be home in the evening when he got back, even though he seldom spent the evenings with her. She was finding her feet, by now, and was acquiring a smattering of Dutch and a casual acquaintance with the wives of Rauwerd's colleagues and friends. She walked Dickens, shopped, took an interest in the running of the house without interfering with Bep, and schooled herself to assume a casual, light-hearted manner when she was with Rauwerd, never asking him where he went or what he did. He was highly thought of in the medical profession, everyone was at pains to tell her so, but since he never mentioned his work other than casually, she didn't ask him about it.

Dressing for the dinner party, she reviewed their married life so far. There was no doubt about them getting on well; they did, but only up to a point. They liked the same things, shared a sense of humour, and, on the face of things, were a happily married couple; on the other hand it had been disastrous that she should have fallen in love with him when all he had to offer was friendship. Life could be very difficult, thought Matilda, slipping into the rose-pink dress and clasping the pearls around her neck, but she had no intention of giving up hope.

Dinner was a success, even with Nikky there in a slinky black dress that did nothing for her lack of curves. Matilda, confident that she looked nice, smiled and chatted and tried out her Dutch—which pleased Professor Tacx mightily, even when she said it all wrong—and received the compliments about her party with shy dignity. No one hurried away; indeed, they lingered until almost midnight and, when they left, reminded her that they would see her at the ball.

She hadn't had much time to talk to Rose. Only as everyone was getting ready to leave and Nikky said, 'You'll run me back, Rauwerd?' did Sybren, obedient to his small wife's eloquent eye, say, 'No bother, Nikky, we'll drop you off. It's not out of our way.'

He clapped Rauwerd on the shoulder in a friendly fashion, kissed Matilda and swept Nikky out to his car while Rose kissed Rauwerd and then Matilda. She didn't say anything, only winked.

Which meant, thought Matilda, standing in the hall beside Rauwerd, that Rose and Sybren and possibly any number of the other people knew about Nikky. She was going to ask Rose next time they met.

Which was at the ball, when, of course, there was no time for private talk. Matilda, resplendent in the cream satin, danced the first dance with Rauwerd and after that didn't see him again until the supper dance when he came to fetch her from a circle of his colleagues who were chatting her up in the nicest possible way.

'What a lovely time I am having; aren't you?' she asked as they went along to the supper room. 'I do like your friends, Rauwerd.'

'They appear to like you, my dear. I must say, that dress is quite charming.'

They joined a party of friends for supper and then went back to dance until the small hours. As they circled the floor for the last waltz, Matilda said, 'Shall I ask your mother and father over for lunch in a day or two? I'm sorry they decided not to come, but I'm sure your mother would like to hear about it.'

'And see the dress, of course.'

'Oh, yes. I told her about it, of course, when we went there to lunch.'

He leaned back a little to look at her. 'You didn't tell me, Tilly.'

'Well, I didn't think you'd be interested.' She sounded pleasantly matter-of-fact. 'There are some gorgeous dresses here tonight. It's a very grand affair, isn't it? And I've met a host of new people—there was a nice fat man with a beard…'

'The *Burgermeester,* my dear. You've stolen his elderly heart.'

'Oh, good. We'll have him and his wife to dinner, shall we?'

'Aiming to be a prominent hostess, Matilda?' he asked silkily.

She caught her breath with the hurt of it. 'No. I thought that was what you wanted, Rauwerd—someone to run your house and entertain your friends and be in the house when you get home.'

'Did I say that?'

'Yes. But if you want to…' She was forced to stop, for the dance was ending and there were people laughing and talking all round them. Nikky was there, of course; she had come with a professor from the university, but there was no sign of him now. Matilda wished her goodnight and saw her join a group of people at the door. She had smiled at Rauwerd and touched his arm as she left them. She was wearing a vivid green sheath with a slashed skirt and long black gloves. Very dramatic.

Matilda fetched her wrap, lingered to speak to the director's wife and went back to the entrance hall. Rauwerd was waiting for her; so was Nikky, cocooned in black fur. Almost everyone else had gone, Rose and Sybren amongst the first; there was only a handful of local people left and no sign of the professor.

'I'll drop you off, Tilly,' said Rauwerd, 'and run Nikky back—Professor Wijse had to leave before the end and she's without transport.'

'Oh, hard luck,' said Matilda. 'Come in and have some coffee first—Bep will have left some ready and it's quite a long drive.'

Nikky gave a girlish laugh. 'Oh, I'll enjoy it, and Rauwerd loves driving at night, don't you?'

Matilda ushered her unwelcome guest into the drawing-room and went along to fetch the coffee. She was crossing the hall with the tray when Rauwerd came in from the car. 'Isn't it rather late?' he asked mildly.

'Well, yes; but it's so late it doesn't matter any more, does it? Do you have to be at the hospital in the morning?'

He took the tray from her and she sensed his annoyance. 'Yes.'

She made no attempt to hurry over their coffee. Indeed, she engaged Nikky in a rather pointlesss conversation which Rauwerd sat through silently, but at last she put down her cup with a little laugh.

'Oh, dear, I'm half asleep. I'll simply have to go to bed. Do forgive me, Nikky, if I go up now.'

She stood up looking quite superb, her eyes bright and her cheeks flushed, due almost entirely to her smouldering rage. 'I hope we shall see you again soon,' she said insincerely to Nikky. 'It was a delightful evening, wasn't it?'

Rauwerd went to the door and opened it. She paused to whisper, 'I'll say goodnight. There's not much left of it, but I'm sure it will be good!'

She heard his quick furious breath as she swept past him.

Rage and unhappiness upheld her while she undressed and got into bed. Half-way through a sniffing, snuffling weep she fell asleep.

The full horror of what she had done hit her with all its force when she woke. Emma, who had brought her her early morning tea, stared at her face with consternation.

'Miss Tilly, whatever is the matter? Are you ill? Didn't you enjoy the dance?'

Matilda looked at her through red puffy lids. 'It was heavenly, Emma, but I was so tired when we got home...'

'Five o'clock I heard the car go round to the garage. The doctor 'as ter go ter work, but you have a nice lie in.'

'I'll feel fine once I'm up, Emma dear, really I will. I'll be down to breakfast as usual.' Five o'clock! It had been three when she had gone to bed.

She felt sick when she contemplated facing Rauwerd presently, which was why she took extra pains with her hair and spent twice as long as usual disguising her pink nose and eyelids. She wore a new outfit, too—a Swiss knitted jacket and skirt with a matching blouse; its bow tied under her chin, which was really rather fetching.

Rauwerd was already at the table, but he got up as he always did, wished her good morning and picked up his letters once more. He looked tired and very stern and the apology which tentatively trembled on her lips was swallowed again; he was still angry. If he had shouted at her, had a blazing row, it would have been easier, but his chilly politeness stifled any wish on her part to apologise. She took a roll and buttered it. She wasn't sorry; he had deserved every word and a great many more besides. She was no man's doormat.

Rauwerd put down the last of his letters and rather disconcertingly sat back in his chair, watching her. 'You have been crying?' he observed and expected an answer.

'I can cry if I wish,' snapped Matilda.

He got up, preparing to go. 'You mustn't over-react, Matilda. I suspect that your imagination is obscuring your common sense; it is certainly blinding you to the obvious.' He stopped by her chair, looking down at her unsmiling. 'We must have a talk, you and I. I hadn't intended to say anything yet—after all, we have been married such a short time.'

'You're angry?' she muttered, not looking at him.

'Yes. I won't be home for lunch...'

'If there are any calls for you...'

'I shall be over at the hospital,' he said and added silkily, 'not in Amsterdam!'

He whistled to Dickens and went away leaving her to stare at her plate while she fought terror, and tears.

It wouldn't do to mope. She drank several cups of

coffee and went to discuss the day's meals with Bep. Bep wanted to know all about the ball and so did Emma, so Matilda sat down at the kitchen table and described as many dresses as she could remember and what they had eaten for supper. Only when the two ladies were satisfied that they knew everything there was to know, was she able to talk about food. If Rauwerd was going to quarrel with her she would feel sick; she chose a meal which made that prospect less likely, made her shopping list, donned a smart little felt hat and gloves, and, armed with a basket and her purse, set off to the shops.

It was a chilly morning and windy and the town was busy. She stopped to examine the fruit at her favourite stall just outside the supermarket and actually had an orange in her hand when the bomb concealed in the shop exploded.

Chapter 8

Matilda felt herself tossed into the air and then fall, half smothered in oranges, apples and cabbages. Her fall was cushioned by a large crate of tomatoes which puréed themselves all over her person and from which, after the first shocked seconds, she dragged herself upright. The stall's owner was half buried under a mound of potatoes and Matilda dragged her from them, aware of the profound silence almost at once broken by cries and screams and moans from inside the supermarket. It astonished her that she was still clutching her basket and purse; she looked at them in a silly kind of way for a moment and then handed them shakily to the stallholder.

The police and ambulances and fire engines would arrive within minutes; in the meantime there was surely something she could do to help. She picked her way over the debris around her and edged into the supermarket. Its front had been blown out and the floor was knee-deep in tins and broken glass, broken bags of rice and sugar, tea and flour; from the depths of its interior people were staggering, calling to each other, crying for help. She pushed past them; the bomb had gone off somewhere at the back of the store and that was where the injured would be.

There was smoke and dust so that she couldn't see very well, and shelves still tumbling lazily to the ground, carrying their contents with them, making progress difficult. She began to come across the injured then, lying silent, some of them pinned to the ground by falling masonry, others were wandering around in a dazed way, seemingly unaware of their wounds. Matilda, still dazed herself, began to work her way from one victim to the next, doing what she could, which wasn't much, uttering reassuring words, straightening broken arms and legs as gently as she could, pulling away the more easily moved debris, snatching a handful of dusty tea-towels on sale on the shelves still standing and using them to cover the more obvious wounds.

She was joined almost at once by two policemen and three men who had followed them in, and her nurse's training automatically took over. She began to look more carefully at the wounded lying around groaning, mostly women, and she made sure that they could be carried out without more damage being done. More men were making their way towards them now and she was dimly aware of ambulance bells and a good deal of shouting. She felt light-headed but there wasn't time to think about that; some of the people lying there were severely wounded, even dead; they had to be got to hospital as soon as possible. She crawled to a young woman lying unconscious under a pile of milk cartons and began to fling them aside. It was a good thing she was unconscious for she had lost an arm... Matilda did what she could with her remaining tea-towel and watched while one of the men picked the girl up and carried her away.

'*Vlug,*' cried Matilda, thankfully recalling her Dutch lessons, although anyone in their senses would have known that quickness was of the essence. And then, as she caught sight of a battered pushchair and a small child still strapped into it, 'Oh, someone come quickly...'

One of the policemen heard her and made his way to her side. Together they pulled the child clear just as the first of the ambulancemen arrived. A mound of tins had fallen in a great heap between the shelves; Matilda could hear cries from beneath it and began burrowing frantically towards the sound.

'Over here,' she called urgently, but the hubbub was considerable by now, with a great many helpers all willing but lacking someone to organise them. The ambulancemen were too busy getting victims into the ambulances; the police were hampered by frantic people searching for children and friends. She tugged at the end of a broken shelf and a few dozen tins rolled away leaving a gap with an arm sticking out from it. She edged forward, took it in her hand and squeezed it gently and was rewarded by an answering squeeze. She began to move the tins carefully and presently was re-warded by the sight of a face, dirty and pale but alive. She paused for a moment and said joyfully, 'Oh, hello.' The face stretched into a smile although the voice was too faint to hear. Matilda smiled back and began, very carefully, to move the tins.

At the hospital the bomb had, naturally enough, taken everybody by surprise. Rauwerd, at his desk after a busy outpatients' session had lifted the receiver be-fore the last rumbles had died away.

'Yes, a bomb,' agreed the medical director, 'or a gas explosion.' The rescue team was to be ready in five min-utes. 'Deal with the situation as you think fit, Rauwerd—you're free?'

The team was alerted. Rauwerd had scarcely put down the phone when there was a call from the police. 'Give us five minutes. Much damage?'

He dialled again and, when Jan answered, 'Is *Mev-rouw* at home?' He sounded calm and unhurried; it was Jan who sounded worried.

'She left about twenty minutes ago to go to the shops. Shall I look for her? We all three could go...'

'I'm on my way there, Jan. Stay at home and ask Bep and Emma to get things ready in case she has been hurt. Does she shop at the supermarket?'

'Almost never, Doctor.'

'That's where the bomb exploded, Jan, so there is a good chance she's all right.'

He rang off and got into his white coat and went to join the team and the waiting ambulances.

'The supermarket,' he told them. 'Get the ambulance as near as you can and split into teams of three. I'll go in ahead of you with Cor and Wim.' He nodded to the two young housemen standing by him. 'The rest of you follow as we've done in practices.'

It was no distance, a matter of a minute or two, but they were hindered by the people milling around; the police ahead of them cleared a path and the ambulances stopped, unable to get nearer for the rubble in the street. The fire engines had come in from the opposite end, and the police were urging people to stay away so that the rescue work could go ahead.

Rauwerd, making his way over fallen masonry and glass and ruined stalls, saw that there was already a row of victims lying in the cleared space outside the supermarket. He said over his shoulder, 'Tell the second team to organise stretchers and get these people back to the hospital.' He noted the tea towels. 'They've had a very rough and ready first aid.' He switched on his walkie-talkie to warn the hospital and ducked into the dust and smoke of the ruined store.

Matilda was moving the tins very carefully and slowly. The pallor of the face visible in their midst urged her to fling them aside as fast as she could go, but that might bring a cascade on to the owner of the face. She needed help but although there were people round her now, struggling to free the victims, they had their own worries. She didn't allow her despair to show on her face, however, for the sickly white face peering back at her was looking anxious.

'Not long now,' said Matilda with pseudo-cheerfulness. Her hands were cut and bleeding and she was covered in a fine dust which had stuck to the squashed fruit and veg still adhering to her person. She felt dizzy, too, and every now and again her surroundings dipped and swayed around her but she kept doggedly on.

The sight of her, with her hair hanging in a dusty cloud around her shoulders, a trickle of dried blood on one cheek and what looked like the beginnings of a black eye, brought Rauwerd up short. He said, 'Oh, my dear Tilly, thank God you are safe. You're not hurt?'

He had caught her by the arm and she looked up into his face, white and etched with lines she had never seen before. She said in a tightly controlled voice, for she felt rather peculiar, 'Are you the rescue team? How did you know I was here?'

'I didn't—I just hoped that you were all right and safe.'

'Well, I am, but we must get this poor soul out—all these tins,' she cried distractedly.

He shouted to one of the team members and, taking no notice of her protests, sat her down on an upturned shelf. 'Don't move, Tilly,' he told her and although he spoke quietly she didn't dare disobey him.

An ambulanceman joined them and carefully and slowly they eased out the owner of the face, laid her on a stretcher and carried her away.

'And now you,' said Rauwerd. 'You're to go back with one of the team and be taken home, and don't argue, please, Tilly.'

Something in his voice stopped her from protesting

and indeed there was nothing she wanted more than to be at home, in bed, asleep. Rauwerd hauled her gently to her feet and handed her over to a policeman, then immediately turned his attention to the latest victim to be carried out of the ruins around him.

She felt a flash of utter misery that he could do that as she was led away, the policeman's sturdy arm hooked into hers. She was glad of it; once she could get into the street away from the dust and smoke and pitiful cries for help she would feel better.

They were almost at the ruined entrance when her legs turned to cotton wool and she keeled over, to be caught before she reached the ground and carried to one of the police cars. Her companion had seen the doctor's face as he had turned away. The doctor had had to stay, poor devil, thought the policeman, so it behoved him to take care of this pretty English girl who had been so quick to give help. He eased her into the nearest police car and told the driver to go to the hospital. 'And make it quick.'

Matilda, coming to as she was put on a stretcher in the first-aid department, shook the policeman's hand and muttered, *'Dank U,'* and even managed a smile. She added. 'The doctor...' and stopped, at a loss for words.

'I tell him,' said her kind companion.

The Medical Director came himself to look her over. 'Nothing serious,' he assured her. 'An ATS injection, and a nurse will clean up those cuts and scratches. You're going to have a black eye but there's no concussion. I hear that you were one of the first to give aid.'

He patted her hand. 'We are all very proud of you. I'm so glad Rauwerd found you; he was anxious.'

She nodded, furious with herself that she couldn't stop the tears trickling down her dirty cheeks.

'So he knows you are safe. Now we'll see to you and send you home to bed, and that's an order, Matilda.'

Her hands were scratched and torn, she was grazed, and her eye was rapidly turning a rich purple. She was cleaned up, had her injection and was driven home, where she had a rapturous welcome from Bep, Emma and Jan.

'The doctor told us to have everything ready in case you had been hurt,' said Emma. 'You're to have a bath and go to bed. That worried he was, too,' Emma tut-tutted. 'Them nasty old bombs, scaring the wits out of decent folks.'

Matilda, bathed, her hair washed, and made to drink hot milk, got into bed, closed her one good eye, and was asleep instantly.

It was well into the afternoon when the last of the victims had been taken from the ruins and the rescue team had gone wearily back to the hospital, before Rauwerd opened his own front door. Jan, hovering at the back of the hall, heard him.

'You're back, doctor. Coffee? A meal? *Mevrouw* is sleeping.'

'Coffee, please, Jan. I'll change my clothes—I've cleaned up at the hospital, but I need another suit. I must go back at once.' He started up the stairs. 'I'll take a look at my wife.'

Matilda was curled up into a ball, her sore hands

stretched out on the coverlet, her eye, swollen and richly purple, half hidden by her hair. The faithful Dickens, keeping her company by the bed, got up as Rauwerd stood looking down at her; there was a look on the doctor's weary face which, if she could have seen it, would have made the black eye worthwhile. But she didn't stir as be bent and kissed her gently and went along to his own room, taking Dickens with him.

She woke at the end of the afternoon, drank the tea Bep brought her and decided to get up. She felt fine except for the eye and her hands and Rauwerd would soon be home. She put on one of her pretty dresses, tied her hair back with a ribbon because her hands were too clumsy to put it up, and went downstairs, closely shadowed by her faithful household.

The phone had been ringing all day, Jan informed her, and it rang again while he was telling her this. It was Rose, her pretty voice anxious.

'Tilly? You're all right? Sybren drove over to Leiden as soon as he heard about the bomb. He saw Rauwerd just for a moment—he was up to his eyes, of course, and so dreadfully worried about you because he'd had to leave you, but he couldn't do anything else, could he, being in charge of the rescue team? Have you seen him since?'

'No, I've been asleep. He came back to change his clothes but he didn't wake me. He'll be back any minute...'

'Oh, Tilly, I'm so relieved that it wasn't worse for you. Sybren says everyone is talking about the way you waded in and helped and gave first aid. Will you feel like having me to tea in a day or two and telling me all about it?'

'Oh, Rose, I'd love that—what about tomorrow?'

'Lovely. May I bring little Sybren with me?'

She put down the receiver and Jan appeared at her side. 'May I suggest a nice glass of sherry, *Mevrouw?* The doctor would like you to have it.'

He handed her a glass. 'There are flowers, also— from the director's wife and the partners' wives and from Professor Tacx. May I say how proud we are of you, *Mevrouw?*' He beamed at her, picking his words carefully so as to get the English right.

'Why, thank you, Jan, but there were other people helping, too, you know. And it was lovely to come home to you all here.' She glanced at the clock. 'I wonder when the doctor will be back.'

'You would like me to telephone?'

'No, I don't think so, Jan. They must be very busy. I don't know how many people were hurt, though I dare say quite a few were transferred to Amsterdam or den Haag. Could Bep put dinner back for half an hour?'

'Certainly, *Mevrouw.*'

But the half-hour came and went and in the end she dined alone. It was almost ten o'clock when she heard his voice as he spoke to Jan in the hall and whistled to Dickens.

'You should be in bed,' he said from the hall, and he spoke so harshly that she felt the silly, easy tears prick her eyelids.

'Hello, Rauwerd.' Her voice came out expressionless.

'I slept well all day, thank you. Would you like dinner? Bep's got everything ready for you.'

He had come right into the room and she looked at him now. He looked tired to death; she longed to push him into his chair and throw her arms round his neck and hug him and fuss around him with a drink and his supper, while he unburdened himself of his day's work, as any husband would.

Only he wasn't any husband; he was Rauwerd, who had no intention of doing anything of the sort.

'How do you feel?' he wanted to know. 'Is that eye painful?' He sat down opposite her. 'Van Kalk examined you thoroughly; you escaped lightly.'

'Yes, didn't I? Were the casualties high?'

He nodded. 'We've transferred about half of them; there are several in intensive care, though.'

'It was dreadful. You must be very tired. Did you tell Jan that you wanted a meal? I'll go and see…'

'He's bringing me some coffee and sandwiches.'

'I'll get you a drink.'

'Stay where you are, I can get it. By the way, a woman called at the hospital; she was the stallholder where you were standing. Says you were so kind and helpful when you were both knocked over. She found your handbag and returned it; it's in the hall, rather the worse for wear, I'm afraid. You are by way of being a heroine, Tilly.'

'That's nonsense—I was a bit nearer the store than anyone else, that's all.'

He said, 'You might have been killed, or mutilated.'

His voice was harsh again. Jan came in then, which was a pity, for Matilda had hoped that he would say more.

But what was there to say? He wasn't a man to pretend to feelings he didn't have for her and she didn't blame him for that. She poured his coffee and watched him eat the sandwiches, and although she longed to talk she held her tongue. She gave him a second cup of coffee and when he had drunk it he fell asleep.

He woke after half an hour. 'My dear Tilly, I'm so sorry. You should have wakened me...'

She said in a motherly voice, 'Why? You need a nap. I think you should go to bed at once. I suppose you have to go to the hospital in the morning?'

'Yes.' He was staring at her and she met his gaze with her one good eye.

'I am proud of you, Tilly, and there has been no chance to tell you so. I was so scared and when I saw you there, quite oblivious of your danger, I said nothing. I hope you'll forgive me for that.'

She got out of her chair. 'Well, of course I do. There was no chance to talk, was there? And I didn't expect you to bother with me when there were people lying around crying for help. I'm going to bed.' She smiled at him. 'It's been quite a day, hasn't it?'

He went to the door with her and opened it.

'Oh, your father phoned this evening just to make quite sure that we were all right. I missed his first two calls but Jan coped marvellously. Goodnight, Rauwerd.'

She got up as usual in the morning to find that Rauwerd had already left for the hospital, leaving a message with Jan that he thought it unlikely that he would be home for lunch.

The morning was largely taken up with answering the telephone calls. It astonished Matilda that there were so many of them, but then, of course, Rauwerd was well known in the town. Dickens had been left at home, so she donned the eyepatch Rauwerd had left for her and took him for a brisk walk along Rapenburg and then submitted to the anxious attentions of Emma and Bep, eating the lunch they had made with such care although she wasn't in the least hungry and then going to the sitting-room to wait for Rose.

It was quiet there and the sun shining through the window gave out a pleasant warmth. She curled up in a chair with Dickens beside her and closed her eyes. Rauwerd would be working and there would be no let up for a few days to come. Perhaps when things had got back to normal she would be able to persuade him to take a few days off. Go over to England, perhaps, and see a play, or just laze around in his London home or walk in one of the parks.

She was almost asleep when Jan came in and said apologetically, 'Juffrouw van Wijk is here, *Mevrouw,* and she insists on seeing you.'

Matilda sat up straight and assumed an expression of pleased surprise. Just in time.

Nikky pushed past Jan and didn't wait for him to close the door before she said, 'I thought Rauwerd would be here—I came to see him, really. My God, what a fearful shock I had when I heard. He's not hurt? I phoned the hospital but they didn't know where he was; nor did that man of yours when I telephoned yesterday. This morning I was told that he was unable to answer the telephone—I could leave a message for him with his secretary.' She laughed rather wildly. 'His secretary! If he'd known it was I, he would have answered the phone.'

Matilda heard her out and then said politely, 'Do sit down. And do tell me, why should Rauwerd have answered your telephone call? He is a doctor, and they are working almost round the clock at the hospital.'

Nikky fixed her with an angry look. 'Oh, you don't know what you're talking about.' She burst into sudden laughter. 'Oh, poor Matilda, your eye—you do look a fright—and your hands. You look as though you've been scrubbing floors for years. You won't be able to go anywhere for days. Not that it would matter; you don't go out together, do you? I mean, the two of you for fun?' She leaned back in her chair. 'Rauwerd and I always had fun; he'd die of boredom if he didn't have me to visit. Does he tell you he's working late?'

Matilda sat like a ramrod, very pale, her eyes sparkling with rage. Any minute now she knew she would say something rash, or slap Nikky's face. Neither of them had heard Jan answer the door and admit Rose, who was standing at the door Jan had half opened, shamelessly listening.

She flung it wide now and went in, the carrycot dangling from one hand.

'Tilly, dear, how lovely to see you.' She turned an enquiring face towards Nikky. 'Oh, hello. Just going, are you? Jan's in the hall; he'll see you out, and don't you dare to say another word.'

She stood back by the open door and Jan, who had heard every word, went to the front door and held it wide. Rose was small and unassuming but she had a way with her; Nikky went. Slowly, it was true, but she went.

Rose put the carrycot down on the sofa and sat down on the arm of Matilda's chair. Matilda was paper white and tears of rage were trickling down her cheeks. Her pallor threw her black eye into violent relief and she was shaking. Presently she said, 'Thank you, Rose. I couldn't think of anything to say, you know. I just wanted to hit her. She said… Did you hear?'

'Oh, yes,' said Rose comfortably. 'I was standing at the door, listening to every word.'

'Rose, is it true? I mean about her and Rauwerd? Will you tell me?'

Rose said carefully, 'She wanted him—he's quite a catch, you know. She never loved him, only his name and his money and the prestige his work gives him— and I'm quite sure that Rauwerd never considered marrying her, didn't even fall in love with her; he just tolerated her because he's a kind man. No one likes her and I suppose because of that he was her friend. Ask him, Tilly. He'll tell you that Nikky isn't of any importance to him.'

Matilda sniffed, blew her nose and mopped her face. 'Heavens, you must think I'm a silly fool to take any notice of the woman. I'll—I'll have a talk with Rauwerd.'

'You do that. You see, everything will be all right. That's a really lovely eye. Were you terrified?'

'Petrified. It's like being turned to stone for a few moments; you can't move or speak. I ruined a new suit, too.'

'Plenty more where that came from,' said Rose cheerfully. 'I say, I'm sorry I was so high-handed just now, ordering Nikky out of your house, only you looked as though you were going to thump her.'

'I was. I wish I had, too.' They giggled together. 'Oh, good, here's Jan with our tea. Is the baby all right there? He's very quiet...'

'Asleep,' said his proud mother. 'He's so placid, bless him. When's the next Dutch lesson? Isn't Professor Tacx a nice old man?'

Emma and Bep had provided a lovely tea: tiny sandwiches, scones, toasted and buttered, rich chocolate cake and wafer-thin bread and butter. They took their time over it and hadn't finished when Rauwerd came in.

He kissed them both, studied his small godson and sat down by the fire. When Jan came in with fresh tea Matilda gave him a cup and asked. 'Is it still very busy on the ward? Are the patients recovering?'

He studied her face; tears and rage had taken their toll but her voice was quietly enquiring. 'Ordered chaos is the term; we've borrowed nurses from here and there and, of course, it took them a little time to find their way around. But the patients are coming along nicely. Some nasty injuries and still three in intensive care.' He had demolished the rest of the bread and butter and was starting on the cake. Matilda wondered if had had lunch, and put the plate of scones within his reach. He ate those, too, while he carried on desultory conversation until Rose got up to go.

'And may I just ring Sybren,' she asked, 'to let him know that I'm on my way?' When she had done that and kissed Matilda she asked Rauwerd, 'Will you carry the baby down to the car for me?'

With the infant safely stowed in the back of the car she paused as he opened the car door for her. 'Look, this isn't my business and probably you'll never speak to me again, but there is something I must say…'

'About Tilly?' His voice was very quiet.

She nodded. 'Nikky van Wijk was here when I arrived. She just walked in—she wasn't asked. I don't know what she said before I arrived but she was saying a whole lot—I stood at the door and listened—lies about you and her. But there were little bits of truth mixed in and it all sounded plausible.' She looked rather anxiously at his face; he was angry but there was something besides anger in his tired face.

'You're furious. I'm sorry if you don't want to be friends any more.'

He smiled faintly. 'Yes, I'm furious, but not with you, Rose, or with Tilly. I promise you I will do something to put matters right.' He bent and kissed her again. 'Sybren's a lucky fellow.'

She beamed at him. 'Yes, isn't he? I shall tell him all this. Will you mind?'

'I should find it extraordinary if you didn't—you're too close for secrets, aren't you?' He shut the door on her. 'Drive carefully.'

Rauwerd didn't sit down when he went back into the sitting-room; he went to stand at the window, looking out into the garden, but he turned around when Matilda spoke. She had had time to think what she was going to say and to school her voice to matter-of-factness.

'Nikky called this afternoon. She was worried about you. She phoned yesterday but Jan didn't know where you were and I was asleep. She tried the hospital, too, and again today; they told her that you were unable to take calls but she didn't believe them so she came here.'

'And what did she have to say?' His look was so intent that she glanced away.

'Well, she was upset, naturally…'

He sauntered towards her. 'Why naturally, Tilly?'

She hesitated. 'You're old friends—She—she has a great regard for you.'

'What a nice way of putting it. And do you believe that?'

Matilda met his gaze squarely. 'No, but I don't think it matters what I think. Rose came just before Nikky left; she told me to ask you… But I don't think I want to know. I'd like to forget it; it isn't as though…' She paused. 'I expect you would like to go and see Nikky; she was very upset.'

He lounged against a chair but now he straightened up. 'Why, I do believe I'll do just that, Matilda.' He had come to stand in front of her, hands in his pockets. 'You are almost too good to be true, you know, although, of course that should be easy since your own feelings aren't involved. You are also as blind as a bat.' He went briskly to the door. 'Don't wait dinner for me,' he said cheerfully as he went out.

She went to bed shortly after dinner with the excuse that she had a headache, and certainly her eye bore out evidence of the statement. She was sitting up in bed knitting with a kind of concentrated fury when there was a tap on her door and Rauwerd came in.

'Emma says you have a headache.' He took her

wrist in his hand. 'Your pulse is fast; do you not feel
well, Matilda? You have had a bad time, you know.'
He looked at her with narrowed eyes. 'Or have you a
headache?'

'No, I haven't. I said I had otherwise Emma and
Bep would have wondered why I came to bed so early.'

'And why did you?' He sat down on the side of the
bed and took the knitting out of her hands.

She shook her head. 'I thought I felt tired, but once I
was in bed I wasn't.' She smiled at him with determined
brightness, suddenly certain that he had something to
tell her. He had been to see Nikky and they would have
talked, about her probably.

'I'm going over to London on Sunday to give details
of the bombing to a committee of hospital authorities
and discuss the nature of the injuries. I have two consultations as well. I shall be there for three days, and
I'd like you to come with me, Tilly. We will go to the
house in Tilden Street, of course. You could shop if you
wish and we might go to a show.'

She studied his face; it gave nothing away. She asked
slowly, 'Does Nikky know?'

She wished she knew what he was thinking; his face
was so still and his eyes half closed.

'Yes.'

She said wearily. 'And I suppose, when we're there,
I stay and you come back here—there are all sorts of
excuses you could make.'

His voice was so cold that she actually shivered at
the sound of it. 'You think that? You must be out of

your mind, Matilda.' He got up from the bed and stood towering over her.

'Well, I'm not,' said Matilda, 'not any more. And I won't go with you.' She pulled the bedclothes over her ears. 'Take Nikky,' she added into the pillows. But he hadn't heard that. He was already out of the room, closing the door with a deliberate quietness which was much worse than a resounding slam.

Because she lay awake until the small hours, she overslept. Rauwerd had already gone to the hospital by the time she got down and Jan told her, with a shake of his head, that he wouldn't be back until the early evening.

'The doctor is working too hard,' he told her, 'and now he goes to London.'

He cast a quick glance at Matilda's face. 'You will be staying here, *Mevrouw?* The doctor says that you are still not quite well.' He gave her a fatherly smile. 'We must all take care of you.'

She murmured suitably, feeling guilty, nibbled at her breakfast and had a long conversation on the phone with her mother-in-law.

'Rauwerd phoned this morning, my dear; such a pity you aren't well enough to go to London with him, it would have made a pleasant little break for you both, but you are wise to stay at home after such an ordeal.'

Matilda, feeling guiltier than ever, invited her inlaws to lunch the Sunday after Rauwerd got back, and hung up, to plunge into a variety of small chores to keep her busy. She was dreading Rauwerd's return; indeed, she felt sick whenever she thought about it. Unnecessarily so, as it turned out, for he was his usual coolly pleasant self and no mention was made of their conversation on the previous evening, nor of his trip to London.

The five days till Sunday dragged by. A number of people called to see how she was. Rose telephoned and wisely said nothing at all about Rauwerd, only made a date for the following week and Matilda went to two meetings of charities she had been asked to patronise, the black patch covering her eye which was now yellow and green as well as purple. On Sunday, early, Rauwerd left for London.

Chapter 9

Sunday stretched endlessly before Matilda. She and Rauwerd had bidden each other a polite goodbye after breakfast and she had watched him drive away, wishing with her whole heart that she was with him. If he had given the smallest sign that he wished for her company she would have begged his pardon and got into the car just as she was. But he had given no indication of regret at going alone. She watched the Rolls slide away and when it was out of sight, went indoors, got her coat and took Dickens for a long walk. She ate her solitary lunch under the kindly eye of Jan, and then spent the afternoon in the garden, weeding, with Dickens keeping patiently to her side. Rauwerd's mother and father were coming to tea; they were a welcome break in her lonely day and she listened eagerly to his mother's tales

of his boyhood and proud reminiscences of his success
as a medical student.

'He works too hard,' said his fond parent, 'but, of
course, you can understand that, my dear, being a nurse
yourself.' She peered closely at Matilda's wan counte-
nance. 'I must say you have been badly shaken; you are
far too pale and heavy-eyed. When Rauwerd gets back
he must take a few days off and take you somewhere
quiet. You'll know of his small farm in Friesland, but
of course he has had no chance to take you there yet. It
will be ideal for you both.'

Matilda made a suitable reply; it was the first time
she had heard about a farm, but then there was so much
she didn't know about Rauwerd. She doubted very
much if he would wish to take her there. They saw
little enough of each other; to be together on a farm
miles from nowhere, as it probably was, didn't seem
a good idea.

When her guests had gone she took Dickens for another walk, presently ate dinner and then went back
to sit in the sitting-room with her knitting. But she allowed it to rest in her lap, not attempting to do a stitch
of it. She had had time to think during the day and she
knew what she was going to do. She was going to see
Nikky and find out the truth for herself. She had been
cowardly, ignoring a situation which had been bound to
worsen, and which had. There was a second car in the
garage, a small Daimler; when Jan came in to see if she
wanted anything, she voiced her intention of driving to
Amsterdam in the morning. But Jan was unexpectedly
firm about this. With all due respect, he was quite cer-

tain that the doctor would be most uneasy if she were
to drive herself. Her own car would arrive shortly and
no doubt the doctor would take her for several drives
to make sure that she perfectly understood the slightly
different rules of the road in Holland. He pretended not
to see her quick frown, and went on, 'If *Mevrouw* will
allow me, I will drive you myself, wait for as long as
you wish, and bring you back home.'

He looked at her almost pleadingly and she saw no
alternative.

'Well, thank you, Jan, if that will make you easier. I intend to visit Juffrouw van Wijk. I don't know
where she lives, but I expect I can find it in the telephone book.'

'Juffrouw van Wijk has a flat close to the Leidse
Plein, *Mevrouw*. I will drive you there and park close
by until you are ready to return.'

'Oh, will you, Jan? Thank you. I don't suppose I
shall be long. If we got there at about ten-thirty tomorrow morning?'

'Very good, *Mevrouw*. You will be home for lunch?
So that I can tell Bep?'

'Oh, yes. I—I—haven't any plans.'

Which wasn't quite true. Her head seethed with
them, most of them highly impracticable. She sat back
and thought out what she wanted to say to Nikky. If
Nikky would see her…

She took great pains with her appearance in the
morning. The fine wool suit was a perfect fit and her
shoes, elegant and high-heeled, matched her clutch
bag. She had been uncertain about a hat but finally de-

cided that it might make her feel that much more self-confident. It was head-hugging with a stiffened bow at the back and gave her, she hoped, dignity, a commodity she was determined to keep at all costs that morning.

There was a lot of traffic and she was secretly relieved that Jan drove and not she, for Nikky lived in the heart of the city, down a narrow street lined by solid square houses, all of them converted into flats.

Jan drew up half-way down the street and helped her out. 'There's a line of meters just round the corner, *Mevrouw,*' he told her. 'I'll leave the car and stroll around until you are ready. I'll not be far away and I'll keep the block in sight.'

'What good care you take of me, Jan.' She paused on the pavement to smile at him.

'A pleasure, *Mevrouw.* Besides, I had my orders from the doctor to look after you.'

Matilda paused on the pavement; just for a moment she faltered. If Rauwerd knew what she was doing... She could see his face very vividly in her mind's eye, white and angry, his eyes like blue stones. She gave herself a little shake; angry or not, she was hopelessly in love with him. There would never be anyone else for her, she was sure of that, but if Nikky had spoken the truth... But that was why she was there, wasn't it? So that she could find out for herself? She reached the entrance and marched in, found Nikky's name on the cards against the neat row of bells, pressed the second one down and went briskly upstairs. The first floor had four front doors; Nikky opened hers as Matilda lifted her hand to the knocker.

She was surprised, and just for the moment bereft of words, which gave Matilda the chance to say with polite firmness, 'I'd like to talk to you, if I may, just for a little while—about you and Rauwerd.'

Just for a moment she thought that Nikky was going to slam the door in her face, but then she said sullenly, 'Oh, come in then...'

They went into a sitting-room, modern and sparsely furnished with uncomfortable-looking chairs, a coffee-table of mirror glass and some impressionist paintings on the scarlet-papered walls. Not a room to relax in, but then she didn't want to relax. She sat down gingerly on the least uncomfortable chair.

'I'd like the truth about you and Rauwerd. I don't mean just bits and pieces of it, or what you choose to tell me. Are you in love with him?'

Nikky laughed. 'Lord no, nor could ever be, but he's got everything a woman wants, hasn't he? Good looks, money—heaps of it—a life-style to please any girl and highly thought of in his work. He was—how do you say—just my cup of tea.'

'And does he love you? Or did he ever love you?'

'You're a silly kind of woman, aren't you? Of course he didn't and he doesn't. We have known each other for years. I suppose, because I was alone and didn't get asked out much, he took pity on me. If he'd asked me to marry him I would have done, make no mistake about that. But he didn't. He married you. I suppose I hated you, so I decided to have another try at getting him away from you. Only I didn't succeed, did I? You know that he came to see me? Well, that's the end of a beautiful friendship—I'm off to the States. I know a few people there; American men are supposed to be good husbands… I shall miss him, though, always ready to sort things out for me, give me lifts, lend me money, but nothing more than that.'

She had been standing by the wide picture window; now she came and sat down opposite Matilda. 'Do you believe me? Why didn't you ask Rauwerd?'

'No, I couldn't do that. You see, if he had loved you and you loved him, then I would have had to do something about it, wouldn't I? I'd like him to be happy more than anything else in the world.' She paused. 'And yes, I do believe you.'

'You're in love with him, aren't you?'

'Yes.' Matilda got to her feet. 'Thank you for seeing me. I hope you'll be happy in America.'

'Happy?' Nikky asked mockingly. 'Oh, yes, though not your idea of happy—Sunday lunch with mother-in-law, and a pack of children round your feet, and Rauwerd's slippers put to warm each evening.'

There was no suitable answer to that; Matilda went to the door and made her escape.

Jan was waiting. She got back into the car and he turned it and began on the drive back. After a few minutes she asked, 'Jan, I want to go over to London. Can I phone for a place on a flight tomorrow morning?'

'Indeed you can, *Mevrouw.* I'll see to it for you if you will tell me when you want to go, and I can drive you to Schiphol. Would you wish to let the doctor know?'

She felt a gathering excitement inside her. 'No, thank you, Jan. I'd like to surprise him. If I could get a flight about eleven o'clock, I'd be at the house by about two, wouldn't I?'

Back in Leiden again, she had a belated cup of coffee and took Dickens for a walk. She would have liked to have rehearsed exactly what she was going to say to Rauwerd, but her thoughts were too chaotic. She only knew that she would have to apologise before embarking on explanations. She walked along the deserted street, her head in the clouds, while Dickens trotted beside her. She walked until she was tired and then went back for lunch, a meal which Bep served almost an hour late without saying a word.

Jan had booked her a seat on a flight just before midday and she spent a good deal of the afternoon curled up in a chair in the drawing-room wondering what Rauwerd was doing, still trying to think of what she would say when she saw him again. She wandered up to her room presently and went through her wardrobe, deciding what she would wear, and then packing a small overnight bag. She washed her hair and did her nails and went down to eat a dinner she didn't want. She wouldn't sleep a wink, she was sure, but the moment she laid her head on the pillow she did so, and only wakened when Emma came in with her morning tea.

'You'll be coming back with the doctor?' Emma wanted to know.

'Oh, dear Emma, yes. That'll be tomorrow evening late or the following morning. I'm not quite sure.' She bounced up in bed. 'And Emma, if Mevrouw van Kempler phones, will you tell her that I'm in England and we'll both be back in a day or two. I'll telephone her as soon as we get home.'

Emma studied her with a speculative eye. 'I must say you look 'appy, Miss Tilly, though that's as it should be, you and the doctor being man and wife. It's not right for yer to be apart, when all's said and done.'

The plane was full and at Heathrow it took a long time to get through Customs, even though she had no luggage. She found a taxi at length and was driven to Tilden Street. But that took time, too, what with heavy traffic and a delay because of an accident ahead of them.

It was getting on for three o'clock by the time she opened the door of the house in the quiet street near Grosvenor Square, to be met in the hall by Cribbs's dignified, 'Madam, this is a pleasant surprise. Have you had lunch? Perhaps a cup of tea?' He beamed at her with real pleasure. 'You are quite recovered? The doctor said that you had had a bad time of it.'

'I'm fine, thank you, Cribbs. Is—is the doctor at home?'

He shook his head. 'No, madam, he left this morning early to go to some meeting or other, and then he said that he would go on to the hospital—he had two or three appointments there, I understand, and he didn't expect to be back much before this evening.'

Her disappointment was so great that she had to swallow back her tears. But she hadn't come all this way to be put off so easily.

'I'll go over to the hospital, Cribbs. The doctor might be free earlier than he thought. Is he dining at home?'

'Yes, madam. I believe he intended to go back to Leiden tomorrow evening; he didn't know for certain.'

Her one thought was to go to Rauwerd at once, but common sense took over. 'I'd love a cup of tea, Cribbs, and I'm just going upstairs to tidy myself.'

She did her face with great care and brushed her hair until it shone and then wound it neatly, determined to look her best. When she went downstairs Mrs Cribbs had added a plate of dainty sandwiches to the tea tray. Sitting in the taxi Cribbs had called for her, Matilda felt ready for anything.

The hospital entrance hall was empty, save for the porter in his little box. Matilda poked her head through its window before she had time to get scared. 'I want to see Dr van Kempler,' she told him in what she hoped was an assured voice. 'I'm his wife.'

The porter put down his paper and looked her over slowly. 'Does he expect you, ma'am?'

'Well, no…'

'He'll be at the meeting then…began at three o'clock and likely to last for an hour or two. Can't interrupt it, I'm afraid.'

'Oh. Well, can I wait here?'

He said grudgingly, 'I suppose you could. Maybe he'll not be so long. There's no telling.' He nodded towards the back of the hall. 'There's a bench there, between those two statues.'

Matilda thanked him politely although she was bursting with impatience. The seat was hard and cold and not easily seen by those who passed to and fro through the hall. Each time she heard footsteps she looked up eagerly, but there was no sign of Rauwerd. Fewer and fewer people passed by and presently, weary from excitement and anxiety, she closed her eyes.

When she opened them the place was deserted; even the usual hospital noises were hushed. She looked at her watch and saw that she had been asleep for an hour. She jumped to her feet. Rauwerd must have left by now; he wouldn't have seen her there on his way out. She hurried to the porter's lodge and found another man there.

'Dr van Kempler,' she began, 'has he gone? I'm his wife—I've been waiting for him, but I felt asleep.' This didn't sound quite right. She began again, 'He wasn't expecting me, and I've been sitting on that seat by the statues.'

'Really can't say, madam. There's a conference on and there's doctors going to and fro...'

'He's tall and rather large with fair hair.'

He sucked his teeth and thought. 'Well, I do remember a very big man—I thought to myself at the time, "There's a big man", but that could have been yesterday...'

She would have to go home; he might already be there. On the other hand he could still be in the hospital. She asked, 'The consultants' room—where is it? I'll just make sure that he's not there before I go home.'

'Well, I don't know that I can let you go there, madam. It's private like, you see.'

· He was friendly, but she could see that he was going to be firm about it. Desperation made her cunning. 'Oh, well, I'll sit here for a little longer. Thank you for your help.' She smiled at him and went back to the seat and stayed there until she saw him turn his back to attend to the switchboard.

She was down the passage alongside the statues before he turned round again. The passage went on and on, lined with large mahogany doors—Hospital Secretary, Lady Social Worker, General Office…there was no end to them. At its end there was another passage, much wider and winding into a dimly distant curve. The first door said 'Hospital Governors' and the second, 'Board Room', and the third said 'Consultants' Room'. She fetched up before it, breathless from hurrying and fear of being caught. Without pausing, in case her fear took over, she knocked on the door and went in.

There were five persons in the room. Three were strangers to her; the fourth was the tall, thin man who had been kind to her at the geriatric hospital—Rauwerd had called him Dick. The fifth was Rauwerd.

They turned to look at her with unhurried calm, although Rauwerd's calm was shattered by such a fierce delight at the sight of her that she found herself trembling.

He came towards her. 'Tilly, what a delightful surprise!' He took her hands in his, smiling down at her. 'Come and meet some of my colleagues.'

They shook hands with her warmly and Dick said, 'I was so delighted to hear of your marriage. I hope that when I come to Holland you will let me visit you?'

Matilda, struggling with all the sensations of someone who had expected one thing and become involved in another, murmured politely, exchanged small talk with the gentlemen, very much aware that Rauwerd's hand on her arm was sending delightful thrills up it. She listened with apparent interest while one of the learned gentlemen, grey haired and bearded, told her about his recent visit to Leiden, all the while wondering what she was going to say to Rauwerd and, for that matter, what he was going to say to her.

It seemed an age, although it was barely ten minutes before Rauwerd said easily, 'Until ten o'clock tomorrow, then? In the board room?'

They all shook hands again and she went ahead of Rauwerd to the door. She couldn't trust herself to look at him but walked silently beside him back along the corridors and passages to the entrance. The hall was empty, save for the porter reading his paper over a cup of tea. Half-way to the door Rauwerd stopped, took her in his arms and kissed her soundly, and then walked on again, his arm tucked into hers. It took only a few moments to reach the car, just time enough for her to ask, 'Why did you do that?'

He paused, his hand on the car door. 'Because I love you, my dearest Tilly; it is something I have wanted to do since the moment we met—I fell in love with you then.'

He opened the car door and shoved her gently in and then got in beside her.

She said in a voice she strove to keep normal, 'But I didn't like you very much…'

He glanced at her sideways, his eyes gleaming in his calm face. 'No, I know that. That is why I suggested our marriage should be on a friendly footing—to give you time to change your opinion of me.'

Matilda digested this remark slowly and with mount-
ing excitement. She wanted to sing aloud, fling her
arms around Rauwerd's neck. Everything she had been
wanting to tell him bubbled up on to her tongue, but
she clenched her teeth; it was neither the time nor the
place to do any of these things. She kept silent until he
stopped before the house and then skipped ahead of him
through the door Cribbs was holding open.

'Tea, madam?' asked Cribbs, so that she was forced
to stop and answer him.

'Oh, yes please, Cribbs.'

She glanced at Rauwerd who smiled and said blandly,
'In half an hour, my dear? In the study, perhaps. And we
don't want to be interrupted, Cribbs. Keep all the phone
calls unless it's something urgent, will you?'

He crossed the hall and opened the study door and
Matilda went past him into the centre of the room. She
turned to face him almost as soon as he closed the door.

'I went to see Nikky,' she began.

'I thought that you might do that.' He sounded un-
concerned and she felt a prick of peevishness.

'Why should you think that?'

'You're my wife, and, even though you weren't aware
of it, you were in love with me—still are, I hope.' He
crossed the room and took her hands in his. 'Although
you didn't know that for a long time, did you?'

She stared up at him. 'No, no I didn't and when I
did, I thought that you and Nikky loved each other—
she told me...'

'My dearest love, if I were to tell you, just once, that
I have never loved, nor ever shall love Nikky, would

you believe me, so that the whole tiresome thing can be forgotten? There are so many other things I would rather talk about and we have wasted so much time.'

He drew her close in a satisfying, gentle hug and kissed her. 'Can't I ever talk about her again?' demanded Matilda into his shoulder.

'Well, perhaps when I am an old man and you are a delightful old lady, we might discuss it, but not, of course, when the grandchildren are around.'

'But we haven't any children,' observed Matilda, unaware of the silliness of the remark.

'Easily remedied, my darling.'

She leaned back to look into his face. 'I think I'm going to cry,' she said in a watery voice. Then, when she saw the look of love and tenderness in his face, she added, 'But I don't think I will.'

She put up her face to be kissed instead; so much more pleasant. Indeed, she was enjoying it so much that she didn't hear Cribbs come softly in with the tea tray, and, after a swift pleased look, go softly out again.

* * * * *

"Why are you armed with pepper spray? Did something
happen to you?"

She didn't look up.

"Yes. Something happened."

"Here?"

She shook her head, her body trembling so badly
she didn't trust her voice. The only sound was Nick's
wheezing breath. He finally cleared his throat.

"Okay. Something happened." His voice was gravelly
from the pepper spray, but it was calmer than it had been
a few minutes ago. "And you wanted to protect yourself.
That's smart. But you need to do it right. I'll teach you."

Her head snapped up. He was doing his best to look at her, even though his left eye was still closed.

"What are you talking about?"

"I'll teach you self-defense, Cassie. The kind that actually works."

"Are you talking karate or something? I thought the pepper spray…"

"It's a tool, but you need more than that. If some guy's amped up on drugs, he'll just be temporarily blinded and really ticked off." He picked up the pepper spray canister from the grass at her side. "This stuff will spray up to ten feet away. You never should have let me get so close before using it."

"I didn't know that."

"Exactly." He grimaced and swore again. "I need to get home and dunk my face in a bowl full of ice water." He stood and reached a hand down to help her up. She hesitated, then took it.

Don't miss
A Man You Can Trust *by Jo McNally,*
available September 2019 wherever
Harlequin® Special Edition books and ebooks are sold.

www.Harlequin.com

HSEEXP0819

Need an adrenaline rush from nail-biting tales
(and irresistible males)?

Check out **Harlequin Intrigue®**,
Harlequin® Romantic Suspense and
Love Inspired® Suspense books!

New books available every month!

CONNECT WITH US AT:

Facebook.com/groups/HarlequinConnection

 Facebook.com/HarlequinBooks

 Twitter.com/HarlequinBooks

 Instagram.com/HarlequinBooks

 Pinterest.com/HarlequinBooks

ReaderService.com

**ROMANCE WHEN
YOU NEED IT**

SGENRE2018R

Looking for inspiration in tales
of hope, faith and heartfelt romance?

Check out **Love Inspired**® and
Love Inspired® **Suspense** books!

New books available every month!

Love Inspired®

LIGENRE2018R2

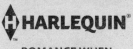